together with you

Books by Victoria Bylin

Until I Found You
Together With You

together with you

VICTORIA BYLIN

BETHANYHOUSE

a division of Baker Publishing Group
Minneapolis, Minnesota

Published by Bethany House Publishers
11400 Hampshire Avenue South
Bloomington, Minnesota 55438
www.bethanyhouse.com

Bethany House Publishers is a division of
Baker Publishing Group, Grand Rapids, Michigan

Printed in the United States of America

Library of Congress Cataloging-in-Publication Data
Bylin, Victoria.
    Together with you / Victoria Bylin.
        pages ; cm
    Summary: "Responsible for his young daughter and two teenage sons for
the summer, Dr. Ryan Tremaine wants to reconnect with his children, but after
hiring Carly Mason as his daughter Penny's nanny, Ryan's attraction to Carly
complicates his plan"— Provided by publisher.
    ISBN 978-0-7642-1153-9 (softcover)
    I. Title.
PS3602.Y56T64 2015
813'.6—dc23   2014041331

Unless otherwise noted Scripture quotations are taken from the King James Version
of the Bible.

Epigraph Scripture quotation taken from the Holy Bible, New International Version®.
NIV®. Copyright © 1973, 1978, 1984, 2011 by Biblica, Inc.™ Used by permission of
Zondervan. All rights reserved worldwide. www.zondervan.com

This is a work of fiction. Names, characters, incidents, and dialogues are products of
the author's imagination and are not to be construed as real. Any resemblance to actual
events or persons, living or dead, is entirely coincidental.

Cover design by Paul Higdon

Author is represented by the Steele-Perkins Literary Agency

15   16   17   18   19   20   21   7   6   5   4   3   2   1

To Deborah Raad
and
Southland Christian Church
in honor of
Faith and Friendship

*Let us then approach God's throne of grace
with confidence, so that we may receive
mercy and find grace to help us in our time
of need.*

—*Hebrews 4:16* NIV

1

The clerk at McGill's Sporting Goods, a sandy-haired college kid, pushed a button to feed the paper tape through the register, but it jammed for the third time. Scowling, he tossed the crumpled receipt in the trash. "Sorry, sir. I know you're in a hurry."

"Yes, I am." Dr. Ryan Tremaine spoke through gritted teeth, but he didn't blame the clerk for his predicament. He'd been a fool to let his two youngest children, Penny and Eric, out of his sight, but he'd lost patience with Eric for pouting and Penny for pulling the tags off rugby shirts. Expecting to be right behind them, he'd allowed them to go to the food court for ice cream while he paid for the baseball cleats for Kyle, his oldest son.

It was a bad decision, and Ryan knew it. The mall, crowded on this Saturday afternoon in June, was a dangerous place, especially for a little girl with special needs and a thirteen-year-old boy who had what a family therapist called "issues."

Kyle slung the bag holding the shoebox over his shoulder. "This is taking forever. Maybe I should check on Eric and Penny."

Ryan was about to agree when the register spit out the mile-long receipt. The clerk tore it off and handed it to him with a flourish. "There you go, sir. Sorry for the delay."

Snatching it, Ryan spun on his heels. With Kyle at his side, they sped out of the store to the main mall. He'd given Eric a twenty-dollar bill and instructions to buy whatever treats he and Penny wanted, then to wait in front of the ice cream place. Striding toward it now, he scanned the counter, empty except for a trio of giggling teenage girls. His gaze zipped to the tables in front of the shop, also empty, then to the sea of half-filled wooden chairs and gray Formica tables.

"Do you see them?" he asked Kyle.

"Not yet."

Ryan focused on one face at a time. An ophthalmologist by profession, he had better than 20/20 vision, which made his failure to spot Penny and Eric even more alarming. In spite of the icy air conditioning, droplets of perspiration beaded on his neck and dripped down his spine.

Kyle pointed to the far side of the food court. "There's Eric."

Ryan spotted his son coming out of a video arcade filled with shadows, flashing lights, and kids who looked as rebellious as Eric in his zombie T-shirt and baggy pants. Eric had no business in that place, especially with Penny. She was five years old and a victim of FASD, Fetal Alcohol Spectrum Disorder, a condition that affected her in myriad ways, including sensitivity to noise, light, and smells. If Eric had taken her to the arcade, anything could have happened—a meltdown, her running away, maybe hiding. She had done that a couple of times at the house, and Ryan had battled panic until he found her.

Five steps beyond the arcade, Eric ground to a halt. Panic glinted on his face like sunlight on a mirror, ricocheted back to Ryan, and blinded him with a terror so fierce he stopped breathing. There was only one explanation. Penny was missing.

It was Ryan's fault, not Eric's. The FASD was his fault, too.

Penny had been conceived in the affair that wrecked his marriage—a byproduct of impulse and enough gin to drown his conscience, at least for a time. When Penny's mother had died six months ago, he'd taken custody and made a solemn vow to never fail his daughter again. It was a promise he broke daily, it seemed. No matter how hard he tried to connect with her, she still called him Dr. Tremaine instead of Daddy.

His relationship with his sons wasn't much better, but his ex-wife was away on a mission trip, and he had the boys under his roof for three months. Determined to rebuild their trust, he'd written out what he called the SOS list—things a family did and enjoyed together, things that made them close. Traditionally, SOS stood for Save Our Souls, but Ryan didn't believe in God. For his purposes, SOS stood for Sink or Swim, which is what he and his kids would do this summer.

With Penny missing, they were sinking hard and fast.

Eric spotted him and broke into a run. Behind him, a uniformed security officer gave chase while speaking into a microphone clipped to his collar. It didn't make sense, unless the man knew something about Penny.

Terror shredded through Ryan like a riff on an electric guitar, though no one would know it to see his face. Carefully blank and in control, he shoved aside the rising panic in spite of the mental picture of Penny lost in the mall. With her blond ponytail and blue eyes, she was a beautiful little girl. And vulnerable . . . more vulnerable than most children because of the way fetal alcohol affected her brain. Instead of being naturally shy, she would go to anyone, especially a nice man with candy . . . a nice man who would take her for a nice ride in his nice car.

Stay clinical, Ryan told himself. *Get the facts*. But he couldn't turn off the ugly pictures or the fear, and when he swallowed, acid burned the back of his throat. Forcing down the bile, he called to Eric over the rumble and clatter in the food court, "Where's your sister?"

Eric's chubby face wrinkled into a knot. "I told her to stay in the arcade."

Kyle caught up to them. "I don't see her anywhere."

"Where is she?" Ryan repeated to Eric.

"I don't know."

Frantic, he scoured the line at the candy store and the island of bubblegum machines. He looked everywhere, but there was no sign of Penny.

"Sir?" The deep voice came from over Ryan's shoulder. Turning, he saw the security officer with his thumbs hooked on a thick black belt.

"Is this your son?" the man asked.

"Yes, it is."

"I'm Officer Lewis, and I'm here about a shoplifting incident." Before Ryan could react, the officer lowered his chin at Eric. "You were at the prize counter, weren't you?"

Eric looked down at his shoes. "Yes, but—"

"The manager saw you take two candy bars. You put them in your pocket and ran for the door."

Ryan's mind spun with frightening implications, but Penny was in the greatest danger. "Officer, wait. My daughter is missing."

The man's attention snapped to Ryan. "How old is she?"

"Five."

Chin down, he spoke into the microphone clipped to his collar. "Code Adam. Repeat. Code Adam. Roger that."

As a choir of voices responded in the affirmative, Ryan flashed to the famous picture of seven-year-old Adam Walsh, wearing a red baseball cap. The child had been abducted at a mall much like this one, murdered, then decapitated. *No. No. No.* Terror screamed through his brain, drowning out logic, hope, everything except the gong-like echo of yet another failure.

Officer Lewis focused on Ryan. "Would you describe your daughter, sir?"

"Blond hair. Blue eyes." He held out his arm to show her height, saw his shaking hand, and pulled it back. "She's about forty inches tall." He knew, because she'd just been to the pediatrician.

"What is she wearing?"

"Denim overalls and a pink T-shirt." Both wrinkled because the fourth nanny had quit yesterday, leaving him to add *Find a new nanny for Penny* to his SOS list. He'd planned this day so differently . . . just Kyle and himself shopping for baseball cleats and grabbing burgers for lunch. Now, instead of happily crossing *Buy cleats for Kyle* off the SOS list, he silently berated himself for the bad judgment that put his daughter in danger and his younger son in the middle.

Officer Lewis repeated Penny's description into the radio, then explained a Code Adam to Ryan. The outer doors of the mall were being locked as he spoke, and no one would leave without being observed by a designated mall employee. Penny's description would go out on the PA system, and managers would walk the aisles of their stores. If Penny wasn't found in ten minutes, law enforcement would be called, the doors would be opened, and the alert canceled.

Ryan nodded, his face carefully blank, but his heaving lungs revealed his panic. He blinked and imagined Penny in a nondescript sedan, clawing at the windows, calling for help. He blinked again and pictured her frail, broken body in a shallow grave, then in the morgue, covered in a white sheet, lost to him before he could make up for how she was conceived.

Most people blamed the mother for fetal alcohol exposure, but Ryan considered himself as accountable as Jenna. He'd bought the gin and wine they'd consumed. They had made this child together, told lies to each other and to those they loved. What a fool he had been. One impulsive fling and Penny had paid dearly.

So had Jenna.

And Heather, his ex-wife.

And his sons.

together with you

That snowball of damaged lives needed to stop. Heather had found God and was at peace, but the rest of his family was a mess. It was up to Ryan alone to rebuild the family he'd destroyed, and that's what he intended to do this summer by using every ounce of his intelligence, will, and heart.

Officer Lewis clicked off the microphone and pulled a notepad and pen from his pocket. "What's your daughter's name?"

"Penny Tremaine." Except she didn't like her new last name and refused to learn it. "Or Penny Caldwell. It's complicated."

Officer Lewis scribbled on the notepad. "We don't broadcast the child's name. It could give a predator an edge. It's for the female officer checking the restrooms." Turning slightly, he spoke again into the radio.

Ryan faced Kyle. "Keep looking for her."

When Kyle took off with a nod, Eric moved to follow him. "I'll help."

"No." Ryan stopped him with a hand on his shoulder. "You saw Penny last. How long has she been gone?"

Eric shook off the touch. "I don't know."

"Take a guess."

"I said I don't know!" Eric's face pulled into a doughy knot that made him look younger than he was. "We went to the arcade. She saw the purple horse and wanted to ride it."

"I told you to go for ice cream." Ryan's voice shook as badly as his hands. "Eric, this is serious. Penny's in danger."

Eric tried to look tough, but his gaze shifted to the floor. Shoulders hunched, he looked as lost and vulnerable as Penny.

And it was Ryan's fault. In a fit of impatience, he'd heaped the responsibility for Penny on the immature shoulders of a thirteen-year-old boy. If Penny wasn't found, Eric would suffer from guilt he didn't deserve, guilt that belonged only to Ryan.

The security officer ended the call and reported back. "Someone's checking the ladies' room now."

"Good," Ryan said crisply, as if sounding in control would make it so.

"While we're waiting, I need some basic information. Your name, sir?"

Like a prisoner of war giving his name, rank, and serial number, Ryan rattled off his name, address, and three phone numbers—cell, home, and office. Surrounded by noise and strangers, fearful of pedophiles, trapped and smothered with remorse, he heard the most condemning words of his life blast from the mall PA.

"Code Adam. Repeat, Code Adam. The missing child is a five-year-old female with blond hair and blue eyes. . . ."

~

The instant Carly Jo Mason heard Code Adam on the Animal Factory PA, she locked the cash register and prepared to walk the aisles of the stuffed animal boutique where she worked as assistant manager. Furry creatures lined the shelves, along with outfits that turned them into everything from ballerinas to soldiers, anything a child could imagine. Carly loved it—except when a Code Adam blasted over the mall's public address system. Children went missing everywhere, but it happened a lot more in Los Angeles than it did in her hometown of Boomer, Kentucky.

How she, a girl from Boomer, ended up in Los Angeles was a painful story, one she didn't like to tell. Maybe someday she'd put the trouble in Lexington behind her, but it wouldn't happen today—not with a Code Adam reminding her of Allison Drake, an FAS teenager nicknamed Allie Cat. It had been two years since Allison had vanished from Sparrow House, the home for troubled teens where Carly had been employed as a counselor, two years since Carly had thrown a vulnerable seventeen-year-old girl to the wolves.

She still searched for Allison online and hoped the girl would send her a text out of the blue, even call the phone number Carly would keep forever, or until Allison was found, dead or alive. The old pain congealed in her throat, thickening until she swallowed it back. The Bible said she was forgiven by the grace of God, but how did she forgive herself?

Pocketing the register key, she headed for the front corner of the store, scanning the aisles even before she started the Code Adam protocol. The first leg of the search took her past the Bear Pit, crowded today with a birthday party. She studied the group but didn't see a girl fitting the Code Adam. Jungle Land came next. There were only boys in the aisle, paired with two watchful adults.

With only the Friendly Forest left to check, she sent up a prayer for the lost little girl, for lost children and teenagers everywhere, including Allison. Carly's heart thudded sluggishly, maybe from caring too much for too long, but then she spotted a little girl playing with the stuffed rabbits, and her pulse sped into a gallop. With a blond ponytail and denim overalls, the child matched the Code Adam perfectly. Carly needed to call Mall Security, but she didn't want to leave the child for even a minute. She had slipped away once and could do it again. With her coworker supervising the birthday party, Carly decided to take the girl to the front counter where she could use the phone.

Children this age were typically shy and suspicious of strangers, so she snagged a lion off the endcap, ambled to the girl's side, and crouched down. Using the stuffed animal as a puppet, she spoke in her growliest voice. "*Grrr.* I'm Lance the Lion. Who are you?"

The child broke into a smile. "I'm Penny. I have a dollar, and I'm going to buy a rabbit."

"Excellent," Lance declared with a shake of his tawny mane. "I'll lead you to the cash register."

"Okay, but I have to pick which one." Penny turned back to the bin and resumed her hunt for just the right rabbit.

Every second was an eternity for a worried parent, but Carly didn't want to frighten the child by rushing her. There was something oddly intense about the pinch of her eyebrows, the careful way she inspected each rabbit before hurling it to the floor. With a BA in biology, a masters in social work, plus a year of PhD work at UCLA, Carly knew kids. Something about Penny's expression struck her as atypical.

Hoping to nudge the girl along, she picked up a brown rabbit with a white tummy and black button eyes. Wiggling the rabbit's head, she made her voice squeak. "I'm Tiffany Rabbit, and I need a home."

Penny's blue eyes lit up. "Me too."

"You do?" Tiffany asked.

"I do," Penny repeated. "My mommy's not here."

The poor woman had to be worried sick. Using Lance again, Carly spoke in his voice but with more authority. "Come with me, Miss Penny. I'll help you find her."

"She's in heaven."

No . . . No . . . Not this sweet child. An old wound split open, and Carly swallowed a familiar lump of grief. She'd been fourteen when her mother died of a fast-moving cancer, leaving her to be raised by her father and older brother and sister. The gold locket hidden under her red polo shirt, warm from her skin and memories, had belonged to her mother and was Carly's most treasured possession. She made Lance dip his head in a kind of prayer. "I'm sad for you, Miss Penny."

Penny nodded solemnly. "I'm sad, too."

"Do you have a daddy?" Lance asked.

"Sort of." Penny heaved a very adult sigh. "Mostly I have nannies. Dr. Tremaine—he's my daddy—he works all the time. Kyle is nice, but I *hate* Eric. He took me to the arcade, and I *hate* the arcade. It smells bad." Her lower lip popped out, stiffened, and trembled with the threat of tears.

Tiffany Rabbit hippety-hopped to the rescue. "I need a mommy, too. Can I come home with you?"

Penny raised her skinny little arm and patted Tiffany on the head. "I want this one."

Tiffany turned to Carly, who looked at Lance, who did another puppet shake of his mane while speaking to Carly. "We *both* want to go home with Miss Penny. Is that okay?"

Carly finally used her own voice. "I think we can work something out." She had already decided to buy both animals for Penny, who probably didn't understand the price tags. Every dollar counted for Carly, but she could live on Cup O' Noodles a few extra days. Aware of the Code Adam and the ten-minute limit, she tucked Lance under her arm and reached for Penny's hand. "Let's go pay."

Penny took Carly's fingers as if they were already best friends, and they walked together to the counter where Carly made the call to Security.

"Keep her there," the operator said. "Her father's on his way."

Good, Carly thought. She wanted a word with the man about his daughter. She understood a child getting lost in a mall. It happened. They were little human beings with minds and feet of their own. But Penny's instant attachment indicated a dangerous lack of healthy suspicion. If Carly could win her trust with a stuffed animal, so could a predator. Penny needed to be taught to protect herself, especially with her mom in heaven.

Carly paid for the toys with her employee discount, then handed Tiffany Rabbit to Penny, who told the rabbit she'd get to sleep in Penny's bed tonight along with a bunch of other stuffed friends. Carly joined in the conversation with Lance, who did lots of growling while they waited for Penny's dad—the man she called Dr. Tremaine. The more Carly thought about the circumstances, the more she worried.

"Penny!"

A deep voice shot through the store. Turning, Carly spotted a tall man with close-cropped dark hair, narrowed eyes, and a lanky build striding toward the cash register. Presumably this was Dr. Tremaine. Dressed in khakis and a navy polo shirt, he dodged children and parents with the agility of an athlete. She supposed he was handsome, even striking, but his steely gaze lacked warmth of any kind.

Carly laid a protective hand on Penny's shoulder. "Your daddy's here."

The child looked at her father, her expression blank as she lifted Tiffany Rabbit and made her talk. "Hi, Dr. Tremaine," she said in a squeaky voice. "I'm Tiffany Rabbit, and I'm going home with Penny. Lance is coming, too."

The man stared at the rabbit, speechless. He clearly didn't know how to play with a child, and Penny plainly needed someone who did. When his gaze shot to Carly's face, his blue eyes collided with her brown ones the way an empty sky touches flat brown earth. Fear glittered in his irises, but so did arrogance. Carly didn't like that cold glare, not one bit. Penny needed a daddy, not this man who oozed tension, maybe anger.

Determined to make her point, she raised Lance and gave an enthusiastic growl. "*Grrr*. I'm Lance the Lion. Nice to meet you, Dr. Tremaine."

2

Ryan owed this woman a huge debt of gratitude, but the
talking lion irritated him. So did the sparkle in her big
brown eyes. Something about the situation seemed to
amuse her, or maybe she was one of those annoying women who
made lemonade out of life's lemons by adding too much sugar.
After the trauma of the past ten minutes, her playfulness grated
like fingernails on a chalkboard. So did her long blond hair and the
red polo shirt sporting the store logo of a toothy lion. He guessed
her to be in her midtwenties—too old to be working in the mall
with teenagers, perhaps a sign she'd failed Adulthood 101. All
that aside, he was bone-deep grateful that she had found Penny.

With his throat still tight, he clipped his words in an effort to
appear steadier than he was. "Thank you for finding my daughter."

The woman studied him for a moment, her gaze now serious.
"I'm glad I could help. I'm Carly Mason, the assistant manager.
If you have a minute, I'd like to tell you about how I found her.
Frankly, I'm a little worried."

*Here we go again. Another ignorant do-gooder with advice
about a situation she doesn't understand.* On the outside, Penny

seemed like an ordinary child. She was classified as having Fetal Alcohol Effects, not full-blown Fetal Alcohol Syndrome, so her disabilities didn't always show, even to someone with a trained eye. A psychologist, Miss Monica, was helping her cope with both the FASD and her mother's passing, and Ryan valued that woman's training. He didn't want Carly Mason's unschooled advice, but he did want to know what had happened. "I want to hear everything, but not in front of . . ." He indicated Penny with his chin.

"Of course."

With the stuffed lion in hand, Carly dropped to a crouch and spoke to Penny in the lion's gravelly voice. "I want to play with Tiffany Rabbit. Let's go to the play pit."

"No." Penny's face pinched, her lower lip trembling as her chest heaved with the opening salvo of a tantrum.

Here we go again. If Ryan didn't control the situation, Penny would. Using a signal he'd worked on with Miss Monica, one that would get her attention without increasing the volume level, he rested a gentle hand on her shoulder.

"No," she cried, shaking off the touch.

He couldn't let Penny win this battle, but her will was as strong as his own and often stronger.

"Dad!"

Ryan turned and saw Kyle racing toward the counter with Eric and Officer Lewis behind him. At the earlier call from the dispatcher, Ryan had bolted ahead of them. Penny loved Kyle. Maybe she'd go with him without a fuss. Before Ryan could ask Kyle for a favor, Officer Lewis propped his hands on his hips and grinned at the woman named Carly. "So you found Penny. I should have guessed she'd be here."

"We're a popular spot." Carly set the lion on the counter, then spoke to Penny in her regular voice. "We've been playing with the animals, haven't we?"

Happily the center of attention, Penny held up the rabbit for everyone to admire. "This is Tiffany."

Officer Lewis gave a satisfied nod. "My job's done except for the incident at the arcade."

With Penny safe, Ryan focused on Eric. The candy bars bulged in one of the deep pockets of his cargo shorts, evidence of confusion rather than a crime, but the matter needed to be addressed. Ryan glanced at Officer Lewis. "I'm sorry for what happened. We'll go back to the arcade to apologize and pay."

Eric's cheeks flushed red beneath his pale skin, the result of too much time in front of a computer screen and a vampire-like preference for the night. "I didn't mean to take them. Penny ran off, and I got scared."

Officer Lewis crossed his arms over his chest. "I believe you, but you still have to pay for the candy."

"He will," Ryan replied.

"I'll let the manager know to expect you." Satisfied, Officer Lewis gave a relaxed wave and left.

Ryan turned to Eric and saw a stony expression he knew too well. Of his three children, Eric was the biggest mystery to him. They had no common interests, a fact evidenced by the SOS list. Ryan had jotted down several ideas, things like *Eat dinner together once a week, Go for ice cream,* and *Have breakfast at Minnie's Pancake House,* a place the boys used to love. He'd also listed things to do with them individually. Between *Go to Kyle's baseball games* and *Swim lessons for Penny,* he'd written *Eric—?*

Juggling the needs of his three children was the hardest thing Ryan had ever attempted. When the boys were little, he'd been in med school and working to be first in his class, then interning at USC and working even harder to be the best. He missed out on their formative years without realizing those years would have also formed him as a father. Dealing with teenage problems when he was absent for the daily trials of a toddler left him handicapped—

and divorced. Heather was right. He'd neglected their marriage in favor of his career, but that career, along with a healthy inheritance from his father, provided handsomely for his family. Surely that counted for something.

With the shoplifting incident resolved, Ryan turned to his sons. "I need a few minutes with Carly. Eric, you can look around but stay where I can see you."

Eric glowered but headed for a barrel of rubber sharks at the end of the glass counter.

Ryan turned to Kyle. "Stay with Penny, all right?"

"Sure." He shifted the bag holding the baseball shoes to his other hand. "How about if I take her to pick out another rabbit?"

"Or an outfit for this one," Carly suggested.

"Good idea." Ryan wished he'd thought of clothes for the rabbit, but that's what happened with Penny. He was so focused on the problems that he forgot to be an ordinary dad.

Kyle reached for Penny's hand. "Come on, Squirrel. Dad said to buy the rabbit some clothes."

It was just like Kyle to have a special name for his sister, and to share the credit for a good idea. He was generous in that way, maybe because he had success to spare. A solid student and natural athlete, he wanted to go to Stanford for premed. Twenty years ago, Ryan had been just like Kyle—assured, optimistic, and ready to take on the world. Now he was empty inside, tired of the fight, and afraid that someday Kyle would be just like him. It didn't help that Kyle had inherited Ryan's dark hair and lanky build. When Ryan looked at his son, he saw an untarnished version of himself, which reminded him just how tarnished he'd become.

He wanted a cigarette. Badly.

And a drink.

But he wouldn't.

Fighting a scowl, he waited while Carly summoned a clerk to take over the register, and then followed her to a couple of chairs on the far side of a play area designed for toddlers. The stuffed chairs were at a ninety-degree angle to each other and offered a view of Eric at the counter and Kyle and Penny at the end of an aisle.

"This is the dad spot," she said lightly. "Have a seat."

"Why the dad spot?"

"Moms never sit down." She sank into the cushions and crossed her legs. "When it comes to dressing up stuffed animals, fathers tend to watch."

Ryan said nothing.

"Don't get me wrong," she said with a flutter of one hand. "The dads aren't neglectful. If something happens, they move fast, like you did when you hurried into the store. Losing Penny had to be terrifying."

He gave her high marks for diplomacy but braced for the inevitable criticism. "It shouldn't have happened."

"Of course not. But even the best parents make mistakes. As my dad says, 'Learn and move on.'" Settling back, she laced her fingers over one knee. "That's why I wanted to talk to you. Winning Penny's trust was extremely easy. A predator could have—"

"I know."

"It's important she learn—"

"Believe me, I understand the situation." He didn't need this lecture, and he saw no reason to explain that Penny suffered from FASD. It was like confessing to child abuse, which was how he saw drinking during pregnancy. Penny was completely unexpected and a terrifying surprise considering they had used birth control.

Ryan shoved to his feet. "Thank you again. But as you heard, I need to take Eric back to the arcade."

She stood with him. "I don't mean to push, but I see at-risk kids every day. How old is Penny? Around four?"

"Five, almost six. She's small for her age."

"That makes her even more vulnerable. Kids are impulsive. They have to learn, and it's our job to teach them. We have to . . ."

Blah. Blah. Blah. Ryan admired her passion, but speeches couldn't change the harsh realities of life. Maybe they could for Carly. After all, she worked in a toy store with talking stuffed animals. But Ryan didn't share her naiveté.

The instant she paused, he drove in a wedge. "Let me assure you, I understand the situation better than anyone."

He must have been glowering at her, because she drew back from him, her expression a bit haughty.

Ryan was done with her and done with the store. He lived in the real world, not a land of make-believe, and he still had to take Eric to the arcade. Kyle's baseball practice started in two hours, the younger kids needed dinner, and someone had to do laundry before they all ran out of underwear. Then there was the matter of hiring a new nanny. With a little luck, the agency would find the perfect person and schedule an interview for Monday.

He summoned Kyle with a look, then gave Carly a curt nod. She meant well even if she was naïve. "Thank you again. If you'll excuse me—"

"Of course."

Kyle said something to Penny. When she shook her head, he tried again, this time attempting to steer her away from the clothes with a hand flat on her back.

"No," Penny shouted. "Tiffany wants a ballet outfit!"

Braced for a meltdown, Ryan strode in her direction. He could carry Penny kicking and screaming through the store, but what did he do then? He still had to take Eric to the arcade. The best approach was to avert a disaster by speaking to Penny in calm, simple sentences. His long strides ate up the distance but not fast enough for him to stop Penny from flinging rabbit clothes all over the floor.

Kyle held out his hands, palms up in a sign of helpless surrender.

"I've got her," Ryan told him. "Wait with your brother." Embarrassment crept up his neck like a spreading rash. After a tug on his collar, he laid a firm but gentle hand on Penny's shoulder. "Pick one outfit."

She ignored him.

"Pick one outfit," he repeated. One command at a time, he reminded himself. Too much information overwhelmed her.

Penny dropped a yellow tutu on the floor, then tossed a pink one. The clothes piled into a disjointed rainbow that matched the chaos in her mind.

Behind him, Carly murmured, "May I try?"

With Penny about to erupt, there was nothing to lose. Besides, they were in Carly's store, and she had a knack for making lions talk and children listen. "Go for it."

Bending at the waist, she placed her hands on her knees and her face parallel to Penny's. "So Tiffany likes to dance?"

Lips in a pout, Penny nodded.

"Does she like purple?"

When Penny nodded again, Carly fingered through the outfits on a higher rack and selected a froth of purple tulle and hot pink sequins. Penny snatched it with her usual lack of manners. "I want to play rabbits with you."

"We can't."

No explanation followed. No apologies. There was only the simple command Penny could understand. Ryan's opinion of Carly Mason rose a notch. Hopeful Penny would obey, he clasped her shoulder. "We're leaving now."

Whirling, she flung herself against Carly's legs with the force of a bowling ball. When Carly stumbled back, Ryan grasped her arm, but momentum slammed her against his chest. With the vanilla scent of her hair filling his nose, she turned and they traded a dazed look. Ryan couldn't help but notice her soft curves. It was a knee-jerk reaction, purely physical, but the awareness nearly caught his hair on fire. Carly's cheeks flushed pink, a sign she was as aware of him as he was of her.

He released his grip but kept his eyes on her face. "Are you all right?"

"I'm fine." Her voice wobbled, and she seemed as stunned as he was, either from the near fall or his touch.

Dismissing the moment as nature at work, Ryan trained his gaze on Penny, still clinging to Carly's leg and demanding to play with her. Her voice rose in both volume and pitch, telling the world she was overwhelmed, not in words but in the unbridled emotion of a coming meltdown. Penny was a mess. His *life* was a mess, and it showed.

Teeth clenched, he picked up his daughter, held her tight against his chest, and used one hand to cup her head against his shoulder. If he shielded her from the noise and glaring lights, maybe she'd settle down. Instead, she howled like a banshee, reared back, and kicked so hard he nearly buckled over.

What made him think he could raise a little girl he didn't understand? Six months ago, he'd been given a choice when Denise Caldwell—Jenna's older sister and Penny's Aunt DeeDee—offered to take custody. Ryan had refused. Penny was his flesh and blood, and he owed her the best life he could provide. But at times like this, with her screams knife-like in his ear, he felt as bereft and alone as Penny.

"I want to stay here," she yelled. "*I want to play with the rabbits.*"

There was no point in trying to reason with her. Once she lost control, she didn't have the ability to regain it. "I'm sorry," he said to Carly over Penny's wailing. "I'll get her out of here."

"No." Carly pointed to a curtained doorway on the back wall. "Let's go to the break room. She needs less stimulation, not more."

The stares of other customers ate into him, their smiles smug and slightly superior, as if their perfect children would never behave in such a way. Ignoring them, he made eye contact with Kyle and jerked his chin to signal where they were going, then he followed Carly to a narrow room with a sagging couch, a mini-fridge, and a low table littered with magazines. Penny's shrieks echoed off the walls.

"I apologize," he shouted over the ruckus. "This is going to take a while."

She acknowledged him with a nod, circled to the side where Penny could see her, then started to hum "Amazing Grace." Ryan didn't believe in God, but he knew the words to the old hymn. His mother had been quietly faithful in the face of his father's intellectual pride, and she'd taken Ryan and his sister to church until he was old enough to protest.

The soft humming shifted into da-da-da's that blossomed into the lyrics about grace and fears relieved. Ryan wished life really was that simple—that a prayer could wipe away FASD like bleach on a stain, but it couldn't. With her hot tears soaking his shirt, he closed his eyes and held her even tighter, his aching arms a small penance compared to the price Penny paid for the worst mistake of his life.

Carly sang the old hymn until Penny's sobs eased into hiccoughs, then silence, and finally the steady breath of sleep. Limp in his arms, his daughter was free from confusion and the chains that bound her.

"She's out cold," Carly whispered. "Why don't you lay her on the couch? I'll get a blanket."

He eased Penny onto the sagging cushions and stepped back, savoring the moment of quiet. Carly covered her with a blanket decorated with stupidly grinning bears, then motioned for Ryan to follow her to the far side of the room.

Considering the intensity of the meltdown, she deserved an explanation and Ryan needed to give it. "This isn't what you think."

"Yes, it is," Carly replied. "She had a meltdown. It happens."

Her compassion stunned him. When Penny fell apart like this, people usually assumed she was a spoiled brat having a tantrum. He wished she was, because then she could learn how to behave. "She has FASD," he blurted to Carly. "That stands for—"

"Fetal Alcohol Spectrum Disorder." The blood drained from her face, leaving her ashen under the buzzing fluorescent light.

"You know what it is?"

"I do." Blinking hard, she knotted her fingers at her waist in a pose that hinted at a prayer or maybe a fist.

He'd been expecting criticism, especially judgment of Penny's mother. Instead pain gleamed in Carly's eyes. Determined to understand, he latched on to the most obvious answer. "Do you have a child with fetal alcohol?"

"No," she said. "I'm single. No children."

"Then how?"

She raised her chin. "It's not important."

But it was—both to Carly, who was struggling to hide some deep reaction, and to Ryan, who needed a nanny for Penny. If Carly was that person, he'd gladly put up with lectures, talking lions, "Amazing Grace," and the treacherous attraction that lit his hair on fire.

"I'm looking for a nanny," he said to her. "Any chance you'd be interested in coming for an interview?"

3

No. A thousand times no.

Carly stared at the smudged floor, her heart shriveling at the memory of that last night with Allison. Closing her eyes, she relived that moment in all its hideous glory—her refusal to take Allison with her to Boomer for the weekend, the teenager's accusations and drama-queen tears, and finally the phone call she'd received the next day from her boss. *"Is Allison Drake with you?"*

"No. Why?"

"She's missing. She told Chyna she was running away because you didn't want her around anymore."

Carly still winced at the memory of her boss's tone, slightly accusing because Carly had been cautioned before about being too open with Allison. It was a mistake Carly would never repeat and the reason she had left hands-on social work.

"Carly?" Dr. Tremaine tilted his head to the side in an effort to make eye contact.

"I heard you," she murmured, dragging her head up. "The answer is no."

"That was fast."

"I'm not interested." No more personal involvement, she reminded herself. With Allison, she'd lost the professional distance meant to protect them both. The teenager paid a price, and Carly had left Sparrow House with a load of guilt and the determination to help FASD kids by preventing the affliction in the first place. That's why she was working on her PhD at the UCLA School of Social Welfare. When she finished, she'd go home to Kentucky and dedicate herself to national prevention programs.

She normally talked about FASD whenever the opportunity arose, but she needed to discourage Dr. Tremaine. "I hope you find the right person. It's not me."

"I'm desperate. Penny's had four nannies in six months. The last one quit yesterday. I didn't want to bring Penny to the mall, but there wasn't much of a choice."

"I know it's hard." Oh, did she ever. "But the answer is still no."

"It pays well."

She shook her head.

"You can live in or keep your own place. I'll even negotiate hours."

"No," she said again.

"What'll it take?"

For Allison to be found alive and unharmed. Maybe then Carly could forgive herself. As things stood, the confident woman who had marched into Sparrow House with a newly minted social work degree had crawled into a hole and died. It was Carly's father who had pulled her out with the suggestion of more grad school. When she'd won a full-ride scholarship, she'd taken it as God's hand, packed her Chevy Cavalier, and sped west.

Somewhere in the tornado-touched plains of Oklahoma, she stopped being Carly Jo and became simply Carly. The name change seemed appropriate, though she missed Kentucky terribly. Given a choice, she'd pick grits over salsa any day of the week. Californians might have lower cholesterol than folks in Kentucky, but they didn't know beans about good cooking.

Thoughts of home put a faint smile on her lips. Maybe she'd cook up a real meal tonight and share it with Bette Gordon, her neighbor and only true friend in Los Angeles.

"You're smiling at something," Dr. Tremaine broke in. "What is it?"

"Fried chicken."

His brows collided in confusion, then lifted with the start of a smile. "I have a big house with a remodeled kitchen. If you live in, you can cook or not cook. Plus there's a view of the ocean, a pool—"

"I'm sorry. I have to get back to work."

"Two more minutes."

"I can't."

"Please?"

He was practically begging, and her earlier impression told her it was something he rarely did. "All right. But I really do need to get to the register. That birthday party's about to end."

He gave a crisp nod. "I'll be quick. If you understand FASD, you know what Penny's facing."

"I do," she admitted.

"I think you know how to help her."

If she revealed her experience, he'd increase the pressure. "That's irrelevant. I don't want the job."

"Are you sure?" He lifted one dark brow. "From what I've seen, you love kids and you know them. You're also compassionate. There's no way you can turn your back on a child who needs you."

"That's not fair—"

"But it's true."

She'd expected a bribe in the form of a high salary, not a jab at her conscience. Who did he think he was, manipulating her like this? Carly propped her hands on her hips and glared up at him. He was a good six inches taller than she was, spit-shined and wearing a designer polo shirt, but Kentucky pride flowed in her veins, and she didn't take guff from anyone. "That's a little presumptuous, don't you think?"

His eyes glinted back at her, a sign that he didn't take guff from anyone either. "Yes, but I'm right. I saw your face when I said FASD."

"So?" Her voice quavered. She hoped he'd take it as a sign of anger, not weakness. But in truth she was fighting tears.

"You care and it shows." He pinned her in place with an unyielding gaze that belonged on a battlefield or maybe in an operating room with a beating heart exposed and in his care. The heart belonged to Penny, and Carly knew unequivocally that this man would fight to the death for his daughter.

Ignore that pull in your gut. Don't feel their need. Don't feel anything.

But even as her common sense lectured her heart, her hands slid off her hips in defeat. He was right. She wanted the job. If she could make a difference in Penny's life, maybe she could forgive herself for failing Allison.

But the risks were too great. Penny would become attached to her. What would happen in the future when she went home? Grad school was temporary; Kentucky was forever. Nothing good would come from forming a deep attachment destined to be broken. There was also the matter of Carly's shattered confidence. She couldn't stand the thought of failing Penny the way she failed Allison.

"You are partially right," she conceded. "I care about kids like Penny, and I know what you're facing. But I can't get involved with your daughter. It wouldn't be wise."

"For you?"

"For her," Carly corrected him, though he was right about her own tender heart. "Penny needs someone who'll stay in her life. That's not me. When I finish school, I'm going home."

He rocked back on his heels. "So you're not from around here."

"No."

"Where do you go to school?"

"UCLA."

"Undergrad?"

He was bulldozing her into an interview, and she didn't like it a bit. But at that moment, Penny rolled on the couch, drew up her knees, and pulled into a fetal position. A lump shoved into Carly's throat, and she answered his question without thinking. "I'm working on a PhD in social welfare. I have a masters' from UK."

"UK? As in England?"

"No." She was used to the misunderstanding. "Where I come from, UK stands for the University of Kentucky."

"Basketball."

"Go, Cats." She gave a little fist pump. If talking Wildcat basketball would change the subject, she'd wear UK blue for a week.

"I hear it now," he said.

"What?"

"Your accent."

"Well, that's where I'm from—Boomer County, Kentucky." She let the mountain drawl come out in full force. People in L.A. were either charmed by it or snobbish—mostly snobbish.

Dr. Tremaine didn't seem to care either way. "How much longer will you be here?"

"At least a year." More like two years. She'd finished most of the class work and was in the preliminary stages of her dissertation.

"To Penny, a year is a long time. At this point I'd be grateful for even two months with the same person. Would you at least think about it?"

Every time he said the child's name, Carly inwardly winced. If he pushed much harder, she'd cave in, and they'd all regret it. It was time to be country tough, so she put her hands back on her hips. "The answer is still no, and there's a second reason for it. A very good one."

"What is it?"

"You."

"Me?" He poked his index finger into his chest.

"Yes, you." With one hip jutting, she lifted her chin even higher. "If we were in Boomer County, I'd know everything there is to know about you and your family for three generations, maybe four. You're a stranger to me, Dr. Tremaine, and my daddy taught me not to talk to strangers. My gut tells me you're a good man, but I've learned to be careful."

"Good for you."

"No, it's not. I don't like being suspicious."

"Here." He pulled out his wallet and handed her a business card. "Call my office on Monday and ask for Fran. She's the office manager, and she's known me for years. She'll tell you I'm not a jerk."

"I didn't say you were."

"I'm not. At least not anymore."

Carly didn't know what inspired his defensiveness, but she recalled Penny saying her mother was in heaven, which meant Dr. Tremaine was a widower. "I'm sorry about your wife."

He hesitated. "My wife?"

"Penny told me her mother's in heaven."

"She is, but we weren't married."

"Oh." A blush stained Carly's cheeks. "Forgive me. I thought—"

"It's all right."

"It's just—"

"I know what she said." He shoved his wallet back into his pocket. "Penny's mother passed away six months ago, and I took custody. The boys are—" He shook his head. "It's complicated."

"I see."

"I wish I did," he said more to himself than to her.

Finally giving up, he crossed the room to the couch and lifted Penny without waking her. Carly gathered Lance the Lion, Miss Rabbit, and the ballerina outfit, then followed him into the retail section of the store, where Kyle and Eric were amusing themselves at the barrels full of sharks, rubber fish, and glow-in-the-dark eels. The sight of them filled Carly with a longing for her own siblings—an older brother who was on deployment with the Kentucky National Guard and an older sister with two kids and a baby on the way.

"You have a nice family," she said to Dr. Tremaine.

He hesitated. "Yes. I suppose I do."

How could he doubt it? Carly was twenty-eight, single, and dedicated to a cause, but she still longed for a family of her own.

As she watched the Tremaines leave the store, she hoped they knew how blessed they were. A family was something to cherish, and not all children had one. Allison had lived in nine foster homes by the time she moved into Sparrow House, including one where she'd been five days shy of a permanent adoption when the prospective parents discovered the wife was pregnant and changed their minds. That was typical of Allison and her life—candy dangled and taken away.

Letting out a sigh, Carly helped with the birthday party until the twelve little girls were happy with their animals and left the store. Famished, she told her coworker she was taking lunch, fetched her tub of yogurt, and sat on the couch still bearing a dent from Penny's body. After a few bites, loneliness struck like a fist to her solar plexus, and she decided to call her father. With the three-hour time difference, Reverend Paul Mason would be finished preparing for Sunday at the sixty-year-old church he'd pastored all of Carly's life.

He picked up on the first ring. "Hey, honey. How are you doin'?"

"I'm fine, Daddy. How 'bout you?"

"Just getting ready for tomorrow." In that singsong drawl she loved, he told her about plans for the Sunday service. "Wish you were here."

"Me too."

"So how's Wild Thing?"

Wild Thing was the butterscotch kitten she'd found in the alley and taken in shortly after renting her apartment. "She's fine."

"And you?"

"I'm all right." Except her voice came out breathy and sad. Knowing her father would hear the struggle, she 'fessed up. "Actually, I'm kind of down right now. A little girl with FASD got lost in the mall. She wandered into the store and everything's fine, but she reminded me of Allison."

He paused, no doubt breathing a prayer. "I don't suppose you've heard from her."

"No."

"She's in God's hands, not yours. All you can do is pray."

"I know, Daddy."

"And while you're at it, stop beating yourself up. It's about time you forgave yourself."

"I wish I could." In her darkest moments, she pictured Allison as a victim of sex trafficking, pregnant and drinking, even dead in a ditch. Where was God in this big messy world? Carly knew the theology, but her prayer life was nothing but static and garbled pleas for help, like an old movie where an island castaway calls desperately for rescue on a broken radio.

Her chest ached with a homesickness so powerful she smelled her father's pipe tobacco. *Home.* She ached for the comfort of the house where she grew up, the serenity of rolling green hills and a sky full of clouds instead of smog. As soon as she finished school, she'd go home for good.

Her father's voice pulled her back to the bargain yogurt and the break room. "Tell me about this little girl."

"Blond. Blue eyes." Like Allison, except Penny didn't have the physical indicators of FAS other than being small for her age. Allison's face had displayed them all: small widespread eyes, the lack of a philtrum—the indentation under the nose, a flattened face, and a smaller than normal head. The clinical aspects varied widely from person to person, but today Carly focused on what mattered most—the child herself. "Her name's Penny and she's adorable. Her father's raising her alone."

"No mother?"

"She died six months ago." Carly told her dad the entire story, including Dr. Tremaine's pressuring her to interview for the nanny job. "I won't call, of course."

"Are you sure about that?"

"Very."

"You know what I think, Carly Jo?"

She laughed, more out of pain than amusement. "I don't know, but you're dying to tell me. Go right ahead."

He paused, maybe to take a long draw on his pipe. "I'm sitting here on the porch looking at the clouds. Some of them are thunderheads boiling up right before my eyes. Others are as wispy as feathers. Way in the distance, there's a wall of gray and no blue sky at all because a storm's headed this way. You know what your mother used to say about the Kentucky weather."

"If you don't like it, wait an hour and it'll change."

"That's right."

When it came to beating around the bush, her father was a master. "What are you getting at, Daddy?"

"You used to love storms. You'd press your little nose to the window and watch the lightning as fearless as can be. The thunder didn't bother you a bit. You laughed at it. Now here's the point . . ." He paused as if he were preaching to his whole congregation, not just to Carly. "You've changed, baby girl. You've lost your courage."

Carly bristled from head to toe. "How can you say that? It took courage to move to Los Angeles."

"Yes, it did. But it might have taken more courage to stay at Sparrow House and face what happened."

Guilty as charged. If she used church lingo, maybe he'd believe her. "I have a new calling now. And the scholarship. God opened that door."

"I don't doubt it. And that's what troubles me. Maybe the Lord's opening a new door with this nanny job. I have to wonder if you're slamming it a little too quickly—and a little too hard."

She jumped to her feet and started to pace. "You know what'll happen if I take this job. Penny will get attached to me."

"I see the logic, but you've never been one to play it safe. Does this doctor seem like a decent man?"

She thought of the business card in her pocket. "He told me to call his office manager for a character reference. She's known him for years."

"That's a good sign."

"I suppose."

Her father said nothing for several seconds. She imagined him puffing his pipe and staring at the sky, until his deep voice broke the silence. "I know you'll make the right choice, but I wish I were there to look out for you."

When it came to protecting his family, Paul Mason had a big heart and the sincerity of a shotgun. A sweet smile lifted Carly's lips. "I know, Daddy. I love you lots."

"I love you, too, sweetheart." A sigh whispered over the phone. "Your mother and I worked hard to give you wings. We just didn't expect you to fly so far away."

He said *we* as if her mother were sitting next to him; then he changed the subject to news about her brother and sister. Carly ate up every detail until her break ended and they said their usual long good-bye.

The rest of the afternoon slipped by, and at closing time Carly locked up the store and drove to her apartment, a first floor studio in an old neighborhood. A year ago the area had seemed safe, but now gang graffiti and burglaries were on the rise. Just last week, someone broke into Bette's car and stole the phone she had carelessly left on the seat.

Vigilant as always, Carly turned down the alley that led to the carport behind her building. After parking, she gripped her pepper spray and headed for the gate leading to a courtyard full of over-grown juniper shrubs. Good lighting illuminated the way, but she trembled as she passed through the squeaky gate.

As she stepped onto the raised slab of her porch, Bette, still wearing her Vons bakery uniform, opened her own door and stepped outside. Her bubble of brown hair sagged a bit and her red lipstick was long gone, but a chunky bracelet—she wore them all the time—still dangled on her wrist. Today it was the pink and silver one Carly had given to her for her birthday.

"I've been waiting for you," Bette said. "You won't believe what I heard at work today."

Carly braced for bad news. "What happened?"

"There was a murder on Mariel Avenue. It was a home invasion by three men. The poor woman was raped and beaten to death. They didn't take anything, not even her purse."

Blood drained from Carly's face. Bad things happened everywhere, even in Boomer County, but a home invasion just two blocks away? Strangers beating up a woman for no reason? Carly didn't bother to ask God why. She had stopped asking that question the day her mother died. Instead of fighting what she couldn't understand, Carly had decided to become a doctor and find a cure for cancer. Her career goals had changed but not her ambition to do good in the world.

"I can't believe it," she muttered. "What's wrong with people?"

"It's the second one around here since April."

Two murders in two months within a few blocks of her apartment. Her belly clenched with a nauseating mix of fear and fury. "We both need to move."

"I think about it," Bette admitted. "But I've lived here twenty-two years. This is my home."

Dr. Tremaine's offer to live in flitted through Carly's mind. As appealing as that aspect of the job was, she refused to abandon Bette. "We could look for a two-bedroom and share it."

"Forget that!" Bette flicked her hand to dismiss the idea. "You know how I feel about my privacy. Besides, you're going home to Kentucky."

Bette's cat, a black male with four white paws, slinked around her ankles and meowed. "Tom's hungry. I better go."

"Me too." But first she knelt and gave Tom a chin scratch.

"Keep your door locked," Bette cautioned.

"Always."

In unison, they stepped into their matching apartments and shut their matching doors, each alone with her cat and her fears. A lamp cast a warm glow as Carly twisted the lock behind her. Unnerved by Bette's news, she placed her purse on the table holding her laptop and research material, and then sat on the bed and stroked Wild Thing.

Somewhat comforted, she went to the kitchenette to fix Wild Thing's supper. As she opened the lid on the trash to toss the empty can, the smell of yesterday's tuna assaulted her nose. Normally she would have run the bag out to the dumpster in the alley, but the trip would have to wait until morning. No way would she venture outside with a woman's murder fresh in her mind. She needed to move, but where? Rents were high in Los Angeles, and she didn't want roommates, especially fellow students who were as idealistic as she used to be.

She had no choice but to stay here . . . or to interview for the nanny job. Determined to push away the temptation, she plucked the business card from her pocket, moved to toss it in the trash, but stopped with it dangling over the garbage. Somehow tossing the card felt a little like tossing Penny.

At that moment, Carly didn't like herself very much. Her father was right. She'd lost her courage.

"Lord, I can't do it," she said out loud. "I just can't."

But neither could she let go of the business card. She was sick of being a coward, sick of the *what ifs* and *if onlys*. Maybe her father was right, and this was her chance to redeem herself. With shaking fingers, she set the card next to her laptop, then stared at the black letters that read *Ryan Tremaine, MD, General Ophthalmology*. She'd call Fran on Monday to arrange an interview, but not the one Dr. Tremaine expected. Carly would be interviewing him, and if her instincts told her she was making a mistake, she'd run from the job as fast as she could.

4

No one could be as perfect for the nanny job as Carly Mason, but Ryan's hopes soared when he opened the front door on Monday morning and saw Mrs. Harriet Howell, a woman the agency assured him was exemplary. Retired after forty-one years with just two families, Mrs. Howell took short-term assignments like this one when the agency couldn't immediately find a good match.

Ryan was particularly worried about today because Penny's Aunt Denise, a flight attendant based in Florida, was in town for the night and expected to pick her up around five o'clock. Ryan didn't mind Denise as a person, but he objected to the hawk-like way she watched his every move. To keep Denise at bay, he needed to find someone like Carly but older, someone without a mane of blond hair and skin as warm as a sun-ripened peach.

At first glance, Mrs. Howell fit the bill perfectly. Pleasantly plump, she was dressed in loose navy slacks, a white blouse, and a floral-print blazer with all the colors of the rainbow.

Smiling at him, she extended her hand. "Dr. Tremaine, I presume?"

"Yes."

"I'm Harriet Howell. It's a pleasure to meet you."

They shook like the business partners they were, and he escorted her into the two-story house. It was over seventy years old, recently updated, and a family heirloom. Ryan's grandfather had built it in the 1940s, passed it on to Ryan's father, who bequeathed it to Ryan at his passing three years ago. Having grown up here, he knew every nook and cranny.

Mrs. Howell glanced up the staircase. "Where's Penny?"

"Still asleep."

"And the boys?"

"Also asleep." He indicated the hall leading to the back of the house. "We can talk in the kitchen."

Thump. Thump. Thump. The ceiling shook with the force of Penny running down the hall to the front set of stairs that ended in the foyer. A second staircase gave access to the kitchen, a necessity and convenience in such a large house. He had told Penny not to run indoors, but she couldn't remember the rule or resist the impulse.

Ryan was about to say something to Mrs. Howell when Penny hit the landing and skidded to a halt with her pajama top misbuttoned and her feet bare on the plush carpet.

Eyes wide, she stared at Mrs. Howell's colorful jacket with trepidation. "Someone painted your coat. It's messy."

Mrs. Howell's eyes twinkled. "I think it's pretty. So are your pajamas. Pink is my favorite color."

Penny trotted the rest of the way down the stairs, then lifted her little chin. "I like purple best."

"Purple is beautiful," Mrs. Howell replied. "Every color is pretty in its own way, isn't it?"

"Especially purple."

Chuckling like a grandma, Mrs. Howell winked at Ryan. "We're going to be just fine."

He breathed a sigh of relief, officially introduced Penny to Mrs. Howell, then led the way to the kitchen with Penny holding Mrs.

Howell's hand and chattering about her stuffed animals. She attached easily to people, a problem with strangers but an advantage with a new nanny. He needed a word with Mrs. Howell before he left, so he waited while she and Penny fixed a bowl of cereal. When Penny was occupied with breakfast, he showed Mrs. Howell the list of phone numbers and household rules pinned to a corkboard.

"It's all very clear," she said, skimming it.

"Kyle will take care of himself," he told her. "And Eric has permission to visit a friend. The boy's mother will pick him up later."

Mrs. Howell skimmed the list, nodding with approval. "You're very organized."

"I try."

"About Penny . . ." She lowered her voice. "The agency explained the situation. We need time to get to know each other, but I'm a firm believer in structure. Children need discipline. I'm sure you agree."

"Yes, but Penny's a little different from most kids." And she'd be different her entire life. "It's not always a matter of *won't*. Sometimes she *can't*."

Mrs. Howell's cheerful expression melted into pity. "Was she adopted from Russia? I've heard about terrible problems with those children."

"Penny's mine," he said, claiming both his daughter and the responsibility. "Fetal alcohol happens here, too." When Mrs. Howell waited for more, he gave his standard reply. "It's complicated."

"Never mind, then." She fluttered her hand. "Is there anything in particular I need to know about her?"

Where did he start? Blaring televisions made her screech, so Ryan kept the volume low. Certain smells made her gag, so he'd switched to a milder aftershave. As for impulse control, she didn't have any. Ryan didn't have time to school Mrs. Howell on FASD, so he settled for the obvious. "Just keep an eye on her. If you turn your back for a minute, she'll get into something."

Kyle walked into the kitchen dressed for baseball practice, saw

Mrs. Howell, and introduced himself. At least one of Ryan's kids had good manners, and he basked in a bit of pride until Eric showed up wearing a frown.

Mrs. Howell took Eric's grunt in stride, then turned back to Ryan. "Go on to work, Dr. Tremaine. We'll be fine."

"You have my number. Call if you need anything."

He palmed his keys, then paused to glance at Penny seated at the table. Droplets of milk were splattered around her bowl, but she seemed happy today. As for Kyle, he was on his second bowl of some granola concoction, and the gallon jug of milk—the one Ryan had bought yesterday—was less than a quarter full. When Eric nearly polished it off, Ryan held back a sigh. He'd have to stop at the store on his way home for what seemed like the hundredth time since the boys moved in. How did single parents work and do all the running around? At least he could afford help.

After a quick good-bye to the kids, he drove to Pacific Eye Associates, where he was partnered with four other doctors in a busy practice. Medicine as a science enthralled Ryan's intellect, but he hated the bureaucracy and business end with a passion. In that way, he was a lot like his father. A famed neurosurgeon, Garrett Tremaine had embodied perfection and expected his only son to do the same. Ryan never did tell him about Penny or the affair. As for his mother, she had died of a heart attack shortly before his father. She knew about Penny, and in that gracious way of hers, she'd encouraged him to make his daughter part of his family.

Ryan loved Penny fiercely, but he hated FASD and the challenges it posed. With the need for a permanent nanny heavy on his mind, he went through the Employees Only door and straight to Fran's office. She was seated at a monitor looking at today's appointments.

With her typical good cheer, she smiled a greeting. "How was your weekend?"

"Awful."

She sat back in the chair. "So what did Penny do this time? Or was it one of the boys?" With two adult children of her own, Fran was an excellent sounding board.

"Penny got lost at the mall." He told her everything, including Carly's involvement and how he'd given her the business card in spite of her resistance. "If she calls, tell her I'm not a jerk."

Fran laughed. "You're not a jerk. In fact, you're the second-best boss I've ever had." Her best boss being Ryan's sainted father. When Garrett Tremaine died, Ryan had snapped up Fran for his own practice.

"Thanks," he said dryly. "That'll convince her."

"I hope so. You need help. If Carly calls, should I set up an interview?"

"Definitely. Anytime. Any place she wants to meet. Just let me know." Talk of Carly reminded him of Denise's visit and the empty milk jug. "I need to get out of here early. How does my schedule look?"

Fran turned to the monitor. "We had some cancellations. If I move up the Carters, you can be out of here by three."

"Do it." He trusted Mrs. Howell, but first days with Penny could be rough. He'd be wise to get home early. He had to stop for milk. Bread too. And more apples and string cheese. It would be just like Denise to open the fridge, see the half-inch of milk in the jug, and wave it under his nose as a sign of parental incompetence.

Fran scribbled on a Post-it. "I'll message you if Carly calls."

"Thanks."

Ryan ducked into his office, traded his blazer for a white lab coat, and headed to the exam room for his first patient. He usually lost himself in his work, but today he glanced constantly at the message function on his computer monitor to see if Carly had called. When there was no word from Fran by lunch, he picked up a file and made some notes.

A tap on the door surprised him. Looking up, he saw Fran with a grin on her face. "Carly Mason just called."

"Oh yeah?"

"She'll be at your house at four o'clock."

"What did you think?"

"I like her," Fran said. "We spoke for twenty minutes. She's e-mailing her resume, references, everything you need for a background check, plus she's bringing a hard copy to the interview. If she takes the job, I'll call it an answer to prayer."

Leave it to Fran to give God credit for a coincidence. It was human nature, pure and simple, that led Penny to the Animal Factory, but he didn't bother to argue with Fran. She knew how he felt, and they agreed to disagree.

"I think she's the one," Fran remarked.

"I hope so." Especially with Denise arriving after the interview. If Carly was as qualified as he hoped, he could introduce her to Denise, and Denise could quiz her to her heart's content. On the other hand, if the interview with Carly bombed, Mrs. Howell was his ace in the hole.

Fran reminded him of the lunch with a drug rep in the office kitchen, then left him to finish his notes. He hurried through the routine reports, but his mind was on the interview with Carly. He didn't know very much about her, except she had experience with FASD and was in grad school. It was a good start. A very good start, but he wished she looked like Mrs. Howell, complete with gray hair and baggy pants.

❧

Carly rang the doorbell at the Tremaine house, waited a full minute, and rang it again. When no one answered, she walked back to the street to check the address painted on the curb. She was at the right house, so where was Dr. Tremaine?

If she wanted out of the interview, this was her chance.

Her gaze shifted back to the white stucco house framed by drooping elms and a horseshoe driveway. It was in an affluent area, an old neighborhood with custom homes, mature trees, and quiet, winding streets. There wasn't a speck of graffiti in sight. Pulled in two directions—to go or to stay—Carly stood by her old Cavalier with the asphalt burning through the soles of her ballet flats. As much as she wanted to flee, she had to be fair. Doctors often ran late, and so did she occasionally. A ten-minute grace period seemed in order.

The minutes crept by until a black Honda coupe zipped into the cul-de-sac, slowed, and veered into the Tremaine driveway. The sporty car looked like something Ryan Tremaine would drive, so she approached with her purse and curriculum vitae in hand. The car door flung wide, the trunk popped, and Dr. Tremaine climbed out of the driver's seat in a rush of energy and motion.

"Sorry I'm late," he called to her as he lifted four grocery bags from the trunk. "Did you just get here?"

"About five minutes ago. I rang the bell, but no one answered."

His straight brows snapped together. "The boys are out, but Penny's here with a substitute nanny. She should have heard the doorbell." With the bags dragging on his arms, he jammed his key in the lock and called out, "Mrs. Howell?"

No answer.

He brushed past Carly and headed down a short hall. Unsure of what to do, she followed him into an airy kitchen that opened into a family room filled with overstuffed furniture, a brick hearth, and a huge television. A red afghan lay in a heap on the sofa, and a hundred colorful blocks were strewn across the floor. Carly turned back to the kitchen, where Dr. Tremaine had left the bags on the counter before approaching a stairwell.

"Penny?" he called. "Mrs. Howell?"

Carly's stomach lurched. With Penny's impulsiveness, anything could have happened.

Dr. Tremaine turned away from the stairs, muttered an oath, and yanked at his tie as if it were choking him. "I have to find her."

"I'll help."

His gaze veered to a sliding glass door, slightly ajar with lace curtains askew and the screen pushed back. "What in the world—"

He strode toward it, shoved the glass wider, and walked into the backyard. A sixtyish woman in a colorful jacket was pacing along the wrought-iron fence on the far side of the pool. With her back to them, she was peering down the hill behind the house. Presumably this was Mrs. Howell, and she was looking for Penny.

After dropping her purse on the table, Carly followed Dr. Tremaine into a beautifully landscaped yard. Ten steps ahead of her, he strode to the edge of the turquoise pool, his neck bent as he paced along the edge, searching the bottom.

Dear Lord . . . No.

Carly mentally ran through pediatric CPR, praying they wouldn't need it. By the time she reached the lip of the tile, Dr. Tremaine had circled to the deep end. Chest heaving, he raked his hand through his hair. If Penny had been in the water, he would have jumped in and dragged her out. Carly breathed easier, but the relief was short-lived.

Across the pool, Mrs. Howell stood frozen by the iron fence that marked the edge of the yard and a steep slope that faced the Pacific Ocean. Any other time, Carly would have savored the view, but today she approached Mrs. Howell with her head full of fear and the old guilt caused by losing a child.

Dr. Tremaine reached Mrs. Howell first. "Where's my daughter?"

"I-I—" Ashen and gray, she broke into choked sobs. "She was incorrigible. I put her down for a nap. I thought it would calm her."

"Where is she?"

"I don't know." Cringing, Mrs. Howell pressed her hands to her cheeks, gasped for air, then turned to Carly with a bleak plea in her eyes. "I've never had this happen before. I lost her. I can't believe it."

"We'll find her." Carly laid her hand on Mrs. Howell's sleeve and squeezed. She'd once stood in this woman's shoes, though instead of facing a parent, she had been accountable to her boss. *"You became too involved with her, Carly. You lost your professional distance, and Allison paid for it."* So had Carly, but she'd learned her lesson. Mustering a new calm, she focused on Dr. Tremaine. "Does Penny have a favorite hiding place?"

He raked a hand through his hair. "Her closet. I've found her there before."

Mrs. Howell sniffed. "I looked there first. I looked everywhere, but it's such a big house. It's just so—"

"How long has she been missing?" he asked.

The woman wrung her hands. "I-I don't know. Kyle left for baseball practice around eleven. Eric left with Nathan after lunch. I tried to read Penny a story, but she wouldn't hold still. She kept kicking the coffee table and wouldn't stop even when I counted to three. I tried everything. I thought a nap would help."

A muscle twitched in Dr. Tremaine's jaw. "When did you see Penny last?"

"An hour ago."

With his lips sealed, he inhaled rapidly through his nose. Carly braced for an explosion, but instead he spoke to Mrs. Howell with the cool detachment of a man in control. "What were you doing for an entire hour?"

"I fell asleep," she admitted. "It's been such a difficult day, and I-I dozed off on the couch. When I went to get Penny out of her room, she was gone. I can't believe this happened. I've never—"

"We'll find her," Carly said again, but her heart sank to her toes. She had spouted the same vain platitudes about Allison and never seen her again, didn't know if the teenager was dead or alive.

All business, Dr. Tremaine gave a curt nod. "I'll check the house. Mrs. Howell, knock on the neighbors' doors. Maybe someone has seen her."

"Yes, sir." She hurried back through the house, leaving Carly alone with Dr. Tremaine.

"Where should I start?" she asked.

"Check the outside, including the old garage over there." He pointed at a low outbuilding behind a block wall. "It should be locked, but Kyle keeps his baseball stuff in there. He might have left it open."

They walked in opposite directions, Dr. Tremaine returning to the house and Carly pacing along the perimeter of the fence. The iron bars were four inches apart, like prison bars, and they didn't bend even a little. Penny couldn't possibly have slipped through them. Even so, Carly scoured the steep hill with her eyes. Seeing nothing, she turned at the corner of the fence and the block wall, saw an open gate, and spotted Miss Rabbit's purple ballet outfit on the ground. Hot on Penny's trail, Carly raced in that direction.

5

Ryan hurried up the stairs to the second floor, repeatedly calling Penny's name in the most normal tone he could muster. "Where are you, sweetheart?"

He listened for a giggle or even a sob, anything to indicate she was breathing and present. "Penny?"

Still no answer.

Methodical by nature, he started the search in her room by pulling open the closet doors. Toys and clothes lay on the floor in a jumble that was uniquely Penny, but there was no sign of her. Leaving the doors wide, he peered under the unmade bed, then turned to the window that looked into the thick canopy of an elm tree. He had picked this room for Penny so she could enjoy hearing the birds. Now he was worried that she'd reached for a sparrow and fallen to the ground. With his heart in his throat, he pushed the lacy curtains aside, checked the screen, and breathed a sigh when he saw the latches securely fastened.

He checked his own room next. It only took a minute, because it was military neat. Orderliness had been trained into him, which made the messiness of Penny's mind even more of a mystery to him.

Next he surveyed Eric's room, a mess beyond description.

Then Kyle's room, a relaxed assortment of clothes, books, and sports posters on the walls.

Ryan checked the bathrooms, the linen closet, even the door to the crawl space over the living room. There were a thousand hiding places in the big old house, and Ryan knew every one of them. He'd grown up here and had spent hours exploring and making up games. If he hadn't become a doctor, he would have been a marine biologist exploring exotic islands. Instead, he followed in his father's footsteps, rebelling only enough to become an ophthalmologist instead of a neurosurgeon.

With Penny missing, he wished he'd become anything but what he was—a failure as a husband and father, a jaded cynic, a prisoner to mistakes he couldn't fix. Even worse, Penny was a prisoner, too, a prisoner who'd escaped and needed to be found for her own safety.

He thudded down the front stairs to check the first floor, including the nanny quarters on the far side of the house. As his foot hit the tiled entry hall, the doorbell rang. Maybe a neighbor had found Penny. Or maybe it was a police officer with horrible news.

In that blink between hope and certainty, Ryan stared down the abyss of utter helplessness. He wished he could pray like his mother and Fran or sing "Amazing Grace" like Carly, but his only comfort was the randomness of fate. With his chest tight, he opened the door. Instead of a neighbor with Penny or a police officer, he came face-to-face with Denise, all smiles and holding a stuffed kangaroo as tall as Penny.

"Pretty cool, isn't it?" She held the toy out for him to admire. "I picked it up in Sydney last week. Penny's going to love it."

"Uh—" Ryan froze.

Denise tipped her head. "I know I'm early. Is this a bad time?"

"No. Yes. I mean . . . uh . . ." He was stammering. Ryan never stammered.

With her hair tight in a bun, Denise exuded the calm authority of someone accustomed to being in control. That authority was well deserved. A few years ago, she had been in a fiery crash landing and saved a hundred lives. The heroine of the day, she'd been interviewed on all the major networks.

Maybe she could work that magic to find Penny. "Come in," he said, steadier now. "I'm in the middle of another nanny problem."

She let out a huff. "So what happened this time?"

"In spite of great references, today's nanny fell asleep on the couch. Penny's hiding somewhere."

"Hiding?" Denise's perfectly shaped brows pulled into crooked lines. "Does that mean you can't find her?"

With each word, her voice hit a new high in volume and tone. Ryan wanted to plead the Fifth Amendment but settled for dodging the question like a bad politician. "It means we're looking for her."

Kangaroo in hand, Denise called up the front stairwell. "Penny, it's Aunt DeeDee. I have a present for you."

Daring to hope, he listened for footsteps pounding down the stairs.

Nothing.

"Penny?" Denise called again. When there was no reply, she marched down the hall to the kitchen, set the kangaroo on the floor, whirled around, and stared at Ryan with the authority of a Supreme Court judge. "I want to know *exactly* what happened."

"Penny likes to run off. It's some sort of game. I'll tell you more after we find her."

Denise snatched her phone out of her pocket. "I'm calling police. How long has she been gone?"

"It's too soon."

"How long?" she demanded. "And is this nanny missing, too? Did she kidnap her? We need an Amber Alert."

Even if Penny had walked out the front door, it seemed impossible that a stranger could have snatched her from this quiet street. But how far could she wander in an hour? Maybe it was time to call the police after all. Except that phone call would be a black mark on his record as a father, and Denise was keeping score. Every minute counted, but logic told him Penny was somewhere in the house or close by.

"Let's finish searching the house," he said to her. "Today's nanny is checking with the neighbors, and a woman I'm interviewing is looking out back. If we don't find her in five minutes, we'll call the police."

Denise lowered her phone, but the glare in her eyes burned hotter. "I'll give you three, then I'm calling for that Amber Alert."

Code Adams.

Amber Alerts.

Denise was right. Danger lurked everywhere. Even two minutes was too long if Penny was in trouble. "I'll call now. Keep looking."

As Denise stepped into the backyard, Ryan picked up the house phone and raised his hand to punch in 9-1-1.

❧

Carly snatched the purple ballerina outfit off the concrete and headed for the old garage next to the house. Designed for one car, it had probably been built with the original residence in a distant decade. Dirt stains marred the white stucco sides, but the overhead door was modern, complete with keypad access. With the ballerina outfit in hand, she brushed by a spindly shrub surrounded by an apron of dark berries on the concrete walk.

When a berry squished under her shoe, she looked down and saw small, purplish footprints leading to a side door left ajar. She eased it open until a fan of light revealed a 1960-something Chevy Impala, a car like the one she'd seen in Polaroids of her grandparents as newlyweds, except this was a pristine white convertible with the top down to reveal a cherry red interior.

The car charmed her, but it was the sight of Penny in the backseat, asleep and hugging Miss Rabbit, that made Carly's heart thump with relief. Bending at the waist, she laid a hand on her shoulder. "Penny, wake up."

Penny rolled to her side. As she pulled her knees to her chest, Carly saw berry-colored footprints on the upholstery. A quick glance revealed Penny's exact entry into the car. She had opened the passenger door, climbed in the front seat, and walked over the console to the back.

Considering the Impala was fully restored, the stains were more than a mess. Penny had done real damage. How Dr. Tremaine reacted to the news would be a telling moment, maybe the moment Carly decided whether or not to take the job. She expected him to be annoyed, but if he valued the car over the child, she'd have a reason to leave.

She gave Penny a second little shake. "Come on, sweetheart. Your daddy's worried. Let's go find him."

With her eyelids fluttering, Penny rolled to her back, saw Carly, and bolted upright with Miss Rabbit flopping in her hand. "You're the animal lady."

"That's right."

"You made Miss Rabbit talk." Penny scrambled across the seat and stood to climb out of the car. "Lance is upstairs. Let's get him."

Unmindful of dings, dents, and berry juice, Penny flung a leg over the side. Carly lifted her up and out, and they left the garage with Penny clutching Miss Rabbit and Carly holding Penny's hand. In a *Wizard of Oz* kind of way, they made quite a trio— a child with a damaged brain, a stuffed animal that needed a child's heart, and an ex-social worker who lacked the courage to care again.

Hand in hand, they walked into the backyard with Carly humming "Follow the Yellow Brick Road." She wasn't ready to take the job, but finding Penny filled her with some of her old hope. With her heart lighter than it had been in months, she could almost forgive herself for losing Allison.

◦◦◦

Penny had once heard a doctor say her brain was like a jigsaw puzzle with missing pieces. She didn't understand what that meant, or what FASD stood for. She only knew she was different. When adults talked, she heard some of the words but not all of them. Other times the words meant something different to the adult than they did to her, like what happened this morning with Mrs. Howell. When the nanny said, *"Make your bed,"* Penny said back to her, *"Make it do what?"*

Things like that happened all the time. Penny didn't care about making her bed, whatever that meant, but she cared a lot about a place called heaven. Aunt DeeDee said her mother was there and looking down at her. If that was true, why couldn't Penny see her? And if heaven was a place, why couldn't Penny find it and be with Mommy again?

That's why she had wandered off at the mall—that and the awful noise and bad smells in the arcade. And that's why today she had hurried to the garage when Mrs. Howell fell asleep. Last night Dr. Tremaine told Kyle his old car took him back in time to when he was Kyle's age. Hoping to go back in time and find her mommy, Penny had climbed in, closed her eyes and . . . it worked! The car didn't take her to her mother in heaven, but it brought Carly from the Animal Factory.

Holding on to both Miss Rabbit and Carly, Penny skipped through the gate leading to the backyard. A breeze blew through the fence and suddenly she wanted . . . Penny didn't know what she wanted, but Carly was here and that made her happy enough to pull free and spin in a circle, which she did, just because she wanted to spin.

Carly lunged after her, took her by the hand, and together they passed the swimming pool where Penny could be a mermaid. She'd seen the movie about Ariel a hundred times, or at least pieces of it, because it was too hard to sit still for so long.

"Can you swim?" Carly asked.

Penny didn't know what Carly meant, but she said yes because she thought that was what Carly wanted to hear. When Penny had lived with her mother, they spent a lot of time in the pool at their apartment. Penny knew how to kick and move her arms, something her mother called *the dog paddle*, which made no sense to Penny, because she wasn't a dog. Dogs scared her, but she liked cats because they didn't bark and jump on her.

She and Carly were five steps from the house when the sliding glass door whooshed open and Aunt DeeDee ran out with her arms stretched wide and her mouth hanging open like a big fish.

"Penny! Oh, my word—"

Aunt DeeDee hugged her so hard that Penny couldn't breathe. Aunt DeeDee was crying, too, like the day Penny's mother left for heaven. Penny didn't understand that trip at all. How did riding in a boat and putting ashes in the ocean get a person to heaven? Aunt DeeDee said Penny was too young to understand, and that someday she would explain it better. But Penny wanted to know now. She had even asked Dr. Tremaine the day he told her he was her daddy, but he just said her mommy was gone forever. If the magic car didn't work, maybe Penny would find a boat and look for her in the ocean.

She wiggled free from Aunt DeeDee and saw Dr. Tremaine come through the door with the big house phone pressed to his ear. He said something like, "We found her. Yes. Yes. She's safe." Then he set the phone on a brick planter, came up next to her, and dropped down on one knee.

"Hey, sweetheart." He laid his hand on her shoulder in a nice way. "Where were you?"

She worried Dr. Tremaine would be mad, so she lied. "I don't know."

"I think you do," he said in his daddy voice. He told her all the time to call him Daddy, or even a special name she made up. He just didn't want her to call him Dr. Tremaine. But nothing else felt right. Only Dr. Tremaine felt right because Penny visited a lot of doctors, and he acted like one.

"Were you hiding?" he said in that same nice voice.

She didn't want to say yes, because the magic car was special and he might move it or lock the door to the garage, so she pointed to the air behind the house. "I went there."

Aunt DeeDee hunkered down and hugged her as hard as the first time.

Her daddy stood straight, then reached down with his big hand and touched her hair. It tickled and Penny pulled away. Aunt DeeDee raised her chin at her daddy like she was mad, stood straight like he was, and told him he had some explaining to do. Penny thought they would yell at each other, but Dr. Tremaine made that tight face that meant he was thinking before he spoke, something everyone told Penny to do.

Finally he turned to Carly. "Where was she?"

"In the garage, sleeping in the old Impala."

Penny wished Carly had kept the secret, but Carly didn't know the car was magic.

Aunt DeeDee hissed air through her nose. "This is unacceptable. What about fumes or . . . or . . ." She kept stammering about bad things like the car rolling backward or Penny getting locked in the garage. Penny understood some of what Aunt DeeDee said but not every word. Finally Aunt DeeDee stopped talking about the magic car.

Mad and upset, Aunt DeeDee scowled at Penny's daddy. "I don't understand it, Ryan. How hard can it be to find a competent nanny?"

"Harder than you think," he said in his doctor voice.

Aunt DeeDee glared at him, then cupped Penny's face with both hands. "Penny, you can't run off alone."

"But I wasn't alone." She held up Miss Rabbit to prove it.

Aunt DeeDee pressed her fingers over her mouth like she was going to cry again, but Penny didn't see the big deal. "It was just like at the mall. I went to the Animal Factory all by myself. It was fun."

Her daddy groaned. "Penny, that's enough."

Why was he mad? She was telling the truth like he said to do. She gave a little huff, then looked up at Aunt DeeDee. "Eric was mean, so I left him at the stupid arcade and went to the Animal Factory, because that's where Bethany had her birthday party. Carly was there and she made Miss Rabbit talk. Then Dr. Tremaine came, and so did Kyle and Eric and a man with the badge, and . . . and . . ." Penny lost track of the story, so she turned to Carly and held up Miss Rabbit. "Make her talk. Okay?"

All three adults stared down at her. Her daddy's mouth was tight like a zipper but twisted. Aunt DeeDee's eyebrows were so high they looked like mountains. Carly was the only person wearing a normal face. She looked at Aunt DeeDee, then at Penny's daddy. "The three of us need to talk." She held her hand out to Aunt DeeDee. "I'm Carly Mason, and I'm here to interview for the nanny job."

Aunt DeeDee shook her hand, but she didn't look happy about it. "I'm Denise Caldwell, Penny's aunt—her mother's sister."

"She's a very special little girl," Carly said, smiling down at Penny.

Penny didn't feel special. She just felt different. Hugging Miss Rabbit, she wished—she didn't know what she wished.

Dr. Tremaine glanced at the house. Penny turned her head and saw Mrs. Howell by the big glass door with her hand on her chest.

Her daddy called out, "We found her." Then he reached for Penny's hand. "Aunt DeeDee and I need to talk to Carly."

"Okay."

When her daddy walked her to the house and told Mrs. Howell to give her Oreos and a big glass of milk, Penny was happy. She liked Oreos the best, and she told her daddy that. He said he liked them too, then he hugged her as hard as Aunt DeeDee did, even harder, and went back out to the patio.

6

Still reeling from the search, Ryan headed for the patio table, a glass rectangle shaded by a beige vented umbrella. Four feet away from it, Carly and Denise were waiting in the awkward way of strangers who'd just met and didn't like each other.

"Let's sit," Ryan said to the women.

As if they were at a cocktail party instead of a job interview, he pulled out two chairs. Denise reached him ahead of Carly, her expression smug as she sat at the head of the table. Ryan indicated Carly should take the chair facing away from the house, and he sat facing the kitchen window, where Mrs. Howell and Penny were in his line of sight.

When he shifted his gaze to Carly, he saw the guarded expression she'd worn at the Animal Factory. He wished he could read her mind. She was either an ally in his fight with Denise or the star witness against him.

"This won't be a conventional interview," he said, folding his hands on the table. "I'd like to start by explaining Penny's remark about going to the Animal Factory and how she met Carly."

"Good," Denise replied, "because Penny's version is terrifying. What was she doing alone in a toy store?"

"That's a good question and a fair one," he admitted. "Penny's nanny quit on Friday. Kyle needed new baseball cleats, so I brought all three kids." Refusing to dodge the truth, he told Denise about sending Eric and Penny for ice cream, the faulty cash register, and the Code Adam. "It was a mistake. A bad one. It won't happen again."

Razors flashed in her hazel eyes. "Let me be clear here. You left my niece—a special needs child—in the care of a thirteen-year-old boy?"

"I expected to be ten steps behind them."

"But you weren't."

"No." A witness box in a stifling courtroom would have been more comfortable than the padded chair shaded by the umbrella. If he were in Denise's place, he'd ask the same outraged questions, just like she asked questions the day they met in his attorney's office to discuss custody and visitation. She'd brought an e-mail from Jenna, written two years ago, asking her to raise Penny if something ever happened to her. His DNA trumped that letter, but she'd pressed him. *"Why do you want her?"*

"Because she's mine."

It really was that simple. As low as he'd fallen before and after the divorce, he couldn't abandon a child with his blood. Penny looked a lot like Jenna, but she had Ryan's eyes and the Tremaine nose. She was part of him—the neglected part he needed to redeem.

Prepared for a lashing, he drew back in the chair and faced Denise. "It was a bad decision. I admit it."

Under the table, someone kicked his foot. Startled, he glanced at Carly. Her eyes were riveted to Denise, giving no indication that she'd signaled him. But who else could it be? Denise was too far away, and the kick wasn't an accident.

Carly broke in. "I think this is where I come in."

Denise raised her perfectly penciled brows. "I'm sorry if this comes off as rude, but you're here for an interview, not to interfere in a family matter. I'd prefer it if you'd wait inside with the other nanny."

"I have a unique perspective," Carly replied. "I'm assistant manager at the Animal Factory. When Penny wandered away, she came to our store, and I found her. The story doesn't start well—not at all. But I saw how Dr. Tremaine handled it. All parents make mistakes. What counts far more is what comes next, how a person makes a bad situation better. That's what a child learns."

Absolution. Ryan craved it.

Denise leaned back in the chair and crossed her legs. "I appreciate your perspective, Carly. Working in a toy store, you must see children and parents every day."

"I do."

"That's nice," Denise said, maybe meaning it. "How old are you, dear? Twenty-two, maybe twenty-three?"

"I'm twenty-eight."

Like Denise, Ryan had assumed Carly was younger. He viewed her age as an advantage, plus he knew she was in grad school, another plus no matter what she was studying. With that kick to his foot, she'd told him she was on his side. But what she brought to the table remained to be revealed. She could still torpedo him by accident.

Denise tapped a crimson fingernail on the arm of the metal chair. "So you're twenty-eight and you manage a toy store. That sounds like fun."

"Oh, it is."

"Yes, but let's be realistic. Managing a toy store hardly qualifies you to judge the situation with Penny. You might not be aware of it, but she has special needs."

"I'm aware." Carly turned her attention to Ryan, giving him both authority over Denise and a look at the intense gleam in her pretty eyes. "My CV is on the kitchen table. I can get it if you'd like."

The fact she said CV, short for curriculum vitae, instead of resume, told Ryan she had more clout than he knew. "Why don't you summarize for us, starting with your education."

"I'd be glad to." Her eyes twinkled at him, then she turned back to Denise. "I have a BA in biology and a masters' in social work, both from the University of Kentucky. A year ago I won the Emma Hanson Scholarship from the UCLA School of Social Welfare and am working on my doctorate."

"What's your focus?" Ryan asked.

"My dissertation is on fetal alcohol prevention." She looked straight at Denise. "FASD is the one birth defect that can be prevented one hundred percent of the time. Education is vital, and that's my long-term goal—to make sure women understand the consequence of alcohol consumption during pregnancy."

So the toy-store manager was an expert on FASD. Ryan rubbed his jaw to hide a smirk, then pitched her another question. "The scholarship's impressive. Any other honors?"

"Phi Beta Kappa and Alpha Delta Mu. That's a national honor society for social workers. My master's thesis was on FASD. It won a prize and was published last year."

With the smirk under control, he risked a look at Denise. "Any questions for Carly?"

"Yes, several." Her lips pulled into a frown, but she erased it with a careless shrug. "You surprised me, Carly. And I admit it— I'm impressed."

"Thank you."

"Let's move on a bit." Denise recrossed her legs. "What hands-on experience do you have with FASD?"

Sitting tall, she emanated confidence, but her eyes lost their sparkle. "Back in Lexington I counseled teenage girls at a group home called Sparrow House. Two had full-blown FAS, but I suspect others were affected by fetal alcohol as well." Her gaze shifted from Denise to Ryan. "I know firsthand how difficult it is to cope with a disability that's unseen and misunderstood. It's hard on the kids and the caregivers alike."

She understands. She knows the fight. Which meant she knew *him* in a way few people did. If they'd been alone, he'd have told her how much her understanding meant, but Denise's gaze stayed hard on his face until she shifted her attention back to Carly.

"I have another question," she said. "How did you become interested in this particular field?"

"A boy back home had FASD. When his parents adopted him, they had no idea what they were getting into. This boy struggled in school and got in trouble, but his parents did everything possible for him. He'll always need some help, but he's seventeen now and works at the grocery store. Love can't fix a damaged brain, but I saw the difference it can make to a child with special needs."

Denise looked down her nose. "That's a lovely sentiment. You started in biology, though. Why the biology degree?"

"I was premed for a while." She focused solely on Ryan. "I had plans to save the world, but medicine wasn't a good fit."

Ryan knew the feeling. His youthful ambitions had been different, but he recalled that naïve passion to explore the unknown and leave his mark, like the astronauts on the moon. Those dreams went up in smoke somewhere in college when he'd succumbed to his father's pressure to go to medical school. He had also met Heather and become infatuated with her. When they eloped, Kyle was already on the way. Ryan had felt trapped at the time, not because of the baby but because of the lost dreams.

Carly, it seemed, had escaped those regrets and he wanted to know more. "When you worked with FASD kids, what was a typical day like?"

"Typical? There's no such thing."

That was Ryan's experience, too, but Denise interrupted. "That's true, but we have to provide Penny with routine."

"Absolutely," Carly replied. "But we also have to remember

Penny has brain damage. Her mind works in unique ways, which means there are things she can't do and things she won't do. There are also things she *can* do, but only if the adults in her life communicate their expectations in a way she can understand. It's all very confusing, especially for outsiders, because she looks perfectly normal. But she's not."

"No." Ryan thought of the tantrums for no apparent reason; her hypersensitivity to noise, smells, tight socks, and bright lights; the storytelling and lying; her learning challenges. Most frustrating for him personally was her inability to understand the consequences of her actions. "She's impulsive," he said. "If she wants something, she takes it."

"That's typical," Carly replied. "Raising children with FASD is a unique challenge. They pull your heart right out of your chest about a dozen times a day, either because you're afraid for them, because you love them so much it hurts, or because you're so grateful for a special moment."

"That's it exactly," Ryan said.

Denise had the annoying habit of huffing through her nose, and she did it now. "You're certainly qualified to work with Penny. But don't you think that leads to another question?"

"Of course," Carly said to her. "Hiring a nanny is a big decision."

"You're highly qualified, perhaps overqualified. Tell me, Carly. Do you really want to be Nanny Number Five?"

❧

Carly didn't care for either Denise's tone or the vaguely superior gleam in her eyes. "I'm not sure yet. I came here today to interview Dr. Tremaine—not the other way around. I didn't expect to meet you, but I'm glad you're here. Penny has strong family support. That's a big advantage."

"Yes," Denise agreed. "I'd do anything for her."

Dr. Tremaine pushed his chair back a few inches, draped a leather shoe over his knee, and looked at her with an appreciative gleam in his eyes. "The job's yours if you want it. What'll it take for you to say yes?"

"I'd like to know more about Penny, how she was diagnosed, and her early years with her mother."

The pool pump kicked on with a hum, and the water rippled to break the silence. Denise hid her face, pinched the bridge of her nose, then wiped away tears with her fingertips. "I'm sorry. It's . . . it's just still so fresh."

After a respectful pause, Dr. Tremaine focused back on Carly. "Jenna died in a car accident. A drunk hit her head on after a night shift at the hospital. She died instantly."

"I'm so sorry," Carly murmured.

"Life is cruel." He spoke in a benign tone, but his voice carried the weight of human suffering. "We deal with it. There's not much of a choice, is there?"

Carly thought of the home invasion in her own neighborhood. "No, there isn't. But it's still wrong."

"It's also real." His gaze hardened into a stare, one that dared her to argue.

Putting her personal angst aside, she lifted her chin. "That's true, but we can strive to make the world a better place." That was Carly's purpose in life and the reason she was working on a PhD.

"Jenna's death was just so wrong," Denise said, her voice breathy. "Penny's my only family. You can understand what she means to me."

"Yes." Carly couldn't imagine being that alone. In addition to her father, brother, and sister, she had aunts, uncles, and a passel of cousins.

"It's just all too much—" Choking on a sob, Denise shoved to her feet. "I'm sorry. I need a moment."

Ryan stood with her. "If you'd like some privacy, you can use the guest room upstairs."

She paused to inhale, then squared her shoulders. "Mostly I need to hug Penny and give her that kangaroo."

"She'll love it," Dr. Tremaine assured her. In a lighter tone, he spoke directly to Carly. "Denise is a flight attendant. She brought Penny a three-foot stuffed kangaroo from Sydney."

"What a perfect surprise."

Denise managed a watery grin. "Ryan, if you don't mind, I'll take Penny to dinner a little early. The other nanny can leave, and you and Carly can finish the interview."

When he stood, so did Carly. She offered her hand to Denise. "I'm glad we met."

"I am, too." Denise squeezed Carly's fingers, then she and Dr. Tremaine went into the house.

Restless and weighed down by thoughts of Allison, Carly wandered to the fence at the back of the yard. With one hand on a black bar, she stared at the ocean and silently asked God whether she should take the job or run from the risk of personal involvement. The only answer was the scrape of palm fronds high above her head. It was a lonely sound, a rustling like the one deep in her soul. She tried so hard to do the right thing, to be a good person. But what if she failed Penny the way she had failed Allison?

She needed help, a sign like the one God gave to Gideon in the Bible, when He'd answered the man's desperate prayer for assurance by dampening a cloth with dew. The picture of Gideon cowering in a winepress triggered the memory of the berry stains on the seats of the Impala, and she decided to ask for a sign of her own. When she told Dr. Tremaine about the mess, he'd probably try to clean it. If the stains came out, she'd stay. If they didn't, she'd take her guilt and leave.

7

Ryan listened to Mrs. Howell apologize for the fortieth time and sent her home. Anyone could make a mistake, but she wouldn't be back. If Carly didn't take the job starting tomorrow, he'd cancel his appointments and stay with Penny.

With the house empty, he grabbed two bottles of water from the fridge and returned to the backyard where Carly was standing at the fence. The sun was in front of her now, low on the horizon and shooting rays of light through her hair. The brightness turned the blond waves into a mane or a halo, maybe a helmet. She'd done battle with Denise today and won. Ryan couldn't remember the last time someone had fought for him instead of against him.

"It's a beautiful view," he called out as he approached. "On a clear day, you can see a couple of the Channel Islands."

Carly turned to him with a faraway smile. "I've never been on an island."

"Really?" He handed her the water.

"Kentucky has rivers and lakes. No islands." She took a swig from the bottle, then turned back to the view of the Pacific dotted with whitecaps. "I have to tell you more about finding Penny. You're not going to like it."

"Have at it. I'm used to criticism."

"It's not criticism."

"What is it?"

"Penny tracked berry juice all over the seats of the Impala. The upholstery's a mess."

She looked at him expectantly, waiting for a scowl or at least a sigh. He cared, of course. The Impala was worth a small fortune, and it held a thousand memories: restoring it with his father, visiting car shows, driving it for the first time down the Pacific Coast Highway. He treasured the old car, but his stomach burned with other memories: his father becoming churlish over a gum wrapper left in the ashtray, polishing chrome that already gleamed.

Ryan aimed his chin toward the garage. "Let's take a look. We can talk salary and hours while I clean it up."

"I haven't taken the job yet," she reminded him.

"No, but I hope you do."

As they headed toward the gate, he raised his hand to touch the small of her back but stopped. He had no business touching her, and he wouldn't have reacted that way with Mrs. Howell. Annoyed with himself, he strode past her to the garage and used the keypad.

Carly pointed at the concrete walk. "She went in through the side door."

"Kyle keeps his baseball gear out here. He must have forgotten to lock up." As responsible as Kyle was, he was still fifteen, though he'd be sixteen soon.

When the metal door was halfway up, Carly leaned down to peer at the back end of the car. "What year is it?"

"1962. It's a Chevy Impala SS. A family heirloom."

"My grandpa owned an Impala. It wasn't a convertible, though. Yours is amazing."

"I enjoy it." He wished his sons shared his interest, but even Kyle glazed over when Ryan mentioned taking the car out for a spin.

When the big door locked into place, he entered the stuffy garage and hit the switch for the overhead light. Hands on his hips, he peered down at a collage of purple footprints and groaned.

Carly stayed outside in the sun, her hands hooked in her pockets and a worried expression on her face. "How bad is it?"

"Bad."

"Penny was oblivious, I'm sure."

"Completely." He sensed she was interviewing him again, so he stopped the inspection and faced her. "This is one of those can't/won't times you mentioned. Penny doesn't think ahead or imagine consequences. I see the berries and make the connection to stains. Penny can't do that."

"So you're not angry with her." It was half a question, half a statement.

"Angry at Penny? No." Ryan reserved his anger for himself. "It's frustrating, of course. And I've been known to raise my voice, but the best solution is to tell the gardener to pull out the berry bush." He wished he'd done it sooner.

"You have a good understanding of her."

"We've been in counseling for three months now. My first lesson from Miss Monica—she's the therapist—is that I have a choice. I can either accommodate Penny's special needs, or I can frustrate us both with expectations she can't meet."

"Exactly. My own view is that it's up to us as adults to adapt to kids with FASD, because they can't adapt to us. We wouldn't ask a blind man to see."

"No."

A hint of battle flashed in her eyes. "But we *would* do everything possible to enable the blind man to function as best as he can, and we'd teach him to read in ways he could understand—like Braille instead of print on a page. From what I've seen, Penny doesn't have any of the physical indicators, except she's small for her age. That suggests Fetal Alcohol Effects rather than full blown FAS."

FAE was the least of the evils on the fetal alcohol spectrum but still significant, damaging, and frequently undetected. Without a clear diagnosis, FAE kids and parents like Ryan were often confused and frustrated by a lack of understanding.

Carly stepped into the garage and looked down at the stain on the seat. "Do you think it'll come out?"

"Maybe."

She waited for more, her head tipped and her brows slightly arched. "Maybe you should try now. The longer it sets, the worse it gets."

Kentucky practicality rang in her voice. "Sure, why not?" He wasn't optimistic, but he lifted a rag and a can of upholstery cleaner off the workbench, squirted a test spot, and set the can down. "It needs to soak. We might as well finish the interview."

Carly scooted onto a tall stool at the workbench behind her and laced her hands in her lap. "Tell me more about Penny."

"Her intelligence is in the 110 range on the Wechsler Intelligence Scale."

"Normal."

"Yes." Though in the Tremaine family, anything less than a gifted IQ was considered subpar.

"How was she diagnosed?"

"Her mother drank during the pregnancy." Ryan knew for a fact, because he had purchased the gin they consumed in a vain effort to drown their guilt over the affair.

"Is she on medication?"

"No, but I haven't ruled it out."

"She's still young." Carly glanced down at the test spot, then back at him. "I don't mean to be nosy, but I'd like to understand your relationship with Penny's mother."

"Does this mean you'll take the job?"

"I'm still deciding."

Ryan hated telling the story, but he'd bare his soul if it would convince Carly to be Penny's nanny, even for the summer. He stood straight and faced her, the car, and the stain between them, the rag dangling from his hand.

"I had an affair. No excuses. I hurt a lot of people, and I'm sorry."

Carly said nothing, her expression tighter than before but carefully blank. If he'd just torpedoed himself with her, so be it. His campaign to be a better father meant telling the truth. "I broke it off before I knew Penny had been conceived. She was an accident." He hated thinking of her in that way, but it was true. "Her mother told me about six months into the pregnancy. I promised to pay child support, saw an attorney, and that was that." Except for the guilt made even worse by Jenna's mercy. *"Save your marriage, Ryan. Save your family. This baby and I will be just fine."*

Instead of easing his conscience, her generosity had shamed him even more. So did the horror on Heather's face when he told her about the affair. Looking at Carly now, Ryan wished for the millionth time that he'd been a better man. "Heather and I tried to work things out but couldn't. We've been divorced four years now. It's hard on the boys."

"Shared custody?"

"Yes, but I have them for the summer. Heather's on some sort of mission trip with her church."

Carly's face lit up. "Where did she go?"

"Haiti."

"My father's a minister. I have a lot of respect for mission trips."

To Ryan, a summer in Haiti sounded like a bad vacation. He tried to blank his face, but he let out a snort. Carly drew back, a sign she'd judged his attitude correctly. Hoping she wouldn't hold it against him, he dabbed at the stain with the rag. "That's the whole ugly story. If I could change it, I would. Especially what happened to Penny. People blame the mother for FASD, but I'm as responsible as Jenna. I bought the liquor, drank it with her—"

"Dr. Tremaine?"

His hand clenched the soiled folds of the rag. Dreading criticism, he lifted his head and faced her.

Carly stared at him with enough fervor to melt the asphalt driveway. "I don't judge anyone. You made a mistake, a bad one. I've made mistakes, too. As my daddy says, 'We're all beggars at the King's table, sinners in need of grace.'"

The music of the Bluegrass slipped into Carly's voice, but the sentiment was Christian claptrap, the same foolishness he'd heard from Heather a year ago when she told him she was a Christian now and had forgiven him. He appreciated the gesture, but he couldn't forgive himself and never would. When it came to his own life, Ryan was judge and jury, and he was guilty as charged. "I appreciate the sentiment, but the facts stand. Penny's brain is damaged because of what her parents did to her. She'll always have certain challenges."

"Just like the blind man." Carly popped off the stool and looked down at the stain. "It's gone."

"I'm surprised." He glanced at the can and made a note to buy more. "This is good stuff. I'll work on the rest of the seat over the weekend."

Carly smiled at him. "I'll help."

Ryan's brows lifted. "Did you just accept the job?"

"Yes."

He set the cleaning supplies on the workbench and put his hands on his hips, ready for more negotiation. "Name your salary."

She gave a figure that was almost exactly what he had agreed to pay Mrs. Howell. "Perfect. Live in or live out?"

"Out," she replied.

He preferred the nanny to live in for the convenience, but Penny's prior nannies weren't in their twenties, pretty, and impressive grad students with long blond hair. It was easy to imagine talking with

Carly and sharing tidbits from the day, something he couldn't do with an employee, or any woman, until he finished the SOS list and made things right with his sons.

"That's fine," he said about her living out. "When can you start?"

"I have to give notice at the Animal Factory, but I'm off for the next three days. How about tomorrow?"

"Perfect."

"What time?"

"Seven a.m.?"

"I'll be here." She glanced at the driveway where long shadows stretched like fingers across the asphalt. "I should go."

After hiring four nannies, Ryan followed a routine that included paper work, giving her keys to the house and van, exchanging phone numbers, and showing her the nanny quarters. Even if she didn't live in, she could use the room during the day. "Can you stay a little longer? I'd like to show you around, give you the tax forms, that sort of thing."

"Could we do it in the morning?"

"Sure."

He wondered if she had a date tonight or maybe a serious boyfriend. For all he knew, she was living with some guy. Not that it mattered to Ryan. Carly's love life was her own business.

She waited while he closed the door with the keypad; then they walked to the house where she picked up her purse but left the manila envelope with her CV. After shepherding her down the hall, he followed her across the street to her car, an old red Cavalier. At the sight of the worn tires, he almost told her to wait while he fetched the keys to the van, a fairly new model with all the bells and whistles.

She unlocked the car door, then faced him. "By the way, does Penny know how to swim?"

"Enough to dog paddle across the pool. She started lessons a few months ago, but it didn't go well. Too much noise and splashing."

"I'll work with her."

"Thanks. She'll enjoy that."

"About the boys . . . How much supervision do they need?"

"Kyle's almost sixteen. He's pretty self sufficient." Pride filled Ryan's chest, though his ex-wife deserved most of the credit. "He'll need a ride now and then, a sandwich or two. Eric . . . Eric's a bit of a mystery to me."

"He's what? Thirteen?"

"Barely. His birthday was last month." Ryan wished he had bought a gift instead of stuffing cash in a funny card, but he didn't know what to buy.

"That's a hard age for anyone," Carly said. "Plus he's the middle child with a brand-new special-needs sister."

Her analysis impressed him. "He's been having a rough time for a while."

"Does he have friends?"

"A few."

"Good. I'll help any way I can."

Ryan couldn't remember the last time someone offered to help. With Carly, he even believed she could make a difference. "The boys already met you at the Animal Factory, but I'll make official introductions in the morning."

"Let's make it fun," she suggested. "If they're anything like my older brother, they like to eat. I'll pick up something from a bakery."

"Perfect." He opened his wallet and handed her cash.

She slipped the money into her pocket, then gave a shake of her head. "This has been the strangest job interview of my life."

"Same here."

"This is a change for me, but taking the job feels right." Her voice pitched a little lower, as if the decision had as much gravity for her as it did for him.

Ryan didn't live by his feelings. They were wild things that ran amuck and led to mistakes. Instead, he focused on the practicalities and took his phone out of his pocket. "You should have my cell. What's yours? I'll call you."

She recited the number, and he punched it in. When the call completed, birds chirped inside her purse. It took him a second to figure out the chirping was her ringtone. Things like that usually annoyed him, especially when a patient's phone went off in the middle of an exam, but with Carly the playfulness struck him as sweet. "Clever."

He opened the car door and held it wide. After climbing in, Carly tilted her chin up to meet his gaze. "Good night, Dr. Tremaine. I'll see you tomorrow."

"Good night, Carly." He moved to close the door but stopped with it still open. "You probably noticed. Penny calls me Dr. Tremaine."

She peered up at him, the streetlight bright on her face. "Do you know why?"

"No, and I hate it." Staring into her eyes, he saw a friend instead of an employee. "Call me Ryan. It might help Penny see me differently."

Carly glanced through the windshield, then faced him again and shrugged. "Okay. Ryan it is."

He nodded crisply, closed the door, and stepped back, watching as she steered down the quiet street. The taillights beamed a steady red, flashed brighter when she braked, then disappeared when she turned the corner. Hopeful his nanny problems were solved at last, he made a beeline for his office, slipped the SOS list out from under the desk mat, and crossed off *Find a nanny for Penny.*

∽

Instead of going straight home, Carly drove to the Animal Factory. Her boss was there, so Carly gave notice and asked if the customary two weeks' notice could be shortened. The newest clerk wanted more hours, so Carly was able to quit immediately.

After hugging her coworkers good-bye, she bought little gifts for Penny and Eric, then popped into a sporting goods store for something for Kyle.

By the time she left the mall, the sky was black except for streetlights and a handful of faded stars. She didn't like getting home after dark, but sometimes it couldn't be helped. The alley, poorly lit, seemed even murkier than usual, and she immediately saw why. Two of the lights in the carport were burned out. She considered parking on the street, but it was late and a good spot would be hard to find.

Choosing the lesser of two evils, she pulled into the space next to Bette's old sedan, clutched her pepper spray, and hurried through the gate to the courtyard. Night-blooming jasmine filled her nose with a hint of exotic islands, and she inhaled deeply. The scent was one of the consolations of dusk, a touch of paradise before the neighborhood exploded with noisy cars, sirens, and the chop of a police helicopter circling overhead.

With the home invasion fresh on her mind, she skipped a stop at her mailbox, hurried to Bette's door, and knocked. Bette knew about today's interview and was waiting for news.

In just a few seconds, she peeked through the side window, turned the deadbolt, and ushered Carly inside. "How did it go?"

"I took the job." She dropped her purse on a chair, a relic from the 1990s and a remnant from Bette's marriage. Tom Cat leapt off the sofa and landed with a plop. "Days only, so I'll be around. But what an interview. Penny got lost, her aunt showed up with a stuffed kangaroo, and I saw a fully restored 1962 Chevy Impala."

Bette's eyes crinkled with laughter. "You sure know how to spin a tale, Carly Jo."

Carly Jo. Bette did that now and then. Battling a wave of homesickness, Carly reached down and stroked Tom's silky black fur.

"The kettle's boiling for tea," Bette said. "Want some?"

"Just one cup."

Carly followed her to the kitchen, fetched her favorite mug, and selected something lemony from the boxes jammed on the narrow shelf. As she removed a tea bag, Tom rubbed against her ankles to demand another scratch. Carly obliged, then carried her cup to the table and sat. "I feel good about the decision, but I have to admit I'm a little nervous about it."

"Why?"

"When you work in a family setting, things get personal fast." She blinked and recalled Dr. Tremaine—now Ryan—standing under the streetlight, the five o'clock shadow evident on his strong jaw, and his business shirt tailored to his lean body. She couldn't help noticing him in a physical way, but the attraction didn't mean anything. It couldn't. He was her employer now. As the recipient of a broken heart in college, she knew better than to fall in love with the wrong person.

Bette poured boiling water into Carly's cup. The steam rose in a cloud between them and filled the air with the scent of lemons. Bette's bracelet—a Southwest style made of chunky turquoise—rattled on her wrist as she set down the pot. Carly dipped the bag, gave it a squeeze, and added sugar. Back home, she drank sweet tea all summer long, strong with lots of ice, but folks in California didn't know how to make it.

Bette broke into her thoughts. "Being a nanny won't be like working at the Animal Factory, that's for sure."

"No." Carly dipped the tea bag a few times. "At the Animal Factory, kids come and go. It's easy and fun."

"It's like me at the bakery." Bette lowered her plump body down to the chair. "I know the regulars, some of them surprisingly well because they blurt their troubles, but no one asks about me. It's funny how that goes."

Carly often thought about the way people in Los Angeles talked so openly to strangers about the most personal things—divorces, problems with kids, plastic surgery. It happened in line at stores, in waiting rooms, anywhere. People in Boomer County talked, too, but they knew one another.

Bette blew on her tea to cool it, risked a sip, and hummed with pleasure. "That sure tastes good after a long day."

"Any word on the home invasions?"

"No, but I'm worried." Bette studied Carly across the table. "Are you sure about not living in with this family? It makes sense, considering what's happening here."

"I'm sure."

"I hope you're not staying because of me."

"Not entirely, but I worry about both of us. We could share a two-bedroom, but it would only be until I finish school."

"No, thanks," Bette said. "The crime scares me, but I'm used to living alone."

So was Carly, but she didn't like it. She missed her family, the little jokes born of a common history, just knowing people cared about her. Her mind leapt to an unsettling future, one where she had gray hair, saggy arms, and only a cat for company. She was twenty-eight, single, and a virgin by choice because she wanted her wedding night to be everything God intended. The thought gave her goose bumps in one breath and filled her with fear in the next. What if that night never came?

She had stopped dating after the mess with Allison, mostly because she was such bad company. As for being social in Los Angeles, she missed Kentucky too much to risk losing her heart to someone who didn't share her roots. Aching for home, she took a long sip of the sweetened tea that wasn't quite sweet enough.

She chatted a little longer with Bette, then went to her own apartment, immediately slipping the two deadbolts into place. She fed Wild Thing and then turned on her laptop. After skimming her e-mail, she clicked on the links to Allison's social media pages. There was nothing new, just the same pictures from two years ago and an old note from Chyna at Sparrow House, saying, *Hey, AlleyCat, where r u?*

Next, Carly checked her post about Allison on a Web site dedicated to finding missing children. Again, nothing.

A car backfired on the street. Carly jumped out of her skin. A cat screeched out on the walk, and a female voice shouting in Spanish penetrated the glass of the locked window. Her heart pounded and not just because of the noise. It was the unknown that plagued her—worry, failure, and feelings she didn't want to have, especially when those feelings included a child with FASD and the child's troubled father.

"Ryan," she said out loud to numb herself to the name.

It didn't work. Instead her heart came alive with the memory of his confessing to the affair. She'd been repelled in one breath, impressed by his remorse in the next. Knowing how it felt to have made a bad mistake, she felt his failure as plainly as she felt her own. The power of that connection couldn't be denied. She liked him as a person, and if she were honest, she found him attractive.

With that awareness pinging from her body to her heart, she wondered if she'd met someone special . . . the man God made just for her.

"That's ridiculous," she said out loud.

Dr. Ryan Tremaine was cynical, snide, not a Christian, and her employer. He also lived and breathed the Los Angeles smog, was a little older than she was, and came with a family tree shaped more like a tangled vine than a sturdy oak. The stain being lifted from the upholstery was God's gracious sign that she belonged with Penny, but no way would Carly care for Ryan any more than she'd care for any hurting human being.

And that, she realized, was a very big problem.

8

Carly sat perched on the top row of the bleacher seats facing the baseball diamond, watching as Kyle's team jogged onto the field with their caps pulled low against the sun. Eric and his friend Nathan were huddled on the bottom bench as far from her as they could get. Ryan had taken Penny for her session with Miss Monica and would arrive any minute. It was four in the afternoon, warm but not hot, and the air smelled of sunscreen, hot dogs, and the red clay dirt of the infield. With her eyes shaded by a white visor, she relaxed in the sunshine, off duty for the moment.

After a full week with the Tremaines, she thought she knew why God had dropped her into their lives. When it came to his sons, Ryan's demeanor was clinical, as if he were diagnosing patients instead of raising children. He loved his kids, but he was missing out on the fun side of life, something Carly observed on that first morning when she arrived with donuts, gifts, and an icebreaker game. The kids had enjoyed the surprises—an outfit for Miss Rabbit, rubber snakes for Eric, and baseballs for Kyle—and they quickly chimed in with answers to the silly questions she pulled out of a bowl. Even Eric had played along, but Ryan didn't crack a single smile.

Carly felt a little like Maria in *The Sound of Music,* her mother's favorite movie. Nothing would stop her from going home to Kentucky, but someone had to help Ryan understand his children, and apparently Carly was the one. But how? She didn't want to be a know-it-all, but she'd gleaned things about the boys he needed to know.

The batter smacked a grounder to the shortstop, who whipped the ball to Kyle at first. Tall and lean like his father, he snagged it with a graceful swipe of the glove.

Carly leapt to her feet, shouted, and clapped with the other adults on the bleachers. Ryan needed to be here. Turning, she glanced over her shoulder and spotted him by the tot lot, where Penny was playing with her friend Bethany under the watchful eye of Bethany's mom. Carly took in his tall frame and long stride, the sun glinting off his dark glasses and the tanned skin that made his short hair even darker. Instead of his usual shirt and tie, he was dressed in Levis and a gray plaid shirt with rolled-up sleeves. The look suited him.

Grinning, she waved so he'd see her. He raised his arm to acknowledge her, a kind of salute that sent a little zing to her heart. Inexplicably energized, she turned her attention back to the game and waited for him. Two pitches later, Ryan arrived at the bleachers and climbed up to meet her.

"Sorry I'm late." He whipped off the sunglasses and put them in his pocket. "Traffic was hideous."

"It usually is."

He hated to be late. Carly knew that about him, along with other things, like his favorite kind of pizza and the fact he played a mean game of chess. She'd gleaned the details during the icebreaker game, along with his favorite color—dark green—and his favorite TV show—reruns of *Seinfeld*.

They'd discussed meeting at the game earlier, and she was free to go if she wanted. Ryan could cram the kids into his Honda, but it was a beautiful day and she liked baseball. He didn't mention her leaving, so she stayed at his side with her legs crossed and a canvas tote bag at her feet. Figuring he might be thirsty, she reached into the bag and handed him a bottle of water, still cold thanks to an ice pack.

An appreciative smile lit up his face. He took a long drag, wiped his mouth with his bare forearm, and surveyed the stands. "Where's Eric?"

"As far from me as he can get." She pointed to Eric and Nathan on the bottom bench, stuffing themselves with popcorn. "How did it go with Penny today?"

"Very well." Enthusiasm, maybe surprise, deepened his voice. "Miss Monica said to keep doing what we're doing. She's glad you're here."

"So am I." Carly meant it. "Any insight into why Penny runs away?"

"No," he answered, more somber. "But as long as the nanny situation is stable, Miss Monica said we should wait and come back in a month. That could be the last visit."

"That's great." Now was the time to bring up the way Eric misbehaved to get attention, or the fact that Kyle had a girlfriend, but Ryan was relaxed and she didn't want to spoil the mood.

He took a deep breath and blew it out. "It's not often all three kids are occupied at the same time."

Carly liked that about him, the way he noticed moments out of the ordinary. He glanced at her with his lips damp from the water, hesitated, then said, "You're off the clock. If you want to leave—"

"No. I like baseball, plus look." She pointed to the scoreboard. "The score's tied and Kyle's up next."

"Good. We can kick back and relax."

The *we* sounded natural enough. They were employer and

employee, but his casual tone and being apart from the crowd made them something else. Friends, she decided. Sharing the afternoon with Ryan definitely beat going home to her apartment.

The opposing team made the third out. Kyle jogged in from first, grabbed a bat, and headed to the plate. He took the first pitch for a strike, missed the next one, then hammered a line drive to left field. Carly and Ryan leapt to their feet, cheering like crazy as he slid into second for a double.

"He's got wheels for legs," she said. "And he's got a great stretch at first. With his build, it's the perfect position for him."

Ryan gave her a curious look. "You know baseball. I thought people in Kentucky were just into basketball."

"The Cats are number one," she said. "But Boomer County's not far from Cincy." Knowing the history of the rivalry with the Los Angeles Dodgers and Cincinnati Reds, a rivalry second only to the Dodger rivalry with the San Francisco Giants, she put an extra note of pride in her voice. "I grew up rooting for the Reds."

Ryan reared back. "That's heresy in the Tremaine household."

With her nose in the air, Carly huffed at him. "May the best team win, and *I* know who that is."

He gave a hearty laugh, the first one she had ever heard. "When the Reds are in town, we'll take the kids to a game."

"I'd like that." A touch of home appealed to her. So did the fun of razzing Ryan about his misguided baseball choices.

They settled into easy banter that shifted into stories about their everyday lives. With smacks of the bat punctuating the conversation, she learned that he liked being a doctor but once dreamed of being the next Jacques Cousteau. He had lived in Los Angeles all his life except for a fellowship at the Wills Eye Institute in Philadelphia, but he enjoyed travel. Given a choice, he'd choose a week on an exotic island over a history-packed trip to Europe, though he'd been to London a few times.

In turn, she told him about growing up in a small town, how

much she missed her family, and how much she disliked the big-city bustle.

They glanced occasionally at Penny and Eric, but mostly they teased each other about their differences.

"So you don't like Los Angeles," he said with a shake of his head. "What's not to like?"

"Almost everything!" *Everything except Ryan and his kids.* Carly pushed that thought aside. "For one thing, the seasons are upside down. Kentucky is brown in the winter, green in the summer, and the sky's always blue. Here it's the opposite. The hills are green in winter and brown in the summer. And the sky—" She gave a disgusted shake of her head. "Half the time it's as brown as the hills. I hate smog."

"Los Angeles at its worst," he said. "But it's home to me."

"You love it."

"I do," he admitted. "It's big, noisy, and impersonal, but the good outweighs the bad. The ocean is close. The weather is just about perfect, and there's plenty to do. Movies, theater, museums, even the zoo."

Ryan's mention of the zoo was her opening to bring up the kids, but she was enjoying his company and didn't want to put her nanny hat back on just yet. "Other than play chess, what do you do for fun?"

"Fun?"

"Yes, fun! It's what we're doing now. Just enjoying this beautiful day."

"I don't think much about fun."

The poor guy really needed to loosen up. Carly had grown up in a family where joy and faith were opposite sides of the same coin. Joy wasn't a matter of simply being optimistic or a Pollyanna. Her kind of joy grew from the rich soil of God's love, serving others, and embracing life in all its complexity. She doubted Ryan would understand, so she searched for common ground. "Do you like birthdays?"

"Sure."

"How about Christmas?"

"What's not to like?" He tossed off a shrug. "Trees. Lights. Christmas music. It's a nice time of year."

She went for the clincher. "How about when Kyle's team wins, or when the Dodgers go to the World Series?"

His mouth relaxed into the promise of a smile, and he bumped her arm with his elbow. "You got me, Carly. That's definitely fun."

His eyes locked on to hers, his blue-gray irises shining silver and somehow murky and mysterious at the same time. She lost herself in those eyes, and for a blink she forgot he was her boss and saw him only as a man—a handsome man with broad shoulders, forgotten dreams, and a smile that sent lightning bolts to her toes.

The bat cracked against the ball. Someone shouted, "Heads up!"

Carly's gaze snapped to the sky where a foul ball was plummeting straight at her. As she cringed to the side, Ryan launched to his feet, leaned sideways, and caught it bare-handed. The leather whapped against his palm. Hauling back, he lobbed the ball over the fence to the pitcher holding up his glove.

"That had to hurt," she said when he sat back down. "Is your hand all right? I have ice in the cooler."

His eyes twinkled in a way that suggested she was being silly. "I'm fine." To prove it, he held out his hand and flexed his fingers. "It didn't hurt a bit."

"Are you sure?"

"Positive."

She gave a shake of her head. "Thanks. That ball would have beaned me if you hadn't caught it."

His brows lifted in what seemed like a smirk, but his twinkling eyes betrayed him. "That's because you're a wussy Reds fan."

Carly laughed. "I walked right into that one."

He was closer to her than when he first arrived, so close she could see the cleft in his chin and the start of a scoundrel's smile.

The faintest trace of his aftershave, a smoky scent, wafted to her nose, and so did the smell of the hot cotton of his shirt. Rolled-up sleeves revealed muscular forearms with a smattering of dark hair, and when he raised his knee and planted his foot on the bench in front of them, her insides did a mischievous leap.

Unnerved, she retreated to nanny land with a glance at Penny. Ryan remarked on how well Kyle was playing. Carly mentioned that Eric and Nathan were on their fourth bag of popcorn, and they settled in to watch the next pitch.

She really did like baseball, at least that's how she explained the shivers still running up her arms. She'd never be a Dodgers fan. Her Kentucky roots were too deep, but she decided to go to all of Kyle's games. It was just plain fun, especially with Ryan snagging foul balls and trading jokes with her.

Five days after Kyle's baseball game, Ryan took Eric and Nathan to the museums at Exposition Park. He wanted to spend quality time with Eric, even have a conversation or two. Instead he was playing chauffeur and busboy to two thirteen-year-old boys. His patience was frayed, and the heat wave didn't help.

What had he been thinking to suggest a trip to see the Space Shuttle Endeavor at the Science Center? This morning, when he had skimmed the SOS list, he was able to cross off just two items—*Go to Kyle's baseball games* and *Swim lessons for Penny*. Thanks to Carly, Penny swam like a fish. On the other hand, *Have a family dinner and enjoy it* had been an abysmal failure with the four of them sitting at the kitchen table saying nothing. He hoped to have better luck taking Penny for ice cream at Dairy Queen sometime.

He had arranged for her to play with Bethany today so he could spend time with Eric, but nothing else went as planned. Eric and Nathan raced to the Natural History Museum, gawked at the T. rex, but ignored everything else. In the Science Center, they called the space shuttle clunky, dashed through the ecosystem exhibit, then charged past the section on technology and inventions. Ryan and Eric exchanged maybe five sentences, and those were about lunch.

Ryan felt like a failure.

And he was lonely. The day would have been a lot better with Carly to run interference, but today he was on his own and determined to break through to Eric. Maybe the IMAX movie would help. It was about the marvels of the ocean, and Eric had seemed interested when they first arrived and saw the five-story poster on the building. At the very least, he and the boys would sit together.

He glanced at his watch, saw it was time to head for the theater, and approached Eric and Nathan from behind. "The movie starts pretty soon. Let's get in line."

"Do we have to?" Eric asked.

"Yes, we do." Ryan sounded stern even to himself.

Eric traded a "my dad's a pain" look with Nathan, who gave a little shrug. "It's okay with me. I kind of want to see it."

"All right," Eric agreed. "But Dad?"

"Yes?"

"Could we sit by ourselves?" Eric's round face turned tomato red. "Mom would let us. We like the front row, and she hates it."

If he told the boys they had to sit with him, Eric would resent him. On the other hand, what good was sitting on opposite sides of the theater? There was no good answer, so he mentally flipped a coin. "You can sit wherever you want. We'll meet outside the exit."

He bought the tickets, and the three of them stood in line, Eric and Nathan keeping their backs to him. When the doors opened, they zipped to the front row while Ryan took a seat in the very back.

The spot reminded him of sitting on the bleacher with Carly. He enjoyed her company, and that was a problem. Nature had a way of asserting itself, something he couldn't allow. His sons needed to see him living with integrity, and Ryan needed to redeem himself in his own eyes. Dallying with the nanny like a lecherous duke in a romance novel was out of the question.

Even so, alone in the crowded theater, he wondered if she'd enjoy the documentary about the marvels of the ocean. When the lights dimmed and the movie started with birds chirping like the ones on her ringtone, he decided she would, in part because Carly enjoyed everything in life except spiders, burnt toast, and smog. The chirping birds segued into plucking violins. An ocean wave exploded on the screen in a roar of blue and white, and the surround-sound shook with the force of nature's power. Ryan didn't believe in God, but sometimes he wished he did. A man couldn't help but wonder about a supreme creator at the sight of such magnificence.

Somehow it made a man feel small.

So did sitting alone.

He tried to lose himself in the story about sea life and food chains, but his eyes kept dipping to the back of Eric's head. The day was far from a success, but Eric seemed to be enjoying the movie. When a great white shark shot onto the screen, everyone gasped, and Ryan heard Eric shout, "Wow!"

The movie ended with a round of enthusiastic applause, the crowd filtered out, and Ryan met the boys at the exit.

"So what did you think?" he asked them.

Nathan, always polite, answered first. "It was cool. Thanks, Dr. Tremaine."

"Yeah, Dad," Eric added. "Thanks. Can we go to the gift shop?"

"Sure."

The boys dashed ahead of him, crossed the sunbaked plaza to the Science Center, and raced to the store in the main building. When Ryan caught up to them, they were in the ocean section and rummaging in a barrel of plastic sharks, whales, and sting rays. Bags containing colorful fish and sea plants hung nearby, and an assortment of books for all ages was displayed face-out on a low shelf.

Ryan saw a chance to be an ordinary dad, took out his wallet, and gave each boy spending money.

Nathan's face lit up. "Thanks, Dr. Tremaine!"

"Yeah, Dad," Eric added. "Thanks."

While the boys shopped, Ryan wandered to the other side of the store. On his own, he bought each boy a T-shirt, one for himself, and a glass paperweight with an ocean scene for his desk. He didn't know if the day had been a success or not, but *"Thanks, Dad"* had a nice ring to it.

9

"You can't have it," Eric shouted at Penny. "It's mine."

Carly raced from the laundry room to the kitchen, where she'd left Eric and Penny at the table just long enough to switch a load of whites from the washer to the dryer. Eric was making a diorama of the ocean in a cardboard box he'd spray painted blue and silver. Since the trip to the Science Center, he'd been obsessed with sharks. He still oozed resentment and barely spoke to anyone—especially not to Ryan—but yesterday he had ventured out of his room and asked for a ride to a hobby store for paint, glue, and glitter. With Ryan's permission, Carly obliged, and Eric had been occupied for several hours with his modeling project.

With his shout in her ears, Carly strode into the kitchen just as Penny reached the foot of the stairs with a plastic shark clutched in her hand. Carly intended to make her return it to Eric, but Eric reached her first. "That's mine!"

"I want it!"

Penny was no match for Eric, who jerked the toy out of her hands. "You brat! I hate you—"

"I hate you, too," Penny yelled back.

Carly winced at Eric's rage but chose not to address it in the heat of battle. As soon as she finished with Penny, she'd talk to him about the difference between hating a person and hating what they did. But first she needed to control Penny. "We're going to the quiet room."

"No."

"Yes." She walked Penny past the kitchen to the maid's quarters, now the nanny room, added on to the side of the house. Carly used it as an office and a personal retreat, as well as a place for Penny to calm herself. With its plain walls, white furniture, and sky blue drapes and bedding, the room suited her purposes to a tee.

Gripping Penny's hand, Carly led her to an overstuffed chair wedged in the corner. She sat on the ottoman, turned Penny to face her, and kept eye contact. "The shark belongs to Eric."

"But I want it."

"It belongs to Eric," Carly repeated.

"But—"

"It belongs to Eric." She spoke the same words in the same cadence with the hope they'd penetrate Penny's brain the way a carpenter deepened a cut with precise strokes of a saw. "It. Belongs. To. Eric."

Penny huffed, a sign she understood.

"You have to say you're sorry."

"I'm sorry," Penny said, though Carly suspected she didn't comprehend the real meaning.

"Let's go say it to Eric."

She led Penny back to the kitchen, but Eric was gone. Assuming he was in his room, Carly took Penny upstairs where, for once, Eric's door was open. She peeked inside, didn't see him but spotted a computer tablet glowing face up on his rumpled sheets. She glanced at the screen, saw foul words on his Facebook page, along with a picture of Penny at her worst and the caption *My Sister, The Monster.*

Carly inhaled sharply. At the same instant, Eric came into the room with a charger he'd probably borrowed from Kyle or Ryan, because his own room was such a mess he couldn't possibly find a thing. When he saw Carly, his eyes dipped to the tablet, and his cheeks flamed red.

She took the embarrassment as a good sign and confronted him with more calm than she felt. "I saw the picture on your Facebook. After Penny says what we came to say, I'd like to talk to you about it."

"It's just a picture," he mumbled.

"A hurtful one." Carly indicated that Penny should face Eric. "Do you remember what to say?"

Penny hid her face against Carly's leg in an attempt to avoid everything—the confusion in her mind and the messy room. Carly gently turned her around, then prompted her with a squeeze of her hand. "You're sorry you took the shark."

Eric glared at her. "I don't care what she says."

"I do," Carly replied. "And I care about you, too. So let's do this. Penny, tell Eric you're sorry."

"I'm sorry," she said, maybe understanding but probably not.

Carly tipped up Penny's face with a finger on her chin. "Now go to your room."

Her bottom lip trembled. "I don't like it in there."

Neither did Carly. With its frilly curtains, bright colors, and gingerbread shelves, the room was a little-girl paradise, unless the little girl had a disorder that made smells, noise, clutter, and bright lights painful to her. Tonight she'd talk to Ryan about the room as well as the shark incident.

Carly gripped Penny's hand and led her out the door. "You can play with Miss Rabbit now."

Consoled, Penny walked with Carly to her room. Carly set her up with Miss Rabbit and Lance, then returned to speak to Eric. He was sitting on the edge of the bed with the tablet in hand, his mouth tight and his eyes burning with anger. As Carly leaned against the doorjamb, he tossed the device on the bed so she could see his Facebook. The ugly picture was gone.

"Did you delete it?" she asked.

"Yeah."

"That's good, but I'm going to be very direct with you, Eric. You're old enough to understand what happened to your sister."

"*Half* sister."

"That's right." Carly shifted her weight, slouching a little to keep the mood casual. "You know the facts, and you're smart. I bet you get good grades."

"Not as good as Kyle."

Sibling rivalry. Carly hid a wince. As the youngest in her own family, she had competed with her sister and brother in everything and lost every time, until she discovered a knack for working with kids.

"You're not Kyle," she said to Eric. "You have your own talents. It takes time to figure out what they are, but I've noticed a few things about you."

His head jerked up. "Like what?"

"You're quiet, but you watch people. You notice things, like Kyle forgetting to take out the trash."

Eric almost smiled. "He does that a lot."

"You notice things about your dad, too. I bet you can tell me what color tie he wore to work today."

"It was blue."

The color of his eyes. Carly had noticed, too. Her mind wandered to this morning and how they had chatted over coffee before Ryan left for the office. He was almost late for work, and she worried until he texted that he arrived in time, a friendly gesture that made her feel important to him, which was silly.

Annoyed at herself, she focused back on Eric. "I've noticed other things about you. For instance, you're good at jigsaw puzzles. That one in the family room—" She'd found the sea-life puzzle in the closet and put it out just to see what would happen. "You finished it in what? Three hours?"

He shrugged, but his shoulders seemed a little broader. "I was bored. There was nothing else to do."

"Sure there was." Carly crossed her arms. "You could have picked a fight with Penny, caused trouble for me, or run off without telling us where you were. But you didn't do any of those things, even if you wanted to. That tells me you have a lot of self-control." It also meant he tamped down his anger. "Penny doesn't have that ability. It's my job to teach her as much as she can learn. And that's the problem—her mind doesn't work like yours or mine. Learning is hard for her."

"That's what my dad says."

"It's true." She had his attention, so she slipped down to the floor and sat with one knee raised. "I don't think you hate your sister. I think you hate some of the things she does, like when she took the shark and messed up the diorama."

"Yeah!" he said, facing Carly fully. "Or when she has a meltdown in front of my friends."

"Or kicks the table."

"She drives me *crazy*! Why does she have to be here anyway?"

The question was as multifaceted as a human life. Why was Penny born in the first place? Why had Ryan broken his wedding vows? Why was she suddenly a forever-piece of Eric's life, sharing his father and living under the same roof? Until Penny's arrival, he'd been the baby of the family. Now he was caught in the middle. As Ryan had said back at the Animal Factory, the situation was complicated.

"I can't tell you why Penny's here on earth," Carly said to him. "But I know God loves her."

"My mom talks like that."

"Your mom's a smart lady." Carly hadn't communicated with Heather personally, but she saw her heart in her boys, and Ryan spoke well of her. "Here's the deal, Eric. I can tell your dad about the picture or you can. I don't keep secrets, because most of the time they hurt people."

Eric kicked at some dirty socks on the floor. "I don't like talking to him."

No surprise there. Carly thought for a moment. "Let's do it this way. I'll tell him the whole story, including how mad you were at Penny for swiping the shark. I'm sure he'll want to talk to you, but this will give you time to think about what to say. By the way, does he have the password to your Facebook?"

"Yeah." He rolled his eyes the way only a thirteen-year-old could. "My mom has it, too."

"We both know you can change it, even set up a ghost account." Like Allison did. Her accounts were all under AlleyCat117. "If I were you, I'd give your dad the password again, tell him you were mad at Penny and you're sorry. I think he'll understand."

When Eric stayed quiet, Carly pushed to her feet and left. He had some thinking to do, and Carly needed to text Ryan to make sure he'd be home on time. She sent the message and was in Penny's room when her phone rang and she saw his office caller ID. Wanting privacy, she slipped into Ryan's bedroom and closed the door. "That was fast."

"Carly, it's Fran."

"Oh!" She hadn't spoken to Fran since they arranged the interview, but they'd hit it off. "What's up?"

"Ryan got your text. Dr. Shaya called in with a migraine, so he's been covering her emergencies. He's slammed today."

"I can imagine."

"There's another problem. Dr. Shaya was supposed to meet tonight with a new doctor they're considering for the practice. The woman's from out of town, and someone has to take her to dinner. The other two partners bowed out, so it's Ryan or no one. Can you stay late tonight? If you can't, I'll babysit."

Carly hated getting home after dark, but the conversation about Eric couldn't wait. "I'll do it. What time do you think he'll be home?"

"Not too late. Maybe ten?"

"That's fine."

"Wait. Hold on."

She heard muffled sounds, then Ryan's deep voice. "Carly?"

A little charge rippled down her spine. "Hi."

"Thanks for staying. What happened with Eric?"

"It's a long story." One she didn't want to tell over the phone when he needed to return to his patients. "Everything's fine, but you'll want to have a sit-down with him."

"A sit-down?"

"That's my dad's expression for a talking-to." Kentucky leaked into her voice. In a year or so she'd be home for good. Homesickness washed through her, and her chest tightened, but it tightened even more when Ryan's deep voice echoed in her ear.

"A sit-down, it is," he said, sounding tender. "Thanks, Carly. I'm glad you're there."

"I'm just doing my job."

"And doing it better than anyone." He paused, maybe to let the compliment soak in. When he spoke again, his voice came out lower, more personal. "I'll get home as soon as I can."

"I'll be waiting."

They said good-bye at the same time, awkwardly but with a lingering warmth that made her soft inside. Unnerved, she sat on the foot of his bed and tried not to think about Ryan having dinner with a colleague. A female colleague. Unwanted pictures flashed through her mind: a cozy table for two, candlelight, Ryan gazing into the eyes of a willowy redhead who shared his view of the world.

Jealousy snaked through her, which was ridiculous. Ryan was her boss, and they were friends. She should be hoping he had a good time at dinner, not reacting as if she had a crush on him. That was just plain silly.

She pushed off the bed and headed for the door, but before opening it, she turned. With its modern furniture and silver and black bedding, Ryan's bedroom reflected the hard edges of his personality. His cell-phone charger sat on the nightstand, plugged in and ready to go. An adventure novel lay face up with a bookmark tucked between the pages. There wasn't an item out of place, except for a bureau drawer left slightly ajar. As perfect as Ryan tried to be, he was still human.

So was Carly.

Determined to hold back her silly feelings, she blinked away the picture of silver and black and went to take care of Penny.

10

Shortly after ten o'clock, Ryan walked into the house with his black blazer slung over his shoulder. The silence reminded him of those nights before Penny came to live with him, when he dated frequently and did as he pleased. On a night like this, he might have poured himself a drink and indulged in a cigarette. He certainly wouldn't have rushed through dinner with Dr. Evelyn Donnelly, but that's what he'd done in his hurry to get home to Carly.

The house was dark except for the stove light in the kitchen and the golden glow of a single lamp in the family room. Approaching quietly, he spotted her curled on the couch and sound asleep, her arm around a white bed pillow. He needed to wake her, but the simple beauty of a woman sleeping struck him as something to be enjoyed, even revered. An ocean breeze filtered through the open window and lifted a wisp of her hair. When it brushed her cheek, she wrinkled her nose, moistened her lips, and settled back into her dreams.

"Carly?" He raised his hand to shake her awake but stopped. If he touched her in such a personal way, he'd remember and want to do it again. When she didn't respond, he lifted a throw blanket off the recliner. They could talk in the morning.

As he unfolded the fleece blanket, her eyelids fluttered open, and she rolled to her side. When she saw him, she bolted upright. "Oh dear! I fell sound asleep."

"You must have needed it," he said. "Sorry to keep you so late."

She shook her head as if to jar loose the cobwebs, then she patted the couch next to her. "Sit. I have to tell you what happened with Eric."

"I've been wondering."

She pointed to a cardboard box under the flat-screen TV. It resembled a fish tank, which in a way it was. Blue and silver spray paint sparkled on the inside, plastic plants stuck up from the sand-covered bottom, and the fish from the museum dangled from the top, including a snarling great white shark.

Carly stifled a yawn. "Eric made that today."

Ryan was impressed, both that Eric had ventured out of his room and his attention to detail. Maybe the museum trip was more successful than he realized. "He did a great job."

"Penny thought so, too. She wanted the shark, so she took it."

As Carly described the quarrel, Ryan wondered if his kids would ever get along, let alone love one another. When she told him about the picture on Facebook, he let out a chest-deep groan. "That's awful. It's bullying. It's just—"

"It's wrong." She laid her hand on his forearm. "Eric knows it and he's sorry. He already took the picture down."

"Good." The warmth of her hand soaked through his shirt sleeve to his skin, filling him with a volatile brew of hope for himself, the longing to be understood, and the certainty that Carly was the answer to bringing his family together. She had an almost mystical gift when it came to understanding his kids. And him.

"I gave him a choice," Carly said. "I told him he could tell you, or I would. " She paused, maybe to soften her words. "Right now, he's struggling to understand the changes in his life, and he's thirteen to boot."

Ryan grimaced. "It's a rough age."

"It was for me, too," she admitted. "But it's also an amazing age, because we learn so much. Eric's expecting you to talk to him about the picture incident. The good news is that I believe he's truly sorry. He was angry and reacted. The bad news is that he's angry about so many things."

Ryan glanced at the shark staring at him with its lifeless eyes. "I'll talk to him tonight. I don't think Denise would ever check Eric's Facebook, but it's the kind of thing that would have her calling attorneys."

"That reminds me." Carly winced a bit. "She called your cell phone around seven."

"I saw it."

"When you didn't call back, she called the house and I picked up. We talked a long time about Penny, but I could tell she wanted to hear even more."

"She can't get enough." Ryan appreciated Denise's dedication, but he felt like a bug under a microscope.

"I think she's lonely."

So did Ryan. "Thanks for talking to her."

"It was nice for me, too. The more I know about Penny, the better. Denise has her baby book. Did you know that?"

A *baby book*, the thing Heather kept for each of the boys, though Kyle's was more complete. The books were full of first smiles, first words, first teeth, and dozens of moments Ryan didn't recall, though Heather had included him as much as she could.

"I didn't know that," he said to Carly.

"Someday Penny will treasure it. From what Denise told me, it's all she has left of her mother. Jenna took a lot of pictures, but they were on her phone, and that was destroyed in the accident. There wasn't much in the apartment, just a few framed photographs of the two of them. Denise has those, too."

"Maybe I should ask her for one. Penny rarely mentions her mother. It worries me."

"Me too."

"At least she hasn't run off lately."

"She's doing great. But there's one more thing I want to talk to you about."

"Just one?"

"Actually more." She disarmed him with a twinkle in her eyes. "To tell the truth, I have a whole list of things for you."

"Have at it," he said, meaning it. With Carly he no longer expected criticism.

"First, Penny's room."

"What's wrong with it?"

"Everything." Her nose wrinkled, a sign she was about to say something he didn't want to hear. "I know you tried to make it nice for her, but it's too stimulating."

"I can see that now." Six months ago, he'd hired a decorator to make it a little girl's paradise. When the woman finished, it had reminded Ryan of a box of new crayons—bright, busy, and full of choices. An abundance of shelves held dolls, games, art supplies, picture books, and educational toys. "What do you suggest?"

"Simplicity. Order. I'd like to redo it—new paint, new bedding, and new curtains. The furniture's fine, but everything else needs to be evaluated from Penny's perspective."

"Go for it."

Victory won, she gave a little fist pump. "This'll be fun."

"I'll help," Ryan offered. "Moving furniture, painting, whatever you need."

"Thanks, but I thought I'd make it a day project and recruit the boys. It'll keep them busy, and it's a chance to be big and strong while I bark orders at them. It's preparation for marriage."

Ryan laughed. "Good plan."

With her eyes twinkling, she laced her hands in her lap. "It also brings up the other thing I want to tell you. It's about Kyle."

Kyle was a good kid, the one who made normal mistakes. Ryan relaxed a bit. "What's up?"

"I think he has a girlfriend."

So much for relaxing. A first girlfriend was something to enjoy, a first date, a first kiss. But teenagers got carried away and made mistakes. Ryan raked his hand through his hair and groaned.

Carly laughed. "I hope you've talked with him about girls."

Her earnest eyes drilled into his, and he wondered just how far apart they were when it came to love and relationships. He knew she was a Christian, but what exactly did that mean? Hands off until marriage? No one he knew lived that way, but he had to admit, there was a time for self-control. Kyle was way too young for that step to adulthood, especially if it led to a teen pregnancy.

Ryan needed to have a serious conversation with his son, but what did he say? *Don't do what I did?* He couldn't, not when he and Heather had slept together before marriage and Kyle was the result. Did he hand the boy a box of condoms the way his own father had done? Ryan came from a world where adults chose their own moralities. Kyle was only fifteen, but his body was maturing even faster than his brain. He'd be a man soon, and Eric was right behind him, Eric who lived like a vampire and stole candy bars by accident.

"Ryan?"

"Sorry." He dragged his hand through his hair. "The whole subject gives me a headache."

"I know you'll handle things with Kyle," she said with far more confidence than he felt. "His girlfriend's name is Taylor Robertson. You haven't met her yet, but I did at the last practice. Her twin brother is on Kyle's team. Her mom's nice and so is her dad, though I suspect he has a shotgun in his trunk to scare away boys."

"Good."

Carly laughed. "My dad had one of those."

"Did it work?" He really wanted to know. "How many boys did he scare away from you?"

"A few." She blushed a little, then scooted to the edge of the couch. Looking down at the carpet, she wiggled her feet into a pair of flip-flops with daisies on top. "I better go."

Stay. Tell me about those boyfriends. Kyle wasn't the only male who had to fight his impulses. So did Ryan, and right now he wanted to enjoy the heady mix of peace and longing only Carly could inspire. Maybe it was her Kentucky roots that made her so easy to be with, or the fact that she was eight years younger and less scarred by life. Ryan was far wiser in the ways of the world, but he admired Carly's country wisdom. With her help, maybe he could cross off the toughest item on the SOS list.

"I need a favor," he said, touching her elbow to keep her on the couch.

Her toes stopped at the edge of her flip-flops. "What is it?"

"I have a list of things I want to do as a family, things that I hope will bring the four of us together." He felt silly confessing, but this was Carly, who didn't judge him for his failures. "I call it the SOS list. That stands for Sink or Swim."

"Or Save Our Souls," she said, sounding wistful. "What's on it?"

"Things like go to Kyle's games and do something with Eric." He elaborated on the museum trip, including how they sat apart. "I'm pretty sure it was a bust."

"Oh, but you're wrong! That trip was a *huge* success!"

"I don't see it."

"That's because you're thinking like an adult, not a thirteen-year-old boy." She laced her hands over her knees. "Kids at that age need their parents, but they don't want them to stand too close. You were there for Eric. That's what matters."

He puffed up a little. "I guess so."

"What else is on the list?"

He named a few more things, like going for ice cream and taking Penny to the park down the street. Mentally he added *Meet Kyle's girlfriend and her parents,* a normal step all parents took. "I can handle most of it. In fact, it's been fun."

"Like at Kyle's game."

"Exactly." He hadn't missed a game since that day. "By the way, I ordered four tickets for a Dodgers-Reds game in July. Want to go?"

"You bet."

Her smile pleased him a little too much, but the favor he needed to ask humbled him. "Ordering tickets is easy compared to the one thing I can't seem to pull off."

"What is it?"

"Sitting down to a family dinner and everyone enjoying it."

She tipped her head. "That shouldn't be too hard."

"It's harder than you think. I tried, and it was awful. If you can stay late one day and have dinner with us, it might help."

When she didn't answer, Ryan followed her gaze across the room to Eric's cardboard box, where the shark was hanging by a thread. Her expression held a touch of fear as she faced him. "You're trying hard, aren't you?"

"Very."

"Just keep at it. It takes time."

"I don't have time." The boys had been with him for six weeks. The summer was racing by. "I could really use your help."

"You don't need me. This list is for you and your kids."

"But—"

"Ryan, I'm right on this."

His name on her lips sounded both sweet and bitter, and he wondered why a simple meal posed a threat to her. "Stay. Just this once."

She started to stand but stopped on the edge of the sofa. "Let's compromise. Name the day and I'll cook something for the four of you."

"That would be great." But it wasn't enough. He wanted Carly to share the meal, but convincing her to stay would have to wait for a more relaxed time. "How about next Tuesday?"

She tapped a finger on her knee. "That should work. Kyle doesn't have practice that day. Denise won't be visiting until later in the month, so Penny will be here. I'll make sure Eric knows, too."

"So what's on the menu?"

"That's a surprise."

"A hint?"

"Nope." After giving him a stern look, she shoved to her feet. "I need to go home."

Standing with her, he glanced at his watch. They'd talked for almost an hour. "It's late. Spend the night in the nanny room."

"I can't. My cat's waiting."

He knew a lame excuse when he heard one. "I thought cats could stay alone now and then."

"She's been alone all day."

Ryan worried about Carly driving home, but he had no right to pressure her. She was a competent, independent woman. Even so, he waited while she fetched her purse from the nanny room, then walked her to her car. He didn't have to do it. She was an employee, a member of the household in a formal way, but a masculine caring, a timeless urge to protect her, took root in his chest and refused to budge.

"See you in the morning," Carly said as she slipped into the driver's seat.

He closed the door and watched her pull out of the driveway. The hush of night descended on him. The sky seemed blacker and the stars more distant, and as he headed to the house, he thought of Carly's head on the pillow on the couch and gave in to a wave of loneliness. He considered sneaking a cigarette, but he needed to speak with Eric. Disciplined as always, Ryan climbed the stairs one at a time. He reached Kyle's room first, saw the door open a crack, and heard Kyle murmur something, presumably into his phone. "I like you too, Taylor . . . a lot."

For a breath Ryan was young and in love again. He blinked, saw Carly's pretty face, and felt like a fool. Falling for the nanny was *not* on his SOS list. Kyle spoke more quietly into the phone, reminding Ryan of that talk they needed to have about girls. It couldn't wait too long, but this wasn't the time.

He passed Kyle's room and tapped on Eric's door. After several seconds, he assumed Eric was blasting music through earbuds, opened the door a crack, then fully. Eric was propped on pillows on his messy bed, staring at his computer tablet. At the sight of Ryan, he yanked out the earbuds.

"Carly told me about the picture of Penny."

Eric remained slouched against the stack of pillows with the tablet against his knees. Ryan wondered what Carly would do and decided she'd be herself—direct, truthful, firm. And kind. Eric's anger was knee-jerk but understandable. His second reaction—to take the Facebook picture down—was the behavior Ryan wanted to encourage.

He walked into the room and sat on the edge of the bed. "The diorama you made looks great."

Eric's brows lifted, maybe with surprise. "I like using spray paint. Carly said it was all right."

Ryan tipped his hat to Carly. He would have said no to the spray paint, but Eric had lived up to her trust. "You did a good job. I hear Penny tried to trash it."

Eric's face was like flint, unmoving, and for a moment Ryan recalled being thirteen and stuffing down every big, confusing feeling. He knew in his gut how hard Eric worked to keep up a tough façade, because Ryan worked just as hard. "I get mad at Penny, too. It was wrong to put that picture online, but you took it down. I'm proud of you for making things right."

"I guess."

"No guessing. You did the right thing."

As Eric shrugged off the praise, Ryan looked into the hazel eyes the boy inherited from Heather. For the millionth time Ryan wished he owned a giant can of the stain remover like the one he used on the berry stains in the Impala, something that could erase the stains on his conscience. But such a thing didn't exist. All he could do was tell the truth and hope Eric would understand.

"Six years ago I made a bad mistake," Ryan admitted. "I'm trying to make things right for all of us, but it's hard for everyone. I need your help."

Eric narrowed his eyes. "What for?"

"I'd like you to be a little extra patient with Penny. Do you think you can do that?"

"Why should I?"

"Because you can." For all of Eric's anger, he possessed a healthy brain and a sharp mind.

Ryan waited for him to say something, anything. Even a sarcastic remark would keep the door open, but his son just stared at him. At a loss, Ryan walked out of the room and closed the door. He'd taken two steps when Eric stepped into the hall and held out a folded piece of paper. "Here. Carly said to give this to you."

Ryan opened his mouth to ask what it was, but Eric slipped back into his room and closed the door with a soft click.

Alone in the hall, Ryan unfolded the note and saw Eric's Facebook info, complete with password. Pride in his son filled his chest, and he paused to savor this big step toward mutual respect. Knowing Carly would still be awake, he went out to the patio to call her.

～∽～

Carly steered the Cavalier into the carport and turned off the ignition. Just as she reached for her purse, her phone chirped. Worried, she checked the caller ID and saw the picture she'd snapped of Ryan. Handsome and unguarded, he filled the screen with a roguish smile.

"Hi," she said. "Is everything all right?"

"It's great. Eric just gave me his password to Facebook."

"Oh, good."

"It is, and that's why I'm calling. He said you told him to do it. Thanks."

"I suggested it, but he made the choice."

"You're home. Right?"

"Just getting out of the car." She opened the door and scanned the alley. It was empty, but she decided to keep Ryan on the phone until she reached her apartment. "Tell me more."

"The conversation was awkward, but we made progress. You were right about Kyle, too." He described overhearing the phone call with Taylor. "Young love. I barely remember it."

"I do! All the drama about dances, those looks across history class." Laughing a little, she opened the squeaky gate.

"What was that?"

"The gate."

"Where do you live, anyway?"

She didn't want to tell him. If he knew how bad the neighborhood was, he'd pressure her to live in, and she couldn't do it. "I'm about a half hour from you. I'm at my door now."

"Good. I'm staying here until you're locked up tight."

"Okay."

Grateful for the protection, even if it was just on the phone, she narrated turning the deadbolt and opening the door. "I'm inside now."

"Sweet dreams," he said.

"You too."

As she closed the door, their good-byes overlapped, touching like a tangle of arms in a first awkward kiss.

She locked both deadbolts, then slumped against the door and succumbed to a wave of fear—not because of crime and helicopters, neighbors with barbed-wire tattoos, or even because of FASD and Allison. It was because of Ryan and how he made her feel. Warm. Safe. Protected. And something more . . . something dangerously close to love.

11

Dressed in a white shirt, flashy tie, and charcoal blazer, Ryan trotted down the stairs ready for work. He'd fallen into the habit of an early morning chat with Carly, and he looked forward to saying good morning enough to set his alarm for it. It was Tuesday, and tonight she'd cook dinner for his family, though she told him repeatedly that she planned to leave the instant the last serving bowl hit the table.

Just as he expected, she was seated at the kitchen table making a list of some sort. The recessed lighting lit up her hair in a way that reminded him of the beach on a sunny day, and he paused at the doorway. No one else brought calm into his life. With Carly, he felt strong, competent, and even wise. That's why he had to convince her to stay for dinner.

She looked up from her notepad with a frown. "Ready for breakfast?"

"Not yet. What's wrong?"

Stifling a yawn, she went to the counter and opened the bread box holding bagels and loaves of wheat, white, and sourdough. The boys ate that much, though the bagels were for him. Carly plopped one in the toaster. "We had a Penny episode yesterday. I would have told you when you got home, but it was a little late."

Since the night he walked her home by phone, he'd been concerned about where she lived and made sure she left well before dark. "What happened?"

"She tried to run away again."

"So the problem isn't solved."

"No. We were in the pool when she asked me about her mother. The entire incident was weird."

"It often is with Penny." He lifted a mug off the shelf and snapped a pod in the Keurig. Carly busied herself with fixing the bagel for him. They were elbow to elbow, surrounded by the aroma of strong coffee. The other nannies didn't fix his breakfast, but Carly was more than a nanny.

Turning, she fetched a tub of cream cheese from the refrigerator. "Penny asked me if her mother still liked to swim—the key word here is *still*. She seems to think Jenna is alive and living somewhere."

"I've worried about that. It's one of the reasons I took her to therapy. With so much going on, Miss Monica said she needed time."

"I can't imagine what it was like for her."

"Me either."

"Death is complicated for any child, but especially Penny. We talked about heaven and what it's like, and I told her what I thought, that heaven is everything that's good about this world but a thousand times better. If her mother liked to swim on earth, she could swim in heaven. Then I told her we can't go to heaven without help from God." The toaster popped, but she faced him instead of removing the bagel. "Religion is personal. I suspect we have different views."

"We do."

"I hope you don't mind what I told her."

"Not at all." He supported anything that would help Penny

cope with her disabilities, even an imaginary god. As for himself, he thought about eternity now and then, at funerals or when he noticed his mother's Bible on the bottom shelf in his office. Once in a while, on a gray day, he picked it up and read, but the logic of needing a savior escaped him. Though there were times with Penny, like when she ran off, that he wished he could believe.

Carly plopped the bagel on a plate. "She won't talk about her mom, but she thinks about her and wonders where she is. Did Penny go to the funeral?"

"You're asking about closure."

"Exactly." She slathered the cream cheese just the way he liked it, then handed it to him. "Maybe you should take her to Jenna's grave."

"Can't do it," he mumbled while chewing. "She was cremated. Denise hired a boat and scattered the ashes in the ocean. Penny didn't go, but Denise told her about it."

"So she has a picture in her mind."

"Yes." Ryan took another bite. Chewing more slowly, he tried to piece together Penny's actions. "What happened after the heaven talk?"

"We sat in the sun to dry off. I was wearing sunglasses, so she couldn't see my eyes. She thought I was asleep and headed for the gate. Rather than stop her, I watched."

"And she headed for the car."

"Exactly." Carly covered the toaster and wiped up crumbs. "I tried to talk to her about it, but she can't explain. Rather than frustrate us both, I let it go. But I'm positive everything is related—her mother, swimming, running away, even the old Impala."

"I understand her mother and the ocean, but why the car?"

"I have no idea." Carly ambled back to the table, picked up the pen, and tapped it against the notepad. "At least she's happier in her room. It feels calmer now, even to me."

Thanks to Carly, the walls were now pale blue, and the open

shelves were filled with white bins labeled in block printing with words like "Crayons" and "Bedtime Books." There was no clutter except what Penny created, and the messes were easily put away in the bins. Problem solved, or at least mitigated.

There was nothing else to say about Penny, so Ryan shifted gears from a problem he couldn't solve to one he could. After setting the plate in the sink, he rested his hands on the counter and crossed one foot over the other. "Is that a grocery list?"

With a flick of her wrist, she flipped the paper upside down. "Yes, it is. And tonight's menu is a secret."

"Stay. I want you with us."

She was already shaking her head. "We've been over this. I'll dish up, but then I'm leaving. You don't need me here. Families eat together all the time. Not as often as they used to, but still, it's normal."

"Not for me."

"Not normal? What do you mean?"

"I was an only child." On the rare occasions he had eaten dinner with his parents, he felt like a grad student giving a presentation. That wasn't all bad. Those conversations sharpened his mind, and he enjoyed them as much as other kids enjoyed having their fathers coach soccer. "Meals with my parents felt more like meetings."

Carly drummed the pen some more. "Didn't you eat with Heather and the kids?"

"Not very often."

"So this really is new to you." She tipped her head, curiosity bright in her eyes. "I can't imagine."

Sensing a crack in her resolve, he tweaked his strategy. When it came to rescuing people in need, Carly would fight and fight hard. Rather than pressure her—he was certain she'd rebel—he waited with what he hoped was a mildly pathetic look on his face.

She drummed again, sipped her coffee, then faced him with a glint in her eye. "You're pathetic. Do you know that?"

He threw up his hands in surrender. "Definitely. Absolutely. I'm beyond hope."

"You're also a bad actor," she said with a hint of a smile. "You're playing on my sympathies with that dreary face."

Confession time. "You bet I am. You might not believe it, but I really am in trouble here. The first time we sat down together, it was awful."

"What happened?"

"Kyle tried to talk baseball, which annoyed Eric, who hates sports. I asked Eric about the movie he saw with Nathan, and he told me it stank. No one said another word until Penny spilled her milk. It was a mess, a complete disaster."

Carly's mouth puckered as if she were hiding something; then she chuckled.

Ryan didn't get it. "What's so funny?"

"You are! Spilled milk and bickering are part of life. My brother was a table kicker, and I can't tell you how many times my sister and I stuck our tongues out at each other over mashed potatoes."

"Hmm." Maybe he didn't want *normal*.

Carly studied him for a moment. "It's your job to teach them manners, but it's even more important to just be with them."

"I'm trying."

"I know you are." She picked up the list, skimmed it, sighed with as much exaggeration as he'd dished out earlier. Finally she set it down. "Oh, all right. I'll stay. But just this once. And only because there won't be any leftovers, and I'm cooking the best meal in the world."

He pushed away from the counter. "Thank you, Carly. It means a lot to me."

"It'll be fun. You'll see."

When she dismissed him with a flick of her hand, he noticed bluish shadows under her eyes. She looked tired, or maybe she was coming down with a cold.

"Are you feeling okay?"

"I'm fine." She surrendered to a massive yawn. "It was a bad night. The police helicopter woke me up around three, and I couldn't get back to sleep."

"Just say the word and you can live in."

"No, but thank you."

He wished she would change her mind and not just for the convenience. He worried about her driving that rattletrap car of hers. If he didn't need the van for hauling the kids around, he'd have told her to drive it like her own. As things stood, the Check Engine light had popped on yesterday.

Carly opened the pantry and lifted a box of pancake mix for the kids' breakfast. "Dinner's at six. Don't be late."

"I won't," he said. "By the way, I'm dropping the van at the mechanic."

"That's fine. I'll take my car to the store. Have a good day."

"You too."

He took a step toward the hall, but his feet stopped, and he turned for a final look at Carly. Out of the blue, he was struck with the urge to kiss her good-bye. Those feelings were pure craziness, nature at work, and as inconvenient as a toothache.

Annoyed, he headed for the van. As he turned the ignition, the amber warning light flashed, a reminder to check the engine before something costly happened. He needed to rein in his feelings for Carly for the same reason.

◈

Carly spent the entire afternoon in the kitchen. With a little luck, her mother's fried chicken would work its usual magic, and Ryan could cross "Have an enjoyable family dinner" off his SOS list. She hoped the meal went well, because after last night's helicopter incident, where the lights scraped across her window, she was determined to be home before dark. How many times did she have to ask the landlord to replace the lights in the carport? She would have done it herself, but it required long fluorescent bulbs, and they were expensive. Besides, that's why she paid rent.

Kyle walked into the kitchen and sniffed the air. "Dinner smells awesome."

"I think you'll like it." Using potholders, she lifted a rectangular Pyrex dish out of the oven. "We're having fried chicken, green beans with bacon, hash-brown casserole, and homemade biscuits."

"Wow." He looked close to drooling. "What's for dessert?"

"Chocolate meringue pie." Ryan's favorite, a bit of trivia she'd picked up talking to the boys. She set the steaming dish on a woven mat. "How about setting the table?"

While Carly dished up, Kyle broke out the silverware. Penny was in the family room playing with stuffed animals in the small tent Carly used to give her a quiet place downstairs. Eric was upstairs on his computer, either playing a game or reading about shark attacks.

Surrounded by familiar aromas, Carly chatted with Kyle about his day. Of the three kids, he was the most content. Yesterday he'd told her he believed in God and liked going to youth group with Taylor. Carly hoped Ryan had spoken to him about girls and respect, then worried about what he might say. Ryan came from a very different world than the one where she'd been raised. There was a good chance his advice to Kyle would be "use protection." Probably not yet. Kyle was far from an adult, but someday he'd be a man and responsible for himself and the woman he loved.

Carly often wondered about phrases like "safe sex." Her personal idea of "protection" had nothing to do with latex and everything to do with love. She wrestled with physical temptation as much as any woman, but she wanted her wedding night, if she had one, to be as special as she imagined, even sacred. That longing had cost her a boyfriend in college, an almost-fiancé who didn't want to wait for marriage to have sex. She cried a lot when he ended the relationship, not for what she lost but for what they didn't really have. In the end, she had realized that he didn't know her at all.

"Carly?"

"Yes?" She set down the biscuits and turned to Kyle. He looked so much like Ryan that she inhaled sharply.

Kyle's cheeks reddened a bit. "I just want to say thanks for everything—driving me to practice, being nice to Taylor and her parents, everything. My mom would like you."

"That's high praise." She was flattered, truly. "Knowing you and Eric, I'm sure I'd like your mom, too."

"She's all right," Kyle said in a way that turned "all right" into "someone special." Then he glanced back at the table laden with food. "This looks great."

"Oh, it is." She'd been put on earth to serve and bless others. That's why she was standing here now—to help the Tremaines become a family. If that meant cooking up fried chicken for Ryan, she'd do it with joy. She just wished that catch in her heart would go away, because when he walked into the kitchen and smiled at her, she could barely breathe.

12

Ryan sauntered into the kitchen after a long day at the office, smelled fried chicken, and congratulated himself on guessing Carly's menu. What else would a southern woman fix for a family dinner? The anticipation was the one bright spot in a day that included bad news from the mechanic. The van needed a part that was back ordered, and it wouldn't be ready until late tomorrow. He hoped the bad day wasn't a harbinger of things to come with the meal.

Carly saw him and smiled. "Perfect timing."

"Hey, Dad." Kyle stuck a napkin under a fork. "You should see what Carly fixed."

"It smells great."

She tossed him a look he interpreted as *"See? Normal talk. That's not so hard."* After setting down the platter of chicken, she surveyed the table and turned to Kyle. "Would you get Eric?"

"Sure."

"Don't forget to wash up," she added.

Next, she glanced at the tent in the family room. Ryan followed her gaze and saw Penny silhouetted against the tan fabric. Giving her a safe place in the middle of the house was brilliant, another one of Carly's innovations. As he turned to comment, she faced him. "I'll call Penny in a minute. How was your day?"

"Long." Five patients didn't show up, a thorn to both the bottom line and his usual busy pace. He'd been distracted all day. "I have bad news about the van. It won't be ready until late tomorrow."

"There's nothing on the calendar. At least no carpool duties. We'll be fine."

There it was again, that *we* that wrapped around them like a lariat and pulled tight. He needed her tonight, so he didn't pull back from her mentally, or from the table set with red gingham place mats and white dishes. "Dinner is served," he said dryly. "Why do I feel like a sacrificial lamb?"

He was looking at the table and his place at the head when Carly laid her hand on his arm. The touch was feather light, but it carried the weight of all her goodwill, the hours she'd spent fixing the meal, and most of all, the fact she was on his side.

"Relax," she said to him. "Families do this all the time. Why don't you change clothes?"

"Good idea." He excused himself to go upstairs, where he put on old Levis and tried to stop thinking about Carly and lambs. She was right. For most people, a family meal was as routine as brushing one's teeth.

Somewhat fortified, he returned to the kitchen, where Eric and Kyle were seated on one side of the table, with Carly and Penny on the other. Only one seat remained—the empty chair at the head of the table.

Feeling more like a CEO than a dad, Ryan sat. All eyes were on him, every ear waiting to hear what he'd say. Carly met his gaze and held it, silently telling him to break the tension. What did he do? Tell a joke? Explain why he'd called this meeting together? None of the above, he decided. After clearing his throat, he put his napkin in his lap. "This sure looks good—"

"We have to say grace!" Penny cried out.

Ryan never said grace. He didn't believe in God, but others did, and that was fine by him. "Okay, honey. You can say it."

"No," she said. "You."

Eric and Kyle knew how he felt about religion. If he said grace, he'd be a hypocrite. But with four pairs of eyes staring at him, he latched onto a compromise. "We'll have a moment of silence. Anyone who wants to pray, can."

He bent his neck and stared at his empty plate, silently counting to ten, when Kyle's voice, as deep as Ryan's, broke the silence.

"Father God, thank you for the food we're about to receive, for Carly who cooked it, and for Dad who earned the money to pay for it. Amen."

Ryan sat stunned. Deep down, he didn't think his kids appreciated what he did for them—food, clothes, doctor visits, college funds. What kid *did* appreciate those things? Ryan hadn't appreciated his own father until he was married and paying his own bills. He swallowed hard and nodded an acknowledgement to Kyle. His throat was too tight to speak, and besides, he didn't like mush and neither did Kyle.

"Dig in!" Carly reached for the chicken, served Penny, and passed the platter to Eric across from her.

Quiet as usual, Eric took a drumstick.

Kyle helped himself, then passed the platter to Ryan.

They repeated the ritual with the serving bowls, sitting in silence, punctuated by the scrape of forks. Even Penny was quiet for a change. He might have enjoyed the quiet after the hectic day, but Carly waggled her brows at him. A cue. *Say something.*

Ryan cleared his throat. "So, Kyle. How was baseball practice?"

"Good," Kyle said between bites. He was a lot more interested in the chicken than in conversation.

Ryan tried with Eric. "How about you, Eric? What did you do today?"

The boy let out a sigh. "The usual."

Whatever that was. Ryan decided not to push. "Penny? How about you?"

She didn't make a sound, not a peep. Maybe she heard him; maybe she didn't. With her auditory deficits, he couldn't be sure. Rather than push Penny into frustration, Ryan focused on Carly, willing her to play social worker and lead the conversation. Instead, she glanced from face to face, saying nothing.

"Good chicken," he said to her.

"Thank you." She smiled at him. "How was your day?"

"Normal."

He sounded just like Kyle and Eric. No wonder his kids didn't talk at the table. Neither did he, and he didn't know how to fill the silence.

❧

Carly couldn't stand the tension. No one put an elbow on the table. The boys kept their napkins in their laps. Not a single drop of milk dripped down a chin. Penny's fidgeting was the only hint of normal behavior, and even she was more subdued than usual. If her own family had acted this way, she'd have lobbed a biscuit at her brother to see if he was breathing.

She didn't think Ryan would appreciate a flying biscuit, and Penny might imitate her. Belching might have done the trick for the boys, but she couldn't bring herself to do it. Still pondering, she reached for the pepper shaker, caught a whiff, and realized the answer was in her hand.

Humming loud enough to draw attention, she lifted the pepper shaker and shook it over her food. She shook and shook until everyone at the table was staring at her plate with reactions ranging from confusion to amusement. Ryan's brows were arched as high as she'd ever seen. Kyle's expression matched his father's. Penny was laughing in that maniacal way of hers. And Eric . . . Eric's eyes were sparkling with a mirth she hadn't seen in him before. She winked at him, and he smiled back.

Carly kept shaking the pepper. Her plate was nearly black with it, but she shook until pepper covered every inch of her meal. Everyone just stared at the mess until Eric burst out laughing. Penny laughed too, then she shouted, "Carly's crazy!"

Kyle looked at her plate with a mix of horror and confusion. So did Ryan, but his face stayed stiff.

Ramping up the joke, she leaned forward and inhaled through her nose. The pepper tickled her nostrils with the start of a sneeze. "Ahh . . . ahhh . . ." Snatching up her napkin, she reared back in the chair with her eyes watering. "Aaaatchoooo!"

She sneezed two more times, then fanned herself. "Well, excu-uuu-use me," she said, like in the old Steve Martin routine.

Kyle burst out laughing. He was in stitches, and so were Eric and Penny. And then suddenly so was Ryan. Carly had never heard him laugh so hard and so freely. Her heart melted into a puddle of warm butter, the best part of eating a biscuit, and she knew she'd never forget this moment.

The entire family was laughing now, and so was Carly. Her chest ached with the force of it, and her eyes watered with bitter-sweet tears. She didn't want this moment to end. Yearning for a family of her own, a husband and children who'd laugh and cry with her, she turned to Ryan. His eyes, twinkling and full of joy, locked on to hers, and she felt a nudge under the table, his foot against hers, a wordless *thank you* that flooded her heart with both joy and trepidation. She didn't dare lose her heart to this man. They were as mismatched as day and night, darkness and light.

The kids were talking at the same time now, about food they hated and food they liked. Forcing her thoughts away from Ryan, she made notes about what to cook for them. Kyle liked corn better than peas, and Eric frowned at gravy. And Ryan, he was on his third piece of chicken and second helping of hash-brown casserole, which he announced was his new favorite food.

The dinner settled into the relaxed meal she'd hoped for, and the family cleaned out the serving bowls except for some of the hash-brown casserole, which she decided to take to Bette. They were all too full for the chocolate meringue pie, but no one wanted to leave the table. Finally, worried about driving home in the dark, Carly prodded the guys into doing the dishes and took Penny upstairs for a bath and pajamas.

"Carly?" the little girl asked as she flopped on her pillow, her hair damp and her eyes shining.

"Yes?"

"Would you read me a story?"

She glanced out the window, saw the elm silhouetted against the royal blue sky, and shook her head. "I have to take care of Wild Thing. Let's ask your daddy to do it."

"No. You do it. You make funny voices."

Carly was about to insist that she needed to leave, when Penny bolted upright, wrapped her arms around Carly's ribs, and squeezed. Warmed to the core, Carly surrendered to both Penny and her own desire. She didn't want to leave, not really. "You pick the book, okay?"

Penny scrambled to the bookshelf, opened the bin that said "Bedtime Books," and climbed back on the mattress. Snuggling against Carly's side, she let out a big yawn as Carly opened the book and started to read. After just three pages, Penny's eyes fluttered shut, and her breathing settled into the rhythm of sleep. Carly turned off the lamp, kissed her warm forehead, and went downstairs.

The kitchen sparkled from top to bottom. Kyle and Eric were in the family room wrestling, literally, for the remote. Ryan was nowhere in sight until he came through the back door. "I took out the trash," he said with a grin. "We did rock-paper-scissors. I lost."

Happiness welled in her heart. "You had a good time."

"Yes, we did." He lowered his voice so only she could hear. "What you did tonight . . . it was amazing."

"You mean the pepper?" She laughed a little.

"I mean everything."

"It's just how I was raised. My daddy loves a good practical joke."

"I'd like to meet him."

She imagined Ryan and her father sitting down for a cigar and a debate on God, life, and everything in between. Sparks would fly, but in a good way.

Ryan indicated the family room with a stretch of his arm. "Eric suggested a *Jaws* marathon. How about it? Want to join us?"

"It's tempting," she admitted.

"Then stay."

What harm would there be in staying just one night? She had clothes and toiletries in the nanny room, and Bette would be glad to feed Wild Thing. Wise or not, Carly wanted to bask in the warm glow of family a little longer. *Family.* The word echoed in her mind along with a hint of warning, because she could have changed *family* to *Ryan*. Even so, a happy shiver danced down her spine. "All right. I'll stay. But I have to call Bette."

Ryan spoke in a husky voice. "We'll wait for you."

Blushing a little, she went to the kitchen and lifted her cell phone off the counter. When Bette's house phone went to voice mail, Carly's brows pulled into a frown. Next she called Bette's cell phone. A second round of voice mail turned the frown into a knot of worry. Bette was always home this time of night. If she'd been asked to work late, she would have called Carly. Maybe she was in the bathroom. Carly waited a few minutes, busying herself by wiping the shining counters yet again, then she tried both numbers a second time.

Again, voice mail.

In Boomer, she could have asked a neighbor to knock on Bette's door. In Los Angeles, she didn't have anyone to call. Jamming the phone in her pocket, she hurried to the family room where Ryan was seated on the couch with his arm stretched across the back. Eric was kneeling in front of the diorama to tweak something, and Kyle was seated in the recliner, a switch because Ryan usually sat in the big chair. The *Jaws* theme played a cruel reminder that danger lurked unseen in even the most tranquil times.

"I have to leave," she said in a tight voice.

Ryan leapt to his feet, concern etched across his angular face. "What's wrong?"

"I can't reach Bette."

"Try again," he suggested. "Maybe the phone's on silent."

"It's not. I've tried twice now—both numbers." Carly glanced at the boys. They were standing now, much like their father, and watching her with concern. The Tremaine males made quite a picture. "Have fun," she said to them. "I'll see you in the morning."

She went to the fridge, put the container of hash-brown casserole in a grocery bag, and headed to the nanny room to get her purse.

"Wait." Ryan caught up to her in the hallway. "I'm going with you."

"It's not necessary."

"Yes, I think it is."

"You belong with the boys." What if the sudden need to go home was God pulling her back from the mistake of becoming too involved?

Leaving Ryan, she fetched her purse and charged back down the hall. Going full tilt, she hurried out the front door before Ryan could catch her. She didn't want to ruin his night with his sons, especially when she was probably overreacting to a phone glitch. And especially when she longed to say yes to his offer to accompany her—not because she needed a man to steady her, but because she wanted to be with him.

She climbed into her Cavalier just as Ryan strode out of the atrium with Kyle and Eric behind him.

"Carly," he called. "Wait up."

Pretending not to hear, she turned the key in the ignition. Instead of roaring to life, the engine groaned and died. She turned the key again, heard an impotent *click-click-click*, and slumped against the seat.

13

As Ryan opened Carly's door, the boys came up behind him, crossed their arms, and stood like soldiers waiting for orders. Pride swelled in his chest. When he'd gone after Carly, Kyle had said to Eric, "Come on, let's help Dad." This is what men did for women. They slayed dragons and fixed cars, and they didn't let vulnerable, hardheaded females drive alone in bad neighborhoods after dark.

Carly looked up at him and sighed. "It's probably the battery. Could you give me a jump? I have cables."

He pulled the door wider and offered his hand, the gesture issuing an order while his eyes bored into hers. "I'm not about to let you drive off with a dead battery. I'll take you home to check on Bette. That's final."

She glanced at his fingers, then looked into his eyes. Ryan lowered his chin. "We're wasting time."

She grabbed her purse and the grocery bag with one hand and accepted his help from the car with the other. When she pressed her palm tight against his, the heat of worry shot up his arm.

Kyle interrupted. "I'll keep an eye on Penny."

"Me too," Eric added.

Carly beamed at the boys. "Thanks for helping. It means a lot to me."

It meant a lot to Ryan, too. Seeing his sons act like men puffed up his chest, and he gave a mental salute to both Carly and the effectiveness of the SOS list. "Eric, would you get my phone and keys, please?"

His son nodded once and took off for the house.

"Kyle," Ryan continued, "make sure to lock up."

"I will."

"And check Penny a few times."

Widening his stance, Kyle propped his hands on his hips. "I'll stay up until you get home."

"Good. It shouldn't be long."

"About an hour or so," Carly added.

Eric returned with the keys and phone. The boys went back in the house, and Ryan guided Carly to the main garage with a hand on the small of her back. He opened the overhead door with the keypad, helped her into the passenger seat, and backed out of the driveway.

The fading sunset turned the trees to silhouettes, and the night air sharpened the scent of Carly's skin lotion. Being with her felt like a date, except her foot tapped nervously on the floor mat and she tried a couple of times to call Bette. He didn't know where she lived, so in between worrying out loud, she gave him directions.

As they approached her neighborhood, he spotted a rundown strip mall. A liquor store with bars on the windows sat between a bail-bondsman office and a cheap haircut place, and the only car in the parking lot was on blocks. A fluorescent light flickered in an empty Laundromat.

"Turn here." Carly pointed to a quiet street full of 1950s-style apartment buildings, the kind built in pairs to make an open courtyard. Fresh paint battled some of the decay, but it failed to hide torn curtains behind burglar bars.

He braked at a four-way stop. "Straight?"

"Go left."

The instant he made the turn, flashing lights smacked the windshield. Glare from a fire truck, an ambulance, and four police cars flooded the interior of the Honda. With adrenaline pumping, he braked to a stop. Carly's hand flew to her chest, and she gasped.

Intending to turn around, Ryan glanced over his shoulder. "We'll go another way."

"No!" She snatched up her purse and flung the door open, leaving the bag with the casserole. "That's my building. I have to find Bette." She leapt out and ran to the crowd gathered four buildings away.

Ryan slammed the Honda into reverse, parked illegally up a curb, and ran after her. The police helicopter beamed a spotlight on him, and he stopped. Blinded, he raised his hands, then his face to give the officers a clear view. If they were looking for a thirty-something white male, six-foot-three, 190 pounds, he was in trouble.

The silver light pinned him in place for ten long seconds, each one marked by stark fear for Carly, until the chopper roared away. Blinking away the blindness, he ran to the crowd gathered at the building cordoned off by yellow tape. He didn't see Carly anywhere. Some faces were black or brown; others were white. Some were old and wrinkled; others belonged to babies in their mothers' arms. Conversations in Spanish, English, and Vietnamese blended in a cacophony of rumor, supposition, and only the most obvious facts. Something terrible had happened. Something violent.

Leveraging his way through the crowd, he shouted Carly's name until she cried out, "Over here!" Her pale arm stuck up from the throng, and she waved.

Muttering apologies, he made his way to her side and pulled her into his arms. She sank into him and held tight. "I can't find Bette."

"We'll keep looking. It's a big crowd."

"Yes, but she'd be here. She's nosy like that. She—" Carly's voice cracked. "I-I'm hearing terrible things."

"Maybe she's talking to the police."

"That could be." Carly took a steadying breath and pulled out of his arms. "I want to know what really happened, not what people are saying."

"Do the police know you live here?"

"No, and I can't get anyone's attention. I tried to get to the front of the tape, but the crowd's too thick."

Ryan was six inches taller than Carly, far more arrogant, and dead set on helping her. With his arm around her shoulders, he maneuvered her to the stretch of taut yellow tape where a uniformed officer stood on the other side. Ryan called out to him.

When the man turned, Ryan indicated Carly. "She lives here. She might know something."

The officer nodded, then spoke into his radio. A minute later, a jowly man in his fifties, presumably a detective, spoke with the officer, who pointed at Carly.

The detective approached them with his mouth in a grim line. "Your names, please."

"I'm Ryan Tremaine. This is Carly Mason. She lives in the building."

"Apartment Five," she added. "I've been trying to reach my neighbor, Bette Gordon. She lives in Six."

The detective lifted the tape a few inches. "Come with me."

Carly went first, and Ryan followed. The officer led them to a patch of dead lawn about ten feet from the crowd but in full view of the rescue vehicles. After introducing himself as Detective Hogan, the man tucked his notepad into his coat pocket. "I'm sorry, Miss Mason. Bette Gordon was murdered this afternoon."

Ryan placed his hand on her back. He expected a shriek, a cry, for her knees to buckle. Instead, she clamped her hand over her mouth and closed her eyes. Death in its natural forms traumatized the living. Murder struck Ryan as a macabre kind of tyranny, mankind run amuck like rats eating one another on a sinking ship. A bitter rage pulsed through him. Some things in this life were just plain cruel—murder, cancer, car accidents, FASD.

Carly lowered her hand. With her eyes glazed, she focused on the detective. "When . . . when did it happen?"

"Around four o'clock. What do you know about Ms. Gordon's habits?"

"She works at . . . worked at—" A cry strangled her, but she held it back. "She worked at the Vons bakery. She came home at three-thirty every single day."

The detective wrote on his notepad. "Have long did she live here?"

"Over twenty years." For the next several minutes, Carly answered questions about Bette's life, the building, anything suspicious she might have seen. With each word, she sounded more Southern and more frightened.

Metal wheels rattled in the courtyard. Spotlights lit up a gurney draped with a white sheet, a body evident beneath it, as a pair of men in coroner uniforms maneuvered the gurney down the walk. Ryan drew Carly into his arms to shield her eyes, but she stood ramrod straight, pathetically small compared to the vastness of the heartache.

She gasped, steadied herself, then turned back to Detective Hogan. "What exactly happened?"

"I'm sorry," he said. "This is an open investigation. I can't share the details."

"I know about the home invasion a few blocks from here. Was she shot?" Carly's voice rose an octave. "Beaten to death? Raped?"

Hogan gave her the respect of an almost imperceptible nod, and silently Ryan thanked him. Not knowing was worse than knowing too much.

"Why?" Carly pressed her knotted hands to her chest. "She didn't *have* anything. Not even a decent television. All she had was her cat."

Hogan's eyelids drooped a little lower. "Home invasions don't always make sense."

"This is pure evil!" Carly cried.

The detective let the remark hang, as helpless as Ryan and every other human being to fix this big ugly broken world. The air thickened with the frenetic hum of the crowd, the smell of food cooking in a nearby kitchen, the rumble of the fire truck leaving the scene. In the presence of death, life asserted itself with the tenacity of a hungry child.

The detective shoved the notebook inside his coat. "Do you have a place to spend the night?" he asked Carly.

Ryan answered for her. "Yes, she does."

"Good." He aimed his chin toward the courtyard where police personnel seemed to be everywhere. "We're going to be here a while. Do you need anything out of your apartment?"

"My cat—" She choked up. "And Bette's cat."

Hogan indicated they should follow him. "I'll check for Ms. Gordon's cat while you gather what you need for the night. I want to prepare you. There are pry marks on your door."

"*My* door? Do you mean—"

"Were the marks there before tonight?"

"No."

"Then it's likely the suspects tried to enter your apartment before they targeted Miss Gordon. Having two deadbolts paid off tonight."

Carly grabbed for Ryan's hand and held tight. He squeezed back, then squeezed even harder when he saw the raw, splintered wood on the doorframe. He considered himself a rational man, but the sight of those gashes burned through every ounce of civility in him. If anyone dared to harm Carly—beat her, rape her—he'd be as capable of murder as any man.

Detective Hogan said the outside of her apartment had already been examined for evidence; then he asked Carly for her key, opened the door, and stepped back. After a long look at the pry marks, she led the way inside. Hogan excused himself, and Ryan followed Carly into the dimly lit room and closed the door.

With a sweep of his eyes, he took in the apartment that was smaller than his bedroom. A desk and a chair were pushed against the wall closest to the door. The kitchen cabinets were a dull white and thick with multiple coats of paint. A set of cheap shelves held books and photographs he presumed were of her family. A twin bed was wedged in the corner and covered with giant green throw pillows to make a sofa of sorts. With the A/C turned off—a cheap wall unit—the room was stifling.

Somewhere inside, a cat meowed frantically.

"Wild Thing!" Carly hurried to the bed and crouched to pull the feline into her arms, but it bolted out of reach.

Standing straight, she hugged herself hard, hung her head, and shuddered. Ryan crossed the room in two strides. With his hands gentle on her biceps, he pulled her against his chest and held tight with his cheek against the top of her head. The long strands of her hair wisped against his hands and tickled, but what overwhelmed every other sensation—the heat in the room, the smell of her skin— was the tremble passing from her aching heart into his.

"I'm so sorry," he murmured.

She clutched his shirt in her fists, knotting it so that it pulled tight over his shoulders. Her chest heaved, once, twice, then she collapsed into bone-wrenching sobs. With the pain pouring out of her, he held her as tight as he could. She wept for several minutes, clinging to him with her face pressed against his chest and her tears soaking into his shirt.

For now, he was a port in a storm, but somewhere in his heart, maybe his soul, he wanted to be more for her. It was a dangerous admission, because being *more* meant risking what they had now.

Common sense told him to deny his feelings with the full force of his will, but something stronger than logic, something dangerously close to love, dared him to kiss away her tears.

His breath quickened to match hers. With their chests heaving in perfect time, he inhaled the shampoo scent of her hair, bent his neck, and brushed a kiss on her cheek. But then he stopped. If he kissed her mouth, the landscape between them would change irrevocably from level ground to high mountains and deep valleys. Never mind the ache in his chest and the longing to kick death in the teeth. Carly didn't need a reckless kiss in the midst of this broken night. She needed the security of a friend.

Swallowing hard, Ryan raised his face to the ceiling and away from hers. More than anything, Carly needed to feel safe with him, because she was moving into the nanny room permanently. This time he wouldn't take no for an answer.

～⌒

Carly clung to Ryan with all her might, soaking in his strength when her own deserted her. *Bette . . . murdered.* And it had happened in broad daylight. Had the thugs followed her from her car, maybe lurked in the courtyard? But why? Maybe the perpetrators had been high on some kind of illegal drugs, or maybe they were gangbangers on a sick initiation. The attack made no sense.

And they'd come to her apartment, too.

If she hadn't cooked dinner for Ryan and the kids, she would have walked straight into blood, screams, and mayhem. Did she thank God for sparing her or question Him for taking Bette in such a violent, awful way? Carly knew the theology of good and evil, but she never could reconcile suffering and hope, especially in the face of tragedies like this one, or Allison's, or her own mother's early death. All Carly could do was try her best to make the world a better place.

Trembling, she thought of how sweet Bette was to the children

140

at the bakery. Her small, gentle life had consisted of work, Sunday visits to her old, small church, and movies on her old box television. She didn't have children, just a niece who lived in Omaha. Carly had the number in her phone. *"Just in case of an emergency,"* Bette had said. *"When you get older and you're alone, you worry about things like that."*

She didn't have to worry anymore.

And in that small fact, Carly found consolation. For all her doubts about God's ways here on earth, she believed in heaven with her whole heart. Fresh tears flooded her eyes, but this time they washed away a bit of the pain.

When her sobs ebbed to shaky breaths, Ryan loosened his grip but kept his hands on her arms, rubbing gently to soothe her. "Get your cat and what you need for tonight. The boys and I will move the rest on Saturday. You're living in from now on."

There wasn't a cell in her body that wanted to argue with him, yet even as she nodded, her brain screamed a warning. Ryan was off limits to her heart for every reason imaginable—geography, their different world views, the risk to Penny and even to the boys, because they needed to see their father as a man of integrity, not a man who took advantage of the nanny. She'd accept his offer to live in, but she'd fight her feelings with all her might.

Stepping back from him, she wiped her eyes with her fists. "Thank you. I'm grateful to have a place to go."

He hooked a thumb toward the closet. "Get what you need. I'm going to call Kyle to tell him we'll be late."

"Good idea."

While Ryan spoke to Kyle, Carly filled a duffel bag with clothes, gathered cat supplies, then lured Wild Thing out from under the bed with a treat. She put the cat in the carrier, fetched her Bible off the shelf, and added it to the duffel. She didn't understand God at times like this, but she'd been born and raised a Christian. She knew there was comfort to be had in God's Word.

Ryan picked up the duffel and cat supplies, leaving Carly with Wild Thing meowing pathetically in the carrier. Shifting things a bit, he opened the door, and they stepped outside. Detective Hogan approached, empty-handed. "I'm sorry, but there's no sign of Ms. Gordon's cat. It probably ran off at some point."

Carly blinked back fresh tears. Tom was an indoor cat, fourteen years old and declawed. He couldn't survive on his own. "He might come back when things settle down. I'll check for him tomorrow."

"I hope you find him." The detective handed her a business card. "Call if anything new comes to mind."

She pocketed it just the way she'd pocketed the card from Ryan a month ago.

Laden with her possessions, Ryan led her down the street to his car. The crowd had thinned, and only a few unmarked police cars remained. Lights glowed from nearby apartment windows, and night-blooming jasmine filled her nose. The helicopter was long gone.

Life had returned to normal, but it was a terrible normal. Carly didn't waste her breath asking God why. Instead, she silently vowed to do whatever she could to hold back the tide of ugliness. Her arms sagged with the weight of Wild Thing in the carrier, and she thought of Tom. Tomorrow she'd come back and attach posters on telephone poles. Carly's record for saving lives was abysmal, but she refused to give up hope, even for a cat.

14

On the first Sunday morning after Bette's murder, Carly awoke to pinkish light pressing through the white blinds in the nanny room, her room now. The past four days were a blur of conversations with the police, Bette's niece in Omaha, and Carly's own father, who had threatened to hightail it to California and fetch her home. *Home.* She craved the peace of her father's porch and her mother's kitchen. Instead, she was under Ryan's roof and exquisitely aware that he had held her while she cried.

A brother would have done the same thing, she told herself as she climbed out of bed. But Ryan's embrace didn't feel at all brotherly. She'd lost herself in that moment, and she'd been grateful for his strength, even the bossy way he demanded she come home with him. He had also bought a battery for her car and test-driven it himself before declaring it safe to drive.

Yawning, she glanced at the boxes she needed to unpack and gave silent thanks to everyone who helped with the move, including Fran, who stayed at the house with Penny. In spite of the sadness, Carly had managed to smile a few times, mostly at Ryan and the boys razzing each other, then at the excitement of the neighbors who took her furniture off her hands. Best of all, Tom had meowed at her door and consented to come home with her.

She blinked and recalled other good moments: Ryan bringing her a Coke and giving her shoulder a squeeze; his hand on her back when he found her crying over a box of tea from Bette; the way his muscles rippled in the black T-shirt; and that strong chest—

"Stop it!" she muttered. Indulging in schoolgirl fantasies about her boss was just plain foolish.

To distract herself, she glanced at Tom on the foot of her bed while Wild Thing slept on a pillow. The cats knew each other enough not to snarl, but they weren't friends yet. Carly gave them each some love, then remembered her promise to call her father before he left for church. After another yawn, she pressed his number. "Hi, Daddy."

"Hey, baby-girl. How'd you sleep?"

"All right." Except for her dream about Ryan in that snug T-shirt. The man looked good in black, good in anything.

"Are you there, Carly Jo?"

"Sorry, Daddy. I drifted a bit."

"It's no wonder. Any news from the police?"

"Nothing." She had spoken to Detective Hogan a few times, but he wasn't at liberty to share details. Without Bette passing along gossip from the store, Carly was as disconnected as a passing car.

Her father cleared his throat. "Thank the Lord you're not there anymore. If I'd known how bad that neighborhood was—"

"Daddy, don't."

"I worry about you, sweetheart."

"I know."

"How are things with the Tremaines?"

If her father heard even a trace of her attraction to Ryan, he'd pry the truth out of her even if it meant flying to L.A. to do it. "Things are good."

"What does that mean?"

"It means I'm glad I'm here."

There was a long pause, then a grunt. "So am I, sweetheart."

Awash in homesickness, Carly choked up. "I wish I could be in church with you today. I'd sit in the second pew just like I used to do with Mama."

A faint hum traveled over the phone. "You look like her, Carly Jo."

"I know."

"She was something else, and so are you." He paused. "I don't like you being so far away, but like your mama used to say, *'Our kids are on loan to us.'*"

"I know, Daddy. But it's temporary. I'll be back home before you know it."

"We'll celebrate with your mama's fried chicken."

Tears flooded her eyes in a swirling torrent. "Oh, Daddy—"

"What's wrong?"

"It's just . . . just . . ." She didn't want to talk about the pepper joke or Ryan and the kids. "It's just too much right now."

"I wish you had family out there. Or at least a real friend."

Ryan's face shimmered in her mind, and her belly tightened with the memory of being in his arms. "I think maybe I do. Ryan has been wonderful this week."

Her father's *humph* gusted over phone. "So it's Ryan, not *Ryan and the kids.*"

Until now, she'd been careful to talk about Ryan only as part of the family. In the upset, she'd slipped. "He's a good man."

"A believer?"

"No."

"Be careful, Carly Jo. God gave you a big heart. I'm proud of you for it, but I worry, too. Sometimes you try too hard to fix things that can't be fixed."

Her brows snapped together. "What do you mean?"

"There are things in life only God can handle."

She wondered what he meant but lacked the mental energy to ask. "I'll be careful, Daddy. I promise."

They chatted another minute, then said good-bye. Carly dressed in khaki shorts, a white shirt, and her daisy flip-flops, then headed to the kitchen to wait for Ryan so she could ask permission to take Penny to church—not a typical church, but one with the sky for a roof and sand for a floor.

When she walked in, he was already at the Keurig. Dressed in lightweight sweats, he hadn't shaved or showered, a side of him she hadn't seen before.

She didn't waste time on pleasantries. "I'm headed to church this morning. I'd like to take Penny."

He lifted a brow. "You don't have to take her. I'm here."

"I want to."

"Can she handle it?" The coffeemaker finished with a gurgle. Ryan lifted the mug and sipped while peering at her over the rim. He looked sleepy and ragged, and she wondered if he, too, had been plagued by dreams. He studied her for a moment, waiting for an answer. He probably thought church would be crowded with people and buzzing with conversations, things too stimulating for Penny.

"She can handle the church I have in mind," Carly told him.

"Where is it?"

"At the beach. It'll be just the two of us." And the gulls and the waves. Carly was a Kentucky girl down to her marrow, but she loved the ocean. During those times when her guilt over Allison swamped her, walking on the beach restored her equilibrium.

Ryan finally shrugged. "Sure, why not? Take her."

"We'll be at Will Rogers." The state beach was at the end of Temescal Canyon Road and Carly's favorite spot in Los Angeles.

Ryan paused with the mug halfway to his lips. For a moment she thought he might offer to join them, and her heart gave a little leap. She'd say yes if he asked. She needed a friend today, and after all, they were going to church. But Ryan didn't ask. Instead, he tossed the used K pod in the trash and walked out of the kitchen with his cup in hand, saying nothing and somehow leaving a chill in the air.

⟨⟩

Penny loved riding in Carly's car, even if she had to sit in the back in her booster seat. They were on the curvy road to the beach, and if she stretched her neck like a giraffe, she could see the water. She was wearing her pink swimsuit under her clothes, and Carly's big canvas tote held sandwiches, apples, slimy lotion, and a big black book with Carly's name on it in gold letters. She'd also brought Penny's orange life vest.

"You have to wear it," Carly told her. "But even with it, you can't go in the water past your ankles. *And* we have to hold hands the whole time."

Penny loved to swim. Thanks to lessons from Carly, she could go all the way across the pool like a mermaid. Carly said the ocean was different. "It's not for swimming, but we can watch the waves from the sand."

Penny didn't care about waves and sand. She just liked being with Carly. But then she remembered what Aunt DeeDee said. Penny's mommy was in heaven now, but Aunt DeeDee had spread her love all over the ocean, and Penny could visit her there. Her heart made so much noise, she heard it in her ears. Unable to contain herself, she kicked her feet against the seat in front of her.

Carly looked at her in the mirror. "Press your hands together, okay?"

That was their signal to remind Penny to sit still. She did, but only for a minute because then she forgot. When she kicked again, Carly said her name. This time Penny remembered all the way to the parking lot.

"Good job," Carly said when she stopped the car.

Holding Penny with one hand, Carly fetched the tote bag from the trunk. Side by side, they walked what felt like a mile to a spot where they could see the waves, but the water wasn't too close. The first thing Carly did was buckle Penny's life vest on her. "Remember, stay with me," Carly said. "The ocean isn't for swimming."

Penny looked at the waves and thought of her mommy going in a boat with Aunt DeeDee. Maybe she'd come back on a boat. In the distance she saw little ones with white sails. Maybe a boat like that took her mommy to heaven. While Penny watched the boats move on the water, Carly spread the blanket into a square. Penny wanted to run somewhere, jump high, eat an apple or dig or . . . a bird landed right in front of her, and she ran after it.

Carly chased her, lifted her up, and flew her in a circle, laughing until they almost fell down. Carly squeezed until a big breath hissed out of Penny's lungs, and she relaxed, forgetting everything except the warm sand under her feet.

"Let's sit for a minute." Carly guided her to the scratchy blanket. "Before we play, I want to thank God for this beautiful day."

Penny yelled at the top of her lungs, "Thanks, God!"

Carly laughed. "I think He heard you. Do you know that God has a name? He knows us, and He understands how we feel. We're special—each one of us."

Penny didn't want to be special. She wanted to be like her friend Bethany, who was already in first grade. "I don't want to be special."

"But you are," Carly said. "So am I, and so is your daddy."

"Is Eric special?"

"Yes, and so is Kyle."

Penny didn't understand. She loved Kyle, and even Eric acted nice sometimes. Both of them were big and strong, and they knew how to work the television. They didn't forget things like she did, and no one ever told them to stop fidgeting. Carly's words didn't make sense. "Are they special like me?"

"Not exactly." Carly cupped Penny's face in her warm hands. "You have to try extra hard because of how your brain works. *It's not your fault.*" She squeezed Penny's cheeks even tighter. "It's not your fault, Penny. But it does make you special in a way that's sometimes hard."

"I know." That's why she visited Miss Monica.

"There's more to it." Carly took her hands off Penny's face. "We all make mistakes and have to learn things—"

"Like sitting still." That was Penny's hardest thing to remember.

"Exactly." Carly smiled at her. "You know how your daddy takes care of you, how he makes sure you have what you need, and he hugs you a lot?"

Penny nodded.

"God is like that, too. He's our Father. He even has a special name. It's Abba. That means Daddy."

Penny didn't have a daddy until Dr. Tremaine. She liked it when he played with her in the big swimming pool, and yesterday they went to the little park, and he pushed her on the big-girl swing. He said something about it being on his list, but she didn't understand.

Carly tucked a piece of Penny's hair back in her ponytail. "God loves you so much, honey."

Her mommy said things like that, too. Aching inside, Penny looked out to the ocean. A bird flew by and she followed it with her eyes to the big puffy clouds. She wasn't sure, but she thought maybe God lived in the clouds. "Maybe it's okay to be special."

"Oh, it is."

Carly kept talking, but Penny didn't hear all the words. Instead, she stared at the clouds and went breathlessly still—something she rarely did. But the sky was so pretty. "Heaven is in the clouds."

Carly didn't answer.

"It is," Penny insisted. "Will you paint clouds on my ceiling?"

"That's a wonderful idea," Carly said. "But it would be hard to paint the ceiling. How about clouds on your wall?"

"Okay." Penny looked out to the line where the sky touched the bluish water. She saw lots of boats with sails, but none of them were coming in her direction. Did her mommy know she was here?

Maybe she had to be in the ocean to feel her mommy's love, and for her mommy to know she was here. The life vest rubbed against her skin, reminding her that she had to hold Carly's hand.

"Can we touch the water?" she asked.

"As long as we do it together." Carly stood and took Penny's hand. Her fingers were warm and dry, and Penny liked how her little hand felt in Carly's bigger one. They walked down to the water but stopped on the edge of the wet sand.

"The tide's coming in." Carly pointed to a big white wave. "If we wait right here, the water will touch our toes."

Penny stared wide-eyed as the wave crested and turned to foam. Just like Carly said, an inch of cold water washed over Penny's feet, and she did a crazy dance. With Carly holding her hand, she pretended to be a mermaid and imagined her mommy swimming with her like they used to do in the pool. Penny felt her mommy's love in her heart, but she still couldn't see her. She was sad until she remembered Dr. Tremaine's magic car and how it took him back to the past. Maybe he could take her to find her mommy.

Suddenly hopeful, she stomped her feet on the wet sand. The water was far away now, so she pulled away from Carly and started to twirl. God and Mommy were in the clouds, and Carly was going to paint the clouds in her room. Laughing, Penny sang out to her mommy and the Daddy in heaven, whom she decided to call Dr. God.

15

Ryan fetched the Sunday *Los Angeles Times* off the porch and took it to his office. Reading it was a lifelong habit, something he enjoyed, but today nothing held his interest. He couldn't stop listening for Carly's car to leave the driveway. When it finally did, he left the paper on the floor in a heap and pulled the SOS list out from under the desk mat. Maybe doing something with his sons would get his mind off Carly.

He hadn't updated the list since the awful night at her apartment, so he picked up a pen and checked off *Take Penny to the park* and *Meet Kyle's girlfriend and her parents*, things he'd accomplished before the tragedy. He also crossed off *Take Eric to an aquarium shop*. He'd squeezed that in after the shark fight with Penny. A ten-gallon fresh-water tank now sat in Eric's room and was teeming with a variety of tetras.

With Penny occupied, Ryan wanted to do something special for the boys. His eyes locked on No. 15: *Have breakfast at Minnie's Pancake House,* a place they'd liked when they were younger.

Before going upstairs, he detoured to the kitchen for another cup of coffee. In spite of the gurgle of the Keurig, the kitchen was too quiet, a reminder of the years he sipped his morning caffeine alone or with a woman who had spent the night. He didn't indulge in one-night stands, but he had dated a lot. He hadn't thought much about it until Penny came into his daily life, then the boys, and now Carly.

Ryan went upstairs to ask the boys about breakfast. Kyle was in the bathroom, so he knocked on Eric's door first.

"Come in," Eric called.

Ryan opened the door, saw a sleepy boy, and recalled the three-year-old who cuddled with a stuffed dinosaur. While Eric yawned, Ryan told him about Carly and Penny going to the beach. "So it's just us guys. How about breakfast at Minnie's?"

When Eric groaned, the pancake house with its signature children's menu seemed all wrong.

"Or we could go somewhere else," Ryan offered.

With the fish tank gurgling, Eric gave a man-sized stretch. "I kind of want to sleep in."

It was a rejection but a mild one. And reasonable considering the sheet wrinkles on his cheek. Leaving Eric, Ryan went to Kyle's room and rapped on the open door.

Kyle looked up from tying his shoes. "Hey, Dad. You know that old barbell set? I thought I'd do some lifting."

Ryan didn't bother to mention Minnie's. The weights and bench, stored in the garage with the Impala, were another relic from Ryan's past. He'd been scrawny in high school until weightlifting put muscle on his lanky frame. "I'll back the car out so you can get to them."

"Cool. Would you spot me?"

"Sure."

Ryan went to his bedroom, put on cargo shorts and a polo shirt, and pocketed the car keys he kept in a box with cuff links, watches, and other treasures, including his father's compass-style key chain. When Ryan was a boy, Garrett Tremaine had showed it to him with the admonishment to always know where he was going in life. Fingering it now, Ryan thought of Carly. He possessed the strength of will to keep her at a distance, but pushing her away, especially with her recent loss, seemed wrong to him, even cruel.

He needed to know how to treat her, and for the first time he could recall, his intellect failed to steer him like that old compass. As much as he admired his father, at times like this he missed his mother's quiet confidence in God. She used to encourage him to pray, something he never did, though a quiet yearning occasionally made him lift his eyes to the sky with the vain hope that God was real. That urge hit now, but he ignored it and went to help Kyle.

When he reached the garage, the big door was open and Kyle was doing stretches on the lawn under a tree where last week Ryan had spotted a wasp nest. The gardener had removed it, but Ryan still glanced around. That's what fathers did. They protected the people they loved, especially women and children. Animals, too, he admitted, a bit chagrined. He didn't particularly care for cats, but Tom and Wild Thing were part of his family now.

Was that call to protect instinctive or learned? Ryan didn't know, but if Kyle was old enough for a girlfriend, it was time for the talk that had been pushed aside in the chaos of the past week. They'd covered the biology a long time ago, but not the tougher questions, like *when* and *who*.

Ryan backed the car into the driveway, helped Kyle haul the bench, the bar, and the weights to the middle of the garage, then leaned against the workbench. Kyle picked up weights and set them down, gauging the heaviness to decide which ones to put on the bar.

Breathing in the smell left from the Chevy engine, Ryan draped one foot over the other. "Before you get started, I'd like to talk a minute."

Kyle selected a ten-pound weight. "About what?"

"Girls."

"Oh." His hand went still with the weight in midair. He attached it as well as the matching one for the other side, then looked Ryan in the eye. "You mean Taylor."

"You're almost sixteen." Ryan let the implication sink in. *You're almost an adult, a man.* "Taylor's a nice girl. You both have college ahead of you."

Kyle's expression turned stony. "Dad, I know all this."

"I know you do. It's just—" *Just what?* Kyle needed an example, not a lecture. And Ryan had set a poor one with the affair. "Just don't forget what's really important."

"You mean school."

"No, I mean Taylor."

Kyle's cheeks reddened. Looking down, he nudged one of the weights with his foot. "I don't want to talk about it."

"I do." To Ryan's surprise, he meant it. He'd spoken with both boys about the divorce and his part in it, but Kyle was old enough for the next layer of reality. "You know what happened between your mother and me. I made a bad choice that hurt a lot of people."

"Yeah." Old pain leaked into his voice. "What are you trying to say?"

Ryan didn't really know, and that was the problem. It was one thing for an adult to set his own moral compass, but Kyle was a teenager. *Make your own rules* struck Ryan as terrible advice. He wondered what Carly would say, thought of the way she cared about people, and saw a simple answer. "Don't be selfish. Put Taylor first. You're too young to be too serious. You might get a do-over in sports, but you don't in real life."

Kyle put his hands on his hips, his chin high. "Dad, I get it. Mom's given me this talk about a hundred times."

Hooray for Heather. Ryan made a mental note to thank his ex-wife for picking up the pieces yet again. They'd both moved on emotionally, but they'd be forever linked through their sons. With nothing more to say, Ryan pointed at the weight bench. "Are you ready?"

"Yeah, sure." Kyle hesitated. "Dad?"

"Yeah?"

"Is it okay if I ask Taylor over for dinner? Maybe next Tuesday?"

"Of course." Tuesdays were Family Nights and the best part of Ryan's week. "Just check with Carly."

"I will." Kyle grinned. "She's a good cook, isn't she?"

"The best."

Kyle stretched flat on the weight bench, flexed his fingers, then gripped the bar and started to press. Ryan stood close, counting out loud and ready to grab the bar if Kyle ran out of steam.

"Seven," he counted. "Eight."

Kyle's arms wobbled. Ryan reached for the bar, ready to grab it, but Kyle squeezed out the ninth rep. On the tenth, Ryan lifted the bar from him, felt the weight, and realized something. As surely as the reps were building muscle for Kyle, Ryan's past mistakes had prepared him for the situation with Carly. He just needed to take his own advice.

Don't be selfish. Put her first.

He hoped she was enjoying the beach, but he sensed she needed more than the vague comfort of waves rolling up dry sand. Grieving for Bette and maybe homesick for Kentucky, she needed a real friend. It was a beautiful day, a perfect day to take the Impala for a spin, so Ryan decided to find her.

But first Kyle needed to finish his workout. With Ryan ready to grab the bar, Kyle did five more series of reps, resting in between. "Man, this is hard."

Ryan laughed. "No pain, no gain."

"Yeah, right," Kyle shot back.

When he finished, they put away the weights. Ryan fingered the key to the Impala. "Are you going to be home for a while?"

"Until four or so. Taylor's mom is driving us to the movies."

"In that case, I'm going to check on Carly and Penny. Eric's still asleep. Keep an eye on things, all right?"

Kyle gave a thumbs-up, draped a towel around his neck, and headed for the back gate. Ryan hadn't driven the Impala since Penny tracked berry juice all over the seat, so he paused to check the upholstery. Sometimes stains re-emerged, but the seat looked as good as new. Pleased, he sat behind the big steering wheel, adjusted his sunglasses, and headed to the beach.

16

Carly glanced over her shoulder at an incoming wave. "Hurry!" she called to Penny. "We don't have much time." While Penny used her feet like bulldozers to build up the mountain they called a castle, Carly used both hands to scoop out a moat. The sun was higher in the sky now, beating down on her shoulders left bare by a white tank top. She'd fight for the castle until the waves overtook it, then go home before she needed to break out the sunscreen for the second time.

A shadow fell across the castle and didn't move. Expecting an obnoxious passerby, she looked up with a slight frown, saw Ryan, and shot to her feet. "Is something wrong? Are the boys all right?"

"Everything's fine." He jammed his hands in his pockets. "I decided to take the Impala for a spin. That's all."

Penny stopped her bulldozing. "Hi, Dr. Tremaine. We're building a castle."

"Want some help?" he asked.

Penny pointed to Carly's ditch. "That's a moat. It keeps the pirates away from the princess. Did you know God lives in the clouds? He makes the ocean move, and He's watching us. He's in heaven like my mommy, and He's a daddy."

Carly glanced at Ryan to gauge his reaction to Penny's rambling. He'd given her permission to share her faith with Penny, but he might not like the result. To her relief, she saw a big smile. "Those pirates can be a problem."

Penny replied, "Help us dig."

He dropped to his knees next to Carly, putting them shoulder to shoulder with the waves behind them. With two swipes of his big hands, he doubled the size of her little ditch. She crouched next to him and worked on the castle, drizzling wet sand to build a turret. When their fingers grazed, a little zing shot to her heart. She had no right to enjoy Ryan's presence in that way, so she focused on the scrape of wet sand on her knuckles.

Penny chattered while they worked. Ryan answered back, making jokes and praising his daughter for building such a pretty castle.

This was why she'd taken the job—to unite Ryan and his children. With her chest tight, their eyes locked in a silent exchange of . . . what? Carly couldn't read his expression behind the sunglasses, and she prayed he couldn't read hers, because her feelings for him pulled at her like the tide.

A wave rumbled in her ears, crashed, and raced up the shore. Enjoying the drama, Penny yelled, "Pirates!" and ran screaming to the blanket. Before Carly could stand, Ryan grabbed her hand and lifted her up. The water pulled the sand out from her soles, and she felt off balance until Ryan tightened his grip. "That was close. Those pirates are tricky."

In more ways than one. Slightly unnerved, she shifted her gaze to the watery lump of the sand castle, ruined beyond repair, and slipped out of his grasp.

Ryan nudged the remains of the castle with his foot. "Nothing lasts forever, does it?"

"Some things do." *Heaven. God. Love.*

Ryan stared down at the lump of wet sand. Carly wished she could see his eyes, but the sunglasses hid them, and his mouth stayed sealed. Finally he looked at Penny on the blanket, still wearing her orange life vest. "Thanks for being so careful with her."

"Always."

He waited, maybe for Carly to say more, but she didn't want to think about Allison and why she was so cautious.

Penny scrambled off the blanket. "Can we make another castle?"

"Not today." Carly tousled Penny's hair. The ponytail had fallen apart a long time ago. "You're on the verge of a sunburn, and so am I."

Ryan's gaze dipped to her shoulder. Her skin felt warm and not just from the sun. Fighting the tingle, she swiped at her arm as if brushing off sand, but it didn't help. The tingle spread down to her fingers, then her toes.

Glancing away, Ryan focused on Penny. "Carly's right. It's time to go home."

Penny didn't seem to hear. She raised one arm over her head, stretched hard, and pointed at the sky. "I'm getting clouds in my room."

Ryan turned to Carly with his eyebrows arched over the sunglasses into question marks.

She told him about the plan to paint a cloud mural. "I was going to ask you first."

He whipped off the sunglasses, finally. "Do whatever you think is best. I trust your judgment more than my own. You have no idea the impact you've had on all of us—"

"It's nothing."

"No," he said. "It's everything."

The compliment warmed her to her toes, but his deep voice gave her shivers—good ones. "I'm just glad to help."

"You have." He paused. "How about brunch somewhere? There's a pancake place not too far from here. Penny would love it."

"You mean Minnie's?"

"That's it. Kyle and Eric used to like it."

He sounded wistful, maybe a little lonely. Carly longed to say yes, but her feelings for Ryan were too close to the surface to be easily shoved aside. "You should go with Penny. Make it a daddy-daughter date."

"Come with us," he urged her. "I have the Impala. We'll cruise down PCH."

The Pacific Coast Highway hugged the shoreline, and it was a beautiful day. The temptation to ride with him clawed at her, but she shook her head. "If you take Penny, I can pick up paint for the mural."

Ryan put the sunglasses back on. "All right. If you need help moving the furniture, ask Kyle. He did some weightlifting this morning. He'd probably like to show off."

"I will."

"Eric will help, too."

Carly's heart melted a little more. "He's coming out of vampire mode, isn't he?"

"We have a ways to go, but things are better." Ryan indicated the blanket with a stretch of his arm. "Let's get your stuff packed up."

They worked as a team, and in a few moments Penny was wearing shorts and a top, and Ryan was carrying the blanket on his shoulder and the tote bag in one hand. Carly took Penny's hand, and they headed to the parking lot, where the Impala stood proudly facing the beach.

Pointing, Penny jumped up and down. "It's Dr. Daddy's car!"

Dr. Daddy. Not exactly *Daddy*, but it was a big step for Penny. Grinning, Carly turned to Ryan. "Did you hear that?"

"I did." His eyes were riveted to Penny, who was pulling Carly's arm out of the socket. Giving up, Carly ran with her to the car, turned, and saw Ryan approaching with long strides. With his dark hair blowing in the wind, he reminded her of the pretend pirates invading the sand castle, except he wasn't imaginary.

160

He put the beach gear in the Cavalier's trunk, then faced her. "This is because of you. Carly, I—"

"It's not me. It's . . ." *Love.* But she didn't want to say that word to Ryan, not with her heart humming for him. "It's just being a family."

"Whatever you call it, you're part of it."

"Not really."

"You are," he insisted. "Without you, I'd be fumbling along on that SOS list. Nothing would be crossed off. Now it's half finished."

"I'm glad."

With the sun bright, his eyes glistened like the ocean and seemed just as fathomless. "I want to be a friend to you, too."

"You are."

An invisible cord formed between them and she wondered if he'd kiss her cheek. She stepped back, but the cord tightened like a rubber band being stretched. She took another step, but the tension only increased. The only way to break the pull was to step closer so that the cord would sag. If Ryan considered her part of his family, she needed to be someone safe, like a sister.

Veering back to his side, she raised her arm and made a fist for a knuckle bump. "Friends?"

"Friends," he said, bumping her knuckles against his.

The bones cracked, and they both laughed. Penny stood at the side of the Impala, bouncing on her toes.

"Ready for a ride?" Ryan asked her.

"Yeah!"

"How about pancakes? I know a place that makes them with chocolate chips."

Chocolate chips didn't register with her. "Can we go *home* in the car?"

"Of course," he said. "But first we'll get pancakes."

"Okay, but then I want to go home."

They moved the booster seat from Carly's car to the back of the

Impala and secured it with the aftermarket seat belt. After buckling Penny in, Ryan turned to Carly. "You can still change your mind about those pancakes."

"No." She hugged herself and shivered. "I want to pick up the paint, but I'm worried about Penny in the convertible. You know how sensitive she is to noise."

"I'll put the top up."

Penny punched both arms in the air. "Hurry!"

"She sure is enthusiastic about the car," Carly said. "Maybe you can figure out the tie to running away." A strand of hair caught on her mouth, and she pulled it away.

Ryan's eyes seemed to catch on her lips, but he glanced up in a blink. "I'll let you know what I find out."

He put his hand on the small of her back and guided her to her car, an unnecessary courtesy but one she appreciated.

"I'll follow you out of the lot," he said.

Carly waited while he started the Impala. He said something to Penny, then pushed a button to raise the top. Twisting her head, Penny watched the cloth drop into place. Ryan leaned across the big car and worked the latches, then signaled to Carly with a wave that he was ready to go. She waved back, headed for the exit, and they drove off in opposite directions.

A little lonely, she thought of sand castles and knuckle bumps, rubber bands, pirates, and the moat around the castle that had been wiped away with a single wave. Pirates needed love, too, but her father was right. She needed to be careful with her heart. It was far safer to befriend the entire crew of the pirate ship than to fall in love with the captain.

Ryan pulled the Impala into the garage, cut the engine, and turned to make eye contact with Penny in the backseat. Brunch at Minnie's had been a big hit, but this was the moment that could give insight into her reason for running away. "We're home," he said, sounding extra cheerful.

Her eyes darted up to the cloth top of the car, then to the passenger window. She whipped her head left and right, then let out a cry. "This isn't *home*!"

"Honey—"

"No!" Straining against the booster straps, she kicked the seat as hard as she could, shouting, "No, no, no, no" over and over.

Ryan bolted out of the car, worked the buckle, and lifted her into his arms while she fought with the fury that was uniquely Penny. Hurting for them both, he paced the driveway until she cried herself to sleep. With his muscles aching, he carried her to his bedroom, tucked her in with Lance and Miss Rabbit, then kissed the top of her sweaty head, and paused to breathe in the silence.

He hoped Carly had some insight, because Penny's meltdowns were excruciating for everyone. Tense and stirred up, he followed the paint smell to Penny's room, paused at the open door, and took in the sight of Carly in a loose shirt and a pair of cutoffs that showed her tanned legs. Brush in hand, she stood on her tiptoes to reach the top of a cloud, unaware of him until he cleared his throat.

She turned her head but kept the brush close to the wall. "How did it go?"

"Horrible."

She hurried to spread the brush load of paint, then lowered her arm. "I saw you put her down. Tell me about it."

He crossed the room and leaned against the windowsill. "She had a major meltdown."

"At the restaurant?"

"No. In the garage." Dragging his hand over his neck, he caught a whiff of maple syrup on his shirt. "The instant I said we were home, she exploded."

Carly laid the wet brush over the open can, turned Penny's desk chair to face him, and sat. "What did she say?"

"That this wasn't home."

"So that's it," Carly said, matter-of-factly. "The way her mind works, *home* is likely to be a specific physical place rather than an abstract concept. If I had to guess, I'd say she's thinking of the condo where she lived with her mother."

"I think so."

"So this house isn't home to her yet."

"No." It pained Ryan to admit it, but the facts stood. "Until the meltdown, we had a good time. She calls me Dr. Daddy all the time now."

"That's wonderful." Carly smiled, but he heard a touch of melancholy in her voice. "It won't be long before she drops the 'doctor' altogether."

"I hope so."

"She will," Carly assured him. "I can see how much she loves you, and we've made the whole house more comfortable for her. It'll take time, but she'll make the leap. The question is, how can we help her do it."

"Any ideas?"

Carly glanced at the top of Penny's dresser, bare except for a little white jewelry box she liked. "Penny needs to understand that her mother's gone, but she also needs the comfort of memories. Let's ask Denise for a picture of Jenna."

There it was again, the *us* that tied them together and kept them apart at the same time. "I'll call her tonight, but I can't say I want to talk to her."

"I don't blame you. She's pushy to say the least."

Ryan gave in to a grimace. If Denise wasn't out of the country on a flight, she texted him on every whim. *Tell Penny hi!!! Tell Penny Aunt DeeDee loves her!!! Bought a new friend for Penny— a panda!!!* The exclamation points alone drove Ryan a little nuts. Carly, on the other hand, sent short texts that served a purpose, pictures of the kids, and silly memes that made him laugh.

They locked eyes from across the room, the silence thickening until a cry burst out of his bedroom.

Carly leapt to her feet, but Ryan reached the doorway first. Penny ran straight into his legs. Crouching down, he peered into her watery eyes. "Honey, what is it?"

Instead of answering, she shoved him back, flung herself into Carly's arms, and shouted, "I want to go home! Please, Carly. Take me home *now*!"

❧

Carly guided Penny to the bed, pulled her into her lap, and hugged her tight. Wrapping her this way was a little like swaddling a baby. Carly needed the physical constraint as much as Penny did, because the rubber band tying her to Ryan was pulling hard. When he first walked into the room, it had almost boomeranged her into his arms.

With Penny still clinging, Carly sought his gaze. He'd taken a few steps back, crossed his arms, and was studying Penny with a clinical air. If they could understand Penny's fascination with the car, maybe she'd stop running away . . . like Allison.

When Penny's sobs faded to sniffles, Carly eased her back a few inches. "Honey, what's wrong?"

Penny answered with a forlorn sniff.

Carly tried again. "Are you afraid?"

"No."

"Are you mad?"

She wiped her nose but said nothing.

"Are you sad?"

Penny buried her face against Carly's shoulder. The gesture suggested avoidance, but avoidance of what? The smell of paint? The fluttering curtains?

Frustration hammered at Carly with a vengeance. Even with her training, a conversation with Penny was like untangling a knotted

165

gold chain. If she pulled the wrong strand, the knot tightened and new tangles formed. Holding back a groan, she looked at Ryan. The clinical air was gone, and in its place she saw a worried father.

Without warning, he strode out of the room. A few seconds later, he came back with Miss Rabbit and Lance dangling in his hands. Lifting them, he shot Carly a look as if to say, *What do you think?*

She nodded, almost furiously, then shifted Penny to face forward. Ryan handed Miss Rabbit to Carly but kept Lance, pulled up the little desk chair, and sat in front of them. This is what fathers did—they made fools of themselves for their children, at least fools in their own eyes. Carly thought Ryan was wonderful. Handsome beyond words. Generous to a fault. And so full of love for his family that she wondered if he knew God after all, in some small way.

Penny focused on Lance but didn't talk. Wisely, Ryan turned the stuffed lion toward Miss Rabbit. After a throaty growl, he said, "Hello, Miss Rabbit. You look pretty today."

Carly blushed a little. "Thank you, Lance."

"Miss Penny is pretty, too," the lion said. "But she's sad. I'm worried about her."

"Me too," Miss Rabbit squeaked.

Lance tipped his head, shook his mane, and gave another *Grrrr.* "Does she have a tummy ache from all those paaaancakes?"

Penny smiled a little at Lance's pirate-like drawl, and so did Carly. Miss Rabbit dipped one ear and tilted her fuzzy head toward Penny. "Are you sad?"

Penny gave a very slow nod.

Asking *why* was the wrong approach with her. She understood concrete images and direct questions, not abstractions. Carly tilted Miss Rabbit's head again. "Did your daddy's car make you sad?"

Penny's mouth trembled. "It broke."

Carly turned to Ryan, who made Lance growl. "Did the car go to the wrong place?"

"Yes." Penny focused on Ryan instead of Lance. "You said the car took you to the past. But it didn't work."

Ryan set Lance aside and talked to Penny as her daddy. "Honey, the car doesn't go to the past. It makes me *think* of the past."

"But I want to be with my mommy again."

"I know, honey," he crooned. "But you can't."

Oh, but I wish you could. I wish I could, too. Carly raised her eyes to the painted clouds, blew her mother a kiss, and held Penny tight. "We can't visit heaven, but you can feel your mommy's love in your heart."

Penny pushed off Carly's lap and stood with her fists at her sides. "But heaven is real. Aunt DeeDee told me, and so did you. I want my mommy."

Ryan set Lance on the floor. "I'm so sorry, Penny. We can remember your mother, but we can't visit her."

"But heaven is *real*," she cried again. "Carly said so. It's in the clouds."

Ryan looked at Carly, his expression both sympathetic and mildly accusing, as if her faith had caused this mess for Penny. What could Carly say to either of them? How did you explain heaven to a child who took everything literally, who saw the world in a purely practical way but with some distortion? And Ryan . . . he prided himself on logic and personal competence. He didn't directly disparage her faith, but a gentle criticism wafted off his stiff shoulders.

Explaining heaven was too big a job for Miss Rabbit, so Carly set the toy aside. "Penny, your mommy *is* in heaven, but heaven isn't a place we can visit."

"Yes, it is." She waved her hand at the cloud on the wall. "It's there! That's what you said. It's in the clouds."

The child's pain punched Carly in the gut. She'd blown it again. She'd failed a child who needed her. With a weight in her belly, she searched for the right words. "I believe in heaven with my whole heart, but we can't visit your mommy."

"But why? Why can't we?" Her voice rose to a shriek. Before Carly could stop her, she hauled back and kicked the open paint can so hard it tipped. Gray paint spread across the plastic tarp.

Ryan lifted Penny and held her against his chest. She kicked against him, harder and harder. The room reeked of paint and misery, and Penny's cries echoed off the walls. But what hurt Carly the most was the superior look on Ryan's face.

17

On Monday morning Ryan came downstairs as usual, but Carly wasn't in the kitchen. He glanced down the hall to her room, saw the closed door, and let out the breath he'd been holding. He didn't know what to say about yesterday's fiasco with Penny, except that he wanted to protect his daughter from hurt, and he didn't understand Carly and her faith at all.

Relieved to avoid the conversation, he left the house quietly, cruised through a drive-thru, and arrived at the office an hour before the first patient. With breakfast in hand, he retreated to his desk to read e-mail and scan the news. He was halfway through the bagel, which wasn't as good as the ones Carly made, when his phone buzzed with a text. This early in the day it had to be her.

Frowning, he glanced at his phone. Instead of the photo he'd snapped when Carly wasn't looking, he saw a message from Denise. *Am in LA!! Big news!!! When can we talk w/o Penny?*

He couldn't imagine what the news might be. A promotion seemed likely, or maybe she was getting married and would finally get out of his hair.

Lifting his coffee to his lips, he ordered himself to stay detached.

Knowing Denise, *w/o Penny* meant *about Penny*. And *about Penny* meant questions, criticism, and advice he didn't want. He had a full load of patients today, but he respected the limits of her flight schedule, so he texted back. *Anytime after 5 pm. Where?*

She texted back a street address in El Segundo, a neighborhood on the south side of Los Angeles International Airport. The locals called it the Mayberry of Los Angeles because of its quiet streets and small-town atmosphere.

The residential address surprised him, but a lot of airline personnel lived there. Denise was probably staying with a friend, or maybe the airline rented a house for layovers. He texted back that he'd be there but paused before texting Carly about Denise's visit. She deserved a phone call, but he didn't want to disturb her. Setting the phone aside, he decided to call her later in the morning between patients.

Unfortunately, an epidemic of conjunctivitis filled the waiting room with irritable children and cranky adults. Overloaded, he skipped lunch, asked Fran to call Carly, and barely managed to leave the office on time.

He was in a sour mood when he turned down Denise's street. With one eye on the GPS, he drove by houses typical of an old neighborhood being dragged into the future. The oldest homes were small and flat-roofed, relics from the 1940s. Others were drastically remodeled, and a few were new from the ground up.

The address Denise had given him belonged to an old bungalow on a street about a half mile from the beach. Taking in manicured lawns and mature trees, he parked under a sycamore, climbed out of the Honda, and strode up the front walk.

Denise opened the door wide and smiled, something she didn't do around him very often. Even more disconcerting was her clothing, a faded jersey and old jeans. Her hair was in a ponytail instead of a bun, and she was wearing flip-flops. Sadly, she reminded him of Jenna, and he recalled his promise to ask for a photograph of her.

"Thanks for coming over," Denise called out to him. "Traffic must have been terrible."

"It always is." Determined to be friendly, he asked his usual question. "How was your flight?"

Her lips tipped into a smug smile. "I didn't fly. I drove."

"You *what*?"

"I drove," she repeated. "I turned in my retirement papers a month ago, rented out my condo, and here I am." She held out her hand to indicate the house. "Come on in. I'll show you around."

Ryan's feet stuck to the welcome mat. "This house—"

"I'm renting it, but the move to Los Angeles is permanent." Chin high, she watched him with a dare in her eyes.

The thought of having Denise so close grated on his last nerve, but he feigned calmness and followed her inside. The house was bigger than it appeared to be from the street. A family room stretched into a backyard lined with rosebushes, and a dining area connected to a walk-through kitchen decorated in retro black-and-white. The far end of the kitchen opened into a small den, where cardboard boxes lined one wall. The bedrooms were off to the right.

"It's small," Denise said. "But it's perfect for two people."

"What's going on?" He knew where this conversation was headed but wanted to hear her explain it.

She headed for the rose-colored sofa in the living room. "Let's sit down. I'll tell you the whole story. But first, can I get you something to drink? Water? Iced tea?"

"Nothing. I'm fine."

"Coffee?"

The flight attendant in her sometimes took over. Next she'd be telling him to buckle his seatbelt and put his tray table in the full upright position. Jet noise echoed in the distance, building from a rumble to the full-throated roar of takeoff. If Denise heard the noise at all, she ignored it.

She sat across from him on a chair that matched the couch. "I'm going to be as honest with you as I can."

"I appreciate it."

"I hope you'll return the favor."

"Of course."

She inhaled deeply through her nose, then straightened her spine as if she were about to give a speech. "This isn't a sudden decision. I was considering retirement even before Jenna died. She needed help with Penny, but my job made it impossible to be there for her. As much as I loved flying, it came at a cost. I never married, never had kids. Penny's my only family aside from some cousins I haven't seen in twenty years."

Ryan had the same kind of cousins—distant and forgotten. "You love Penny. I know that, and I respect your ties to her."

"Yes, you do. And you've been good about sharing her. But monthly visits just aren't enough, especially when I hear about her getting lost at the mall or running away."

"We're working on why she does it. You know how it is."

"What I know is that she has to be watched." Denise's gaze flicked proudly around the living room filled with feminine touches—fake flowers, lacy curtains, throw pillows. "This little house is perfect for her. There's no pool, and I'm the only one who'll have a key to the back gate. I'm also changing the door locks to keypads. It's safer for children who tend to wander."

Another jet roared overhead. Denise didn't notice, but Penny would. "Did you consider the jet noise?" he shouted over it.

"She'll get used to it."

"I don't think so."

"Of course she will. It just takes time."

As quickly as the noise erupted, it faded to silence. Maybe Penny would adjust, but Ryan doubted it. "I suppose you want to work out a schedule for Penny to visit."

"Yes . . . or maybe more."

"Like what?"

"I want Penny to live with me. I'm home now, so you won't have to depend on a nanny."

"Denise, no."

The corners of her mouth deepened into a frown. "We both know what Jenna wrote to me in that e-mail."

"Yes, we do." He had read it in the attorney's office, when he and Denise sorted out caring for Penny. Jaw tight, he saw the printed computer page in his mind. *If something happens to me, would you raise Penny as your own? Ryan Tremaine will pay support, but he's not father material. He's too perfect. He'll never understand her.*

When Jenna wrote those words, they'd been true. Except the part about him being perfect. A perfect man didn't cheat on his wife. That failure still shamed him, but he was trying hard to be a good father. He knew Penny now, and he loved her just as she was. She had weaknesses, but who didn't? Even Carly had a few, like her need for religion.

Ryan opened his mouth to tell Denise to back off, but she cut him off. "I can give Penny as much as you can. She needs a mother. As her aunt, I'm the best person to fill that role. I love her more than anyone or anything else."

The implication being that Ryan didn't love her as much as Denise did. He leaned back on the couch and stretched his arm. "Forget it, Denise. Penny's my daughter. I'm going to live up to that responsibility."

"But do you love her?"

"Of course I do."

"Then do what's best for her."

"I am."

Denise shot to her feet. "You ruined my sister's life, and now you're going to ruin Penny's just to prove something."

Ryan bristled, but part of her claim was true. He yearned to redeem himself, but his personal life was none of her business. The meeting was over, so he pushed to his feet. "My motives are none of your concern. We both want what's best for Penny, and for that reason, we're going to work together."

"But I can help her," Denise said, her voice rising over the roar of yet another jet. "I can be a mother to her."

"And I'm her father."

The roar faded as rapidly as it had begun, leaving them tangled in a wash of silence. With their eyes locked, they both heaved a sigh.

Making it a point to be diplomatic, even kind, Ryan offered a faint smile. "In a way, she's lucky. We're fighting over keeping her. A lot of FASD kids get tossed into foster care."

Denise's frown melted a little, and she sat. "That's true. But still . . ."

"What?"

"With all the trouble you've had with nannies, I'm worried Penny won't have the stability she needs."

"Carly's working out great."

"For now. But how long will she stay? She's been very candid about going back to Kentucky."

"Maybe she'll change her mind." He hoped so, and not just for Penny's sake. The boys loved her, and so did—*No.* He wouldn't go down that road. He'd written off marriage the day he signed divorce papers, but Carly made him believe in himself. He wanted to be the man she thought he was, the man she deserved.

He'd gotten way ahead of himself, but when it came to Carly his emotions took off like the jets at LAX, one after another in defiance of gravity. Maybe Denise was right—he'd get used to the background noise, but his feelings for Carly were revving up again, and he felt the reverberation in his ribs.

Denise arched her brows at him. "It's none of my business, Ryan. But are you two involved?"

"No." A truthful answer, but only if he focused on his behavior and not his feelings for her. "Carly and I have a professional relationship. I'll be as straight with you as you were with me. That relationship includes a friendship like I'm friends with Fran, my office manager. Do you have a problem with that?"

"No, but I'm not blind." Denise's voice softened a bit. "I've gotten to know her, and I have to admit I like her."

"She's a nice person."

"She's also young and pretty. You're both adults—"

"Don't go there."

A dry little laugh escaped from her tight lips. "I've had a few relationships in my time. You're human and so is Carly."

"There's nothing between us," he said again. "We talk about family matters, and she's great with Penny. She's intelligent, kind, and more compassionate than anyone I know. You can think whatever you want about me, but don't question Carly's professionalism."

"I wasn't." Denise flattened her hand on her chest, the picture of someone falsely accused, but her eyes narrowed with suspicion.

He'd defended Carly too quickly, said too much, but he wouldn't take back a single word even if he could. Matching Denise's superior stare, he changed the subject. "Let's set a schedule for Penny to visit you. She's not in school yet, so we have some flexibility. What do you think of one overnight visit a week?"

"I'd like more, of course."

"That's my offer." He wasn't denying Denise for spite. He truly believed Penny was better off at home with Carly.

Denise huffed through her nose and paused, maybe to debate the wisdom of negotiating with him. He hoped she didn't try, because he wouldn't budge, especially when another jet blasted into the sky. El Segundo had a lot going for it, but with Penny's sensitivity to noise, he thought Denise had made a mistake in choosing to live here. Ryan didn't hold it against her. He had made mistakes, too, like hiring that over-the-top decorator to do Penny's room. She was happier now without the clutter, though the cloud murals and her confusion about death and heaven still concerned him.

"By the way," he said to Denise, "I'd like a picture of Jenna for Penny's room. She can't grasp that her mother's gone. Having a picture might help her understand."

"Oh." Denise seemed to shrivel in front of him.

"Do you have one handy?" Ryan hated to push, but he agreed with Carly about the picture.

Denise glanced at the boxes on the other side of the kitchen. Sorrow dimmed her eyes, and she turned hurriedly away. "I'm still unpacking. I'll dig one out later."

"That's fine."

She took a breath, maybe to fortify herself. "Would you like to see Penny's room? The furniture's coming later today."

Ryan followed her through the kitchen and around the corner to a tiny bedroom. Square footage meant nothing to Penny, but she desperately needed order. "You might want to talk to Carly before you do any decorating."

"Thanks, but it's not necessary."

For Penny's sake, he tried again. "You know how she is. Too much stimulation—"

"Penny will love what I have in mind. I'm going with a zoo theme."

He hoped Penny would like it, but it was hard to trust Denise's judgment with yet another plane taking off. As a flight attendant, she'd been in charge of passengers but not weather, turbulence, or flight plans. Raising Penny presented a similar mix of circumstances. He hoped Denise planned to pass out headphones to block the noise.

"So . . ." She flashed a smile. "When can Penny spend the night?"

"Any day except Tuesday." Family Night was carved in stone, and he looked forward to it.

"How about Thursday?"

"Check with Carly, but that should work. You two can arrange the details."

With their plans settled, he said good-bye and headed to his car. Perhaps visiting Denise would help Penny understand her mother's passing. Ryan hoped so, but the umpteenth jet revved its engines into a whine. Lumbering down the runway, it picked up speed until it went wheels up, came into his field of view, and shot toward the clouds.

Thanks to Carly, Penny thought God lived in the clouds and that Jenna was with Him. It was nonsense, so why was Ryan staring at the sky with a catch in his throat and an ache in his gut? An inexplicable longing welled in his belly, but a longing for what? Meaning? Purpose? Love? At times like this, he wanted to believe in a loving, all-powerful heavenly Father, but he just couldn't.

Logic was logic.

Faith was faith.

And love was love. Blowing out a slow breath, he steeled himself against all those feelings he didn't want, especially his feelings for Carly.

18

Carly hoped Ryan would get home soon, because he was missing a good time. Earlier, when Kyle had asked if Taylor could stay for dinner, Carly broke out the charcoal grill and roasted hot dogs to go with chips, coleslaw, and baked beans. They'd eaten, and now the kids were enjoying the pool while Carly played lifeguard.

Kyle and Taylor were sitting on the edge with their backs to her, their feet in the water and their heads tipped together. In the shallow end, Eric was wearing a mask and snorkel, gliding underwater, pretending to be a great white shark hungrily stalking Penny and her pink swan.

Kicking and screaming with glee, she yelled, "Shark! Shark!" about a thousand times.

The kids were having a blast, but Carly was concerned about Ryan. Denise's request to meet without Penny worried her, and so did his annoyance over Penny's misunderstanding about heaven. Carly felt bad about Penny's confusion, but there was nothing wrong with teaching a child about God, and she wouldn't apologize. At the same time, Ryan was Penny's father and had the right, even the obligation, to raise her as he saw fit.

The sliding glass door whooshed behind her. After a quick tuck of her hair behind her ear, she turned and saw Ryan. He was still wearing his business shirt, but the tie was missing and the collar was unbuttoned below his Adam's apple. With his hands on his hips, he surveyed the scene at the pool, keeping his distance until Penny spotted him.

"Dr. Daddy!" she shouted. "There's a shark after me!"

"You better swim fast!" he called to her.

Penny kicked ferociously, but Eric roared up and out of the water in front of her. With a playful scream, she splashed him with all her might. Kyle and Taylor turned and waved to Ryan, grinning like the teenagers they were.

Finally he focused on Carly. His smile faded, but he approached the table. Pulling up the chair across from her, he indicated the grill. "Something smells good."

"Hot dogs," she said, feeling a little nervous. "Have you eaten?"

"No, but I'm fine."

After the past five weeks, she knew his habits. He skipped meals when he was worried or troubled, an inclination that made her a little crazy, because she wanted to make things better any way she could, even with hot dogs. "How did it go with Denise?"

"She ambushed me." Ryan's gaze stayed on Penny and Eric. "She retired from the airline."

"Really? I thought she loved her job."

"Not as much as she loves Penny. She rented a house in El Segundo. It's small and loud, but she wants Penny to live with her full-time."

Carly bolted vertical in the chair, her mouth agape and her eyes burning. "That's ridiculous. It's absurd." She swept her arm to indicate the house and yard. "*This* is Penny's home. You're her father. And—" *And I love her, too.*

She cut off the words, but they burned on her tongue like salt, a reminder of her vow to maintain a professional distance. *Allison, I'm so sorry. I lost control and you got hurt.* Carly couldn't bear to lose control again, but frankly, she'd already lost a piece of her heart to each of the Tremaines, with the biggest part—the center of it—going to Ryan.

Forcing air into her lungs, she sat back on the chair. "Sorry. But Denise gets under my skin."

"Mine too," he muttered. "But we worked out a compromise."

He described the weekly sleepover, then relayed his concerns about the jet noise. It was possible Penny would adjust, but they both doubted it. Carly was about to ask about the house in general when Eric sloshed up the pool steps with the mask and snorkel in hand. Penny raced past him and straight into the fluffy towel Carly held out for her. The conversation about Denise would have to wait.

As Carly patted Penny dry, Eric flung a towel over his shoulders and stood about three feet from Ryan, silent but without the old hostility. Ryan shoved a chair in Eric's direction with his foot, an invitation to sit. "How's the fish tank working out?"

"Good." Dripping wet, Eric plopped down on the cushion so hard it hissed. "The tetras are cool. I was wondering about something . . ." He chewed his lips, a habit Carly recognized as a sign of nerves.

"What is it?" Ryan asked.

"It's kind of big."

With Penny in her lap, Carly shifted her gaze between Eric and Ryan, taking in their cautious expressions as they sized each other up. Silent, she prayed for them to find common ground.

Ryan draped a foot over his knee. "Does it involve fish?"

"Definitely."

"Big fish?"

"The biggest."

"Let me guess," Ryan replied. "You want a two-thousand-gallon fish tank, salt water with all the bells and whistles."

"Close," Eric replied. "I want to go shark hunting. You know, in one of those cages—"

Deathly white, Ryan leapt to his feet. "Eric, no!"

Carly paled along with Ryan, but Eric roared with laughter. "I got you, Dad! I got you good! You believed me, didn't you?"

Ryan blinked hard, then dropped down on the chair as if he'd been shot. Laughter rumbled out of his throat. Eric had played a joke on his dad, the kind of joke all kids played. Even better, he'd done it well. Carly couldn't stop grinning.

Ryan's gaze locked on to hers, and they had one of those wordless conversations that made her chest ache. Ryan broke the moment with a blink, then high-fived Eric. "You nailed me."

Eric slapped his hand. "I don't really want to hunt sharks, but I think I want to be a marine biologist, and there's a place we could go snorkeling. It's not very far."

"Where is it?" Ryan asked.

"Anacapa Island. We could camp there."

Carly had never heard of the island, pronounced with the emphasis on the first syllable—*ANN-a-capa*. "Where is it?"

"It's about twelve miles off the coast," Ryan answered. "I've been there."

"It's part of the same chain of islands as Catalina," Eric told her. "But it's a lot smaller and completely undeveloped."

He sounded a little like a professor and a lot like his dad. "How many islands are there?" she asked.

"Eight," Eric replied. "But only five are in the Channel Islands National Park. I've been researching it."

For the next few minutes, he described the islands as remote, primitive, and rich in history. The Chumash Indians had inhabited them, and the larger islands had been home to sheep and cattle ranches after Europeans arrived on the scene. "The sea life is amazing around there."

"Nothing beats real life." Ryan nodded. "I was in college when I camped there with some friends. We snorkeled all day. It was great, but Anacapa's about as primitive as you can get. No electricity. No water. We'd have to haul in everything."

"That makes it better. Can we go?" Eric asked.

"If you're willing to do some toting and lugging, so am I." Ryan thought a minute. "I have vacation scheduled for mid-August. I'll check into the boat and camping reservations. If we can get a space, we'll do it."

"Cool." Eric hunkered forward in the chair. "Can I ask Nathan to come? We can all go, right? Even Penny."

Ryan's brows arched with surprise. He looked at Carly as if to say, *Can you believe it?* She was happy for him, but she liked camping about as much as she liked car trouble and root canals. "Count me out," she said, holding up one hand. "Penny and I will stay here. You men might not mind pit toilets, but I do."

Eric and Ryan traded a look and chuckled. Penny sat up and giggled with them. So did Carly, though she was dead serious about those pit toilets.

Kyle called from the edge of the pool. "What's so funny?"

"This!" Eric made a rude sound, proving to the world he was a thirteen-year-old boy.

They all broke out in a chorus of laughter. Carly's gaze shifted to Ryan. In the same instant, his eyes locked on her face. Her heart sped up, because deep down she wanted to go with him to that desert island, even with pit toilets and no running water. But she didn't belong on the trip.

"You and the boys will have fun," she said to him.

He didn't respond, except to stop drumming his fingers on the chair.

Kyle and Taylor sauntered up to the table. Kyle pulled out a chair for Taylor, then sat next to her. "What are we talking about?"

"Camping on Anacapa," Ryan answered.

Taylor's face lit up. "I did a report on sea lions last year. You can see them there. I bet the island's amazing."

Kyle glanced at Taylor, his eyes so full of puppy love that Carly ached for them both. His dark hair and angular face contrasted perfectly with Taylor's auburn curls, apple cheeks, and a sweet smile that showed off her braces. At fifteen-almost-sixteen, they were adorable together. Heartache might come later, but someday these memories would be sweet to both of them.

Kyle waggled his brows at Taylor to ask a question without words. When she nodded back, Kyle turned to Ryan. "Can Taylor come with us?"

"Sorry," Ryan said, his voice thick with regret. "It's guys only. Carly and Penny are staying here."

Shifting in the chair to face Carly, Kyle gave her a beseeching look. "You could change your mind. We'd all help with Penny."

"I would, too," Taylor added. "I think my parents will let me go if my sister comes along. Nicole's in college, and she loves little kids." Taylor leaned forward and patted Penny's arm. "We could play mermaid together."

"Yes!" Penny shouted.

"Come with us, Carly!" Eric chimed in. "It'll be fun."

All four kids kept up the pleading, breaking her heart and filling it to the brim at the same time. Even so, she shook her head. Aside from the pit toilets, she worried the trip would be too much for Penny.

But then she glanced at Ryan, who was studying his daughter with such longing that her own heart hitched. Her mind flashed to her father's advice to do what's hard, and how she used to run toward a challenge and not away from it. Was she protecting Penny or denying her the experience of a lifetime? How did an FASD caretaker know a child's limits if they didn't occasionally push the envelope?

Kyle grinned at her, a younger version of Ryan and a reminder of how simple life could be. "Please, Carly? It'll be fun. Say you'll do it."

"Do it!" Eric repeated. "Do it! Do it!"

The other three kids joined in. *Do it* turned into a chant complete with hand clapping and foot stomping. Carly tried to shake her head no, but she was paralyzed by love for everyone at the table, even Taylor, who was the teenage girl Carly wished Allison could have been. Desperate to hold back the tide of longing, she pressed her cheek against Penny's wet hair. The longing swelled in her chest to the point of physical pain.

The kids chanted louder, louder still, until Ryan let out a piercing whistle.

Instantly the clapping stopped. When Carly raised her head, she saw all four kids focused on him. He'd become the head of his household, a father they respected and admired. There would be bumps along the way, but this part of Carly's job was done. Satisfaction swelled in her chest, but it disappeared when she imagined leaving them forever and returning to Kentucky.

Ryan's gaze swept across the row of smiling faces. "Carly and I will talk about it. I'll let you know what we decide, whether it's guys only or coed."

Carly nodded her support, not quite trusting her voice. Everyone at the table was staring at her, the teenagers with hope in their eyes, and Ryan with the detachment that had started yesterday in Penny's room. They needed to come to an agreement about Penny and Carly's faith, but she dreaded confronting him. What would she do if he told her not to mention heaven to Penny? For Carly, that kind of silence was both a lie and impossible. Her faith defined her.

"That settles it for now," Ryan announced to the group. "Eric got the ball rolling, so he and I will do the planning."

Taylor smiled at Kyle. Penny wiggled in Carly's lap, and Ryan gave Eric a high five. Taylor's cell phone signaled a text, and she glanced at it. "My mom's here."

"I'll walk you out," Kyle said.

Typically Carly would have trailed after them and said hello to Taylor's mom, but Penny was almost asleep. So Ryan went with the kids.

Alone with Eric, Carly asked him about the island. His enthusiasm rang in every word as he talked about everything from kelp beds to orange Garibaldi fish to lava formations. After a few minutes, Ryan returned with his laptop and set it on the table. "We have some research to do."

Carly stood with a sleepy Penny in her arms, pausing to look down at Ryan and Eric seated with their heads together in front of the glowing screen. "I'll find you later."

He met her gaze, but glare from the computer screen hid his thoughts about Carly going on the trip. "I'll be out here."

She slipped away, leaving Eric and Ryan engrossed in research. As enchanting as Anacapa seemed to be, Carly doubted she'd ever see it. A guys-only trip made the most sense, and that was just fine, she told herself. In fact, it was wise. The last place she needed to be with Ryan was on a desert island with spectacular sunsets, crashing waves, and emotional riptides threatening to pull her more deeply into his life.

～

Camping on Anacapa fit perfectly on the SOS list under *Take a family trip,* but Ryan had to say no to Penny coming along. Anacapa was just three islets with camping on the flat eastern portion. It was essentially a big rock poking out of the ocean like a tooth. The sides were sheer towering cliffs. He wouldn't take any small child to such a primitive place. The risk of Penny wandering off was too great.

Without Penny, it seemed best to go with just Kyle and Eric. He didn't think Carly would mind, and he had to confess to being relieved. Even with five teenagers for chaperones, a night on an island struck him as ridiculously romantic and something to avoid.

Eric was clicking through computer screens when Kyle came

back to the patio and dropped down in a chair. "I hope Carly goes with us, because Taylor would love it."

"Look at this." Eric angled the screen so Kyle could see a picture of sea lions sunning themselves on a porous rock.

"Cool." Kyle said *cool* to everything, even brushing his teeth. Ryan suspected his enthusiasm for the trip had less to do with sea life than it did with Taylor.

Maybe the "guys only" decision wasn't such a good idea. Kyle didn't care for snorkeling. And there was no beach on the island. He'd enjoy the trip if Taylor came along. Without her, he'd be bored silly.

He turned his attention to Eric and the computer. With Kyle texting Taylor and occasionally muttering, "Sure," "yeah," and "cool," Ryan and Eric checked out Web sites for the charter boat and campground. None of the campsites were booked during Ryan's vacation time, which meant they'd have the island all to themselves except for the ranger who lived in a private residence.

Eric scrolled through more photographs, his eyes bright in the glow of the screen. "Do you think Penny will like it?"

"That's a problem," he said to both Eric and Kyle. "It's too dangerous for her. You can see the cliffs for yourselves. The top of the island is wide open. No railings. Nothing."

Kyle's fingers stopped in midtext, and he looked up. "Carly can still come, right? Penny could stay with her aunt."

"She and I will talk about it."

For once, Kyle didn't say *Cool*. "If Carly doesn't come, do I have to go? It's a cool trip and all, but I'd rather stay home."

Eric shoved away from the computer. "Come on, Kyle. It'll be fun. I've sat through a hundred of your boring baseball games. You should do this."

"Baseball's not boring," Kyle shot back.

"It is so," Eric replied, more confident than usual. "It's the most boring sport in the world. It's worse than golf."

Ryan considered intervening, but he liked seeing Eric stand up for himself. If his sons could hammer out their differences on their own, they'd both be stronger. Unless the situation turned mean, Ryan preferred to watch it unfold.

Kyle narrowed his eyes. "You don't like baseball because you're not good at it. You can be such a nerd—"

"You know what you are?" Eric leapt to his feet, his fists knotted. "You're a—"

"Hey," Ryan said. "No name calling."

"You're a conceited jerk," Eric finished.

The boys glowered at each other, Kyle looking smug and Eric fighting to control himself, rivals to the core as brothers often were. This kind of bickering would ruin the trip, which meant Carly needed to put up with those pit toilets so Kyle could invite Taylor and her sister. If Eric invited Nathan, everyone would have someone to pal around with.

As for his feelings for Carly, Ryan would have to draw some thick lines and stay behind them. There would be no sharing a romantic sunset. No quiet moments listening to the waves, and definitely no kisses. He could control his impulses. He was sure of it. Except with thoughts of Carly filling his head, he wanted a cigarette.

"We're done here," Ryan said to his sons. "I'll tell you tomorrow what Carly and I decide about the trip."

Still not speaking, the boys went into the house. Ryan waited a moment, then took the computer to his office. There was a pack of Marlboro Reds in the bottom drawer. Carly was giving Penny a bath, so he had time for a smoke. Some impulses, he had to admit, were harder to control than others. With that thought plaguing him, he put a couple of cigarettes into his pocket and returned to the patio to wait for her.

19

Thanks to her catnap in Carly's lap, Penny jarred awake when they reached her room. Carly tried to settle her down but couldn't. As eager as she was to speak with Ryan, Penny's needs trumped her own, and she decided to give her a bath with lavender-scented bubbles.

Sometimes the fragrance calmed her, but not tonight. The instant Penny sat in the water, she kicked her feet and splashed with her hands. "I want to go on the boat. I want to go on the boat."

The chant echoed like a song until Carly helped Penny out of the tub, wrapped her in a towel, and held her tight. "Penny. That's enough. The boat trip is up to your daddy."

"I want to go," Penny repeated. "My mommy rode in a boat to heaven."

Carly ached for the child, but this wasn't the time for such a sensitive conversation. Hoping the subject would evaporate with the bubbles, she tucked Penny into bed and read to her. Despite Carly's soothing voice, Penny couldn't unwind, and an hour passed before she dozed off. Carly fetched a light sweater from her room, went to the patio to find Ryan, and saw the empty table. Thinking he would return, she sat down to wait.

With the pool bright and the ocean dark in front of her, she lifted her heels to the edge of the chair and hugged her knees. She missed Bette terribly but not the police helicopter. The murderers were still on the loose, though Detective Hogan told her they had a strong lead. The world was such a violent place, such a broken place. Aching for the familiar, she imagined the scent of the loamy Kentucky earth and inhaled.

A whiff of smoke tickled her nostrils. For an instant she worried Eric was sneaking cigarettes. Or maybe the situation was worse. Maybe a careless passerby had tossed a cigarette into the brush behind the house.

She rushed to the fence and scanned the steep hill. Nothing. No flames. No smoke. But in the corner of the yard, the tip of a cigarette flared like a marigold, and she spotted Ryan. Slipping the cigarette from his lips, he looked up and blew out a stream of smoke.

"Ryan?"

Startled, he dropped the cigarette on the concrete and ground it out. "You caught me."

"You smoke."

"Occasionally. It's a bad habit."

"We all have them." Nail-biting. Overeating. Cussing. Losing one's temper and telling a confused FASD teenage girl to just get out. Carly swallowed so hard her throat ached.

Ryan kicked the butt into a flower bed and buried it. "The kids don't know. They need a good example. Not that I'm setting one by sneaking around. I guess that makes me a hypocrite."

"Or human."

"Or just weak."

"It's the same thing." They were back to the faith issue—her belief that human beings made mistakes and needed a savior, and his belief that he controlled his own destiny. She wasn't ready to talk about Penny, so she steered the conversation to safer ground. "About the trip—"

"Penny can't go. It's just not safe for her."

"Oh." Carly paused. "So you don't need me."

"No, I do. In fact, more than ever. We need to bring Taylor and her sister. After you left, Kyle and Eric got in a shouting match. If we make it 'guys only,' Kyle will be miserable, and Eric and Nathan will gang up on him. Kyle doesn't like the ocean all that much, so he won't have anything to do. The island itself is just a big rock. If you don't kayak or snorkel, there's not a lot there."

"I see."

"I need you to chaperone the girls." Ryan scrubbed his hand through his hair, leaving small furrows in the wake of his fingers. "It's an old-fashioned idea, isn't it?"

"Not to me." In Carly's experience, teenage girls needed more protection than they typically received. "It's a good idea, but I'm not sure."

"I am. I don't want the boys to bicker the whole time, and I can't take Taylor and her sister without you."

"Maybe just you and Eric should go."

"That's a last resort. Eric's always been the little brother, and now he's the middle kid. For once he wants to be the star."

"He wants to stand out, and he needs an audience to do it." As the baby in her own family, Carly knew the feeling. "He's also the younger brother and competitive." A lesson from both her psychology classes and Cain and Abel.

"Exactly. Eric's itching to rub Kyle's nose in something. This trip is his chance."

"Boys . . ." Carly shook her head. "I'll never understand what makes them tick."

Ryan laughed. "It's not all that complicated. Boys like to fight, and they like to win. Eric needs this trip the way Kyle needs baseball. The way I needed . . ." He shrugged. "Whatever it was I needed."

"Medicine? Your career?"

"I suppose." Except his voice sounded hollow. "If you come on the trip, Kyle can hang out with Taylor and her sister, I can snorkel with Eric and Nathan, and you can cheer for everyone."

"Oh dear," she muttered.

"What's wrong?"

"Cheering for people is my favorite thing to do." She laid her hand on the black iron and stared into the night. Without Penny, there would be no buffer between herself and Ryan. They'd be a team, a couple chaperoning a boatload of teenagers. Common sense told her to say no, but how could she deny Eric his moment in the sun? She couldn't. Not when she'd been raised to trust God and be brave. "You sold me."

Ryan's eyes lingered on her face. That rubber band feeling was pulling them close, so she raised her fist for another knuckle bump. Ryan copied her, but his hand opened, and so did hers. Instead of bouncing off each other, their fingers laced together and held tight.

"Thank you, Carly," he murmured. "I can't imagine this summer without you."

"It's—it's been good." Weak words meant to hide strong feelings. She loosened her grip, but Ryan held tight. Their gazes locked, and she felt so admired, so beguiled, that she wondered if his feelings for her were as vibrant as hers for him. Maybe, but what did they do then? They were more than just Mars and Venus, or Los Angeles vs. Kentucky. When it came to matters of the soul, they were darkness and light—opposing forces that couldn't occupy the same space.

She eased out of his grasp and stepped back. The patio seemed to sway like the deck of a ship. Grabbing the fence again, she tried to joke. "I hope I don't get seasick on the boat."

"You won't," he drawled, as if he commanded the waves. "I'll get you a motion sickness patch."

Carly wished there was a patch for lovesickness, because surely that's what she had. Looking at Ryan now—tall and strong, lonely, troubled, and sometimes cynical—she told herself to just stop it. This wasn't the forever love that led to marriage. It couldn't be. She was infatuated with him. That was all.

Forcing air into her lungs, she told him about Penny's latest remark about her mother taking a boat to heaven. "I didn't say anything. I have opinions, of course. But she's your daughter, and it's up to you to guide her."

"Yes, it is." That was all he said.

"Do you mind if I tell her Bible stories, or if we talk about Jesus and believing in Him? I know you don't agree, but it's what I believe."

"That's fine. Tell her whatever you feel is appropriate. Maybe it'll help her in the long run."

"I worry—"

"Don't."

"But—"

"Carly, drop it." He patted his shirt pocket as if looking for another cigarette, then lowered his hand without taking one. "Your faith is your business. I worry about Penny being confused, but she's confused about a lot of things. That's my fault."

She hated his guilt. *Hated it.* She hated her own with an equal intensity. Like a riptide pulling a swimmer out to sea, guilt dragged her away from the solid shore of God's love. Why couldn't she let go of that mistake with Allison?

Ryan gripped the fence again and squeezed until his knuckles turned white. "I'd give anything to free Penny from fetal alcohol."

Without thinking, Carly laid her hand on top of his. Slowly he turned to her, his stare as piercing as a nail whacked by a hammer. The force of it rattled through her, but she held his gaze with the iron determination to be his friend, nothing more, despite the electricity snapping between them. She couldn't bear to see him hurting like this. With her throat tight, she took a chance.

"God loves you, Ryan. You're forgiven."

She was, too, if only she could believe it. And as for loving

Ryan, she knew exactly how God felt about this strong, troubled, handsome man who didn't love Him back.

She couldn't hide the truth any longer. She was a lot more than infatuated with Ryan. She was head-over-heels in love with him.

❧

The last thing Ryan wanted to hear was a spiel on Christian forgiveness. Forgiven? By whom? A figment of the human imagination? He knew the theology, thanks to his mother, but religion was the one area where he was firmly in line with his father's intellectualism.

Sometimes Carly was naïve to the point of foolishness. Surely at the age of twenty-eight, she had a few scars, a few regrets, a boyfriend or two, maybe a broken heart. She couldn't possibly be that naïve about human failings. People hurt each other all the time, which is why he vowed to remember she was just a friend. It was the only way to protect her from the risk of heartache.

He wasn't worried about resisting the physical attraction. Past mistakes gave him the control of a robot. What he feared far more was wounding her with his intellect. More than once, he'd seen his father rip his mother's faith to shreds, leaving her in tears and angry with him. When Ryan tried to defend her, his father cut into him, too. Ryan refused to do that to Carly, but neither did he want to hear her namby-pamby, Jesus-loves-you version of faith.

"Let's not go there," he said with a hint of warning.

"Why not?" She lifted her chin high. "I *am* a preacher's daughter."

"I know that."

"Born and raised." She gave a little shrug. "My daddy talks about grace all the time. He likes a good fight."

"A fight?"

"To debate," she clarified. "If he were here, he'd hand you a fat cigar, and you two would have at it. He'd have the time of his life."

Ryan stifled a groan. Just what he didn't need—a snake-handling country preacher bellowing at him.

"Maybe another time," she said. "It's late, and Kyle and Taylor are waiting to hear what we decided."

"I'll tell him when I go upstairs."

"Good. I guess we're done. Good night, Ryan."

"Good night."

She took four steps toward the house before he couldn't stand the stifling silence and called out to her. "Carly?"

She turned so suddenly that her hair swished. "Yes?"

He didn't have anything in particular to say. He just didn't want her to leave. "I don't have to tell Kyle tonight. If you're not sure, you can think about it some more."

"I'm sure."

He wished he could see her face, but her features were blurred by tree shadows. All he could see was the glow of the moon on her white shirt and that tangle of blond hair cascading over her shoulders. He blinked and imagined tunneling his hands through that mane, tipping up her face, kissing her thoroughly.

Maybe he wasn't a robot after all.

And maybe he wasn't as much like his father as he thought, because Carly's soft words—*God loves you, Ryan. You're forgiven*—filled him with a yearning so strong he had to grit his teeth to hold it back. Swallowing hard, he fought the urge to call out to her again, to reach for her hand and ask her to stay.

She disappeared into the house without another word, and this time he let her go. Turning his back, he took the second cigarette out of his pocket, lit it, and stared through the bars of the fence, blowing smoke rings at the wispy clouds dotting the night sky.

The cigarette tasted stale, so he stubbed it out and went inside. Television didn't interest him, so he decided to grab a book off the shelves in his office. He skimmed titles, but nothing interested him until he reached the bottom shelf that held his mother's books, including her Bible.

He lifted it, settled in at his desk, and hoped by some miracle he'd understand the mystery of it all.

He skimmed a few Psalms and deemed them nice poetry.

He read a chapter of Proverbs. A little offbeat, but most of it offered good, practical advice.

Next he turned to the gospel of John and read the first verses. *In the beginning was the Word and the Word was with God and the Word was God.* It didn't make sense to him, not in a logical way.

Sighing, he flipped to the book called Revelation, skimmed the strange visions about horsemen and lamp stands, and decided the author was delusional. Who could believe in this craziness?

Carly did.

So did countless people from countless generations. Maybe Ryan was the fool. But logic told him God was a figment of the human imagination, a vain attempt to ward off the fear of death . . . fear of everything. Determined to be strong like his father, he jammed the book back on the shelf and went to bed.

Four hours later, he jarred awake in the dark. Haunted by dreams of Carly, he lay twisted in the sheets with the unwanted images mocking his resolve to control his feelings for her. He had a choice, a clear one. But how did a man resist the tug and pull of nature—the forces that carved the Grand Canyon, shifted the tides, and pushed up mountains with earthquakes? He thought of those Psalms that were just poetry, the advice in Proverbs, the craziness of God made man, dying for sins, and rising from the dead, the God that supposedly gave men the strength to resist temptation.

If that God was watching, Ryan wanted to know. "If you're there," he said to the dark, "let the wrestling match begin."

20

Shortly after Carly's decision to go to Anacapa, the Cincinnati Reds arrived in town to play the Los Angeles Dodgers. She was nervous about going with Ryan and wisely so. The plan originally called for Eric and Kyle to go with them while Fran watched Penny, but when Eric begged off, Kyle asked to invite Taylor. It made sense, except pairing off with Ryan made the evening feel like a date.

She rode next to him in the front seat of the Honda, while Kyle and Taylor held hands in the back. At the stadium he helped her out of the low-slung car, grasped her elbow on the steps to their box seats, then surprised her with nachos because he'd heard her tell Taylor they were her favorite. Carly knew this wasn't a date. He was showing Kyle how to treat a woman, but it *felt* like a date.

The next morning, she woke up humming "Take Me Out to the Ball Game." Not ready to let go of that good feeling, especially since the Reds had bested the Dodgers 12–10 in extra innings, she put on an old Reds T-shirt and made her way to the kitchen.

Ryan, dressed for work and already sipping coffee, glanced at the shirt and grunted. "Go ahead. Rub it in."

But somehow she couldn't. A nanny didn't joke around with the boss. She didn't sit next to him for fourteen blissful innings, occasionally brushing his knee and sharing the last bag of peanuts. A nanny didn't do a lot of things that had become habit for them, like watching old sitcoms after Penny went to bed, or talking late into the night about everything from the kids to politics to their worst high school memories.

Ryan was waiting for her to say something about the game when her phone rang in her bedroom. "It's probably my dad. I better get it."

She retreated down the hall, lifted the phone, and saw LAPD on the screen. Grief for Bette sunk its fangs into her, but she steeled herself to handle the call. "Hello?"

"Miss Mason? This is Detective Hogan."

"Yes . . ." She hoped she sounded calmer than she felt. "Is there news about . . . about what happened?"

"Perhaps. Can you come to the station around two o'clock?"

"I'll make it work."

Shaking inside, she ended the call and returned to the kitchen. Ryan was waiting for her. "Is everything all right?"

"No. I mean . . . yes. Everything's fine." She chewed her lip. "That was Detective Hogan. There's news about the murder. I'm going to the station at two o'clock."

He took a step toward her but stopped. "I'll go with you."

"But you're taking Penny to see Miss Monica."

"I'll reschedule."

"No. Penny expects to see her. We need to stick to her routine."

Ryan's straight brows collided. "I don't mind canceling, and she won't either."

"I can handle it," Carly assured him. And she could. What she *couldn't* handle was the yearning to say yes because she wanted to spend the afternoon with him.

He gave her a careful look, then laid a hand on her shoulder. "Call if you change your mind."

~~~

Seven hours later, Carly walked into the West L.A. police station, told the desk sergeant about her appointment with Detective Hogan, and waited nervously in the lobby until Detective Hogan lumbered toward her. That awful night roared to life in her mind, and she approached him with questions on the tip of her tongue.

"Miss Mason." He extended his hand. "Thank you for coming today. I know your time is valuable."

He probably said that to everyone. "Do you have a suspect in custody?"

"Let's talk in private."

He led her down the long hall to a room with six desks, ringing phones, computer screens, and the low hum of conversation between a mix of men and women, some in uniform and others in suits or ordinary clothes. Family photographs sat on desks, along with mugs, pens, and the flotsam of life. She could have been in any office, but then her gaze landed on Detective Hogan's desk and an 8 x 10 photo of a gaudy bracelet with pink and silver beads.

A chill swept down Carly's spine, and she gasped. "That belonged to Bette. I gave it to her. How did you get it?"

The detective guided her to the chair at the side of his desk. "Would you like something to drink? Water? A soft drink?"

"No. But thank you." She wrung her hands in her lap, aware of the sheen of cold sweat.

Detective Hogan sat in his big chair and rocked back. "A woman found that bracelet in her seventeen-year-old son's room, along with some narcotics and drug paraphernalia. She brought it to us in the spirit of tough love and the idea we'd scare him about the drugs. She had no idea what the bracelet meant, but his fingerprints in the apartment made the link to Ms. Gordon's murder indisputable."

A feverish anger burned in Carly's brain. "But why? Why did he keep the bracelet?"

"It's a souvenir, a trophy, if you will. We made the link because almost everyone we interviewed said Ms. Gordon liked flashy bracelets. One of the bakery workers even described this one to us. Apparently it was Ms. Gordon's favorite."

Sick to her stomach and seething, Carly stared at the photograph until she thought she might scream.

Detective Hogan let out a sigh. "At least we know who did it."

"Yes." A small consolation, but Carly latched on to it. "What's going to happen next?"

"Arraignment. Plea bargaining. Maybe a trial." He could have been talking about the weather. "There's a chance the kid will turn on his friends."

Carly nodded, as if she understood, but none of it made sense to her—not the violence or the madness behind it, and especially not the internal clash in her soul between wanting mercy for a boy younger than Allison and justice for Bette. All she knew was that she wanted to go home to Boomer County and stay there.

Detective Hogan advised her to keep in touch in case she was needed for the trial; then he cleared his throat. "That's it, unless you have questions."

"No." Carly leapt to her feet. "I have to go."

He walked her to the lobby. After a quick good-bye, she shot across the street to the parking lot. The summer heat slapped her in the face, and her nose burned with the stench of melting asphalt. When she looked up at the sky for solace, she saw an ugly brown haze. A lump ballooned in her throat, but she forced it down. If she couldn't go home to Kentucky, she'd do the next best thing. She'd find Ryan and Penny at the Dairy Queen.

"She's doing very well," Miss Monica said to Ryan. "You're fortunate to have Carly."

If Ryan were a believing man, he'd think God had answered Fran's prayers for him. Sometimes life was too good to be true, and lately that was the case—even if the Dodgers had gotten slapped down by the Reds. It was worth it to see Carly having such a good time. He hoped her meeting with Detective Hogan went well. As soon as he and Penny were settled at Dairy Queen, he planned to call her.

Miss Monica pushed her big red glasses up on her nose. "Penny's still confused about her mother, but you're handling it as well as anyone could."

"So you agree about that photograph of Jenna?" He'd discussed it with her before she took Penny into the playroom.

"Yes, I do. The sooner, the better." Miss Monica gave him a warm smile. "She really is doing well. As long as Carly's in the picture, I don't need to see her anytime soon. I'll leave the next appointment up to you."

Ryan thanked her for all her help, called Penny away from the play table, and walked her out of the office. The Dairy Queen was in the same shopping center, so they headed toward it, Penny clinging to his hand. Getting ice cream was a post-therapy ritual, and one of the things he'd crossed off the SOS list.

"So what should we get today?" he asked as they neared the glass wall of the ice cream shop.

Penny looked up at him and grinned. "Vanilla!"

Her favorite, but he knew that now. As he pushed the door open, frozen air slapped him in the face. Even more startling was the sight of Carly waving from a booth near the play area. In spite of the warmth in her eyes, she looked pale, tired, and a little lost. Penny pulled away from him and ran to her. Carly hugged her;

then she looked back at him. Their gazes locked like magnets on metal, but they both stopped short, a foot apart with an invisible wall between them.

Instead of hugging her like he wanted, he jammed his hands in his pockets. "How'd it go?"

"It was hard, but I'm better now. Seeing you, being here." She touched Penny's cheek, but Ryan felt as if she'd touched him, even more so when she raised her eyes and sought his. "It helps to be with a friend."

"Let's get ice cream, then you can tell me everything."

They ordered their favorites—a cone for Penny, an Oreo Blizzard for Carly, and a hot fudge sundae for himself. Then they sat at the booth she'd staked out. It was early afternoon, between lunch and dinner, so the place was almost empty. Penny wolfed down the cone, then scampered to the play area. The instant she was out of earshot, Ryan turned to Carly. "What did Hogan have to say?"

Her face paled in the bluish light. "They have one of the suspects in custody. He's just seventeen. His mother—" She shook her head. "She found Bette's bracelet in his room, along with a stash of drugs. She called the police, but she had no idea her son was part of a murder."

"That's rough."

"It's awful for everyone. I can't imagine what she's feeling right now." Carly let out a slow breath, glanced through the front window, then turned back to him with a calm expression carefully arranged on her face. "There's nothing more to tell, really. Right now, I just want to feel normal."

Ryan couldn't change the ugliness of Bette's death, but he could give Carly a bit of a respite. "Want to hear about my day?"

"Sure."

"An elderly couple came into the office. New patients. The Wigglebottoms."

"*Wigglebottoms?*" Laughter burst out of her mouth. "Is that seriously their name?"

"No," he said. "It's Wiggleworth, but the new receptionist couldn't read the handwriting on the registration forms—"

"Or she reads children's stories."

"Anyway, that's what she put on the file, and I called the wife Mrs. Wigglebottom. Try saying *that* with a straight face."

"Oh no! What did she do?"

"Fortunately, she thought it was hilarious." Ryan's cheeks warmed with the memory of Mrs. *Wigglebottom*, age eighty-three, shaking her ample hips. "Fran razzed me about it all day. I'll never live it down."

"What about the new receptionist?" Carly asked. "I hope you didn't fire her for it."

"No, not even close." What he was about to say surprised him. "I've loosened up. A few months ago, I'd have been an ogre about it. Now I see it for what it was. A mistake by a nervous new employee. No harm done."

"I'm glad."

"Me too." Relaxed now, he stretched a leg. "You can bet I'll never forget Mrs. Wigglebottom."

Fresh laughter spilled out of Carly's throat, a little too loud and out of control. It built into all-out giggling that wasn't giggling at all but a mess of the day's emotions. When a tear slipped down her cheek, Ryan reached across the table and wiped it away with his knuckle. Her eyes drifted shut, and she leaned into his touch. But then her lids flew open, as if she remembered where they were, who they were.

He remembered, too. "Must be the doctor in me," he said, sounding gruff. "I see watery eyes and feel compelled to check them out."

She snatched up a napkin and dabbed at the tears. "I'm all right."

"Good, because I—" *hate to see you cry*. Sealing his lips, he whipped his gaze to Penny going down a red plastic slide. Instead of settling him down, the sight of her happy face stirred him up even more. He owed Carly so much. He needed her, wanted her in his life. But how did he pursue a relationship with a woman who was already a part of his family?

The counter girl called their number. Carly moved to leave the booth, but Ryan stood first. "I'll get it."

He turned his back and walked away from her, exquisitely aware of the dried tears on his knuckle.

21

Penny, are you ready?" Carly called up to her from the foot of the stairs. They were leaving for Penny's overnight stay with Denise and running late.

"Here I come." She tromped down the steps with her purple backpack bumping behind her. Packing was an opportunity to teach Penny a practical lesson, though Denise insisted she had everything Penny needed, including a wardrobe.

While Penny stayed with Denise, Carly planned to work on the cloud mural. She needed the connection to home and her roots, especially after the moment with Ryan at Dairy Queen, where he touched her cheek and she almost forgot who she was and where she belonged.

Taking Penny's hand, she walked her to the minivan and lifted her into the booster seat with a playful whoosh. The midday traffic was light, and it took less than thirty minutes to reach Denise's place. As Carly parked, a jet took off at LAX. The closed windows and A/C muted the noise, and Penny didn't seem to mind, but Carly shared Ryan's concern. She planned to mention it to Denise, along with reminding her about a picture of Jenna. For Penny's sake, the three of them needed to work as a team.

Carly helped Penny out of the van, handed her the backpack, and together they approached the house. They were halfway up the walk when Denise flung the door wide and ran to Penny, her arms outstretched like wings. Hugging Penny hard, she buried her nose in her hair and inhaled. "I'm so glad you're here."

"Me too." Penny clung just as hard, then wiggled free and did a twirl, capped off with a curtsey.

Denise applauded, then turned to Carly. "Thank you for bringing her. I'm waiting for the cable guy."

"I'm glad to do it." Carly took a breath. "Could I come in for a minute? I'd like to tell you about Penny's routine."

Denise's brow furrowed. "If you'd like. But I know what she needs."

"It won't take long."

Penny grabbed Denise's hand in both of hers and dragged her toward the door. "Do you have a toy for me, Aunt DeeDee? I want it now."

Denise tossed a helpless shrug at Carly and let herself be hauled into the house.

Carly held back a wince. It was one thing for Penny to expect a little spoiling when her aunt made a special visit, but if Denise wanted to give Penny a second home, the indulgences created a potential problem. Keeping a few steps back, she followed them into the living room, where a large, sparkly gift bag sat on a brick hearth.

Penny broke from Denise and ran to it. After tossing a mountain of tissue paper onto the floor, she pulled out a two-foot stuffed dolphin. "It's a fish!"

"A dolphin." Denise knelt next to her. "Your mommy loved dolphins. What should we name this one?"

"Donna," Penny said with authority.

Carly smiled from across the room, but her thoughts ricocheted to Penny's infatuation with boats and her search for her mother. The dolphin could bring clarity or cause more confusion, depending on how Denise explained it. With Jenna's death still so raw, Carly decided not to bring it up. This was a happy moment, and she didn't want to spoil it.

Denise played with Penny and the dolphin for a moment, then stood and patted Penny's shoulder. "Can you play with Donna while I talk to Miss Carly?"

Penny wiggled Donna's head to say yes.

With her eyes beaming, Denise led Carly to the dining area where they could keep an eye on Penny but not be overheard.

"The dolphin's great," Carly said. "Penny swims like a fish now, but you know that from the pictures." Carly had sent several of Penny in the pool. The ones with Ryan pulling her in the plastic swan were her favorites.

Denise rested a hand on the dining room table, her fingers drumming lightly. "What do you want to tell me?"

So much for being friendly. If Denise wanted to get to the point, so be it. Carly slipped a piece of paper from her purse. "I wrote out her routine."

Denise skimmed the schedule, then gave it back at Carly. "I appreciate the effort. But when Penny's here, we'll follow my rules."

"She needs consistency. I thought—"

"Thank you, Carly. But I know my niece."

Denise took a step toward the door, but Carly didn't budge. She cared about Penny enough to fight, but she needed to pick the battles that most impacted Penny. Routine was important, but Penny's biggest heartache concerned her mother. "There's one more thing." She kept her tone casual, even warm. "Ryan asked about a picture of Jenna for Penny's room. Her therapist thinks it's a good idea."

Denise looked down her nose. "I haven't opened that box yet."

"I know it's hard—"

"Do you?"

"Yes. I lost my mom." She didn't mention Bette, but pink-and-silver pain cut through her. "Grief is awful for anyone, but it's especially hard for Penny. She can't process what happened."

Denise glanced at Penny wiggling the dolphin, almost smiled, but turned back to Carly with the same tight-lipped expression. "I'll see what I can do."

"Thanks. I'm sure Ryan would appreciate it." Carly didn't want to leave with the tension lingering, so she turned to a lighter subject. "He told me you're using a zoo theme for Penny's room. She'll love it. You know how she feels about animals."

"Of course I do. She's my niece."

That tone! Denise had probably used it on difficult passengers refusing to buckle up. "I just thought—"

"I appreciate your interest, Carly. But this isn't necessary. I know Penny as well as you do. Maybe better, since we're flesh and blood."

Carly was just the nanny, but even nannies deserved respect. Full of Kentucky pride, she propped her hands on her hips. "For Penny's sake, you and Ryan need to communicate. I'm part of that equation."

"Temporarily, yes."

"I'm here now, and I'm part of Penny's life."

"But for how long?" Denise shot back. "When you leave, Ryan will be on his own again. Frankly, it worries me. She's run away twice now. His judgment is questionable."

"I disagree."

"It's true."

"There's a reason she runs off. We're trying to—"

"She runs off because she's unhappy!"

"She's confused. She's—" *looking for her mother, because you told her she left in a boat!* With her lips sealed, Carly inhaled through her nose. "Ryan's a good father. You haven't seen him with her at the dinner table, or the way they play in the pool. He reads to her at night, and—"

"Does she still call him Dr. Tremaine?"

"No. They have a special name now."

Denise's shoulders sagged inside her crisp yellow shirt. "Does she call him Daddy or something else?"

"Dr. Daddy."

"That's a little formal, isn't it?"

"I wouldn't say that at all." Carly barely kept her voice level. "They're building a relationship—a good one. Ryan spends a lot of time with Penny. He loves her. I see it in his eyes, how he talks to her. When she has a tantrum, he holds her. He—"

"You're awfully quick to defend him."

"Because he deserves it! He's a good father. If you could see him the way I do, you'd be impressed. Denise, he's . . . he's . . ." *the man I love*. Blood rushed to Carly's cheeks. Hoping Denise would see anger instead of longing, she kept her chin high.

Denise raised one eyebrow. "It's clear how you feel about him."

"I *respect* him."

"Of course you do."

Oh, that same arrogant tone! It was full of doubt and derision, suspicion and a haughty know-it-all-ness that sent bolts of fury through Carly's veins. Determined to put Denise in her place, she squared her shoulders. "What are you implying?"

"Nothing."

"I think you are."

"Is there something to imply?"

"Not a thing." Except her cheeks were on fire, and her heart was pounding. She wished she'd kept her mouth shut, wished she hadn't tried to talk to Denise at all. Instead of building a safety net for Penny, she'd given Denise ammo to use against Ryan. "If you're jumping to the conclusions I think you are, you're wrong. Ryan's my employer. I'm a professional and so is he. There's nothing between us."

"Whatever you say," Denise said mildly.

Annoyed with herself for bickering, Carly gave up and walked over to Penny. "I'll see you tomorrow. Okay?"

Penny held up the dolphin. "This is Donna. She swims like I do."

"Yes, she does." Carly absently smoothed a strand of Penny's hair, then kissed the top of her head.

Penny lifted the dolphin with both hands and made it swim. "Do dolphins play in the clouds?"

"They live in the ocean."

"But the clouds touch the ocean," she said, still waving the dolphin. "My mommy likes dolphins. Do you think she swims with them?"

A lump shoved into Carly's throat and refused to budge. The issue of heaven, Penny's mother, and boats needed to be clarified and soon, but she couldn't do it now with Denise so hostile. With her chest tight, Carly headed for the front door. Denise opened it and stepped back. A jet roared in the distance, its engines whining into a vibration that shook the entire house. Penny shrieked and covered her ears.

Denise hurried to her side and hugged her. "It's just an airplane, sweetheart. You'll get used to it."

Carly hoped so, but as she closed the door, the picture of Penny pressing her hands to her ears stayed with her. So did the knowledge that she'd given Denise a new reason to criticize Ryan. Carly needed to tell him about Denise's accusation, a prospect she dreaded down to her toes, and something she needed to do quickly in case he wanted to call Denise himself.

Instead of going home, she drove straight to Pacific Eye Associates. By the time she arrived, Ryan would be done with his last patient. She could speak to him in his office, then go shopping or get coffee or walk on the beach, *anywhere* but to his house after what promised to be an awkward conversation.

When Ryan finished with his last patient, he went to his office to finish making notes in the computer. It was better than dictating, but he disliked the chore, especially now that he looked forward to being home for dinner. He was in the middle of the fourth report when Fran's voice came over the intercom.

"Carly's here. Shall I send her back?"

"Yes, please." This was her first visit to the practice, and he wondered if there was trouble with one of the kids. He shoved out of the chair and met her in the hallway.

Her rueful expression put his mind at ease. What she had to say wasn't a matter of life or death. Maybe she'd dented the van. "What's up?" he asked, indicating she should step into his office.

She crossed the threshold, took in the big desk and the art on the walls, but stayed on her feet. "I'll only be a minute. I have to tell you about my conversation with Denise. It was mildly crazy."

"Just mildly?"

"More than mildly." She gave a mock shudder. "I can't believe I let her get to me, but you know how she is."

"All too well." She'd stopped texting him with exclamation points since moving, but he felt even more like that bug under a microscope. "If you told her off, I'll give you a raise."

"I tried."

"So what happened?"

Carly winced in that sweet way of hers. "This is a bit awkward, but—"

His desk phone gave two short rings, a signal from Fran. "I better take it," he said as he hit the speaker button. "Yes?"

"Sorry to interrupt, but a drug rep needs a signature."

"I'll be there in a minute." He turned back to Carly. "Maybe we should get out of here after I see the rep. It's going to be one thing after another."

She glanced at his desk loaded with mail and files, then at the computer monitor that promised even more work. "I guess we can finish at home."

Ryan had a better idea. "Eric's with Nathan, right?"

"Yes, for a sleepover."

"Penny's gone and Kyle's hanging out with Taylor. Let's have dinner out for a change."

While Carly gnawed on her lip, his phone rang again. This time he ignored it. "What do you say?"

"I was going to run some errands."

"Could it wait?"

A long silence hung in the air. "I guess, but don't you have a lot to do?"

"There's nothing urgent. Just the drug rep, and that'll take a minute."

Her nose wrinkled in a way that reminded him of a rabbit pondering the way to escape a coyote. "Okay," she finally said.

"How about a tour before you go?" He enjoyed sharing what he did.

"Sure. I'd like that."

Mindful of the drug rep, he put on his jacket, turned off the light, and headed for the closet holding samples. With Carly next to him, he gave the rep one minute to give him the spiel, signed the man's tablet, then motioned for Carly to follow him down a corridor decorated with lithographs by a local artist.

At the end of the hall, he flipped on a light in a room he used two or three times a day for laser surgery. As she took in the sophisticated equipment, he told her a little about the procedures he performed.

Carly ran her hand along the table holding a laser. "It's amazing what you can do."

"It's science."

"It's healing," she said, lifting her chin.

Ryan expected more from her, maybe a pitch for Christianity, but she walked out of the room, leaving him with a thought that often plagued him. As an ophthalmologist, he understood the workings of the human eye, but he couldn't explain the randomness of conditions like macular degeneration, retinopathy, cataracts. Some people lost their vision; others didn't. No matter how skilled Ryan was, he couldn't make the blind see. Some things in life really were a mystery.

He showed Carly the four exam rooms, the break room, and the optical shop with its wall of eyeglass frames. She plucked a pair off the wall, put them on, and faced him. "What do you think?"

They were big, black, and goofy. Ryan laughed. "Those are the Groucho glasses." He reached for a pair above her head. "Try these."

They were from a line named for a Hollywood actress, diamond studded, and a deep purple. Old ladies loved them. Carly put them on and giggled. "Does anyone actually *wear* these?"

"Only Mrs. Wigglebottom."

Chuckling, she plucked them off her nose. Ryan handed her another pair. They were like the Groucho glasses but for women. He had a hunch she'd look cute in them.

She balanced them on her nose, then made a goofy face in the mirror. "Nerd girl!"

"Or a librarian." *A sexy one.*

As she pouted into the mirror, it occurred to him that taking her out to dinner bordered on a date. And if he told the truth, he didn't mind that idea at all.

❧

As soon as Carly walked with Ryan into the candle-lit restaurant, she wished she'd turned down his invitation. She had no business eating alone with him, especially in a place lit almost solely by pillar candles in wrought-iron sconces. There were even more candles on the tables, and the high-backed booths made each table private.

They had agreed on Rosa's Hacienda because of the food. Without Penny, whose taste buds rebelled at anything spicy or slimy, they were free to indulge in enchiladas, salsa, and guacamole. Normally Carly's mouth would have watered at the delicious aromas, but when she thought of the conversation about Denise, dread stole her appetite. Nervous, she followed the hostess to a booth in the back corner, Ryan trailing behind her. A waiter brought chips and salsa and they ordered.

As soon as the menu left his hand, Ryan turned to her. "So what happened with Denise?"

Where did Carly start? A slow buildup or a running jump off the cliff? Taking a breath, she jumped off the cliff. "She thinks you and I are romantically involved. It's ridiculous, of course."

Ryan said nothing. Not a word. But candlelight danced in his eyes as he reached for a chip. "I don't think it's ridiculous at all. It's not true, but it's not ridiculous."

"Of course it's ridiculous."

"Why?"

Refusing to be flustered, she ignored the roguish quirk of his dark brows. "It has to be ridiculous."

"Why?"

"Because it is. Denise is looking for trouble."

"Maybe." Ryan dipped a chip in the salsa. "A lot of people would make the same assumption. You and I are both mature adults. It's how most people live now."

"Unfortunately."

"What do you mean?"

Carly had all sorts of opinions about the modern dating culture, especially as a social worker who'd seen both teenagers and twenty-something moms struggle to raise their kids alone. The teens, unable to support themselves, ended up with a parent or relative. The twenty-somethings broke her heart even more. They were stuck in dead-end jobs in retail or call centers. On their own, they juggled rent, day care, child-rearing, and dating in a never-ending battle for both financial and emotional security.

Carly loved talking about relationships, romance, and everything in between, but she didn't want to have that conversation with Ryan, especially not the part where she talked to teenage girls about treating their bodies with respect. When her father preached about purity from the pulpit, he spoke for Carly, too. *"The God-given instinct to procreate is one of the strongest forces of nature, and what do we do? We put off marriage until we finish school, have jobs, and buy houses with big mortgages. That's a long time, folks. I have to wonder if we've put material needs before the need to love and be loved."*

With Ryan seated across from her, his eyes glinting with something indecipherable, she understood her father's lament in a deeply personal way. She struggled with that exact trade-off. She loved her work, but she very much wanted to be a wife and mother. And, like her father said, physical desire was one of the strongest forces of nature, one she battled as much as any human being.

Seated across from Ryan now, she couldn't help but notice his strong jaw, the width of his shoulders, the amused-yet-serious set of his mouth.

He reached for a second chip. "You know what I'm saying, Carly. Surely you've had a boyfriend or two."

Her almost-fiancé in college was none of his business, but if she reacted too strongly, he'd wonder why. Determined to be true to herself, she kept her voice casual. "A few. A serious one in college."

"So you get it."

"Get what?" She knew what he meant but wanted to hear his idea of what *it* was. He stared at her as if she were an idiot, which she wasn't. "Of course I know what *can* happen. But we all make choices—*personal* ones." She'd made hers to wait for marriage, and while the choice wasn't easy, she had no regrets.

"Is 'personal' code for 'mind your own business'?"

"Yes."

His hand rose in mock surrender. "You brought it up. Not me."

"*Denise* brought it up." Carly nudged the chip basket closer to him. "I thought you should know."

He opened his mouth to respond, but the waiter arrived with their meals—carne asada for him and chiles rellenos for her. The food smelled delicious and she was hungry. With a little luck, Ryan would be quiet now and eat.

When he cut into the steak, she relaxed. But he stopped short of lifting the fork to his mouth. With his hand poised over his plate, he studied her. "I have the feeling I hit a nerve."

"You didn't."

"Are you sure? Because if I crossed a line, I want to apologize."

"Drop it. Please." She did *not* want to have this conversation. He was too male, too strong, and a reminder that she was twenty-eight and single. Determined to shove her rattled nerves back into place, she cut the chile relleno with her fork, pressing so hard metal scraped on the plate.

As she raised the bite to her lips, she glanced at Ryan. With the candle throwing shadows on his face, he was the most handsome man she'd ever seen, ever met, ever known as a friend. A wanting took root in her belly, and she thought of the teenage crushes she'd had on movie stars, even the boy in her chemistry class. Those crushes had been safe, because they were pure fantasy, even the crush on the boy in chemistry, because he was a football star and didn't notice her.

But Ryan was sitting across from her. He was real, one hundred percent male, and studying her as if she were an exotic flower. His thoughts were a mystery to her, which she supposed was for the best. He belonged in "crush" land, not in reality.

"Carly?"

She saw determination in his eyes and braced for a battle with two enemies—her heart, because her feelings had to be hidden, and with Ryan, who needed to be told again to mind his own business. Except dodging him seemed cowardly. If she didn't stick up for her beliefs, who would? The thought unnerved her, but she was also her father's daughter *and* her Father's daughter. If Queen Esther could stand up to a powerful Persian king for the sake of her people, surely Carly could handle an awkward conversation with Ryan.

With that thought firmly in her mind, she met his gaze and held it. "All right, we'll talk. What do you want to know?"

22

I don't mean to pry, but I wonder if someone hurt you."

Carly's mouth was full, so she couldn't reply. But displeasure shot from her eyes and she chewed faster, obviously eager to tell him to back off.

Ryan took advantage and spoke his mind. "Whoever the guy was, he was an idiot."

Finally she swallowed. "That's not it."

"Then what is it?"

She paused with the fork poised over the plate, her eyes slightly narrowed and her chin up. The coolness in her expression rankled him, or maybe what rankled him was the intensity of his curiosity about that boyfriend.

She set down the fork. "You won't agree with what I'm about to say."

"Say it anyway." Ryan inhaled the scents of cilantro and candle wax, distinct smells that burned into his consciousness. There was no reticence in Carly's expression now, only a quiet confidence.

She set down her fork, blotted her lips with the napkin, and met his stare with a strong one of her own. "I don't take sex casually."

The bones in his spine snapped into a rigid line. "That's candid."

"Like you said, we're adults." She sat straighter, her shoulders square and her chin firm. "I can handle frank talk if you can."

"Go for it."

"For two years I worked with teenage girls at Sparrow House. I saw a little bit of everything—teen pregnancy, abandonment issues, attachment disorders. Every one of the girls at Sparrow House was hurting. Every one of them had an empty place in her heart, one she tried to fill in ways that offered temporary relief but not long-term satisfaction."

"So far, we agree." He snagged another bite of his dinner.

"That part is a no-brainer," she replied after swallowing another bite for herself. "The question is, what do we give them to fill that empty place in their hearts?"

"Are you asking my opinion?"

"Yes."

"The obvious answer is that we give them a strong sense of self. We teach them to be smart and confident, to care for others and work for what they want. I'm trying to do that for Kyle and Eric. And Penny, too."

"Yes, you are." She sounded amenable enough, but Ryan sensed a trap. "And how are you doing that?"

"By being their father."

"Exactly. But the girls I counseled at Sparrow House didn't have fathers. Some of them were victims of tragedy, orphans with no family at all. A couple of the girls ran away from horrible abuse, wisely in my opinion. And the last one—" Carly inhaled sharply. "That's a story for another time."

Ryan wondered again about that raw nerve. He had assumed a man broke her heart, but maybe it had been someone else, maybe that mystery client at Sparrow House.

Carly took another bite, chewed thoughtfully, and swallowed. "This is just my opinion, but I think our social troubles come down to the breakdown of the family. Without love and at least some stability, children suffer. If they're lucky, they find a caring adult, maybe a teacher or a neighbor, someone who'll shield them a little, teach them, and help them to make safe choices."

"You were that person."

"I tried, but—" She clenched her jaw so hard that it shook. "Leave me out of it. Okay?"

"All right." But he'd learned something important. Carly had a secret, and it was festering the way Ryan's failings had festered into a disaster for his family.

She picked up where she left off. "If a girl *doesn't* find that adult, or if the adult fails her, she turns to her friends, television, music, social media. You've seen the messages she gets."

Ryan considered the magazine covers that were all about being sexy, music videos that bordered on pornographic, and news stories about teenagers "sexting." As much as he believed in an individual's right to set his or her own moral compass, how did a teenager set that compass without a sense of morality? "It gets messy, doesn't it?"

"Yes, very." Carly dabbed at her lips with the napkin. "And it gets even messier when a girl is told to define herself through the eyes of others, particularly men. She's told she has to be beautiful and sexy to be loved."

"That's just wrong."

"It's also a reality." She took a sip of her Pepsi. "When a girl matures, nature kicks in. She becomes sexually aware, and she's told sex can be whatever she wants it to be—casual or special, fun or forever. But that's not true. It takes a two-way commitment for a relationship to be special and forever."

Ryan agreed in one sense but not another. "*Forever* is a long time. Not every relationship needs to last that long to have meaning."

"Maybe for some people," she said diplomatically. "But memories are forever, both good and bad. At Sparrow House I worked with a pregnant sixteen-year-old choosing between adoption and keeping a baby she couldn't support. She chose adoption. She'll heal from the experience, but she won't ever forget her son's birthday, the name she wanted to give him, or the one time she kissed his face."

Ryan felt a pang. Who wouldn't? But logic trumped emotion in his world, and he enjoyed a good debate. He also liked to win, and Carly was running circles around him and eating her meal at the same time.

"There's more." Excited now, she swallowed fast. "Everyone agrees teenage girls are vulnerable, but what about older women? What about the woman who doesn't want marriage and kids in her twenties but changes her mind in her thirties?"

"Women like Denise."

"Exactly." Carly set down the fork. "She had a great career and saw the world. She's never said anything, but I assume she had a few relationships."

"Yes." Ryan knew the details through Jenna. "She dated an attorney for ten years, but they never married. Back then, she didn't want kids."

"But now she wants Penny." Carly's voice softened, maybe with her own longing for children. "I have to wonder if Denise feels a little cheated by life. She had a great career, and it fulfilled her in important ways, but a job won't love you."

He agreed but only in part. "It's a little old-fashioned to say women have to be married and have kids to be happy."

"I'm not saying that at all. But I *do* think human beings have a hole in their hearts that's meant to be filled by God and other people."

He ignored the "God" part. She had faith. So what? It made her a nice person. It shaped her the way being Japanese or Hispanic shaped other people. It was a matter of culture. A Kentucky culture, unsophisticated but genuine. "So no man—or woman—is an island."

An earnest glow beamed from her eyes. "To paraphrase John Donne, a poet and a clergyman, yes."

Ryan saw a hole in her argument. "If no man's an island, what's wrong with two people connecting in a way that meets their needs, whether it's long-term or short-term?"

She opened her mouth, closed it again, then studied him with the saddest expression he'd ever seen on her face. "I don't mean to be callous here, or harsh. But I think you know the answer."

She meant Penny, the devastation to Heather and the boys, the guilt he wore like a hair shirt. As much as Ryan wanted to argue with her, his own life testified against him. They both knew it, but he felt compelled to fight for his convictions. "You said earlier that we all make choices."

"I believe that."

"So if two people want the same thing and are willing to be responsible for the risks, what's wrong with that?"

"A one-night stand?"

Her gentle tone unnerved him. He felt judged, even condemned, but he couldn't accuse Carly of casting stones. The pressure welled from some place deep and internal. He blinked and recalled his mother's reaction to the divorce. She'd hugged him and told him to forgive himself and start over. *"You're human, Ryan. I pray for you every day."* A peculiar yearning to embrace that mysterious deliverance tugged at him, but he forced it back with a sneer aimed at Carly. "You're being unrealistic. What's wrong with adults doing what adults do? It's just nature. Sex is part of life."

"Of course it is." She held his gaze without blushing. "God created it, and I hear He did a bang-up job of it."

Like honey dripping from a wooden spoon, the implication of what she admitted sank into Ryan's mind. *I hear . . .* Carly was a virgin. He knew she was a Christian, but the depth of her commitment—and innocence—stunned him. He didn't know anyone who had resisted the temptation to have sex before marriage, not a soul, and he didn't know what to think now, except she was the strongest woman he'd ever met.

And the most beautiful.

And the kindest.

And so much more.

The man who earned her love would be the luckiest fellow on earth, a thought that filled him with jealousy in one breath, hope in the next, and a love so strong he barely kept from telling her how deeply he cared about her. She deserved a man like herself, not someone with Ryan's lousy track record and semicynical attitude.

Had she meant to reveal her innocence? Apparently not, because her cheeks looked sunburned. The blush implied more than embarrassment over a sensitive subject. It revealed awareness of him as a man, awareness of the attraction simmering between them. Denise wasn't nearly as off base as Carly wanted him to believe. She had feelings for him, the same kind he had for her.

Back off, he told himself. But this was Carly, and he cared about her. He worried about her, too. The world was a big bad place, especially for Little Red Riding Hood with her tender heart. A long time ago, Ryan had been the Big Bad Wolf. He'd never repeat that mistake, but what did he do with this attraction to Carly? Unsure and annoyed by his weakness, he finished the meal in silence. So did Carly, until she set down her fork.

The blush had faded, and in its place he saw a quiet determination. "So that's my opinion," she said with dignity. "And my choice."

"Yes," he agreed. "It is."

A busboy took their plates. Ryan settled the bill, and they headed to the car with the awkwardness sharp until Carly mentioned the weather. Ryan agreed it was a tad bit chilly. The atmosphere between them was chilly, too. He supposed it needed to stay that way, but he didn't like that choice at all.

~⌒

Penny hated the airplanes at Aunt DeeDee's house, but she loved Aunt DeeDee because they talked about Penny's mother. Aunt DeeDee had the same pretty voice. Best of all, tonight she'd made Penny's favorite kind of soup for dinner, the one her mother made with chicken and lots of noodles.

They were eating now, and Penny was happy—except for the noisy airplanes. When a big one zoomed by, she dropped her spoon and covered her ears the way Carly told her. Carly said it gave her *control*. Penny wasn't quite sure what *control* was, but Carly helped her all the time, and Penny trusted her.

Aunt DeeDee set down her spoon and said something.

Penny couldn't hear, because her hands were on her ears. When the airplane was gone, she lowered her hands.

"You'll get used to it, honey." Aunt DeeDee patted Penny's arm. "You know what it sounds like to me?"

Penny shook her head.

"A cat purring. A great big cat," Aunt DeeDee said in her fun voice. "Maybe we should get a kitten. Would you like that?"

Penny forgot all about the jets. "A cat like Wild Thing?"

"Who's Wild Thing?"

"She's Carly's cat. So is Tom, but he's not cuddly." Penny thought Wild Thing was the sweetest cat in the world. Sometimes Carly would sit with Penny on the couch, and they'd pet Wild Thing together. That way Wild Thing wasn't scared, and Penny wasn't too rough.

"You like Miss Carly, don't you?"

"A lot." Carly did special things for her, and she didn't get too mad when Penny messed up, which was a lot. No matter how busy Carly was, she talked in a nice way that Penny could understand. *"Your mind fills up,"* Carly had said to her. *"Sometimes mine does, too. Not because of how my brain works, but because my heart gets too full."*

Penny understood being filled up, because the airplanes were filling her head with noise. Carly said Penny should close her eyes and picture the clouds when she needed to be quiet, so she did it now.

"Penny?" Aunt DeeDee tapped her shoulder with her fingernail. Penny's eyes popped open, but her mind stayed in the clouds.

"Pay attention," Aunt DeeDee said. "I asked what you wanted to do tomorrow. We could go to the zoo or a big toy store. Whatever you want."

"Really?"

"Yes, really." Aunt DeeDee smiled in that giant way that showed lots of teeth. "Where do you want to go?"

Penny knew exactly where she wanted to go. She wanted to go where her mommy lived. Last weekend, when Dr. Daddy's magic car took her to his house instead of home to her mother, she wondered if she needed to ride in a boat like the one that took her mother's ashes to the ocean. "I want to go to the beach."

Aunt DeeDee's eyebrows scrunched together like worms. "I don't think the beach is a good idea, honey."

"But I went with Carly. I chased the birds, and we went in the water."

Aunt DeeDee's mouth fell open. Penny saw even more of her teeth, even a big one in the back with gold all over it.

"You went *in the water*?"

Penny nodded and it wasn't a lie. The white foam had touched just her toes, but in her mind she ran into the waves and turned into a mermaid. "The waves were big, and I swam in them. Carly came with me, and we went far."

"You *swam* in the ocean?"

Penny nodded. "Carly made me wear my life vest to be extra safe."

"But—but—"

Aunt DeeDee sounded like she was choking on her spit. Penny hated when that happened. "Carly says I swim like a fish. It was fun."

Aunt DeeDee scooted her chair close, cupped Penny's face in her cool hands, and leaned close. "Honey, this is *very* important."

"Okay." She knew what important meant.

"How far did you go in the waves?"

"Far."

"Did you get all wet? Even your hair?" Aunt DeeDee squeezed Penny's cheeks so hard that Penny's mouth turned into what Eric called a "fish face." He made her laugh when he did it in the pool, but she wasn't a fish. She was a mermaid, and she lived in a sand castle under the water. "We went all the way in the ocean." She wasn't sure what Aunt DeeDee wanted to hear, so she told the best story she could.

"Oh, Penny."

"I went underwater."

Aunt DeeDee cried out like she'd stubbed her toe; then she snatched Penny's hand and they went to the counter where Aunt DeeDee kept her phone. "How would you like to watch a movie while I make a call?"

"All right."

"You pick."

"Do you have *Little Mermaid*?"

Air blew out of Aunt DeeDee's nose, and her eyes turned into slits. "I do, but you should pick something else."

Penny stuck her lower lip out. "I want to be Ariel."

Aunt DeeDee hugged her again. "I guess it's all right."

She put in the movie and brought Penny a cherry popsicle. The movie started, and in Penny's mind, she was back at the beach with Carly. She didn't know who Aunt DeeDee called, but Aunt DeeDee told the person about Penny going to the beach with Carly. She sounded worried and scared, especially when she hissed that a home visit couldn't wait until next week.

"This child could be in danger," she said.

Penny's ears perked up, but then Ariel swam onto the screen, and Penny didn't hear anything else until Aunt DeeDee came to sit with her. They watched the movie together until Penny lost interest.

Aunt DeeDee hugged her for the millionth time. "I'm going to take good care of you, Penny. Always. It's what your mother would want."

"How do you know?"

Aunt DeeDee swallowed hard. "I just do, honey."

Maybe Aunt DeeDee knew how to get to heaven in the clouds. She'd been the one to take her mommy in the boat. Penny pushed back from her. "Do you talk to my mommy?"

"Sometimes."

"Can she hear you?"

"I-I think so."

Penny wanted to ask Aunt DeeDee how a person visited heaven and if a boat could take her there, but an extra loud airplane made her cover her ears. Like Carly said, Penny's brain was too full to think anymore, and her heart was so full it hurt. With tears spilling down her cheeks, she slipped into a world where no one else could go.

23

When a person cared for a child with fetal alcohol, some days were harder than others. A few days were so impossible even a saint pulled her hair out. Carly was no saint, and Penny had been particularly difficult since returning two days ago from her overnight stay with Denise.

A minute ago, as Carly was hauling paint cans down the hall, Penny informed her, in a particularly entitled tone, that she didn't have to listen to Carly anymore, because Aunt DeeDee said Penny was a little princess, and she let Penny do whatever she wanted.

Carly's blood was boiling as she veered into Penny's room. This was precisely the sort of conflict she had sought to avoid when she spoke to Denise and ended up in that awful conversation with Ryan. They had barely said a word to each other since that night, and Carly didn't know whether to be hurt, angry, or relieved. She needed to talk to him about Penny's behavior, but that meant bringing up Denise. Unwilling to dredge up the conversation at the restaurant, Carly had been handling Penny herself.

"We have rules here," Carly said to Penny as she stepped into the room. "You know that."

Penny sashayed behind her. "I don't care about rules."

"I think you do."

"No, I don't." For good measure, she tossed in a twirl and curtsied.

Carly set the paint cans down on the tarp she'd laid out earlier, then crouched in front of Penny. "We have rules here," she repeated.

Penny twirled again, spinning with her arms wide until she stumbled into a paint can. It tipped and the lid fell off. Gray paint spread across the tarp like polluted water.

Mercifully the can was only a quarter full. Carly righted it quickly, then gripped Penny's arm. "That's enough."

When Penny tried to spin again, Carly grasped her shoulders. "Penny. Stop."

"No!"

"I said *STOP.*"

Penny, her face knotted, stomped in the puddle of paint. Gray droplets spattered Carly's face. Gasping, she wiped her mouth with her sleeve, tasted rancid paint, and tried to work up some spit.

Penny saw her contorted face and laughed.

Fighting a helpless shriek, Carly hunched forward with her hands knotted at her chest. Her mind tumbled into a black hole. Nothing about this moment was funny. Not the spilled paint or Penny's show of temper. Not Carly's undeniable feelings for Ryan and Denise's meddling in their lives. It hurt. Every bit of it. And there wasn't a thing she could do to change the circumstances.

She sucked in a lungful of air and raised her face back to Penny, still spinning in her paint-covered socks. Carly pulled her down to her lap, tugged off the socks, and called through the open door. "Kyle? Eric? I need some help."

"On my way!" Kyle yelled.

He said something to Eric as he came down the hall, saw the mess on Penny's floor, and made a face. Before Carly said a word, he held out his hand to Penny. "Come on, Squirrel. Let's build something with Legos."

"A castle?" Penny asked.

"Whatever you want."

Carly mouthed a silent *thank you* to Kyle. With Penny in hand, he led the way downstairs to the family room.

Sometimes life was just too much. Her anger slid into a murky pool that had grown deeper and wider all week. Filled with the steady drip-drip of her ambivalent feelings for Ryan, that pool became a lake as murky as the spilled paint. She cleaned up the mess from Penny's tantrum, dipped a brush in another can holding a darker shade of gray, and swiped it across the flat bottom of a storm cloud.

In her mind she heard rain hammering her father's roof, saw black clouds and feathery wisps, the turmoil in the Kentucky sky. Like her mother used to say, *"If you don't like the weather in Kentucky, wait ten minutes and it'll change."*

Carly wished her feelings for Ryan were as transient, but they were more like the sky above the clouds—unchanging, bright, and true blue. This wasn't a schoolgirl crush. She loved him. Stupid or not, she had lost her heart to a worldly man who didn't understand her at all, lived in Los Angeles, and preferred "for now" to "forever."

Could he really love her if he didn't understand the most basic part of her character? Not that he loved her. She was sure he didn't.

Because he couldn't.

But what if he did?

She'd seen his expression when he realized how serious she was about marriage and her own sexuality. Surprise had morphed into fascination, then desire evident in a look that seared her skin. Every cell in her body had leapt to life, and she felt that leaping now.

"Carly!" Kyle's voice shot up the stairs.

Surrendering to a groan, she hurried to the kitchen where Kyle was at the sink running water and Penny was . . . *painting the wall*? Gasping, Carly took in smears of ketchup and mustard as high as Penny could reach. Her hands were covered with the red and yellow slime, and she'd gotten it on her face and in her hair.

Carly grabbed Penny's hand to stop the damage. "*What* did you do?"

Her bottom lip poked out. "I'm painting—like you!"

"This isn't painting," Carly ground out. "It's a *mess*."

Kyle squeezed water out of a sponge. "I went to get the Legos but couldn't find them right away. When I came out—" he indicated the wall with a disparaging nod. "That's what she was doing."

Carly glared at the mess. Next to her, Penny whimpered, "My hands are icky."

"Kyle, hand me a paper towel—"

"We're out." He headed to the laundry room for a fresh roll.

"Get it off me!" Penny shrieked. *"Get it off me now!"*

A meltdown was coming. If Denise had walked into the room at that moment, Carly would have given her an earful. They all suffered when she spoiled Penny, with Penny suffering the most. Shaking with fury, Carly gripped Penny's slick hands and crouched. "What's the rule about the refrigerator?"

Penny's bottom lip trembled. "I-I don't know."

"You're not allowed to open it."

"But Aunt DeeDee said—"

"Your daddy makes the rules here." Carly paused to let the words sink in, then repeated them. "Your daddy makes the rules. In this house, you are *not* allowed to open the refrigerator."

When tears flooded Penny's eyes, Carly let go of one of her hands and pulled a tissue out of her pocket. Before she could wipe Penny's face, Penny rubbed her eye with her mustard-covered fingers.

"Penny. No!" But it was too late. The mustard got in her eye and started to sting.

"It hurts!" Screaming, Penny stomped her feet so hard the floor shook.

Carly swung her up into her arms and raced to the kitchen sink.

Kyle came back with paper towels. "Do you need me, because if you don't—"

"Go," she said over Penny's shrieks. "I'll handle it from here."

He took off like a cat on fire. Carly cranked the water back on and made it lukewarm. As she stuck Penny's hand under the stream, the doorbell rang. No one ever dropped in on the Tremaines, not even Taylor or Eric's friends. It had to be the UPS man or FedEx. Ryan hadn't mentioned a delivery, but they weren't speaking, so how would she know?

"Kyle?" she shouted. "Could you get that?"

He called back yes, leaving Carly to wrestle with Penny. The child's tears had washed away most of the mustard, but she was in a full-blown panic. With one hand firm on Penny's shoulder, Carly used her own hand to squeegee the mess off Penny's cheeks. If her eyes were at all irritated, she'd rush Penny to Ryan's office.

"It hurts!" Penny cried again. "Make it stop!"

Kyle walked back into the kitchen. "Uh, Carly?"

"What is it?"

When he didn't answer, she looked up and saw a pinched expression on his lean face. "There's someone here for Dad."

"Who is it?"

He held out a cheap white business card. "I don't know, but she's from the Department of Family and Child Services."

"She's from *where*?"

Kyle repeated himself in the exact same tone, much like Carly spoke to Penny.

Her vision tunneled into a black hole. This woman was here to investigate an allegation of some sort, but who would call? Then it hit her. There was only one person in the world who doubted Ryan's ability to care for Penny, and that was Denise. How dare she call Social Services! No matter what misunderstanding had led to the report, Ryan deserved the respect of a direct confrontation.

Clutching Penny with one hand, Carly pinched the card with her stained fingers and read, *Louanne Stuart, LCSW, Dept. of Family and Child Services.*

Penny shrieked again, her anguish echoing off the walls. *"It hurts! Make it stop! It hurts!"*

Carly knew what Louanne Stuart was hearing and thinking. If the social worker had a lick of sense, Carly and Ryan had nothing to fear. On the other hand, if she was young, inexperienced, and determined to save the world, or perhaps overly cautious, Ryan would be in for the fight of his life.

With her hand shaking, she returned the card to Kyle. "Did you invite her in?"

"Not yet."

"Do it, then call your dad. If he's with a patient, tell Fran to interrupt. This is an emergency."

~~✆~~

Ryan finished with the last patient of the morning and stepped into the hallway. As he headed to his office, Fran waved frantically from the front desk. "Kyle's on line two. He says Carly needs you."

A thousand awful pictures flashed in Ryan's mind—Penny missing again, a car accident, Carly and his kids injured and headed to the ER. Inwardly cringing but outwardly calm, he snatched up the phone in an empty exam room. "Kyle?"

"There's a lady from the county here. She's some sort of social worker."

"She's *what?*"

"A social worker. Carly said to tell you it's an emergency."

"I'm on my way. I'll call you back from the car."

Ryan slammed down the phone, told Fran to cancel his afternoon, then jogged to his car without bothering to snag his suit coat. At the first red light, he called Kyle and learned the details about the mustard fiasco, Penny's shrieks, and Ms. Stuart's ill-timed arrival. The goop in her eyes didn't greatly concern him. He could handle it. On the other hand, Ms. Stuart posed an unknown threat.

A nondescript sedan sat in the driveway, a testimony to the bureaucracy he was about to face. Burying his anger, he strode into the house but paused in the foyer to straighten his tie. If Denise had called DFCS, as it seemed, Ryan was going to war with Denise, DFCS, and anyone else who dared to cast aspersions on his ability to raise his daughter or Carly's abilities as a nanny.

He strode into the family room where a tall African-American woman rose to greet him. Everything about her struck Ryan as severe—the navy blue suit with a pressed white blouse, her close-cropped silver hair, even her pointy black shoes and dagger-like earrings.

She stood and offered her hand. "Dr. Tremaine?"

He crossed the room in long strides and accepted the handshake. "You must be Ms. Stuart."

"I am." Her eyes stayed locked on his. "Do you know why I'm here?"

"Not exactly. But I'm fairly certain it has something to do with Denise Caldwell. She's Penny's aunt."

Ms. Stuart didn't blink, didn't twitch. Nothing betrayed her thoughts as she perused his face. "As soon as Penny is finished with her bath, I'd like to speak to her alone. Do you have any objections?"

"Of course not."

She sat back down on the armchair, but Ryan stayed on his feet. "If you don't mind, I'd like to take a quick look at my daughter's eyes. You probably know I'm an ophthalmologist."

"Yes."

"My son told me about the mustard incident."

Ms. Stuart maintained her blank expression, but he detected a hint of suspicion. Did she think he was going to plot with Carly? That was ridiculous. They had nothing to hide. On the other hand, if he didn't check Penny, Ms. Stuart might consider him negligent.

If he was going to be judged, he wanted to be judged for doing the right thing. "If you'll excuse me for a moment . . ."

Again, no response. Just those hawkish eyes studying him. Ryan stared back, weighed the needs of the moment, and decided to say a few things to Ms. Stuart before checking Penny. He was ninety-nine percent certain her eyes were fine, while he was a hundred percent certain any hint of collusion with Carly sent the wrong message.

Ryan faced her. "Before I check Penny, I'd like to clarify a few things."

"I'm listening."

"Kyle tells me you walked into one of Penny's tantrums."

"I did."

"I'm sure you thought—"

"I don't assume anything, Dr. Tremaine." She sounded matter-of-fact, even a little tired. He guessed her to be in her fifties, a good sign because it suggested she was experienced. On the other hand, she could have an axe to grind, or maybe a past failure that made her overly suspicious. As a physician, Ryan was required by law to report any suspected child abuse. He'd been in the position just once, and the weight of it still burned in his brain. He was judge and jury when he made that phone call. As things turned out, he'd done the right thing.

"You have a difficult job," he said to Ms. Stuart.

"At times."

He was tired of dancing around the visit. "I'd like to know exactly what you're investigating."

"We received an anonymous tip that Penny was placed in a dangerous situation. I'm here to check out her home life and to talk about an incident at the beach."

"What incident?"

Ms. Stuart raised a brow. "You don't know about it?"

"I know Carly took Penny to the beach last Sunday."

"Were you there?"

"Part of the time."

"So you don't know everything that happened?"

"Not everything, but I know Carly. She'd never put Penny in danger. I have to say—" Jaw tight, he took a breath. "I'm relatively certain Denise made this report without the facts and for reasons of her own. I'm going to be blunt, Ms. Stuart. Denise wants custody. That isn't going to happen. This is Penny's home. She's my daughter, and she's loved and safe."

"That's why I'm here, Dr. Tremaine—to make sure Penny's safe."

"Then we're in agreement."

"Yes, we are. And I assure you, this isn't my first rodeo." She gave him another strong look. "I've been in the middle of family disputes more times than I can count. If Penny is in good hands, you have nothing to fear. On the other hand, the person who reported the endangerment believes Penny almost drowned."

"That's impossible!"

"I'd like to talk to Penny before we go any further."

"Of course."

Ms. Stuart opened a portfolio and made some notes. As she capped her pen, Penny emerged from the hallway with Carly hurrying after her. Ryan took in Penny's clean face and wet hair, strode forward, and cupped her chin so he could check her eyes. They were red-rimmed but clear. She was no worse for wear, but Carly looked awful. Dressed in her painting clothes, now spattered with ketchup, mustard, and paint, she approached them with a look as detached as the one worn by Ms. Stuart.

She'd worn that same look while talking to the detective about Bette's murder. He knew her well now, and that look was a mask. Worried, he turned from Carly and focused on Penny. "This is Ms. Stuart. She wants to talk to you about going with Carly to the beach."

"Okay." Penny waved at her. "Do you like mermaids?"

"I like mermaids just fine," Ms. Stuart said with a smile.

"There's one in my tent."

When Penny scooted away to fetch one of her favorite toys, Ryan called after her. "Tell Ms. Stuart everything that happened."

Penny didn't answer. Not a surprise considering her attention span.

"Ryan?" Carly sounded tentative, even worried. "Ms. Stuart might not know about Penny's background."

He hoped Ms. Stuart was knowledgeable about FASD, because explaining it was a challenge. "Penny has some special needs. If we could chat a few minutes—"

"There's no need," she said, almost kindly. "The reporting party provided that information."

Ryan frowned. "I'm not sure Denise understands—"

"I'll speak to Penny first," Ms. Stuart said. "Then I'll sit down with you. Now, if you'll wait somewhere else, Penny and I will get to know each other."

Penny popped out of the tent with her mermaid doll. "This is Annabelle. I named her myself."

"She's pretty," Ms. Stuart replied.

Carly met his glance, and they slipped outside to the table where he and Denise had interviewed Carly all those weeks ago. So much in his life had changed for the better, and it was because of her. His heart swelled with that forever feeling he didn't believe in, at least not the way she did. She'd brought light and love to his home, but looking at her now, he saw the pinched look of someone in pain.

He pulled out a chair for her. "Sit. You've had a rough day."

"It's been awful." She collapsed onto the cushion, slumped forward, and massaged her temples with bone-white fingers.

Ryan had no right to put his arm around her shoulders or even squeeze her hand. But at that moment, Carly was hurting, and he didn't give a rip about boundaries. He shifted his chair closer to hers, sat, and lifted his arm, but before he touched her, she scooted her chair a foot away.

24

Carly longed to rest her head on Ryan's shoulder, but she couldn't allow herself that comfort—not with Ms. Stuart in the house, and not with guilt and a secret eating her alive. Thanks to Denise's accusations, Carly was reliving the nightmare of Allison's disappearance, something she had never mentioned to Ryan. Her supervisor's voice echoed in her mind. *"We all make mistakes, Carly. The trick here is to learn from it."*

Apparently Carly hadn't learned a thing, because she loved Penny as if she were her own, and she loved Ryan, too.

"This is because of Denise," he said, hunkering forward with his foot tapping.

"Wrong or not, she thinks something bad happened." Carly's conscience was clear concerning Penny, but she was far from innocent when it came to Allison, a problem now because that guilt still stewed in her belly. If she didn't shake it off, Louanne Stuart would see it and assume Carly was hiding something. All this because Denise had gone nuclear instead of speaking directly to Ryan. "Do you have any idea what she reported?"

"Something about Penny almost drowning at the beach."

Carly bolted upright. "*Drowning?* She barely touched the water!"

"I know. It's insane. But this is Penny. Who knows what story she made up?"

"This is awful." Even worse than Carly had imagined. "It could come down to my word against Penny's."

They commiserated for the next fifteen minutes, each of them speculating about Penny's thought processes without having the facts. People with FASD experienced life through a different lens, sometimes a kaleidoscope of lenses that colored every word they heard, or didn't hear.

The slider opened with a metallic whoosh. Carly and Ryan both stood and saw Ms. Stuart, her face as blank as before. "Would you come inside, please?"

Carly led the way with Ryan behind her. Once indoors, Ms. Stuart motioned them to the kitchen table where her portfolio was open, her notes exposed and ready to be addressed.

Carly and Ryan sat across from each other, traded a look, then focused on Ms. Stuart putting on a pair of black reading glasses. "Penny is playing in her tent," she said, looking over the frames at Carly. "That's an excellent device for a child with special sensitivities. She told me it's her quiet place, and I had to be invited inside."

"That's the rule," Carly replied.

"The reporting party told us you were the nanny. But in talking to Penny, I see far more than the usual nanny skills. If I may ask, what exactly is your background?"

Before Carly could reply, Ryan touted her qualifications. Ms. Stuart made a few more notes, then turned back to Carly. "I suppose that's what confuses me about Penny's statement. You have tremendous knowledge. Knowing what you do, it seems odd that you'd take Penny into the waves—"

"I didn't."

"She told me otherwise." The social worker removed the glasses, then laced her hands over the notes. "I fully understand the complex relationship with the party reporting the endangerment. Stories become exaggerated, and we all have our motives."

"Yes," Ryan said firmly.

Ms. Stuart shot him a quelling look, then turned back to Carly. "What concerns me is Penny's account of the day. She said you put her in an orange life vest, then took her out past the waves where she swam by herself. I believe the phrase was, 'Carly says I swim like a fish, and I did. I went underwater and everything.'"

"That's absurd!" Ryan shoved back in the chair so hard the legs screeched against the hardwood floor. "I was there. I saw her. Her hair was dry and brushed. She was—"

"Allow me to finish, Dr. Tremaine." Ms. Stuart lifted one brow. "As you admitted earlier, you weren't there the entire time."

"No, but this is crazy! Denise is—"

"Ryan, stop." Carly appreciated his support, but the moment called for diplomacy. "Ms. Stuart is doing her job. I'm not afraid of the facts."

He settled back in the chair, but his eyes stayed on her face. "I'm not either, but the accusation is outrageous."

Carly angled her chair to face Ms. Stuart. "For the record, I did *not* take Penny into the ocean. We played in the sand, and she got her ankles wet. That's all."

"Are you sure?"

"Positive."

Oh, how Carly hated being questioned like this! It was too close to that awful moment in her boss's office. *"Are you sure you don't know where Allison went? Are you sure she didn't give you a hint?"*

Ms. Stuart picked up her pen. "In that case, I have a question. If you didn't take Penny into the water, why was she wearing a life vest?"

Carly hesitated. "As a precaution."

The social worker made a note. "So you put her in a life vest to play in the sand?"

"She's unpredictable—"

"And you were worried."

"A little." Carly was always worried about Penny, in part because she couldn't forget her mistakes with Allison.

Ms. Stuart sat poised with her pen high, perhaps ready to write "guilty as charged" on her yellow legal pad. "Here's my problem, Carly. You understand FASD far better than most nannies and far better than I do. If you were worried enough to put Penny in a life vest, why go to the beach at all? I have to wonder if you're a little overconfident because of your knowledge."

Overconfident? Since Allison, she worried about every decision she made. "That's not accurate."

"Is there another explanation?"

"Yes." She started to say Penny made up stories, but tears flooded her eyes. *Allison, where are you?*

Ryan's gaze pierced her from across the table. "Carly, there's no guilt here. You didn't do anything wrong."

"But I did. Not with Penny, but . . . but before." She pressed her knuckles to her mouth to fight a sob, but it came out in a groan. "Back in Lexington at Sparrow House . . . with a girl named Allison. I h-hate what happened."

Ms. Stuart placed her strong, brown hand on Carly's shoulder. "Honey, let it out."

Why did she have to collapse in front of this woman acting as judge and jury? "I feel so guilty."

"Tell me what happened at Sparrow House." Ms. Stuart gave Carly's shoulder a squeeze. "And call me Louanne."

Carly blurted out the whole ugly story. "It was Friday. Allison was having a bad day, and so was I." Carly's bones ached with the memory of the headache building behind her eyes, the fatigue, the start of menstrual cramps. When she spoke, her Kentucky accent thickened with every word. "I had plans to leave for Boomer, that's my home county. I loved my job, and I loved those girls, but I needed some breathing space. You know how it is."

"I do," Louanne replied. "Sometimes you have to shut the door."

"That's right." Carly wished she had shut it sooner. "But I didn't do that. I lived in at Sparrow House. I wanted to leave early that day, but things kept happening—little things, but someone had to handle them. When Allison came to my room around six o'clock, the door was open and I was packing. She wanted to come home with me. She said she just had to get away. But so did I. I was at low ebb, so I told her no."

"That's reasonable," Louanne assured her.

"Yes, but I should never have given her the idea that we were close enough for that kind of weekend. Allison started shouting that I didn't care about her. I lost it. I yelled back." She sniffed hard. "Instead of taking the time to calm her down or to take her to the house leader filling in for the weekend, I left her."

Louanne nodded, her expression full of understanding. "Sometimes we just run out of gas."

"Yes, but she needed me." Carly wiped her eyes with her fist. "The next day, when I was home in Boomer, the house leader called and told me Allison was missing. One of the other girls saw her get in a car with a man she barely knew. We learned later that they spent the night together, then he drove her to the bus stop. She bought a ticket for Chicago, and that was the last I ever heard of her."

"Oh, Carly," Louanne murmured. "I'm so sorry."

"I'd do anything to have that night back." *Anything at all. Lord, what will it take?* She tried to raise her eyes from her lap but couldn't. "That's how I know I'm not overconfident with Penny. I'm scared to death of making the mistake I made with Allison."

Ryan's voice filled her ears. "You're human, Carly. We all make mistakes."

She dragged her gaze up from her lap, saw compassion in his eyes, and felt almost forgiven.

Louanne broke in. "I see now why Penny was wearing the life vest. You're not overconfident at all. You're overly cautious."

"I suppose I am," Carly admitted. "Penny got her toes wet, but we didn't swim the way she told Denise. FASD kids make up stories. It's part of the condition. I hope you believe me."

"I do." Louanne straightened her glasses. "Kids make up stories to protect themselves. So do a lot of adults. I hear it every day, and I'm sure you did, too. It's my job to dig down to the facts, which is why I'd like to know more for my report. Do you have any idea why Penny spun that particular story?"

❧

So that was Carly's secret. Ryan sympathized with her, deeply, but her guilt surprised him. How many times had she told him to forgive himself for contributing to Penny's FASD? She'd preached it several times, and here she was—as remorseful and self-condemning as he was.

The guilt didn't make sense in the context of her Christian faith. If she believed in a Savior who had died for her sins, why was she carrying that burden on her own shoulders? Wasn't she supposed to roll it off and shout hallelujah, as if nothing had ever happened? Where was her faith now? Or more to the point, what was her faith in? Did she believe in God, or was her faith a remnant from her childhood, the stuff of memorized prayers and the habit of going to church?

Ryan didn't share her faith, but he cared deeply for Carly. She didn't need to know what he thought, but she very much needed absolution. After being helpless in the presence of her tears, he could finally do something. "Let's talk to Penny," he said to Louanne. "If we ask the right questions, she might reveal something."

"I hope so," Carly said. "A lot happened that day."

"Get her," Louanne said to Ryan.

He crossed the family room to her tent, crouched, and peered through the open flaps. Penny was in the corner surrounded by her stuffed animals, including Miss Rabbit, Lance, Joey the Kangaroo, and the dolphin, whose name he didn't recall. Without thinking twice, he reached for Lance.

"Miss Penny!" he said in a growly voice. "Come with me!"

Giggling, Penny scrambled after Lance, took Ryan's hand, and pulled him to the table, where she climbed onto Carly's lap. "I'm hungry."

Carly patted her shoulder. "We'll have a snack in a few minutes."

"Now!"

"In a minute," Carly said, hugging her. "Miss Louanne and your daddy want to ask you some questions."

Ryan kept Lance in his lap. If Penny didn't open up, he'd make a fool of himself and bring in the lion. "So," he said to her, "you had fun at the beach. What did you do?"

"We made a castle."

"Did you go in the water?" he asked.

"It was cold." Penny shivered to make her point. "Fish like it and so do mermaids. Annabelle is my mermaid friend. She swims in the ocean. I saw her."

Glancing occasionally at Penny, Louanne scribbled notes.

"Where did you see Annabelle?" Ryan asked.

"In the waves." Penny kicked the table leg while she spoke. "I wanted to be with her, because she lives in the ocean. Aunt DeeDee took my mommy's ashes to the ocean. She lives in heaven now, and I want to visit her."

Ryan tossed a look at Louanne to be sure she heard the link. When she nodded, he continued. "Did you tell Aunt DeeDee about Annabelle?"

Penny shook her head. "No, Annabelle's my secret friend. But I told Aunt DeeDee about the waves."

He didn't want to ask leading questions, but Penny understood best when people were direct. "Did you tell her you swam in the waves?"

"It wasn't a lie." She buried her face against Carly's neck, then mumbled, "*My feet* swam in them."

With his eyebrows raised, Ryan looked pointedly at Louanne, who capped her pen. "Thank you, Penny. I understand now."

Penny twisted her neck for a better view of Carly. "Can we have cookies now?"

"Yes, we can." Carly lowered Penny to the floor, then spoke to Louanne. "I'm sure you have a busy schedule, but you're welcome to a cup of coffee."

"No, thank you." Louanne scrawled something on her business card and handed it to Ryan. "This is the case number. You can request a copy of the report in ten days or so, but I assure you, there's nothing to worry about."

Ryan slipped the card into his shirt pocket. "Do you want to talk to my sons? Is there anything else?"

"We're done." She stood and picked up the notebook. "I'll be on my way, but Penny?"

As the child turned to her, Louanne offered her hand. Penny stared at it, then grabbed it with both of hers and shook.

"It was nice to meet you," Louanne said. "You have a very vivid imagination."

Just about mermaids, Ryan thought. When it came to imagining the consequences of her actions, like running away or crossing a street without looking, Penny possessed no imagination at all. She lived in the moment, something he related to as a man who'd once given in to impulse.

Ryan walked Louanne to the door, thanked her, then strode back to the kitchen. Penny was back in her tent and out of earshot, so he took his phone out of his pocket.

Carly saw it and frowned. "What are you doing?"

"Calling Denise."

"No. Wait."

Because she asked, he paused. "I'm calling her now. If she has a problem, she needs to call me, not DFCS."

"Yes, but you want to be calm. Tell her what happened. Include her. Don't make her an enemy."

"Well, she is." Not only had she threatened his custody of Penny, she had attacked Carly's character and that clawed at him. He longed to go to Carly now, put his arms around her, press her face to his shoulder, and tell her . . . tell her what? That he admired her? Loved her? He couldn't say either of those things, but he could protect her from false accusations.

With his temper hot but under control, he called Denise and relayed the story. She didn't apologize like he expected. Instead, she defended herself. "I have grave concerns—"

"I get that, Denise. But—"

"Penny shouldn't even be at the beach."

"That's ridiculous. She has to be watched, but she's still a child."

"It's just not safe," Denise protested. "I don't care how competent Carly is, I think she made a mistake."

"Well, I don't."

"You're defending her." Denise's tone reeked of suspicion. "It makes me wonder what else is going on. Remember, Ryan, I know your track record."

"That's not fair." And it insulted Carly, who was staring out the window, her eyes still shiny and her nose a little red. He laid a hand on her shoulder. When she nodded to show her support, he spoke again to Denise. "I'm Penny's father. I respect your ties to her, but you don't have the right to interfere in our lives."

"I do if your nanny is incompetent."

"Carly does an excellent job, and you know it. She's amazing. She's more than competent. She's—" He stopped in midsentence, aware that his defense hinted at that ridiculous idea that wasn't ridiculous at all. He let go of Carly's shoulder and stepped back.

She headed to the sink, and he focused solely on Denise. "This is about Penny, and it's between you and me."

"Fine. But that doesn't change the facts."

"What do you want me to do?" Ryan lashed back. "Keep her in a cage?"

"Of course not. But the beach isn't safe."

"Sometimes neither is flying. Any close calls?" He knew the answer, otherwise he wouldn't have asked.

"A few."

He leveled his voice. "Human beings take chances all the time. It's just life, and I want Penny to have the biggest life I can give her."

"So do I, but I also want her safe!"

"Absolutely." He saw a chance to mollify Denise and took it. "That's why I need a favor. I'm taking five teenagers on a camping trip. I need Carly's help. Could you watch Penny for a few days?"

"Of course. When?"

He named the dates in August.

"I'd be glad to watch her. I love her so much—"

"So do I, Denise."

A labored sigh hissed into his ear. "You're off the hook this time, Ryan. But please be careful. Penny is precious to me, and I promised Jenna I'd love her like my own."

"And you do." He didn't doubt Denise's sincerity, only her judgment. "We can make this work. Just don't call Family Services again—not without talking to me first."

"You're right," she admitted. "It was a knee-jerk reaction, and I'm sorry. I was just so worried."

"I understand." He managed a courteous good-bye, pocketed his phone, then watched Carly chug down a glass of water. If she weren't Penny's nanny and an employee, he would have asked her out weeks ago. But there was also the matter of her faith and Bible Belt roots. She didn't need a skeptical divorced man whose life was a mess.

But looking at her now, he realized her life was a mess, too. Her eyes were dull and puffy, and somehow she seemed diminished. She didn't need Ryan's skepticism, but she *did* need to stop feeling guilty over Allison. It might linger forever the way Ryan's guilt lingered, but he couldn't leave her hurting like this.

She set the half-empty glass on the counter. "I'm glad that's over."

"Is it?"

"Of course. Louanne is gone."

"That's not what I meant." Without thinking, he picked up Lance. "Grrr, Miss Carly. Don't be sad!"

"But I am," she confessed to Lance.

"Dr. Ryan says you did everything right." Lance looked at Ryan, and they both nodded. Then Lance turned back to Carly. "Dr. Ryan is going to play with Penny so you can have a rest, but tonight he wants to have a little talk."

Carly gaped at Lance, then lifted her eyes to Ryan's face. The sparkle returned and was bright, maybe because of the sheen of tears. But just as quickly, she looked away. "No thank you, Lance."

"Aaargh," the lion said, pirate-like. "Dr. Ryan might have to kidnap you. If you don't do what he says, he'll make you walk the plank."

As he hoped, Carly smiled a little more. "I guess he's serious about this conversation."

"I am," Ryan said in his own voice. "I'll find you after Penny's bedtime."

She gave him a hopeless look and shrugged. Ryan took it as a challenge. If she needed to bare her soul even more, he'd listen. And if it was at all reasonable, he'd hire an investigator to find Allison.

25

The instant Ryan left the kitchen to be with Penny, Carly fetched her phone, raced out the front door, and walked a half mile to the narrow park that cut between Ryan's neighborhood and a ravine that carried runoff to the ocean. In the shade of a towering wall of eucalyptus trees, with the cough-drop scent filling her nose, she went to the playground, dropped down on a big-kid swing, and pulled her hair into a ragged ponytail. Then she called her dad.

"Hey there," he said. "How's my girl?"

"Awful."

"What happened?"

"Denise reported me for child endangerment because I took Penny to the beach." She told him everything—about the mustard mess, Ryan's defense of her, and Louanne's absolution. "But Daddy, it stirred up all the stuff about Allison. I just can't stand it!"

"What can't you stand?"

"Not knowing what happened to her! You know that."

When her father stayed silent, Carly knew what was coming and wished she hadn't called. He was going to challenge her to think, and she didn't want to think right now. If she thought too long or too hard, her feelings for Ryan would leak into her voice, and her father would show up on Ryan's doorstep with his shotgun. Not literally, but he'd want to meet the man who had stolen his daughter's heart.

Determined to keep the talk about Allison, Carly tossed a challenge back to him. "Go ahead. Say it."

"Say what?"

"You're going to tell me to stop beating myself up. You're going to say to put Allison in God's hands—like that's the easiest thing in the world. But it's not. I just can't do it. You know I've tried—"

"Maybe the answer isn't *trying.*"

"Then what is it?"

"The work is done, Carly Jo. *Trying* won't get you there. This is about trusting God."

"I know that." She knew everything about being a Christian because she'd been one her whole life. She pushed off the swing so hard it flew back, then forward, and whapped her in the rear end. What an awful day this had been! And now Ryan was acting like a pirate and caring about her, when she could hardly look at him without her heart leaping out of her chest.

"Carly Jo?"

"I'm here, Daddy."

"Maybe you should come home for a visit. I'm worried about you."

Aching to say yes, she inhaled sharply. Dust filled her nose, along with smog and the ocean air that smelled all wrong. If she went home for a visit, maybe she could forget her feelings for Ryan, or at least figure out how to control them. "I'd like that, Daddy. Maybe after the camping trip."

"Just keep it in mind, sweetheart."

"I will." She imagined lush grass, the smells, the booming thunder that gave the county its name. "So what's the weather like?"

"A storm's rolling in."

With her eyes closed, she listened while he described a sky full of gray and white clouds, some wispy and others heavy with rain. It was the exact picture she planned to paint on Penny's wall. A coincidence? Or was it God telling her He understood how she felt? Carly didn't know, but she felt a burning need to finish Penny's mural.

"Thanks for listening, Daddy. I have to go, but I'll call you tomorrow. I promise."

"You know I love you, Carly Jo." The sweetness of home thickened his voice. "If you'd care to call back tonight, you do that."

She pocketed the phone and walked back to Ryan's house, her fingers itching to pick up the paintbrush. Knowing the front door was locked, she went through the back gate. As she rounded the corner of the house, she heard loud splashing, Penny's high-pitched giggles, and Ryan roaring like a sea monster.

Don't stop. Don't look. He'd be shirtless, of course. Water would bead on his shoulders and chest. *His chest* . . . Was it hairy or smooth? Muscular, definitely.

"Hey, Carly!" he called from the shallow end. "I caught a mermaid. Come and see."

Penny shouted, "I can fly, too!"

Carly pasted a fake smile on her face and detoured to the pool. Ryan saw her, flashed a grin, and tossed Penny high into the air. Shrieking, she landed with a splash. Fresh droplets landed on Ryan's tanned shoulders, caught the sun, and sparkled like glitter.

His gaze locked with hers, but Penny popped up in front of him and tried to climb into his arms. "Again, Daddy! Do it again!"

Not *Dr. Tremaine*. Not *Dr. Daddy*. Just *Daddy*. Carly pressed her hand to her chest. With her eyes on Ryan, she treasured the surprise exploding on his face. He was focused on Penny now, his mouth open until his lips pulled into a smile that gleamed white in the sun. Intending to slip away, she headed for the slider.

"Carly?"

She turned and smiled. "I heard."

Penny clung to him like a monkey and patted his face for attention, but he kept his eyes on Carly. "Thank you," he called out to her.

"I didn't do anything. It's just . . . just love."

Afraid he'd see her heart in her eyes, she fled into the house and went straight to Penny's room to finish the mural. Someone, probably Ryan, had covered the cans to keep the paint from drying out. With clumsy fingers, Carly pried open the lid, dipped in the brush, and slashed a thick gray line across the base of the billowing clouds.

She painted a few more squiggly lines, traded the thick brush for a thin one, then added streaks of rain and a swirl of shimmering wind. Stepping back, she saw clouds melting into rain that would cleanse, refresh, and maybe heal her dry and thirsty heart. It was a meltdown, literally. Slumping to her knees, she gave in to tears and questions, a plea to be free of her guilt over Allison, and the strength to forget Ryan's perfect, not-too-hairy chest.

❦

Again, Daddy! Do it again!

Penny's words trumpeted through Ryan's mind for the rest of the afternoon and into the evening. Carly didn't come out of her room to fix dinner, so he tapped on her door. When she didn't answer, he opened it a crack and saw her curled on the bed under a fleece throw, sound asleep with her head on a pillow and her back to him. The day had drained her, but he hoped his plan to hire a private investigator would lift her spirits.

With Carly asleep and Kyle with Taylor, he took Penny and Eric to In-N-Out Burger, one of the few things remaining on the SOS list. Carly was still in hiding when they returned, so he put Penny to bed and headed to the old garage with the Impala to check the camping gear. He preferred hotels and good restaurants, but Eric's enthusiasm had them all fired up.

He opened the big garage door, flipped on the light, and backed the Impala into the driveway to make room for the gear he needed to pull down from the rafters. He was on his last trip down the ladder, shouldering a sleeping bag, when a shadow fell across the garage floor.

"Ryan?"

"Carly. Good." He took the last few rungs and tossed the sleeping bag onto the pile. "I was about to look for you."

"Here I am."

Her tone struck him as distant, even a little vague. She didn't sound like herself at all.

"Let me finish here, then we'll go to my office. There's something I want to show you."

She hesitated. "Could you just tell me?"

"I'd rather show you, but I need to hang the sleeping bags so they'll air out."

She glanced at the pile on the floor. "I'm kind of tired. Will you be much longer?"

A lame excuse, but he couldn't call her on it without revealing his earlier tap on her door. Rather than keep her, he spoke as he shook out a sleeping bag. "I was going to show you the Web site for a private investigator. A colleague of mine used this woman when his son ran away."

"An investigator? What for?"

"To find Allison."

He was halfway up the ladder when Carly's faint voice reached his ears. "You'd do that for me?"

"It's a long shot, but this woman specializes in missing kids." He hung the sleeping bag, straightened the edges, then peered down at her. "Her Web site gives her credentials, success stories, that sort of thing."

"It seems impossible," Carly said, more to herself than to him. "Allison's been missing almost two years. I check her social media all the time. I've left messages there."

"Any cell phone?"

"Disconnected." She leaned against the doorframe and crossed her arms. "She wasn't good with money. She'd give anyone who asked everything she had, not because she wanted to, but because she didn't understand and thought she had to do it."

He thought of Penny. "It's rough."

"Yes." Carly shivered a little. "It would take a miracle to find her."

From the top of the ladder, Ryan beamed a challenge at her. "You're the Christian. You believe in miracles, right?"

Startled, she glared back. "You're mocking me."

"Not at all." He indicated the sleeping bags still on the floor. "Would you hand one to me?"

"Sure."

She came forward and lifted it. He placed his hands near hers and took the bag. "I was trying to show respect for your values. So what do you say? Shall we go for it?"

"I can't afford an investigator."

"I can." Still on the ladder, he tilted his head down while she looked up. The fluorescent light washed the color from her cheeks and the life from her eyes. "Let me do this for you, Carly. We might find her. We might not. Either way, you can have the peace of knowing you did everything possible."

"It's kind of you. I don't know what to say."

"You don't have to say anything. Just e-mail her picture, anything you have that'll help the investigator. I'll call her tomorrow and forward whatever info you have."

"Thank you. You're a . . . a good friend."

After a quick nod, he hung the last sleeping bag and climbed down the ladder. There was so much more he wanted to say. *You're beautiful. I care about you. I love you.* But he didn't say any of those things. What did a man do when he fell for a woman with an outlook on life incompatible with his own? Tense, he folded the ladder and hung it on the wall. Carly waited on the driveway, her hands jammed in her back pockets as he drove the Impala back into the garage. He climbed out, slammed the door, and crossed to the wall to turn off the light.

"Ryan?"

"Yes?" He paused with his hand on the switch.

"I just want you to know. What you're doing for Allison is . . . it's special to me."

Silence wrapped around them and pulled tight, thickening with every breath. He turned off the light, left the garage, and closed the door with the keypad. As it rumbled shut, they walked side by side down the driveway.

"Oh!" Her flip-flop caught, and she stumbled. Ryan caught her elbow and pulled her upright, turning her slightly to counter the fall. She faced him, maybe to say thank you, but nothing came out of her slightly parted lips. No words. No sound. Only the soft rasp of her breath mingling with his.

The moon beamed down through the branches, and a breeze stirred through the leaves, rustling them like the scrape of silk. She was steady on her feet now. He had no reason to hold her and every reason to let go, but she was female, soft, and beautiful. Kissing her was a terrible idea . . . a dangerous one.

Pull back, he told himself. *Let her go*. If they kissed, they couldn't go back to being just friends. He'd never forget it, wouldn't want to forget it. And neither would she. Ryan was a confident man, and that included confidence in his ability to kiss a woman senseless.

Their breathing synchronized. One breath, two breaths.

Her lips parted.

So did his.

One kiss . . . one taste of her lips. One moment of comfort for Carly, who was hurting and always so generous to others. For once, Ryan wanted to be the giver. She needed a strong shoulder, a man to hold her, a moment of something sweet and good.

He leaned forward an inch.

So did she.

He cupped the back of her head with his hand, smelled her clean hair, and tangled his fingers in it. And then it struck him . . . *tangled*. If he kissed her, their lives would be tangled together in an all new way—a way that could cost Penny her nanny, Ryan a true friend, and Carly—he didn't know what it would cost her. She wasn't like the women he used to date. Those women were satisfied with a "for now" relationship. Carly wanted forever.

If he kissed her, he'd hurt her.

He couldn't take that chance.

Jaw tight, he drew her head down to his shoulder and held it there. Her breath raced along his neck and down his throat, a gust that told him she'd been holding it. She sagged a bit, then her fingers let go of his shirt and slid off his shoulder blades. Still fighting the desire to taste her lips, he planted a kiss on her temple, set her upright, and took a big step back. With her face in shadows, he cleared his throat. "Are you all right?"

"I-I'm fine," she murmured.

They took a few steps together, but the almost-kiss haunted them with a silent demand to be taken and enjoyed. Those feelings needed to be pulled out by the roots, so he stopped Carly at the gate. "We both felt something."

She inhaled softly. "Yes."

"It was just nature. Let's forget it."

"Of course," she said, a little breathy. "Like I said before, it's a ridiculous idea."

"Definitely," he agreed.

"Absolutely," she replied.

Ryan opened the gate, and Carly went ahead of him, leaving him to ponder the almost-kiss that wasn't ridiculous at all. Ryan had a problem and he knew it. *They* had a problem. He didn't know how they were going to fix it, and for once in his life he felt outmatched, because all the self-control in the world couldn't stop his heart from loving her.

~❧~

Carly dropped down onto her bed, rolled to her side, and buried her face in the pillow with the hope of clearing her mind, but nothing could wipe away the sensation of Ryan's hand in her hair, his breath caressing her cheek, that smoky look in his eyes as he leveled his face over hers. If he'd kissed her, she would have kissed him back.

But he didn't do it. Instead he'd written off the almost-kiss as just nature, when to Carly it would have been special and forever.

He didn't understand her. And he never would . . . unless he changed or she did. Carly would never go against her most basic beliefs, but was there room for compromise? If she demanded that Ryan share her faith before they moved to the next step, did it mean she was close minded, even self-righteous? She didn't know what to think at the moment; she only knew she loved him and wanted to make a life with him.

But what kind of life?

The pool pump hummed, and she wondered if Ryan was sneaking a cigarette at the back fence. Curling into a ball, she begged God to change her feelings or to change Ryan, because she couldn't bear the pain of loving a man who didn't know how to love her back.

26

As promised, Ryan hired Brie McCarty to search for Allison. A retired LAPD detective in the Juvenile division, Brie was an expert in runaways and sex trafficking. She went to work immediately. Over the next two weeks, she updated Carly and Ryan with several e-mails, though the news was generally disappointing.

Ryan and Eric made plans for Anacapa. It was Monday now, and tomorrow they'd head out on the trip. Seated at the desk in his office, Ryan started up the laptop, intending to pay a few bills. In a little while, Denise would pick up Penny, and tomorrow he, Carly, and five teenagers would take the Cal-Island charter boat to Anacapa for a one-night stay.

Everyone was excited, but Ryan was in a quandary. He and Carly bantered when the kids were around, but otherwise they avoided each other. In spite of his efforts to be friendly in a normal sort of way, the feelings between them were as strong as ever. Someone had to compromise, and he didn't want that person to be Carly. Between her naïve faith and his realism, he preferred the effects of her faith, even if he didn't share it. He was willing to accept their differences, even change for her, but he couldn't make himself believe in God.

While the computer started, he glanced around the office. His gaze went to his mother's Bible, so he picked it up, carried it to his desk, and skimmed through the dog-eared pages like he'd done a month or so ago.

Nothing caught his eye until he saw a note in his mother's handwriting. A little melancholy, he read his name written in the margin and surrounded by four dates—his thirtieth birthday, the day of his divorce, the day he told his mother about Penny, and a date that shamed him, because it was *her* birthday, and he'd forgotten it. When he sent flowers a week later, she told him they were even more special because they made her birthday last another week.

That was his mom. Always thinking of others. Forgiving them. Loving people even when they let her down. Wishing he could fix that mistake and everything else, Ryan read the verse underlined in purple ink. *"Let us therefore come boldly unto the throne of grace, that we may obtain mercy, and find grace to help in time of need."*

There was no way he could go boldly to a throne of grace, or a king he didn't understand. When Ryan messed up, he went to the individuals he hurt and tried to make things right. He wasn't a Christian, but he was a moral person and took responsibility. When it came to behavior, he and Carly were very much alike. He could easily live with their differences. Why not build a life on what they had in common?

A knock on the doorjamb pulled his gaze upward, and he saw Carly looking shell-shocked. Forgetting the Bible, he launched to his feet. "What's the matter?"

"I can't believe this." She held up her phone as if she'd never seen it before. "I just talked to Allison's great-aunt. Her name is Velma. She lives in Cumberland, and Allison is with her."

Ryan gave a silent salute to Brie McCarty. "So she's safe."

"Yes."

He came around the desk, gave Carly a hug, then pointed at the loveseat. She dropped down on the thick cushion and so did he. Their knees bumped, touched again, and this time stayed close. "Tell me everything," he said.

"Brie sent an e-mail last night. It said she had news and wanted to talk. We set a time for later today. But then twenty minutes ago, my phone rang. I saw the Kentucky area code, and would you believe I almost didn't answer? I figured it was a wrong number."

"But it wasn't."

"No, and the news couldn't have been better. Allison is living with Velma."

"That's great. Did you get to talk to her?"

"Not yet. She's away at a church camp for kids with special needs. She's a counselor for girls Penny's age. Adults oversee everything, but what counts is that she's there and being useful. Velma took my number, which Allison had lost. And now I have Velma's number." Carly clutched at his hand and squeezed. "I can't thank you enough—"

"You just did." He turned his palm to match hers and held tight.

Their breathing synchronized, and they turned their heads at the same time. The moment called for a celebration, so he brushed his lips against her cheek. Then, being the man he needed to be, he went back to his desk but stayed on his feet.

Carly gazed at him, adoration in her eyes and her face bright with the joy of finding Allison, or maybe from that brush of his lips on her cheek. When he remained silent, she pushed off the loveseat. "I better get back to the laundry. I just wanted to share the good news."

She took a step toward the door but stopped to look at the floor-to-ceiling bookshelves. The office was Ryan's private domain, even more private than his bedroom, because she did laundry and put his socks in his drawers. Carly didn't come in here at all.

She tilted her head like a curious bird. "You have more books than the Boomer County library."

"Most of them were my father's."

She ran her fingers down the spines of the science and history books, then the biographies and accounts of true crime, each a testament to his father's fascination with the human mind. After browsing Ryan's paperbacks—mostly adventure stories and mysteries with dark covers—her gaze dipped to the bottom shelf where he kept his mother's books. A gap revealed the spot reserved for the Bible now open on his desk. Ryan hurriedly closed it and moved to slide it under the morning paper, but before he finished, Carly turned.

Her gaze flicked to his face, her expression unchanged. If she spotted the Bible, she chose not to mention it. Instead, she turned to the shelves. "Your parents had very different tastes."

"That's right."

"I'm curious about something."

Aside from the news about Allison, it was the first time in days she'd started a conversation. Pleased, he leaned his hips on the edge of the desk. "Ask away."

"Did your father share your mother's faith?"

"Not at all."

"Did they get along?"

It was a nosy question—unless she was asking Ryan if he thought *they* could get along. He hoped so, because he very much wanted to find that middle ground. "My father called himself an agnostic. He was brilliant, and he let everyone know it. My mother's religious streak embarrassed him."

"Oh." She nibbled her lip. "That's too bad."

"It doesn't have to be that way. Two people can have different opinions and still respect each other, don't you think?"

"Of course. It's just . . ." She fluttered her hand. "Never mind. It's none of my business."

"Tell me."

She glanced back at the upper shelves, the ones with the medical books. "I have to wonder if respect is enough, or if it *would* have been enough for them . . . in marriage."

Her stammering charmed him. It also told him she was thinking the same way he was. They just had to find a middle ground. "Respect is a good place to start." They were alone. The office was private. Should he tell her he was reading the Bible out of respect for her? He was considering it when the doorbell rang.

"That must be Denise." Carly hurried down the hall.

Ryan followed in her wake, but his mind stayed in the study where books with conflicting ideas sat on different shelves but in the same room. From his perspective the differences between Carly and himself were merely philosophical. As far as everyday life, they could do things her way. So what did that mean?

Marriage, definitely.

Church on Sundays? Sure, why not?

Children? He hoped so, and he had no qualms about good-night prayers and Bible stories.

An idea formed in his mind, one that skipped dating and went straight to wedding rings. With Carly, there could be no in-between, because their relationship affected his entire family. It was all or nothing. And Ryan wanted it all. The sooner they got married, the better. But some conventions had to be observed, like meeting her father. As a father himself, Ryan knew what *he'd* think of a man proposing to his daughter without the guts to introduce himself first. He'd think that man was rude or a coward.

Ryan was neither. As soon as he finished with Denise, he'd call Reverend Paul Mason and invite him to surprise Carly with a visit. Ryan hoped the man wouldn't be overwhelmed by either Los Angeles or Ryan's sophisticated lifestyle. Los Angeles was a big change from Boomer County, especially for a small-town preacher.

He also hoped they could agree on how to make Carly happy,

because mentally, Ryan added a final item to his SOS list. It was just two words: *Marry Carly.*

                                                      ∽

Carly handed Penny off to Denise with a kiss and a hug. Ryan walked them to the car, and she fled to the laundry room. There were shirts to hang or they'd wrinkle, but mostly she needed to breathe without smelling Ryan's tangy aftershave or thinking about that brush of his lips on her cheek.

Or that open book on his desk, the one he had tried to hide.

Just before he shoved it out of sight, she had noticed the hole on the shelf between *Redeeming Love* and *My Utmost for His Highest,* two of her personal favorites. Intending to ask him about it, she turned just in time to see him slide a thick book under the morning paper. It had to be his mother's Bible.

With her stomach churning, she reached into the spinning clothes dryer, snatched one of Ryan's shirts, and draped it on a blue plastic hanger. He'd picked up the Bible for a reason—maybe because of his feelings for her. She straightened the shirt with trembling fingers, smoothed the sleeves, and wrestled with the question that had plagued her since that almost-kiss. Was respect for her faith enough? She longed to say yes, but doubt squirmed through her. Maybe she'd call her father for advice. But what would she say? *"Daddy, I'm in love with Ryan. He doesn't believe in God, but he loves me and respects my faith. Surely that's enough."*

With another of Ryan's shirts hot in her hand, her mind leapt to a future where she went to church alone, worshiped alone, then tucked their children into bed with a prayer their father didn't understand.

"Carly?" It was Eric.

"What's up?"

"I'm packing, and I can't find the T-shirt my dad bought at the museum."

She reached in the dryer, found the shirt with the Science Center logo, and handed it to him. He wore it constantly. "This one?"

"That's it!" He took it and left but turned at the door. "Thanks for doing laundry . . . and everything else, like driving me around."

"It's my . . ." *job.* But she couldn't say that and didn't want to say it. Working for the Tremaines was more than a job. She loved them, though she knew better than to say *that* to a thirteen-year-old boy. "I'm happy to be here."

"Cool, 'cause I hope you stay a long time."

He darted back down the hall, leaving Carly with the scent of dryer sheets in her nose and a hole in her heart. She loved this family. *Loved them all.* She loved them too much to ever leave, even if it meant visiting Kentucky instead of living there permanently. That's what women did for love. Men too, sometimes. Geography was the least of her worries. The real differences between herself and Ryan were cosmic and personal.

Gloom as thick as dryer lint muddled her thoughts. Fighting it, she hung up Ryan's navy polo shirt, then buttoned the collar so it would hang straight, because that's what he liked. It annoyed her to do it, but it was a matter of respecting her boss's wishes.

Marriage, too, required compromise. But what if she married Ryan and they drifted further apart? If he respected her faith, she'd be obligated to accept his lack of it. But how could she? The path he chose would set the compass for his immortal soul. How could she possibly hold her tongue when the stakes were so high?

With her heart aching, she finished hanging up the shirts, closed the dryer, and went to her room to beg God for wisdom.

27

When the charter boat left the Ventura marina, the seven members of the Tremaine party were its only passengers. Ten miles away, Anacapa Island rose jaggedly from the blue-gray water, a chain of three islets with steep cliffs and jagged faces. The sky burned its brightest blue, and the salty air sparkled with the promise of adventure.

It was a glorious day, but Carly found it difficult to share the enthusiasm spilling off Ryan and the kids. Seated alone in the stern of the boat, on a red cushion that squeaked when she moved, she took in the tableau on the bow. Kyle and Taylor stood on one side, their shoulders touching as they stared across the water. Taylor's older sister, Nicole, stood next to her. Eric, Nathan, and Ryan were lined up on the other side of the bow.

Ryan pointed at something in the distance. Eric jabbed Nathan in the ribs, then called to Kyle and the girls. The boat engine quieted to a burble, and Ryan faced her, his sunglasses in place.

"Carly!" He waved her forward. "You have to see this."

Balancing against the rock of the boat, she made her way forward, peered into the distance, and saw countless flashes of silver arching out of the water. Dolphins! They were directly in front of the boat, leaping and shining and so beautiful she caught her breath.

The captain's voice crackled over the PA. "This doesn't happen every day, folks. We've encountered a pod of dolphins, one of the largest I've ever seen. We're going to stick around and enjoy it."

Carly hurried along the side of the cabin. Ryan walked back to meet her, gripped her hand before she could dodge, and together they moved to the front. "This is incredible," he said just to her. The boat dipped and threw her off balance. Still holding his hand, she leveraged against the strength of his forearm, acutely aware of both the need to let go and the desire to hold on.

When Eric stepped closer to Nathan for a better view, Ryan guided Carly to the spot at the tip of the bow. Just twenty feet away, a single dolphin broke through the water in a perfect arc, its gray body glistening in the sun. Another dolphin leapt into the air, then another. There were dolphins as far as she could see, swimming and leaping in unison.

The captain cut the engine completely, plunging them into silence, punctuated by the ripple of the dolphin ballet. *Glory to God!* It was all Carly could think. Who could doubt the existence of a creator at the sight of such perfection?

The captain, a man in his forties, called down from the cockpit. "I'm in no hurry, folks. How about you?"

Ryan answered back. "No hurry at all."

"Anyone want binoculars?" The captain dangled a pair down to them.

Eric tore his eyes off the dolphins just long enough to take the lenses and call out, "Thanks!"

Kyle, Taylor, and Nicole were all on their toes, straining to catch every leap and effortless splash. Ryan laid his hand on the small of Carly's back and smiled at her. He was usually clean shaven, obsessively so, but three days ago he'd announced at dinner he was on vacation and not shaving. The bristle made him rugged and rebellious, a bit of a rogue, and the pirate who had almost kissed her. When he beamed a smile just for her, she could barely breathe. Their eyes locked until she blinked, then they both turned back to the dolphins shooting past the boat.

They watched in silence until Ryan murmured, "It's astonishing, isn't it? They're in complete sync with each other."

"What do you mean?"

"They're individual creatures with differences we can't see. But they're going in the same direction. In the ways that count most, they're the same—like you and me."

Carly longed to agree with him, but she and Ryan weren't dolphins driven by instinct. They were human beings capable of moral choices, mistakes, and powerful emotions like the ones coursing through her now. Determined to hide that painful brew, she shielded her eyes and watched the last of the dolphins swim by.

"What do you see in all this?" he asked her.

"I see God's handiwork."

"Anything else?"

He wanted something from her, but what? Carly didn't know, but when a man began to search for God, the majesty of creation was a good place to start, especially on a day as blessed as this one. Her heart gave a little leap. "I see beauty. And intelligence. Even love, because the dolphins stick together through thick and thin."

"We see the same things. We just start in different places."

"I suppose we do." But that starting place mattered.

Before she could explain, the captain revved the engine and swung the bow toward Anacapa. Gravity pushed her against Ryan's side. He steadied her with an arm around her shoulder, held her close for a stolen moment, then released her and joined Eric and Nathan.

Eric stared at the last of the dolphins through the binoculars, savoring every minute.

"That was remarkable," Ryan said to him.

"Yeah." Eric lowered the lenses. "I've read a lot about dolphins, but to see them in the wild . . . wow."

"We're just getting started." Ryan pointed to the chain of islets ahead of them. "Keep your eyes open for sea lions. They hang out on the rocks."

Eric started to raise the binoculars but stopped. "Hey, Carly. Would you like to look?"

She preferred watching Eric enjoy himself, but the proud look on Ryan's face reminded her this trip was about boys becoming men, Eric getting center stage, and Ryan finishing his SOS list.

"Thanks," she said, reaching for them.

With the lenses pressed to her eyes, she studied the chain of giant rocks, carved by eons of waves, wind, and bad weather. The eastern islet, where they would camp, was flat on top and mostly brown from the dry summer. A lighthouse jutted up from the center of it, and she spotted a couple of white buildings used by the park ranger.

The west and center islands were jagged, accessible only by boat, and eerily gothic in their isolation. The sight of them depressed her, because she felt a lot like one of the rocks, a part of something but not quite connected. The weight of the binoculars tugged her hands downward, but she kept her bare eyes on Anacapa. With her face to the wind, she silently begged God to show her how to love Ryan like He did.

∽

Ryan was worried about Carly. She wasn't herself, a surprise considering Brie had found Allison and how well the kids were getting along. He expected her to rejoice and celebrate, even praise God, but her occasional smiles didn't reach her eyes.

Maybe that upcoming visit from her father would chase away the gloom. Paul Mason had grunted a lot when Ryan spoke to him yesterday, but he didn't seem surprised by the call. Either he was good at masking his reactions, or he wasn't very articulate.

Either way, he told Ryan he would do some planning and get back to him with dates.

At Ryan's request, they agreed to wait to share the news with Carly. If Ryan told her now, the call would raise the question "why," and he wanted to romance her a little before he proposed to her. The island was the perfect spot for a walk at sunset, maybe that first kiss. Or maybe not. He needed to set high standards for his sons, and that meant holding himself back.

Sighing, he dug his hands in his pockets and peered into the rectangular cove where the boat would dock. The captain slowed the engine to a chug, steered past the kelp beds, and navigated between the thirty-foot sheer rock walls. The cove was dark and chilly, silent, and preternatural in its mood.

Carly looked up at the patch of sky and shivered. "I'll be glad to get back in the sun."

"Me too," Taylor said.

Ryan couldn't put his arm around her without raising eyebrows, so he settled for his second choice. "I'll get your hoodie from the cabin."

"I'll do it." Before he could protest, she slipped away.

The captain backed the boat against the dock. A worker from the charter company greeted them and unloaded the gear that included two tents, a camp stove, a cooler, sleeping bags, duffels, food, and water—all for just one night, and it had to be carried up the hundred seventy-eight stairs zigzagging across the face of a cliff.

As much as he wanted to focus on Carly, he and his sons had a job to do. "Okay, guys. Let's get this stuff up the stairs."

Kyle lifted the ice chest, then told Taylor to put her duffel on top. She insisted she could carry it herself, along with two sleeping bags. Nicole picked up her things; Eric and Nathan grabbed the tents; and Ryan took the two five-gallon water jugs. Carly did her part with her duffel and a sleeping bag, but several items remained to be carried up the stairs.

"Looks like two trips," Ryan said. "Ladies, why don't you wait here?" The females didn't need to be coddled, but Ryan wanted to give his sons a lesson in gallantry.

Carly must have understood, because she made a show of looking up at the stairs as if they were Mt. Everest. "That sounds good to me."

"Not to me!" Taylor lifted the two sleeping bags like dumbbells. Before Kyle could say anything, she sprinted for the stairs. He stumbled after her with the clunky ice chest, and Nicole followed them. Eric and Nathan passed the others at full speed.

With a shake of his head, Ryan turned to Carly. "At that pace, they'll be winded halfway up."

"They're enjoying this," she said, smiling a little.

"How about you?"

"I'm good."

"Are you sure?" He set the water jugs down with a thunk. "You're kind of quiet."

"I'm all right. I just need to get my land legs back."

He'd given her a motion sickness patch, but they didn't work for everyone. "How's your stomach?"

"No problem at all." To prove it, she gave him a big thumbs-up. "Go on now. Be with your sons. This is the last thing on the SOS list."

Not quite. But the last item—*Marry Carly*—had to wait until he met her father. If Ryan was going to live Carly's way, he wanted to start off on the right foot. Leaving her on the dock bothered him, but he needed to set up the campsite. "Are you sure you're okay here?"

"Positive."

Eric's voice shot down from the middle of the staircase. "Hey, Dad. You better hurry. The last one up the stairs is the loser!"

Looking up at Eric, Carly shaded her eyes with her hand in a salute of sorts. "Y'all have come a long way."

The "y'all" told him she was tense, maybe as concerned as he was for their future. If she married him, she'd be leaving her home and family. There was always Skype and air travel, but it wasn't the same as sharing a meal now and then, or taking a loved one to a doctor's appointment. In one of life's ironies, joining his family would take away her own. He wanted her to know he understood. "You've made a huge difference here, Carly Jo."

She tipped her face up to his. "You've never called me that."

"There's a first time for everything." A first kiss . . . a first date. And for Carly, a first night with her husband. He loved her for her goodness and strength, even her faith, and he wanted her to know. Maybe he'd kiss her, just a peck. But he didn't want a peck. He wanted the kiss to be special. For that, he was willing to wait.

He picked up the water jugs and adjusted his grip. "I'll be back for the rest."

"Don't rush." Her eyes twinkled, but just a bit. "I'll stand guard against the pirates."

Ryan smiled at the joke, then climbed the first flight of stairs. When he reached the landing, he stopped and gazed down at Carly waiting on the dock. The only pirate she needed to worry about was him, and he had every intention of taking her captive for the rest of their earthly lives.

～

As soon as the campsite was set up, the group hustled down to the cove for snorkeling. Kyle and Taylor paired up, and Ryan joined Eric and Nathan. That left Carly to swim with Nicole. They enjoyed seeing the orange Garibaldi and smaller fish, but the biggest thrill was a sea lion circling through the cove. As tame as Anacapa was compared to the big blue Pacific, it was still beautiful and wild.

Carly and Nicole were the first to climb out of the water. Wrapped in beach towels, they climbed the stairs to the campground, put on shorts and shirts, and headed for the hiking trail that made a crooked figure eight around the island. They laughed at the clumsy sea lions hauling themselves out of the water at Pinnipped Point, then moved on to Inspirational Point to the west.

The lookout faced the two other islets that made up the official island. Jagged with sharp ridges and pitted by wind, they were uninhabitable. The only life was a thin coat of lime green moss.

Nicole took a deep breath. "This really is like stepping back in time. No phones. No Internet. It's a nice break, but I hate feeling cut off."

"I don't mind it." Carly enjoyed the quiet. "It reminds me of home in a way."

"You're not from L.A., are you?"

"No." And she never would be. "I'm from Boomer County in Kentucky. It's mostly farmland."

"Do you miss it?" Nicole's tone hinted at more than idle curiosity, and Carly wondered if she was asking for a reason. During the hike, they had traded stories and tidbits about their lives. Nicole was a junior at UCLA, a music major, and hoping to earn a masters' at Juilliard in New York. If her dream came true, her future would take her far from home.

"I miss Kentucky a lot," she admitted to Nicole. "I miss my dad, of course. And my sister and her kids. My brother, too, though he's in the National Guard and deployed right now."

"Are you going back when you finish school?"

"That was the plan." *Was.* She should have said *is.*

"So you don't know?"

"It's complicated." She sounded like Ryan back at the Animal Factory.

"I know what you mean," Nicole replied. "I'm asking because I'm worried about moving to New York someday. I have a boyfriend. His name's Justin, and it's serious. But he's from Houston. That's where his mother is, and here I am in California and planning to move to New York. How does a woman juggle it all?"

"I don't know." Carly wiped a strand of hair away from her cheek. "My dad's a preacher. He'd say to pray about it."

"I do. All the time." Nicole took a long drink of water, lowered the bottle, and sighed. "I can't imagine living away from my parents, but I love Justin with everything in me. He feels the same way, but he's applying to law schools all over the country. I've worked hard on my music. I can't just give it up, but . . ." She shook her head. "I want to be with Justin, too."

Carly knew the feeling.

"And there's more." Nicole crushed the water bottle with one hand. "We want to get married, but when? At this rate, I'll be thirty before we even think about having kids. It's just too long to wait."

"I'm twenty-eight," Carly admitted. "The clock's ticking for me, too."

"Exactly! And what do I do about my parents when they get old and need help? My grandmother broke her ankle two months ago, and it's not healing right. My mom visits her every single day."

Carly offered a silent prayer of thanks for her sister who lived a mile from their dad and had no plans to move.

Nicole turned to her. "I just don't know what to do."

The wind tugged harder at Carly's hair. Messy and tangled from the swim, it was almost dry, thanks to the breeze and the sun. Her gaze shifted to the islets. Eons ago, the island had been a single entity, but water and time had broken it into pieces and given each chunk its own distinct shoreline. The island had changed.

People changed, too.

They left home, married, and had children of their own. It was nature at work. And God, too. A pelican soared past the cliff, and she followed it with her eyes. Somewhere it had a home for itself, maybe a nest full of chicks. Carly wanted that for herself—enough to follow Ryan to the ends of the earth. But pelicans mated with pelicans, not eagles.

Nicole, too, watched the pelican. Then she turned to the mainland dulled by the brown haze. "We're so close, but so far away."

"Exactly."

Carly stepped back on the main trail. So did Nicole, and together they walked back to the campground, each wrestling with her dreams.

28

"This is the best day of my life," Eric said as he chewed a bite of his fourth hot dog.

Ryan thought so, too. They were all seated around a picnic table covered with a red checked cloth, eating hot dogs and chips and reliving a day full of snorkeling, exotic wildlife, and magnificent views. A bonfire would have been nice, but open fires weren't allowed on the island. Not that it mattered. The day had been a resounding success for everyone, though Ryan was still worried about Carly.

During dinner she'd been surprisingly quiet. The lively woman who'd sprinkled pepper all over her food was nowhere in sight.

Kyle helped himself to more chips, passed the bag to Taylor, and squirted mustard on a bun. "I'm with Eric. This has been great."

"I think so, too," Taylor said.

"So do I," Nicole added. "I'll never forget the dolphins."

While the kids bantered about everything from sea lions to college to why ketchup didn't belong on a hot dog, Ryan shot looks at Carly. Not once did she look directly at him. Instead, she busied herself with gathering trash and wiping off mustard bottles. Ryan watched her from the corner of his eye until Eric pushed his paper plate away. "Dad?"

"Yes?"

"Snorkeling is fun, but I want to see even more. Can I take scuba lessons?"

What a difference from eight weeks ago, when he refused to leave his room. Ryan didn't want to spoil his kids by giving them stuff they didn't earn, but he wanted to encourage Eric. "Let's see what your mom says."

Ryan already knew Heather would love the idea. They e-mailed often about the boys, and she'd been delighted with Eric's interest in the ocean—everything except going down in a shark cage. She'd been generous to Ryan with praise—her prayers, too, judging by the Bible verse in her sig line, something about God making all things new. After today, Ryan could almost believe it was true.

He tried again to share a look with Carly, but she was opening a box of graham crackers.

"Who wants s'mores?" she asked without looking up.

A chorus of "me's" filled the air, and Ryan fired up the stove again. Carly laid out the crackers and Hershey bars while he handed out skewers and the kids passed the bag of marshmallows. A few minutes later, they were all eating the gooey treats. Ryan was on his feet by the stove, Carly was putting away the food, and the kids were scattered around the campsite with their mouths full.

Eric broke the silence with a smack of his lips. "I kind of miss Penny."

"Me too," Kyle added.

"So do I," Ryan said wistfully.

Finally, Carly looked at him and smiled. Her cheeks glowed with too much sun, and her hair was a tangled gold mess. The look they traded said everything that needed to be said, but it asked a question, too. *Where do we go from here?* She turned away first, leaving him to wish they were alone instead of surrounded by teenagers.

"Let's clean up," he said.

Everyone pitched in, and they were done in five minutes. Kyle and Eric started a play-boxing match, Taylor and Nicole braved a trip to the outhouses, and Nathan ducked into the tent to put on a sweatshirt.

Carly jammed her hands in her hoodie pockets. "I think I'll take a walk."

"Where to?" he asked.

"Cathedral Cove. It's not far."

Ryan almost invited himself along, but Kyle and Eric had stopped boxing and were watching him. He settled for handing her a flashlight. "Be careful. It gets dark fast."

"Thanks." She took the light and walked down the trail, her shoulders square and that long hair fluttering in the salt-scented breeze.

Ryan watched her until the path curved out of sight; then he turned back to Kyle and Eric. The boys traded a look. "What is it?" he asked.

"It's Carly," Kyle said. "She seems kind of sad."

"You think so?"

"I do," Eric answered.

Kyle stood a little straighter. "Maybe you should go with her. You know, talk to her or something."

"Yeah, Dad," Eric added. "Talk to her."

Ryan glanced from one boy to the other. "So she seems sad to you?"

"Kind of," Kyle answered, less certain now.

Eric nodded with confidence. "I think she feels left out." This, from the boy so often caught in the middle and sometimes overlooked. "I like her a lot, Dad. Mom will always be, you know, Mom. But Carly's like an aunt—the fun kind."

Kyle wrinkled his brow a second time. "I don't know how to say this exactly, but if you wanted to ask her out, we'd be cool with that."

"Super cool," Eric added.

"Yeah." As usual, Kyle snagged the last word.

With his sons standing shoulder to shoulder, Ryan saw the wise men they were destined to become. "So you like her?" he said.

"A lot," they both said.

"I like her, too," he told them. "And you're right. She's not acting like herself. Can you two hold down the fort while I check on her?"

The boys nodded, but Ryan hesitated until he spotted Nicole and Taylor ambling toward the campsite. With all five kids safe and secure, he signaled the boys with a wave. "We'll be back in a while." There it was again. *We.* And this time it sounded exactly right.

A short walk took him to Cathedral Cove and a lookout that faced north. The sun, low on the horizon, tinted the sky with shades of orange, and a smattering of city lights dotted the shoreline with silvery specks. Distant whitecaps glistened with an energy of their own, but the most beautiful sight of all was Carly, standing with her toes against a railroad tie marking the edge of the lookout. The sunset lit up her hair, but what struck him most was the determined lift of her chin.

She didn't hear him approach. Maybe the waves drowned out his footsteps, or maybe she was lost in the beauty, or praying. He paused to watch, drinking in the moment, until her shoulders slumped and she crumpled down on a flat wood bench.

❧

What a beautiful, awful day this had been. Alone for the first time, Carly gave in to tears streaked with both joy and misery. Overcome, she hunched forward and buried her face in her hands.

A strong male hand clamped down on her shoulder. She lifted her face, met Ryan's gaze, and choked off a sob. There was no place to hide, no way to deny the truth behind her tears. Dropping down next to her, he laced their fingers into a single fist and raised it off her lap. Neither of them spoke, except for squeezing their hands tighter, until Ryan murmured in a low drawl, "We have a problem, don't we?"

"No, we're fine," she choked out. They had to be fine for the sake of the kids. "I'm just a little emotional."

He quirked a brow. "A little?"

"A lot. But I'm all right."

"Ah, Carly—"

"What is it?"

"I feel it, too." He cupped her jaw and stared into her watery eyes. They were a breath apart, an inch from the kiss they both had denied for weeks. But instead of taking her breath away with that first kiss, he squeezed her heart with words. "I love you."

Orange light burned all around him. In the cove below, a wave slapped against the rocks. "I love you," he repeated in an even huskier tone. "I think you feel the same way."

"I do," she admitted.

"Say it."

"I love you," she said in a full voice.

He kissed her then, and all she could feel was the burning imprint of his mouth, the warmth of his hand on her cheek, the heat of his body chasing away everything except hope. There was nothing tentative between them, no shy questions waiting for answers, no hesitation whatsoever. Every nerve in her body, every cell, was attuned to how good and right it felt to be in Ryan's arms.

She gave herself willingly, savored the heat, the light, the love, and surrendered to the tender glory of a kiss long denied. Every worry sank to the bottom of her mind. But then a gull squawked a warning, and she heard the slosh of waves eating away at the island. Quaking inside, she pulled back. "Ryan, I-I don't know what to do. Everything is so—"

"Complicated."

"Yes." She raised her hand to his jaw, trailed her fingers down the bristle, aware of every spike and prickle, both the ones on his jaw and the ones in her soul. "We're just so different."

"That's true," he said. "But we're also a lot alike."

"Like the dolphins."

"Yes. They live a full, beautiful life. So can we."

"How?"

"The way I see it, there's just one answer." He reached across her body, gripped her left hand, and stroked her ring finger. Then he looked into her eyes, took a breath, and dropped down to one knee. "I love you, Carly. Apart from the miracle you worked with the kids, you've worked a miracle in me, too. I see the world differently because of you. You've given me a new life, hope for the future—"

"Ryan, stop."

"Marry me, Carly. Be my wife."

Tears flooded her eyes. Choking on a sob, she covered her mouth with one hand and shook her head.

"I know I'm asking a lot of you." He lifted her free hand from her lap. "We'd have to live in Los Angeles, but you could finish school. Kentucky's just a flight away. We could go for Christmases. You could visit anytime you wanted."

Every word pounded another nail, because geography was the least of their problems.

Undeterred, he squeezed her fingers. "Say yes. It's the only way."

She tried to say something, anything to stop the craziness, but her tongue stuck to the roof of her mouth. Needing a glimpse of God, she focused on the dying sun shooting gold beams across the horizon. The churning waves filled her ears with the roar and hush of life. Beauty surrounded her, but so did the coming darkness.

Ryan remained on one knee. In the distance a sea lion barked a hoarse, lonely cry. The breeze riffled through his dark hair. When she didn't reply, he hauled himself up to his full height and put his hands on his hips. "It looks like I have some persuading to do."

"It's not that simple."

"I think it is."

Annoyed with his height and his certainty, she leaped to her feet and took three steps before pivoting to face him. "I don't take marriage lightly."

"Neither do I."

"I know." He worked hard to show his love, both to her and to the kids. "It's just that you and I don't see things the same way."

"What things?"

"Almost everything!" She threw up her hands in frustration. "A man and woman need a common foundation. They need to work together to build a future, to be a family, even to decide on who takes out the trash. I'm not sure we have that."

"I am."

She longed to believe him but couldn't stop thinking about the ocean eating away the island. "Convince me," she pleaded with him. "How can this work?"

He jammed his hands in the pockets of his Levis and rocked back on his heels. "I've given this a lot of thought. We already live in the same house, and we've dealt with some tough problems. We know each other better than a lot of couples do. But most important, I love you, Carly. I'd take a bullet for you, and I think you'd do the same for me. I know you'd do it for the kids, because that's who you are."

"I would," she admitted.

He paused. "Your turn. Tell me what's missing."

If she spoke from her heart, would he look down on her? Call her closed-minded? Even mock her for believing in a God he put in the same category as the tooth fairy? She thought of his soul, and she knew unequivocally that she had to test his respect by speaking from her heart, as foolish as she might sound.

"You don't share my faith," she said simply. "It's important to me."

"I know that."

"It defines me."

"And I love you for it." He took a step closer, just one. When she stiffened, he remained three feet away. "I don't believe in God like you do. That's true. But I respect your choices. You know that."

"I do, but those differences matter." The bluegrass twang came out in full force.

He stood taller, arms folded across his chest. "Name them."

"Jesus. Forgiveness. Grace."

Silent, he lifted a brow and waited.

"That's it," she said.

"Is that all?" He sounded amused, even superior.

"It's everything." Peace wafted over her. "It's because of what Jesus did on the cross that I am who I am. We love, because He first loved us. If you don't know what that means, you don't know me."

"But I do know you." He took another step. "You're the most beautiful, generous, caring woman I've ever known."

"Ryan, don't—"

He moved closer, then closer still. "We can live your way. Church. Saying grace. Whatever you want to teach the kids is fine—both Penny and the ones we have together."

He stopped just inches from her. His arms, long and loose, stayed at his sides, but he looked like a lion ready to pounce. If she swayed forward, he'd crush her to his chest and drown her resistance with a kiss as deep and powerful as the first one. She loved this man, wanted him, feared for him. But after all was said and done, they weren't dolphins.

"I love you," she said in a quavering voice. "But what you're describing isn't enough. It's not Christianity. Jesus wasn't just a wise and good teacher, or even a prophet. He was God made flesh so we could have a relationship with Him. What you're describing is just going through the motions."

Ryan didn't say anything. Not a word.

She felt sick inside. "I don't want to live *my* way or *your* way. I want to live God's way."

"You can. I'm not stopping you."

"You don't understand," she repeated. "I want God's way to be *our* way. I know there are successful marriages where people have different faiths, but I'm just not that way. I need to know the man I love is praying for me, and that he leans on God like I do. I'm sorry, Ryan. But I'm afraid anything less would be a disaster for both of us."

"Ah, Carly." He bent his neck, stared at the dirt, and raked his hand through his hair. Finally he met her gaze with a piercing stare of his own. "I love you, Carly Jo. And I think I *do* understand you."

Her full name, her true self. But coming from Ryan, it sounded patronizing. "But you don't. That's what scares me."

"It shouldn't."

"We're so different."

"Not really." He paused, maybe to consider his next words. "I don't want to debate religion, but I have to ask a question."

"What?"

"You're a Christian, and you believe Christ died for your sins. Right?"

"Yes, I do."

"So why did you feel so guilty about Allison? It seems to me if you believed in God that strongly, you'd have set that burden down a long time ago. But you didn't."

"I'm human. I have feelings."

"And those feelings trumped your faith."

"No. That's not right. It's just that . . . that . . ." Carly stopped with hollow words dead on her tongue. She was raised in the church. She read her Bible every morning. She'd been baptized in a muddy pond at the age of seven. She had lived her faith as best as she could, but Ryan was spot-on about her failure to accept forgiveness for hurting Allison.

He was so close she could smell the smoke from the camp stove on his skin and hair. He raised one hand, slowly, and trailed his fingers along her jaw. "Deep down, we're the same. You know that."

His voice was soft, even kind, but his words scraped away everything she believed about herself. Without meaning to, Ryan had accused her of being a fake. She opened her mouth to defend herself, but the words came out in a confession. "If what you said is true, I'm a hypocrite."

"No," he said firmly. "You're not a hypocrite. Just naïve."

"But I'm not naïve. That's not it."

"This isn't important—"

"But it is!" She twisted her neck to escape his touch. "I have to understand."

He gave her a careful look. "All right, then. Here's a diagnosis for you—"

"A *what*?"

"A diagnosis," he repeated. "A scientific determination, a description of a condition."

Carly gaped at him. "Christianity isn't a condition, and it's certainly not a disease."

"No, but it *is* a state of mind. You believe in God because it's how you were raised. It's in your emotional DNA, and that's okay. We're all shaped by our upbringing, society, and our physical makeup."

"And our choices."

"Yes. Especially those. The way I see it, we've both made mistakes and learned from them. We love and respect each other. What more do we need?"

All her life, she'd viewed herself as a sincere believer, not a Sunday-only Christian spouting Bible verses off coffee cups. Now she wondered if Ryan was correct, and if her faith in God was more habit than holy. Alone and lost, she blurted, "I want to go home."

"We will. Tomorrow."

"No." Her heart pounded against her ribs. "I mean home to Kentucky. I need to see my dad."

A pleased look softened the lines around his eyes and mouth. "I talked to him."

Carly gaped at him. "When?"

"Yesterday. I called to invite him for a visit. It seemed like the right thing to do before I popped the question like I just did." He gave a sheepish half smile. "I jumped the gun here, but I'm not sorry."

Carly's heart melted a little. He'd called her dad to show respect, and she appreciated it. "That was nice of you. But I still want to go home. I feel so lost."

He grasped her hands and held tight. "We can be lost together."

But she didn't want to be lost. She wanted to be found. And to be found, she needed to smell the loamy earth and gaze at real clouds painted on God's canvas of blue sky. She slipped her hands out of his, slowly, aware of every scrape of skin. "I'll book a flight when we get to the house."

"When do you want to go?"

"As soon as possible." She'd have to dip into her savings for a last-minute ticket, but she needed to see her father that badly. "I'm sure Denise will help with Penny."

"No doubt," he muttered. "How long will you be gone?"

"Not long." Classes started in September, and if she decided to move out of Ryan's house, she'd need time to find an apartment in a safe neighborhood. She hated the thought of leaving Ryan and the kids, especially Penny, but living under his roof was just too much now.

The sun was almost gone, and the sky was purple with just a strip of lavender on the horizon. "We need to go back to camp," she said to him.

A frown creased his brow, barely visible in the fading light. "What do we tell Penny?"

"Just that I'm visiting my dad in Kentucky and I'll be back soon. She'll be okay as long as we don't make a big deal about it."

"And then?"

"We'll deal with the rest when I come back."

Ryan closed the last few inches between them, then cupped her face again in his warm hands. "Go home to Kentucky, Carly Jo. But promise me you'll come back."

"I will."

"And know this"—his fingers tunneled into her hair—"I'm going to fight for you with everything I have. If it means wrestling with God, I'll do it."

"Ryan, I—"

"I love you." He tipped her head back, drew her fully into his arms, then brought his mouth down to hers in a crushing kiss.

Carly swayed into him, clutched his back, his shoulders, and returned the kiss with all the love and longing in her soul. If this was her only taste of "special and forever," she wanted it to be branded on her heart in all its bittersweet glory.

29

Penny loved Aunt DeeDee very much, but she wanted to go home to her room with the clouds. She'd been here for two whole nights, and she couldn't find the quiet place in her mind. The airplanes flew *all the time,* and she missed swimming with her daddy. "Mermaid" was her favorite game, and it was a lot more fun in the water than it was in Aunt DeeDee's living room. Penny wanted to go to the ocean, but Aunt DeeDee wouldn't take her. The water was close, too. Penny knew, because a blue sign on the corner pointed to it.

She wished she was at the beach now with Carly, but she settled for picking up Donna Dolphin and running into the kitchen. Aunt DeeDee was at the stove with fat gloves on her hands, lifting a big silver pot.

"Shark!" Penny shouted to warn her.

"Penny, no!" The pot clattered down on the stove. Water sloshed, and the orange burner hissed.

Penny ran back through the kitchen. The sharks were after them, so she made Donna swim extra fast.

Aunt DeeDee grabbed Penny from behind and spun her around.

The fat gloves were gone now, and her face was as white as her shirt. "Penny, stop!"

Penny tried, but her legs were wiggly today.

"I said, stop."

"Shark!" Penny lifted Donna so Aunt DeeDee could see her. "The sharks are after us!"

Aunt DeeDee pulled her into a hug. "You can't run through the kitchen like that. It's not safe with hot things on the stove."

Penny knew the rules. She just forgot them. Aunt DeeDee didn't understand how hard it was, but Carly did. She had even painted a meltdown on Penny's wall. Tears pushed into her eyes. She wanted to go home to her daddy and Carly, even to her brothers. Aunt DeeDee's house was just *too loud*.

"I need my tent," she told Aunt DeeDee.

"Oh, sweetheart . . ."

Aunt DeeDee's phone played some music. Holding Penny by the shoulder, she answered it. Penny didn't pay much attention, but she thought it was her daddy calling to say they were back from the island. That meant he would come to pick her up, or maybe Carly would come by herself. Penny clapped her hands until Aunt DeeDee put her big hand over Penny's smaller ones and held them still.

"Yes, that's fine," she said into the phone. "As long as you need . . . Of course. I'm thrilled . . . Yes, she's right here."

Aunt DeeDee handed the phone to Penny. "It's your daddy."

Knowing she had to be careful because the phone was smart and expensive, she held it lightly with both hands. "Hi, Daddy."

"Hi, sweetheart. How are you?"

"I'm okay."

"Are you having a good time?"

"Uh-huh." She wanted to say more, but her thoughts were tangled up.

When her daddy told her they all missed her, she felt nice inside and calmed down enough to think. "Can I talk to Carly?"

"She's not here right now. She went to the bathroom."

"Oh."

"She said to tell you hi."

Penny closed her eyes, found the quiet place in her mind, and used her best voice, not the whiny one. "I want to go home."

"Not just yet, honey." He sounded funny, like he'd swallowed a cracker without chewing it. "You're going to stay with Aunt DeeDee a little longer. It'll be fun."

She wanted to tell him no, but Aunt DeeDee was holding Donna and smiling at her. Distracted, Penny waved at them.

Her daddy broke in. "Let me talk to Aunt DeeDee again."

Penny traded the phone for Donna and made her swim. Aunt DeeDee talked some more to Penny's daddy; then she said good-bye. Crouching, she looked at Penny. "I bet you're wondering what's going on."

Penny was more interested in making Donna swim, but Aunt DeeDee put her finger on Penny's chin and turned her face. "Carly's going on a trip, so you're going to stay with me. We'll have a good time. I promise. I know surprises are hard sometimes, but this is for the best. I'm going to take good care of you."

There were too many words for Penny to understand, especially words like *Carly, trip,* and *surprise.* The kitchen blurred, and so did Aunt DeeDee's face. In a deep, convoluted way, Penny's mind mixed together all the puzzle pieces of her broken life, and she was reduced to her most basic need. "I want my mommy!"

Aunt DeeDee held her tight. "She's gone, honey. She can't come back."

"W-Why not?"

Aunt DeeDee stroked Penny's hair. "It's just the way it is. When people die, they say good-bye forever, but their love stays here. That love is inside you."

If her mommy's love was inside her, Penny didn't have to look for her. But she still wanted a mommy here and now, and she wanted her new mommy to be Carly. Aunt DeeDee was fun and special and Penny loved her, but she felt safe with Carly, because Carly helped her to think.

Aunt DeeDee hugged her hard. "I miss your mommy, too. But at least we have each other."

Aunt DeeDee tried to rock Penny, but Penny didn't want to be rocked. Her feelings were too big for her heart, and she wanted to go home. If she couldn't ever be with her mommy again, she wanted *home* to be with her daddy, her brothers, and especially Carly. That's what she told Aunt DeeDee, who gave her a serious look.

"Penny, listen."

But she couldn't. Not really.

"Carly is leaving tomorrow. That's what nannies do. They come and go. I will be here always."

The only words Penny took in were the ones about Carly leaving. What if Carly didn't come back? What if she went to the ocean and got in a boat and went to heaven and Penny never saw her again? Panicked, she broke away from Aunt DeeDee and ran to the door. "I have to see her."

"She'll be here tomorrow to say good-bye."

"No!" Penny pulled on the knob, but the door was locked with a special lock with a keypad like the one on her daddy's garage. Penny didn't know the magic numbers, but when Aunt DeeDee opened it, she made a square with her fingers starting with the 1. In the morning, when Aunt DeeDee was sleeping, Penny would try to make the same square.

If the lock made the whooshing sound, she could walk out the door and follow the blue signs with waves on them to the beach. The first one was on the corner of Aunt DeeDee's street and not very far. Once she found the beach, she could walk on the sand to her daddy's house—and to Carly.

Penny hoped Dr. God would help her, because she desperately wanted to ask Carly to be her new mommy.

Ryan clicked off the phone with Denise, walked back to the van, and helped Eric and Kyle with the camping gear. Knowing Penny would be upset, he had specifically told Denise to keep the information to a minimum, and that he would speak to Penny after Carly made travel plans. Ryan could only imagine what Paul Mason would think about his daughter's emergency trip home.

When the van was loaded, the kids climbed in the back and Carly took shotgun. They all chattered about the trip, but Carly didn't look at Ryan once. He didn't regret anything he had said or done on the island, certainly not the marriage proposal or kissing her. Carly might have God on her side, but Ryan had Mother Nature.

Two hours later, after taking Nathan and the girls to their respective homes, he pulled the van into his U-shaped driveway, saw a white sedan with a rental sticker, and parked behind it. A tall man with a craggy face and a head full of white hair was leaning against the trunk, his arms crossed and a carry-on at his feet.

"That's my dad!" Carly cried out.

As she leaped out of the van, Ryan locked eyes with Paul Mason through the tinted windshield.

The reverend offered a single curt nod. As Ryan nodded back, Kyle leaned forward for a better look. "He looks mean. Did you know he was coming?"

"I invited him." But Paul Mason's arrival now was a surprise.

The boys piled out the side doors, but Ryan stayed in the driver's seat, watching as Paul Mason hugged Carly so hard that her feet lifted off the black asphalt. It was the kind of hug that squeezed the life out of a person, or maybe it squeezed life *into* a person. The reverend didn't look at all like the country preacher Ryan expected. He was taller, more trim, and well dressed in navy slacks and an oxford shirt tailored to his lean frame. He could have been a college professor, a surgeon, even a high-priced attorney.

Bracing himself for inspection—rotten timing, considering his five-day beard and how badly he needed a shower—Ryan headed toward them with Kyle and Eric in his wake. With her eyes beaming, Carly introduced the boys first.

"Daddy, this is Kyle." They shook hands.

"And Eric." Another handshake.

Their good manners made Ryan proud. "Go on in," he told them. "We'll unpack later."

They walked off, leaving Ryan face-to-face with Carly's father. Paul Mason's piercing eyes didn't miss a thing, but Ryan, too, had excellent vision.

Carly laid her hand on her father's arm. "Daddy, this is Ryan."

"Reverend Mason." Ryan thrust out his hand.

Paul Mason took it and shook. Hard.

Ryan shook back. Harder.

"Call me Paul," the reverend said. "My daughter says fine things about you."

"She's told me a lot about you, too." He knew her father liked to fish, enjoyed cigars, and would fight for his family to the death. So would Ryan, and he wanted his family to include Carly. "She's a very special woman. You must be proud of her."

"Oh, I am." He smiled, but those silver eyes shot daggers.

Carly interrupted. "Daddy, what's going on? I know Ryan invited you to visit, but this is a surprise."

The hard lines of his face melted into a tender look meant just for his daughter. "My daddy-radar's been going off for a week now."

Carly laughed. "I know what *that* means."

"What?" Ryan asked.

The look she gave him was hesitant, even shy. "Daddy-radar means he's been worrying about me. He's usually right, too."

The men locked eyes like a pair of lions prowling in a circle. Neither of them wanted to fight, at least not yet. But the possibility burned in their eyes. "The guest room's all yours," Ryan said graciously. "I hope you're planning to stay with us."

"I will. Thank you."

"Good. The boys and I need to unpack." Then he'd shave, shower, pull out some good cigars, and invite the reverend for what Carly called a sit-down. "Carly can get you settled. If you'll excuse me—"

She shot him a grateful look, but the reverend interrupted. "Hold on, Ryan. I came to see you, not my daughter."

Carly's mouth fell open. "But, Daddy! We just got back."

"I know, sweetheart." He kept his gaze on Ryan. "But when a man makes a call asking to meet a girl's father, he deserves to make his own first impression."

"But—"

"Go on," he scolded her. "Everything's going to be all right."

She glared at her father before turning to Ryan with the anguish of the past twenty-four hours stamped on her sunburned face. Ryan laid his hand on her arm. "We'll be fine."

"I just think—"

"It's okay." He didn't need Carly to protect him. "Your dad and I want to get to know each other."

After a final imploring look, she headed for the atrium. Ryan watched until she stepped into the house; then he faced Paul. Those gray eyes stared at him, not with hostility but with compassion, like a hospital chaplain sent to deliver bad news. Bracing himself for what Carly would call a sit-down, Ryan indicated the house. "Come on in. We can talk in my office."

30

Paul Mason didn't budge. "If you don't mind, I'd rather see that car of yours."

"The Impala?"

"Carly says it's a beaut."

"It is." Paul was either passionate about classic cars, or he wanted to have this conversation as far from Carly as possible. Either way, Ryan was proud of his life and hoped Paul would be impressed by the financial security he could offer Carly.

Ryan led the way to the side garage, punched the code into the keypad, and watched Paul's face as the door lumbered up. When it creaked to a halt, Ryan stepped inside and turned on the fluorescent lights.

Paul let out a whistle. "Ain't that a prize!"

"You can drive it if you'd like," Ryan offered. "Anytime."

"I just might do that. My daddy owned an Impala." Circling the car with his arms crossed, Paul remarked on everything from the upholstery to the pristine paint to the AM radio. Ryan popped the hood, and they talked horsepower. When the conversation lulled,

Paul led the way out of the garage, paused in the driveway, and faced Ryan.

Both men knew why they were here, so Ryan cut to the chase. "I love your daughter, sir. I want to marry her."

"I can't say I'm surprised."

"I wanted to meet you before proposing to her, even ask your blessing. But the Anacapa trip stirred things up. I asked her last night."

"I figured that." His gravelly voice scraped away what was left of the car banter. "Judging by that pitiful look on her face, it didn't go well."

"No."

"I'll be straight with you, Ryan." Paul hooked his thumbs in his pockets and jutted one knee. "I know my daughter inside and out, and your phone call was no surprise. She has feelings for you— strong ones. But she's fighting them tooth and nail. What I want to hear from you is why."

Let the grilling begin. "I'm an agnostic," Ryan said bluntly. "Carly's bothered by that."

"Bothered, huh?"

"More than bothered," he admitted. "But I love her. And I respect her faith and yours. That's why I invited you here. I want to do things her way."

"Do you, now?"

"Yes."

The reverend paused a moment. "Are you sleeping with her?"

Ryan's brows shot up. "No, sir. Like I said, I respect her views."

"Well, good," he said. "I won't have to haul you into church for a quickie wedding."

Was he *serious*? It's not like they were living in 1899, or even 1955. Ryan barely kept his jaw from dropping, but then he saw Paul's eyes crinkle into a smile, and he knew he'd been hoodwinked.

Paul clapped him on the arm. "Don't worry, son. I left the

shotgun at home. But you just told me something important. I believe you about respecting Carly's faith."

"Good."

"But I have to wonder if respect is enough."

"I believe it is."

"Maybe. Maybe not." He folded his arms again. "We'll have that talk another time. Right now my concern is for Carly Jo. The way I see it, you have a problem. My little girl loves you. She also loves God. If you don't understand that part of her character, she won't be happy with you. And because she loves you, she won't be happy without you."

"I'll make her happy."

"You can't."

Ryan balked at his arrogance. "I can try."

"I respect your good intentions, son. But you'll fail." The reverend paused to let the words sink in. "No man can love a woman as much as God loves her. And if that man doesn't love God"—Paul indicated the Impala with an open palm—"he's like a car without gas in it. You can press the pedal all you want, but you won't get out of the garage."

"I can't argue about the car," Ryan admitted. "But human beings aren't machines. We make choices. Like I said, Carly and I will live her way."

"But you can't," Paul said, a bit exasperated now. "To do things Carly's way, you have to be the spiritual head of your household."

The notion struck Ryan as old-fashioned. "I'd say we're equals."

"Oh no, you're not." Paul's eyes twinkled. "My daughter is better than you six ways to Sunday."

Ryan laughed. "You're right about that."

"You bet I am." Paul held up his hands in seeming surrender to all womankind. "My wife was too good for me, too. You know how the Bible describes creation in the book of Genesis, how it evolves from dirt to plants, then animals, and finally to human beings? Every time, what God created became more complex. He made woman last. That tells me she's the best thing he ever made." His eyes twinkled some more. "I happen to agree rather strongly."

"So do I." Ryan liked Paul a lot. No wonder Carly was so solid. She and her father were a lot alike.

"I have one last question for you." As quick as a blink, the humor drained from his face.

"What is it?"

"Are you willing to die for my daughter?"

Ryan opened his mouth to say *of course,* but Paul held up a hand to stop him. "Don't give me drivel about taking a bullet for her. You need to think about what dyin' for a person really means."

That *drivel* echoed what Ryan had told Carly on the island. He meant it, and he still did, but the claim sounded juvenile compared to the question hanging in the air now. *Dying* for Carly meant more than giving his physical life for her. It meant offering up his heart and mind on the altar of blind faith.

After a long look, Paul walked away. Ryan stared at his ramrod spine until curiosity got the better of him. "Sir?"

Paul stopped, turned slowly, then stood with his hands loose at his sides while he waited for Ryan to speak.

"You're not what I was expecting."

Puckering his lips, he rubbed his chin with his thumb. "Lemme guess here. Y'all were expectin' a country preacher with a snake in one hand and a Bible in the other, or maybe a prune-faced killjoy preachin' at folks to shape up or ship out."

"More or less."

"Let me set you straight." Paul spoke without a hint of Kentucky. "I hold a degree in physics from MIT and a doctorate from Harvard Divinity School. I've visited sixteen countries, written two books, and read a thousand others. But don't let that pedigree fool you, Ryan. The degrees are nothing compared to the wisdom in the

Bible and the experience of knowing Jesus Christ. Now, if you'll excuse me, I need to speak to Carly."

"Of course."

Ryan stayed behind until Paul strode through the back gate; then he went to unload the van. It promised to be an interesting visit for everyone, especially Ryan, who had a sudden craving for a cigarette.

⁓

While her father spoke with Ryan, Carly took a hot shower, put on fresh clothes, and wrestled with the chaos of the past twenty-four hours. She didn't know what she expected her father to say when he tapped on the open door to her room, but it wasn't a request for one of her mother's pecan pies. She knew the recipe by heart, so they headed to the supermarket for the ingredients. They were in the baking aisle, talking about Moon Pies and Ale 8, when her father laid his hand on her arm. "Carly, I want to ask you something."

"What is it?"

"If you had one day left on this earth, who would you spend it with?"

It was just like her father to catch her off guard. She put a bag of pecans into the cart, or the buggy, as she would have called it back home. "It would be Ryan. I love him."

"I thought so."

"I tried to stop the feelings, but Daddy, I just couldn't." She couldn't bear to look into his eyes. If she married Ryan, she'd miss her family terribly. "It's all too much, too strong—"

"Love is like that." Absently, or maybe deliberately, he nudged her forward. "What else do we need for your mother's pie?"

"Corn syrup." She ambled down the aisle with her dad at her side. It was like being at the new Kroger in Boomer, and she felt more like herself than she had in days. "I'm glad you're here, Daddy. The situation is just so complicated."

"Because Ryan's not a Christian?"

"Yes, but there's more." *Just say it,* she told herself. "It's about my own faith, who I am. After he proposed, we got into an argument. Ryan tried to be nice, but he said if I really believed in God, I'd forgive myself for what happened with Allison."

"He's a logical man." Her father indicated the corn syrup on the top shelf and out of her reach. "Light or dark?"

"Light."

He put it into the cart, and Carly moved on. "I might as well get milk while I'm here. The boys drink it by the gallon."

Her father sauntered along next to her, saying nothing so she could think for herself. When she picked up the milk, she faced him again. "Ryan thinks I'm a Christian only because I was raised that way. I wanted to say that it isn't true, but in some ways he's right. Like with Allison. If I really believe I'm forgiven, why couldn't I set down the guilt before we found her?"

"You're human and you care."

"I do," she said, pushing the cart toward the bread aisle. The boys ate a lot of that, too. "I tried my best to help Allison, but I failed. I just wasn't good enough."

Her father put his hand on her shoulder. "Ah, Carly."

She faced him. "What?"

"I hate to see you hurting, but I'm relieved."

"Why?"

"Because Ryan made you see something I've worried about since your mother died. Somehow you got it in your head that you have to save the world. But you can't."

"I know that."

"In your mind, yes." His eyes drilled into hers. "But in your heart, you're hanging on to the notion that if you're good enough, bad things won't happen. That's just not true."

She scowled at the criticism, or maybe it was her pride putting up a fight. "What do you mean?"

Her father lowered his hand but kept her pinned in place with his eyes. "What we want from God and what we need don't always match up. We want pecan pie, and God serves up porridge. We want happy endings, but sometimes people suffer and die. It's trite to say everything works out in the end, but it does—as long as you know the end is eternity and beyond our grasp."

He gave her a chance to speak, but nothing came out of her mouth.

"Do you know that, Carly Jo? Or are you grasping at straws in the here-and-now, hanging on to what *you* can do rather than trusting God, because you're afraid and reasonably so. Sometimes He takes us to dark places, like when your mama died."

She opened her mouth to say *of course* she trusted God, but the words died on her tongue. With the lights glaring down from the high ceiling, she saw herself as exhausted, full of guilt, and light-years from the little girl who sang "Jesus Loves Me" with a full and trusting heart. Tears flooded her eyes. "But Daddy, I try so hard—"

"I know you do, honey." He held her hand as if she were small again. "But there are things in life you can't fix. When your mother was sick, we prayed for her day and night, but God still took her home. Ever since then, you've been a fighter."

The old grief wrapped itself around her ribs and squeezed. How many times had she thought, *If only I'd prayed harder . . . If only I'd done more . . .* She had accepted her mother's passing as best as she could, but deep down, she had never quite trusted God again. Suddenly furious, she pounded her fist on the red handle of the cart. "It's just not fair!"

He didn't ask what she meant.

"I try so hard," she repeated.

"I know you do."

"And it's not enough. It's never enough."

"No, it isn't." Her father put his big hand over her fist. "Frankly, I'm relieved you figured that out, especially with your feelings for

Ryan. You can't fix his life or save his soul. I won't tell you what to do, honey, other than to pray."

Inhaling deeply, Carly let the wisdom sink into her. If she learned anything from her mistakes with Allison, it was that she didn't have the capacity to love anyone as perfectly as God did. Not Allison. Not Ryan. Not even herself. She couldn't save the world, couldn't save even a small part of it. She couldn't save Penny, Allison, or Ryan. Especially Ryan.

They all needed grace.

A gift.

Mercy.

And she knew in the dark corner of her heart, in the place where grief for her mother was always fresh, that she needed to trust God for the outcome, *whatever it was.* He loved Ryan even more than she did. Carly loved both God and Ryan, but she loved God more. With that love blooming into trust, she placed Ryan in God's hands like Abraham placed Isaac on the altar. If that offering meant leaving him, she didn't know if she could stand it, but somehow she'd find the strength to rely on God alone.

She hugged her father hard. "Thank you, Daddy."

"Come on, now," he grumbled. "Let's get the rest of what you need for that pie."

Carly wiped her eyes. "I miss Mom."

"She'd be proud of you, honey. I know I am."

Here she was—a teary, frightened mess, and her father loved her just as she was. That was grace. That was Jesus. That was the kind of person she wanted to be.

31

Shortly before six a.m., Ryan's cell phone played the ringtone that signaled Denise. Instantly alert, he snatched the phone off the nightstand and swung out of bed. "What's wrong?"

"It's Penny. I-I can't find her."

"Have you looked in all the closets?"

"I did that first."

"The backyard?"

"Of course I did!" The words blurred into a shriek. "Ryan, she's g-gone. The front door's open—"

"How?"

"*I don't know!*"

"I'm on my way." He grabbed pants and a shirt out of his closet. "Tell me exactly what happened."

He put her on speaker and set the phone on the nightstand. While he pulled on Levis and a shirt, she described finding the front door left ajar. "I-I thought someone had broken in. But her backpack is gone and so are some of her stuffed animals."

"But how did she get the combination to that lock?"

"She must have watched me. It's a simple pattern . . . a square."

Denise inhaled sharply. "That's why I picked it—so I could re-member it."

Ryan's fingers flew over the shirt buttons. "Have you called the police?"

"I'm waiting for them now."

"We need to check the neighborhood." Like that day at the mall, horrible visions shot through his mind with the added terror of cars speeding down a busy street. "I'll be there as soon as I can with the boys and Carly. Her dad's here, too."

"The more, the better." Denise's voice cracked. "Just hurry. Okay?"

He shoved the phone in his back pocket, strode into the hall, and pounded on all the bedroom doors. "Guys, wake up! I need you."

Eric stepped into the hall first, then Kyle. Sleep clouded their eyes. Paul stepped out of the guest room wearing plaid pajamas.

"It's Penny," Ryan told them all. "She's missing. We need to search Denise's neighborhood."

"Oh, man," Kyle muttered. "That's bad."

"We have to find her fast," Eric added. "If she gets scared, she'll have a meltdown."

The boys stepped back into their rooms, but Paul stayed in the hall. "You and Carly go on ahead. I'll take the boys and meet you there. Just text me the address."

"I'd appreciate it." Ryan palmed his phone, shot off the text, and raced down the stairs to wake up Carly.

She was already in the kitchen, dressed but barefoot, and beating the life out of a bowl of pancake batter with a handheld electric mixer. The high-pitched whine muted his steps, and she didn't turn until he laid his arm across her shoulders. Light danced in her eyes until she saw his face and flicked the Off switch. "What's wrong?"

"Denise just called. Penny ran away."

She dropped the mixer, leaving it to sink down in the batter like an animal in quicksand. "She hasn't run away in weeks. Why? How?"

"She figured out the combination to the deadbolt. I don't know why she ran off or where she's going, but I could guess."

"Home," Carly murmured. "To us."

Ryan gave her shoulder a squeeze and released it. "Your father's driving the boys. You can come with me or—"

"I'll take the van."

"Good. She might recognize it." As steady as Ryan sounded, his insides quaked as he dragged his hand through his hair. "We have to find her. I couldn't stand to lose her—"

"I know, Ryan. Oh, how I know." She hugged him hard.

Life and hope flooded into him. "Carly, I—"

"Don't try to talk." She gave him another fierce squeeze, then stepped back. "Go. I'll be right behind you."

With his chest tight, he strode to the old garage. If Penny saw the Impala and came running, this time it really could take her home, especially if Carly married him. Longing swamped him, but fear for Penny's life turned him into a robot. With his brain half frozen, he set up his phone for hands-free, backed out of the driveway, and drove to El Segundo in an icy sweat. He wished he could pray, but asking God for help felt like talking to Lance the Lion.

He reached El Segundo in twenty-six long minutes, turned down Denise's street, and slowed the Impala to a crawl. Swiveling his head from side to side, he peered between houses and around cars. There was no sign of Penny, nothing out of the ordinary except a black-and-white patrol car in front of Denise's house.

Ryan parked behind it, headed for the door, but stopped when he spotted the van coming up the street. Carly leapt out and ran to him. He put his arm around her waist, and they hurried into the house together. Without a faith of his own, maybe he could borrow hers.

Carly hurried to Denise. While the women exchanged a desperate hug, Ryan focused on the policewoman. "What's happening now?"

"We've alerted our officers to keep an eye out for her. There's no sign of abduction, which is a plus."

"So no Amber alert?"

"No." She paused. "At least not yet."

Not until they find her backpack in an abandoned car, or a witness comes forward, or—no! Blocking the awful pictures by an act of sheer will, he slid into an icy pool of surrealistic calm, where time slowed to a crawl and voices, even his own, were off-key and distorted. "My sons and Carly's father are on their way. We'll search the neighborhood."

"Good," she answered. "You know Penny best."

Ryan turned to Denise. When he looked into her bloodshot eyes, he knew exactly how she felt. "Do you know what Penny's wearing?"

"Jeans, a purple T-shirt, pink sneakers." Her voice cracked. "She took her backpack and some of her animals."

Kyle and Eric walked through the open door. Paul followed a second later. After hurried introductions, Ryan took control of the search. "We need to think like Penny."

"She likes the beach," Eric suggested.

Ryan nodded. The south end of Dockweiler State Beach was about a half mile from Denise's place, and the route was marked with blue signs. "I'll start there." He turned to Paul. "El Segundo is laid out in a grid, with a business district in the middle. Take Eric and drive up and down the streets."

Next he faced Denise. "Is there a park nearby? Someplace with swings?"

"There's a playground about a mile from here." She dabbed at her eyes with a crumpled white tissue. "We've been there a few times. There's also the Plunge."

"What's that?" he asked.

"The pool in the rec center. I didn't take her, but she saw posters at the library and wanted to go."

Carly signaled him with a lift of her hand. "I'll check out the park and the Plunge. If I don't find her, I'll help you search the beach."

Ryan accepted the offer with a nod, then turned to Kyle. "Knock on neighbors' doors. Maybe someone saw her."

"Got it," he replied.

He swung his gaze back to Denise. "I don't want to miss something obvious. What happened after I spoke with her on the phone?"

She pressed her fingers tight against her mouth, then slid them to her burning cheeks. "I can't believe what I did. I-I'm so sorry—"

"What happened?" he repeated.

"I told her nannies came and went. That sometimes they didn't come back." A sob tore from her throat. "I'm so sorry."

Ryan gritted his teeth against a rush of anger, but the fury dissolved in a flood of compassion for this flawed, misguided woman who loved Penny as much as he did. He had no right to condemn or berate her. Wanting to help her, he laid a gentle hand on her shoulder. "You made a mistake, Denise. We've all been there."

She shook her head. "I should have given you the picture of Jenna. I should have—"

Carly dropped down onto the couch. "Denise, stop."

"But—"

"You didn't mean for this to happen." She slid to the floor, landed on her knees, and grasped both of Denise's bone-white hands. "I've been where you are right now. It happened in Lexington. I made a mistake, and a girl with FASD ran away. I thought I'd never get over it. But I did."

"How?" Denise broke down again. "*How* did you do it?"

"I had to forgive myself," Carly murmured. "I'm at peace now, but it took a long time and someone being honest with me."

Ryan thought she meant her father, but she turned to *him*. Stepping forward, he offered his hand with the intention of helping her to her feet. She grasped his cold fingers in her warm ones, held his gaze as she stood, then bent and kissed his knuckles. It was a benediction of sorts, an acknowledgement of the forgiveness they all needed.

He longed to savor the moment, but each passing second put Penny in greater danger. After giving her hand a squeeze, he focused on the task at hand. "Kyle and Paul, give your phone numbers to Denise. She'll stay here and coordinate communication."

Leaving them behind, Ryan strode to the Impala, cranked the ignition, and made a beeline for Grand Avenue, the street that led to the beach. Clogged with morning traffic, the two-lane road curved past houses and small apartment buildings. With traffic moving at a crawl, he peered into overgrown yards and along the sidewalk, but there was no sign of a little girl with a purple backpack.

Vehicles inched forward, then picked up speed. The residential area faded to brown hills surrounding an industrial power plant with red-and-white smokestacks. They were the kind of thing that would attract Penny's attention, and he wondered if she'd wandered into the brush. Uncertainty plagued him, but when he rounded a curve and saw the ocean, his gut told him to keep going.

He pressed the accelerator with the hope of flying through the green light, but it turned yellow, then bright red. Stifling an oath, he stomped the brake and skidded to a stop. While cross traffic sped by, he peered up and down the highway, dreading what he might see—an ambulance with flashing lights, police cars, even a coroner's van. Finally the light turned green. He hit the gas, shot across the intersection, and took the access road to an empty parking lot. After steering to the sandy edge, he cut the engine.

The ocean stretched in front of him, limited only by the horizon and a jetty made of gray boulders that marked the end of a storm drain. Pulse pounding, he climbed out of the Impala and slammed the door. A wave crashed and rolled up the shore, faded to foam and vanished, its power and noise forgotten. Cupping his hands around his mouth, he shouted Penny's name at the top of his lungs.

Helpless and hating it, he spotted an old van on the southern edge of the lot, ran to it, and pounded on the door. When no one answered, his mind twisted into a picture of Penny inside it, bound and gagged, abused, dying or dead. Frantic, he searched for a rock big enough to smash the window. He found one on the edge of the beach, lifted it, but stopped when he spotted a couple of teenagers riding the waves. With no other vehicles in sight, the van had to belong to them.

The ice in his veins thawed into steam. Choking back bile, he crossed the bike path and stepped onto the shifting sand. A faded turquoise lifeguard station, empty except for an orange float on the railing, sat useless and blind fifty feet from the waves. A handful of sailboats dotted the water, and the silhouette of an oil tanker stood out against the murky sky.

Sick with dread, Ryan tried to think like Penny. She associated boats with going home. If she had approached the water, even a small wave could have knocked her down and swept her away. Stumbling in the sand, he ran toward the waves, shouting her name as he searched the shore for a sign of her, footprints, anything except her small, cold body washed up on the beach. Out of breath with his heart thundering in his ears, he stared at the water and sky.

There was nothing.

No sign of Penny.

Nothing except a vastness he couldn't fathom. Carly would have seen God the Creator. Ryan wished he could see the loving, almighty, all-powerful hand of God, because he desperately needed to find his own little girl. But when he looked out to the horizon, first to Catalina Island, then to the faintest shadow of Anacapa in the north, he saw nothing but a disintegrating rock . . . a rock like the one in his chest.

Which way would she go? Had she even come this far? A gull

swooped past him and veered to the south. Hoping it was a harbinger, he ran in the same direction as the bird, calling Penny's name
until he decided she couldn't possibly have gone so far. Hoarse
from shouting, he pivoted and ran toward the distant jetty cutting
into the water.

Dizzy and out of breath, he ground to a halt thirty feet from the
rocks and collapsed to his hands and knees. Grains of sand scraped
through his pants and clung to his palms. He tried to think logi-
cally, but all he could do was listen to the waves, a reminder of his
helplessness, his insignificance, the fragility of his own humanity.
He couldn't help his daughter, couldn't see her or hear her. He was
as helpless as a starving babe left to cry out for its mother.

A choice as plain as black and white flashed into his mind. He
could believe in his own abilities and surrender to a fatalistic view
of life, death, and everything in between, or he could cry out for
help like that hungry baby. Just like that baby needed to willingly
suckle its mother's breast, Ryan needed to surrender to the God
he didn't understand.

A groan crawled out of his throat. Fists clenched around handfuls
of sand, he raised his face to the sky and shouted, "Where is she?"

He sucked in a lungful of air, blew it out, and waited. But nothing happened . . . except he felt a wave of something so powerful,
so strong, it made the ocean seem small. That feeling was love . . .
for his family, for Penny, and for Carly, who loved him just as he
was and yet remained true to herself and to her God. He felt her
presence in an abstract sort of way. He couldn't see her, touch her,
hold her. But she lived in him. *Love.* He couldn't see it or explain
it, but it swelled in his chest like the waves rising and crashing up
the beach.

Love was real.

And God was love. Ryan had read those words somewhere in
his mother's Bible, and they were real to him now because of his
love for Carly, his sons, and for Penny, with all her imperfections.

Ryan hated himself for her FASD, hated how he had hurt people he loved, but with his life shattered, he knew that love was powerful, forgiving, and full of grace. Like the water eroding Anacapa Island, love changed his heart of stone to a heart of tender flesh.

Love. Ryan couldn't get his arms around a lot of things in the Bible, but this one word burned in him, leveled him. Still on his knees, he stared at the horizon.

"I give up," he said to God and the man named Jesus. "I don't understand, and I'm full of doubt and anger. But you're all I have left. Protect my daughter. Bring her home."

Even as Ryan prayed those words, he knew a hard truth. If God was God now, He'd be God no matter what happened to Penny. Ryan wasn't making a deal with the Almighty or asking for a sign. He was waving the white flag of surrender with both hands. The war was over.

Drained of all emotion, he lumbered to his feet. He didn't hear a voice. There was no thunder. The ocean kept up its steady pounding. Absolutely nothing was different in his surroundings or in his mind.

But he started to cry.

He never cried.

But wet, sloppy tears leaked from his eyes. Utterly overwhelmed, he embraced the silence—and the peace—that settled over him. Then he heard it. The whimper of a child. He ran full speed toward the jetty. And from the corner of his eye, he caught sight of Carly climbing out of the van.

32

Penny woke up hungry and cold, took in the walls of a big round pipe, and let out a frightened squeak. She had crawled in here an hour ago, maybe longer, because the pipe reminded her of her tent at home and she felt safe. But now the pipe was cold and wet. The waves were too loud, and her legs and bottom were so cold she couldn't feel them.

She wanted to go home to Carly, Daddy, and her brothers, but she was lost and confused. With tears stinging her eyes, she hugged Miss Rabbit, but the rabbit couldn't talk without Carly. Lance was in her backpack, but he couldn't talk to her, either. Penny pressed her hands together the way Carly said, but she couldn't stop the scared feelings from spinning in her tummy. They went faster and faster until they came out in a scream.

She was scared . . . so scared . . . scared of the loud water, of being lost, of never seeing Carly again, because she was just the nanny and nannies left.

"Penny!"

Her daddy's big voice! Penny longed to shout back, but she couldn't stop kicking and screaming. He called her again, louder than before. Her ears heard him, but her mind wouldn't let her crawl forward. All she could do was clutch Miss Rabbit to her chest, kick her feet, and scream at the top of her lungs.

A shadow blocked the entrance to the pipe, then she saw Daddy's legs. "I found her!" he shouted to someone.

He crouched down, and she saw his face. It was all red and puffy like hers.

"Penny! Thank you, God."

He dropped to his hands and knees and crawled to her like a big dog or maybe a lion. Only instead of growling like Lance, he said her name over and over. Finally, he hauled her into his lap and held her so tight that all the cold vanished from her body. She hugged him just as hard, because he was having a meltdown, and Penny knew how that felt. They sat close and warm until he took a big breath. "Let's go see Carly."

Penny arched back so she could see his eyes. "She's here?"

"You bet."

"But Aunt DeeDee said Carly was leaving." Penny sniffed hard. "I want her to stay forever."

"So do I," Daddy said.

He gave Penny another big squeeze, then put Miss Rabbit in her backpack, hung it on his shoulder, and scooted with her to the opening in the big pipe. The light made her squint, but she saw Carly's legs pacing back and forth.

"Denise!" Carly shouted. "We found her. That's right . . . the beach. She's fine. Call my dad and Kyle. Yes. We'll wait for you here."

Penny pushed away from her daddy and crawled faster. With her heart so full it hurt, she scrambled out of the pipe and into the light. Carly swooped her into her arms and spun her around so fast Penny thought she would fly to heaven.

Her daddy came up next to them. Carly stopped spinning, and he put his arms around them both. Everyone stayed quiet, even

Penny. But then she remembered what Aunt DeeDee said about nannies leaving, and she knotted her fingers in Carly's shirt. If she held tight enough, maybe Carly would stay.

Penny leaned back so she could see Carly's face. Her daddy made room but kept his hand on her side. With her heart beating fast, she opened her mouth to ask Carly to be her mommy, but then Daddy waved his arm.

"We're down here!" he shouted.

Carly set Penny down but held on to her hand. Aunt DeeDee ran so fast her feet kicked up sand. Behind her, Penny saw Kyle, Eric, and a man with white hair. She didn't know who he was, but he looked like a grandpa.

Aunt DeeDee slid to her knees and hugged Penny hard. Kyle called her Squirrel, and Eric promised to play "Shark" whenever she wanted. The grandpa-man watched with a big smile on his face, and Daddy and Carly kept hugging each other.

It was time for Penny to ask her very important question. Scared but hopeful, because Dr. God lived in the clouds and loved her, she walked over to Carly, looked up, and used her very best voice. "Will you be my new mommy?"

Carly blinked fast, then turned to Daddy. He looked at Carly a long time, so long that Penny wondered what was wrong. Maybe they needed Miss Rabbit and Lance to talk, or maybe Carly was leaving like Aunt DeeDee said.

Daddy knelt down and touched her arm. "Carly and I are going to talk about that."

"I want her to stay!" Penny wailed.

"We all do," Kyle said.

Carly crouched next to Daddy. When she spoke, the words came out slow. "Penny, listen. Your daddy and I need to have some grown-up time."

Penny's lips trembled. She wanted to understand what was happening, but there were too many people and too many words.

Carly took both of her hands. "It's going to be okay."

"But—but—"

"It will," Carly said. "Wait for us at Aunt DeeDee's house."

Penny clung to her, but then Carly kissed her cheek. "I won't leave you, Penny. I promise."

Promises confused Penny, because sometimes people broke them by accident, but then a gull caught her attention, and she watched it fly to the parking lot. Her daddy's old car was there, and she remembered how she used to think it could take her to her first mommy. It couldn't, but it could take her home with Daddy and Carly.

"All right," she said to Carly and Daddy. "I'll go with Aunt DeeDee, but come and get me. Okay?"

"We will," he promised.

"And hurry," she added with a sweep of her arm that included everyone. "I want to be together with you!"

～

Carly watched Penny leave with Denise. Ryan extended his arm with his palm up. "Let's take a walk. I want to show you something."

She clasped his fingers, and they headed toward the spot where she'd spotted him on his hands and knees. Gulls squawked as they walked, and the roar and slosh of the incoming tide echoed in her ears. After several silent yards, he stopped on an apron of sand wiped clean by a wave. He looked around to orient himself, then drew an X with the toe of his shoe. "This is it."

Carly didn't understand. "I saw you when I parked the van. I figured you were trying to pull yourself together."

"I was, but it was more than that."

"What happened?"

He shook his head, then shoved his hands in his pockets. "I can't explain it. You could say I hit bottom, or that I reached the end of my rope. You could call it a breakdown or a meltdown. Whatever it was, it—" He shook his head for the second time.

Carly waited for him to say more, but he sealed his lips. His Adam's apple bobbed with a hard swallow, then he blew out a gust of air. "I'm making a mess of this."

"It's all right. I know about meltdowns."

"From Penny."

"And my own." She thought of last night's pecan pie. She'd cried while baking it. "My dad helped me to see something. What you told me on the island—"

"Carly, I'm so sorry." A bleakness dulled his blue eyes to murky gray. "I've been an utter fool, a complete idiot. I had no right to say any of the things I said to you."

But you said you loved me. You asked me to marry you. Her stomach clenched into a painful knot, but she arranged a composed expression on her face. She needed to put Ryan in God's hands alone, and though it hurt, she'd do just that. In a paradoxical way, his criticism had given her the strength to let him go, and he deserved to know it.

"You were right about me going through the motions, at least in some ways. I held on to the guilt over Allison out of a kind of fear. I see that now."

"If I helped you, I'm glad."

"You did."

"Good." He glanced at the ocean, then faced her again. "Criticizing your faith was the first thing I needed to take back. There's something else, and it's going to change everything between us."

Back straight and chin high, she braced herself to hear him say marriage would be a mistake, and she had to move out of the house because it was impossible to be just friends. She would always be close to Penny, but if Ryan didn't want to marry her, it would be an answer to her prayer asking God to guide them, though it wasn't the answer she wanted.

He lifted her hand in his. "I don't want to do things your way or my way. I want to do them God's way. And I want our way to be His way."

Her free hand flew to her chest, and her mouth fell open. "Are you saying what I think you're saying?"

His eyes twinkled in a chagrined sort of way. "Yes, I am. But I'm doing a lousy job of it."

"No!" she protested. "Tell me everything!"

Looking down, he pointed to the X in the sand with his foot. "This is where it happened. I hit my knees and prayed—not that God would lead us to Penny, but that I'd understand that thing you call faith. He must have heard, because I-I'm not the same. I can't describe it. It's just . . . just . . ." He shook his head. "I'm stammering like a fool."

"And you never stammer," she said gently. "I understand completely what you're saying."

"Good, because I don't."

"You will."

"I hope so, but considering I've been a Christian for"—he glanced at his watch—"exactly thirty-two minutes, I have no idea what God's way is. I love you, Carly. I want to marry you, but I also want to be the husband you deserve. Can you put up with a long engagement?"

She caught her breath. Her heart pounded against her ribs, and all she could think was that Ryan had found his way home, and he loved her and wanted to marry her.

"Six months," he said. "Maybe a year. You can plan the wedding of your dreams. We'll shop for rings and go on dates. Dinners. Movies. Even more baseball games. I want to romance you, Carly Jo."

His irises were as steely as ever, but they were no longer cold. The color matched the ocean depths, and so did her love for this man who had wrestled with God and found a faith of his own. She flung her arms around his neck. "Yes," she cried. "I'll wait for you."

He kissed her then, and she savored every tingle and special feeling. The kiss took her to a beautiful, exotic place—an island paradise fit for a honeymoon. Breathless, she stepped back. "I have to move out of your house."

Ryan's eyes smoldered into hers. "It's that, or we elope tonight. And I don't think that's a good idea."

"Probably not," she said in her most sultry voice. "But it's tempting."

He tunneled his hands through her hair, then tilted her face up to his. "Do you remember when I said this kind of attraction was just nature?"

She nodded.

"This isn't just nature, Carly. It's love. Your father asked me if I was willing to die for you, and I am. But even more important, I'm willing to live for God, you, Penny, the boys, and the children I hope we have together."

Carly melted into a puddle. *Ryan. Her husband. Her lover, protector, and friend.* And she'd be the same kind of partner to him. With the sun burning away the fog, and the clouds parting to reveal the true-blue sky, she swayed into his arms, tilted her face up to his, and closed her eyes. He nibbled her ear, caressed her cheek, until at last his lips found hers in a kiss that was nature at its best, special and forever, and not the least bit complicated.

Epilogue

Standing in front of the wedding guests with Kyle and Eric at his side and Paul behind him in a minister's robe, Ryan peered down the beach to a white tent festooned with yellow roses, daisies, and a slew of dahlias. For months he had listened to Carly prattle about flowers and guests, catering and colors, but the one thing she never mentioned was her dress.

He didn't think too much about it until now. The tent shielded Carly and her bridesmaids from his eyes, but in a few minutes, the violinist would strike the first lilting notes of Pachelbel's "Canon in D," and his bride would make the long walk up the beach.

"Are you nervous?" Paul asked him.

"Not a bit." Ryan had never been more sure of anything in his life.

"Well, I am," Kyle muttered under his breath. "What if I drop the ring?"

Eric jabbed Kyle with his elbow. "Don't be an idiot. If you can catch a baseball, you can handle a ring."

A proud smile tilted on Ryan's face. The three of them made

325

a good team now, and today his sons were impressive. Dressed in dark suits but wearing flip-flops because of the sand, with fresh haircuts and a little too much cologne, they had his back. So did Paul Mason, who was a father, mentor, and friend, all rolled into one person.

The violinist stood, raised her bow, and the first notes of Carly's favorite hymn, "Be Thou My Vision," filled the balmy air. Standing tall, Ryan stared at the entrance to the tent. The wind stirred through the flowers, someone pushed the flaps open, and Penny stepped into the bright sun.

What a year it had been. . . . Becoming a Christian, Ryan discovered, was like diving into the deep end of a swimming pool. Once a man took the plunge, he was wet all over, and there was no going back. He and Paul had smoked a lot of cigars together, both during Paul's visits to California and at Thanksgiving when Ryan, Carly, and Penny visited Boomer County. He'd met a slew of aunts, uncles, and cousins, eaten his first "hot brown," a Kentucky specialty, and learned to say "How 'bout them Cats?" and mean it.

He glanced now at the white chairs on Carly's side of their impromptu church and saw half of Boomer County, Allison, her great-aunt, plus Carly's new friends from the local FASD community. The chairs on the other side of the aisle were filled with Ryan's colleagues, old friends, Fran, and new friends from the church he and Carly now called their own. Even Heather and her husband were here—a tribute to forgiveness, goodwill, and the friendship between Heather and Carly. That friendship, plus Ryan's genuine respect for Heather's husband, made it a lot easier to be a dad to his sons.

What had he done to be so blessed? Nothing . . . absolutely nothing. *Grace.* It was a gift from God and one he didn't deserve, yet cherished.

Penny stepped onto the white runner between the chairs, beamed a smile at Ryan, and waved to be sure he saw her. He waved back, and Penny took her seat in the front row with Miss Hannah, the nanny who took over when Carly had moved to a gated apartment complex.

Ryan focused back on the tent. The flaps opened again, and Denise stepped onto the sand. The three of them were good friends now. Once a month they met for dinner without Penny and hashed out any difficulties, but mostly they traded stories and supported one another.

Next came Joanna, Carly's sister and matron of honor. In the absence of their mom, Joanna had been a rock in those moments of bridal insanity. Somehow she'd kept Carly and the wedding on an even keel, even when the florist ran late and Penny lost her white flip-flops for the third time. Smiling as she came down the aisle, Joanna winked at her husband and sons in the third row, then joined Denise.

The violinist played a final note. As the melody faded to silence, a hush settled over the crowd. Ryan's pulse sped up, and it raced even faster when Carly's brother, Master Sergeant Joshua Mason, in full military dress, pinned back the tent flaps, pivoted, and stood ramrod straight with his elbow crooked. And on cue the violinist played the opening notes of the Pachelbel "Canon."

Bending slightly, with a bouquet of white roses in hand, Carly stepped out of the tent and into the light. She curled her bare fingers over her brother's elbow, he covered them with his gloved hand, and they began the long walk up the beach.

Her hair, long and loose, shimmered in the sun, and her cheeks glowed with happiness as she sought Ryan's gaze. When their eyes locked, her smile stretched even wider. She was beautiful, and she was his. But what nearly knocked him to his knees was the dress. Somehow the white silk caught the sun and shimmered into a light so bright that all Ryan could see was purity.

The purity of God's love.

The purity of his own soul washed clean.

The purity of a bride coming to her groom with the precious gift of her love and the promise to be his alone.

In a few minutes, he and Carly would take their vows. His SOS list would be complete, and their life together would begin. With his heart overflowing, he gave thanks for his bride, his family, and the unstoppable love of his own heavenly Father.

A Note From the Author

Dear Reader,

Fetal Alcohol Spectrum Disorder (FASD) is a complicated subject. I'm not an expert in any way, but an encounter with a boy in our Cub Scout troop put a face on it for me. I'm going to call him Tommy (not his real name) and share a few stories with you.

This was back in 1997, and at the time I'd never heard of Fetal Alcohol Syndrome. I just knew that among the eight boys in our troop, Tommy stood out. With his small head, narrow eyes, and flattened features, including no dent over his upper lip, he was different from the other kids.

He also behaved in odd ways. While the other boys paid attention (at least some of the time), Tommy didn't even try to focus. When we carved fish out of bars of Ivory soap, he lacked even the most basic coordination. Sometimes he became frustrated, but mostly he retreated into his own world.

I knew Tommy was in Special Ed and didn't think too much about why until a particular conversation with his mom. We were talking about kids and braces when she told me Tommy would never get his permanent teeth. He just didn't have them. I'd never heard of anything like that, and though I wondered why, it seemed rude to ask. My thoughts were simply, "That poor kid."

Flash forward several years.

I'm at the computer researching birth defects for a different book, and Tommy's face pops on to the screen. It wasn't actually Tommy, but the face staring at me from a Fetal Alcohol Web site had the same unique features that characterized Tommy. His condition now had a name—Fetal Alcohol Syndrome, or FAS.

That was the moment when the idea for Penny was conceived. I read a lot of books, including *The Broken Cord* by Michael Dorris, perhaps the first and most well known of the FAS books. There are a lot of blogs out there, but the one that stood out for me was Jeff Noble's FASD Forever (http://fasdforever.com). Jeff's work is inspiring, honest, and full of warmth and humor. On the personal side, I listened to stories from friends with related experiences. Penny's mermaid infatuation was confirmed by one of those conversations, as well as Carly using a tent to give her a safe place.

As the words "spectrum disorder" imply, there's a lot of variation in the effects of fetal alcohol. The amount of alcohol consumed and the gestational time of exposure both make big differences. There's an alphabet soup of acronyms and abbreviations, and research continues to provide new information.

The highest level on the spectrum is full-blown Fetal Alcohol Syndrome, which is where I suspect Tommy fit. The lowest level is Fetal Alcohol Effects. That's where I placed Penny for the sake of a story that's primarily a romance.

I hope you enjoyed getting to know this little girl. I like to think that when Penny reaches adulthood, she'll follow in the steps of Emily Travis, Miss Southern Illinois 2012. Born with alcohol in her system and addicted to drugs used by her mother, Emily is a strong advocate for FASD prevention.

There are two things I hope readers take away from the FASD

aspect of *Together With You*. The first is that FASD is 100 percent preventable. If you're pregnant, don't drink. If you think you might become pregnant, don't drink. No child should sustain what's essentially a traumatic brain injury in its mother's womb.

The second takeaway is that no one is perfect. No matter where we fall on the spectrum of humanity, we all need forgiveness, love, and the grace of our heavenly Father.

With love,
Victoria Bylin

Victoria Bylin is a romance writer known for her realistic and relatable characters. Her books have finaled in multiple contests, including the Carol Awards, the RITAs, and *RT Magazine's* Reviewers' Choice Award. A native of California, she and her husband now make their home in Lexington, Kentucky, where their family and their crazy Jack Russell terrier keep them on the go. Learn more at her website: www.victoriabylin.com.

More Romance

When Kate Darby's only living family member suffers a stroke, Kate takes leave from her career to care for her. In the process, she meets her very own knight in shining armor. Too bad she doesn't believe in happily ever afters . . . at least, she didn't until she met Nick.

Until I Found You by Victoria Bylin
victoriabylin.com

After his spontaneous marriage to Celia Park, bull rider Ty Porter quickly realized he wasn't ready to be anybody's husband. Five years later, when he comes face-to-face with Celia—and the daughter he never knew he had—can he prove to her that theirs can still be the love of a lifetime?

Meant to Be Mine by Becky Wade
beckywade.com

Kate writes romance movie scripts for a living, but after her last failed relationship, she's stopped believing "true love" is real. Could a new friendship with former NFL player Colton Greene restore her faith?

From the Start by Melissa Tagg
melissatagg.com

You May Also Like . . .

Ben has always known just how to get under Bea's skin. When their friends decide to play matchmaker, can these two stop bickering long enough to realize the true source of the "spark" between them?

Becoming Bea by Leslie Gould
THE COURTSHIPS OF LANCASTER COUNTY #4
lesliegould.com

On the set of a docudrama in Wildwood, Texas, Allie Kirkland is unnerved to discover strange connections between herself and a teacher who disappeared over a century ago. Is history about to repeat itself?

Wildwood Creek by Lisa Wingate
lisawingate.com

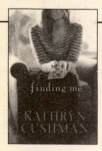

After her father's accidental death, Kelli Huddleston sorts through his belongings and learns a shocking secret: She has a family she's never known. She may want answers, but are some doors better left shut?

Finding Me by Kathryn Cushman
kathryncushman.com